Vincenzo

Or, Sunken Rocks. In two volumes. Vol. 2. Copyright edition

SALZWASSER VERLAG

John Ruffini

Vincenzo

Or, Sunken Rocks. In two volumes. Vol. 2. Copyright edition

Reprint of the original, first published in 1863.

1st Edition 2022 | ISBN: 978-3-37500-456-9

Verlag (Publisher): Salzwasser Verlag GmbH, Zeilweg 44, 60439 Frankfurt, Deutschland
Vertretungsberechtigt (Authorized to represent): E. Roepke, Zeilweg 44, 60439 Frankfurt, Deutschland
Druck (Print): Books on Demand GmbH, In de Tarpen 42, 22848 Norderstedt, Deutschland

VINCENZO;

OR,

SUNKEN ROCKS.

BY

JOHN RUFFINI

COPYRIGHT EDITION.

IN TWO VOLUMES.

VOL. II.

LEIPZIG

1863.

CONTENTS

OF VOLUME II.

		Page
CHAPTER I.	Omens	1
— II.	Pitching a Tent	16
— III.	Promising Prospects	30
— IV.	The "Great Abomination"	43
— V.	Sundry Conjugal Dialogues	64
— VI.	Coup de Grâce	84
— VII.	Welcome Home	106
— VIII.	Heavy Hours	130
— IX.	A Stag at Bay	144
— X.	"Liberta va cercando ch'è sì cara"	164
— XI.	"I can't get out," said the Starling	179
— XII.	Sweets of Home	198
— XIII.	The Blade wears out the Scabbard	209
— XIV.	Currents and Under-Currents	233
— XV.	A Tempest in a Tea-pot	251
— XVI.	The Great Peacemaker	267
— XVII.	Rose seen to Advantage	284
— XVIII.	Vincenzo's Bark in Full Sail	297
— XIX.	Vincenzo's Bark strikes on Sunken Rocks	313
— XX.	Stranded	324
CONCLUSION		334

VINCENZO; OR, SUNKEN ROCKS.

CHAPTER I.

Omena.

"When are we to go back?" asked Rose of Vincenzo, one day.

"Not before we have seen all the marvels of this enchanting city," was the answer.

"I should have thought we had nearly exhausted the catalogue of its sights," said Rose.

"Well, certainly, we have had a bird's-eye view of most of the wonders. Now we ought to try to make ourselves acquainted with details."

"Have you any idea of how long we have been here already, Vincenzo? One-and-twenty whole days."

"Very true; yet not one too many to enable us to acquire a knowledge of the riches of art contained in the gallery of the Palazzo Pitti alone."

"If we are to go on at that rate," quoth Rose, "our sight-seeing will never come to an end."

"Why, surely, my dear Rose, you have not the bad taste to be tired of Florence?"

"Oh! not tired of Florence," said Rose, with a little blush. "Only I do so long to be with papa again."

"That is quite a natural wish in one so affectionate as you are, dearest." Vincenzo paused a second — then added — "My dear little wife, you have not forgotten, have you, that I warned you that our marriage would, of necessity, entail a separation from your dear father? I had hoped that the noble objects of interest in this privileged centre of art would have made your first weaning from home gentle, and less trying. If time hangs heavy on your hands here, what will it be when you are compelled to live, as no doubt will be the case at no distant day, in some provincial town of Piedmont?"

"In any town of Piedmont I shall feel more at home than I do in Florence. Here I have the feeling of being among foreigners."

"I am sorry to hear it," said Vincenzo. "In justice, Rose, we Piedmontese ought rather to consider ourselves the foreigners in Florence. Could there be any distinction drawn between sons of the same land, the Tuscans are best entitled to be called Italians; for they alone have always guarded inviolate the deposit of the national language, that great living sign of our nationality."

This dialogue took place on their way home, late at night, from a large party. Onofrio had procured letters of introduction for Vincenzo and his bride, not only to the Sardinian Legation, but also to several distinguished Florentine families, whose reception of the newly-married pair had been courtesy itself. Rose, however, could not bear these parties; she took no interest either in politics or in literature — the two topics most commonly discussed — nor had the local news any piquancy for her; neither had she any natural or acquired taste for lengthy lucubrations about laces and silks. Moreover, the *dolce parlar Toscano* made her feel her own accent a sore humiliation.

From that moment Rose gave up any allusion as to the time of their return home; in fact, she became less talkative on any subject, often falling into long fits of meditation — a habit quite foreign to her nature. There was evidently a damp on her spirits. Well as Vincenzo knew in what direction her thoughts lay, and much as he felt for her, he chose not to take notice of the change. After what he had said to her on the vexed question of leaving Florence, after his explanations as to the impossibility of their remaining permanently at the Palace, what could a fresh discussion lead to but a fresh expression of useless regrets. In order, however, that she might not misconstrue his silence on this one matter into any want of sympathy, or into anything approaching to displeasure, he made it his study to be more *aux petits soins* than ever.

One morning when their usual hour for going out had come, Signora Candia announced her determination of staying at home.

"Stay at home? Why? Do you feel ill, my darling?"

"Not exactly ill — in fact, not ill at all," answered Rose, "only not disposed to walk. You go out alone, and — enjoy yourself, Vincenzo."

"No such thing," said Vincenzo, taking off his hat and sitting down. "How do you think I am to enjoy myself without you?"

"You take more interest in these sights than I do, and I cannot see any reason against your going without me."

"The reason is that I should have no enjoyment in any of what you call sights without you. I had rather stay with you. Won't you let me do so, dear?"

"Not at the cost of such a sacrifice," said Rose, hastily leaving the room. In a minute or two she came back with her bonnet on, saying, "I am ready."

"My dear girl, you told me you were not inclined to go out to-day," objected Vincenzo.

"I have changed my mind," said she. "Let us go."

"Stop a little — not yet," entreated Vincenzo; "not before we have cleared away this misunderstanding. What do you really wish to do? — stay at home or go out? Tell me frankly, Rose."

The appeal was so feelingly and tenderly made that Rose softened.

"Frankly, then, I tell you," she said, "that I should enjoy a walk very much. It is that perpetual wandering through close galleries, and staring at all sorts of things, that so tires and bewilders me."

"Then," answered Vincenzo, gently, but with a sigh, which he vainly tried to suppress — "then we will walk or drive about, and have done with sight-seeing."

"Not so — not so, indeed," exclaimed Rose. "I will not be the means of depriving you of seeing what you so greatly admire. I am ready to go with you wherever you like, only don't let it last for ever and ever."

"It shall not last an hour longer than you choose," said Vincenzo. "Come, what time will you fix for our leaving this?"

"You must decide that yourself, Vincenzo."

"Shall we say within a fortnight?"

"I should be better pleased if you said within a week," returned Rose.

"So be it," assented Vincenzo — "one more week, and then *en route*."

Rose sprang forward and gave her husband a hearty kiss.

Her step had never been so elastic, her humour so charming, as it was that day. They drove to Villa Albizzi, immortalized by Galileo's sojourn there; and, on their return home, Rose insisted on their entering the church of Santa Croce. Indeed, she it was who took the initiative as to all their visits to galleries or public buildings during the remainder of their stay in Florence. Rose's good humour did not forsake her for a moment; even the many disagreeables of their journey back by Vetturino, the stifling dust of the road, or sudden storms delaying their progress, found her equally placid and cheerful. Vincenzo was too happy to feel any very deep regrets. His cup of bliss was so full, that the drop of gall left in it by the failure of his educational scheme for Rose was drowned in its sweetness. Vincenzo, in short, enjoyed the present, and hoped the best for the future.

Stopping nowhere, except for a few hours in Turin, just long enough to allow of Vincenzo's paying a hasty visit to Onofrio and having a short audience of the Minister, they reached the Palace in the beginning of the last week of July. Thus, the wedding tour had not lasted more than seven weeks.

We leave it to the reader to picture to himself the warmth of welcome which awaited the young couple on all sides. As for the Signor Avvocato, he was never tired of admiring his daughter, or of making discoveries of improvement in her manners and appearance. Vincenzo also came in for a good share of compliments and congratulations on his looks. "How strong and manly the boy had grown — and so bronzed." This fact put the Signor Avvocato in mind of the young rogue's campaign with the hoe. "Ha! ha! ha!" and the old gentleman laughed till his sides ached. Barnaby, in a state of delighted distraction, kept bouncing in and out of the room, and pitching into everybody and everything bull-like.

An influx of visitors soon arrived from Rumelli, but, alas! Don Natale was no longer at their head, as of yore. Don Natale was past walking up the hill now — it was all that Don Natale, in a state bordering on dotage, could do to walk at all, supported on each side, to the end and back again of the small garden attached to the Rectory. He was, indeed, still Rector, though only nominally so, of Rumelli. The effective duties of his office were discharged by a young priest, specially appointed for that purpose by the Bishop of Ibella.

At length the crowd of visitors took their departure, and afforded Vincenzo the desired opportunity of acquainting his father-in-law with the result of his morning's interview with the Minister. He was to be appointed Honorary Councillor of the Intendenza at Chambery, and his official nomination would be forwarded to him within a few days. For the present no emolument was attached to the office — he would receive nothing, in short, but a sum of money sufficient to cover his travelling expenses, and those attendant on his installation. He was to find himself at his post on the 1st of September. The Signor Avvocato was greatly elated by this intelligence; his pride and vanity were tickled, and, in the height of his delight, he bestowed a congratulatory hug on the new Consigliere. It was a good start in life — a better start than many even of the highest functionaries had had. Chambery was a clean, nay, a charming town; agreeably situated, and possessing a most pleasant society. The Signor Avvocato knew Chambery; he had passed through it both in going to and returning from Geneva — how many years ago? full thirty-three years. Ah! a long time that — thirty-three years! and he remembered liking the place very much.

The Signor Avvocato was in a vein of optimism, and went on long in the same strain. Rose said nothing; just as she had said nothing when her husband had first broken the news to her. At last her father turned to her, and, with the undisguised intention of investigating her feelings on the subject, said, "And so, when I see you again, I may expect to find you become half a Frenchwoman, and able to speak French better than papa."

"A superiority, I wish I was not to have any opportunity of acquiring," replied Rose, rather drily.

"Bah!" retorted papa, "you will soon grow fond of the language, and the country too."

"Everything is possible," said Rose; "but suppose we speak of something more agreeable, and let Chambery alone until we are obliged to talk about it; we needn't utter the name before the end of August."

Accordingly the subject was dropped.

The bride's first visit was to Don Natale. The good old priest recognised both her and Vincenzo perfectly well; he laughed and wept in the same breath, talking fast, but incoherently, about old times. There was much of the look and the fugitiveness of impressions of a child about the old man. He manifested, however, one strong abiding feeling, and that was an undisguised horror of the new curate then present. This latter endeavoured to counteract the impression which this evident repulsion might produce on the visitors, by making the warmest protestations of his filial attachment to his venerable superior, as he termed Don Natale, backed by a notable display of affectionate attentions.

But neither the warmth of his protestations, nor his show of devotion, succeeded in impressing Vincenzo favourably; for he observed to Rose as they were leaving the parsonage — "I fear that young priest treats our poor old friend harshly."

"What can make you think so? I should say quite the contrary," replied Rose. "It was impossible to speak more feelingly about the dear old man."

"Speaking and acting are two thoroughly distinct things, my dear Rose. Don Natale's aversion testifies strongly against his curate. Old men in their dotage closely resemble children; and children instinctively know and love those who are kind to them, as they know and hate those who are not so."

Rose contented herself with intimating her dissent from her husband's opinion by a little expressive shrug of her shoulders, and Vincenzo politely abstained from pushing the discussion further.

The abrupt disappearance of the young couple on their wedding day, by no means usual in Italy, had necessarily delayed, till their return, the receiving and paying of the visits which custom has elevated into a duty on such occasions. Ibella and its vicinity now came to call on the bride and bridegroom, and the bride and bridegroom went to call on Ibella and its vicinity; and then a string of dinners and entertainments given and received became the order of the day during the next fortnight. Save when the subject of the internal policy of the country was broached, the doing of which inevitably made the Signor Avvocato fall foul of Cavour and his free trade — for he abominated alike the measure and its promoter — save on these rare occasions, we say, the master of the Palace was in the best of humours and spirits: so were both Rose and Vincenzo, and, in fact, everybody. Rose, playing the part of mistress of the house, was quite in her native element; admirable the clearheadedness and easy graceful self possession with which she did the honours of the Palace. Vincenzo was not a little proud of his young wife, and in the fervour of his admiration registered a vow, that, as soon as they were at Chambery, she should have a charming home over which to preside and shine.

There was only one note on which the married lovers did not sweetly chime. They could not agree in their appreciation of Don Natale's curate. Every fresh meeting increased Vincenzo's antipathy, and Rose's sympathy., for the man. Besides dining at the Palace every Sunday, as Don Natale used to do, he came almost daily to bring news, as he phrased it, of "our dear and venerable friend." The unctuous voice in which he said the words alone sufficed to put Vincenzo out of patience. That the fellow was clever and had a clear insight into the different characters he had to deal with, was evident by the distinct methods he used with father and daughter. Deferential without servility towards the Signor Avvocato, to the Signora he was condescendingly paternal and yet authoritative. It was certainly from no neglect on his part that he failed to ingratiate himself with Vincenzo. At their very first interview he had claimed the privileges of an old school companion, mentioning what Vincenzo very well recollected, that they had once worn similar robes and had lived for three years under the same roof — the first three years that Vincenzo had passed in the seminary. The curate was, however, some six or seven years Vincenzo's senior.

The last week of August had begun. Three weeks previously Vincenzo's official nomination as Consigliere had reached the Palace. The document and its big seals were objects of special admiration and interest to the Signor Avvocato; but, as for Rose, she deigned to take no notice of their visible proof of her husband's success in his profession, turning a deaf ear to all her father's endless comments and oracular speeches upon the subject. Nor, though the last days of August were at hand, the period to which she had herself adjourned all mention of any change — did she drop a word, or give the slightest hint as to the impending move; nor was she busying herself, at least so far as Vincenzo could see, in any preparations for her journey. Vincenzo felt rather cross at her obliging him to be the first to re-open the disagreeable discussion. There was, however, no help for it, and so he made his approaches cautiously and gently, by saying one morning, "Do you know, my dearest, that our time for going away is close at hand?"

"Already?" exclaimed Rose. "Dear me! it seems as if we had only just arrived."

"Nevertheless, we have been here a full month," observed Vincenzo; "and I warned you, my darling, that I was to be at my post on the 1st of September."

"Oh! that's impossible," said Rose; "I have quantities of things yet to do, and which cannot be done in a hurry."

"Well, if it is really impossible that you should be ready, so as to let us be at Chambery by the first, let us fix the second or third. I dare say the Minister will not mind my being a day or two behind time."

"Must we, then, really and truly go?" asked Rose, after a moment's consideration.

"Of course we must; the matter was settled long ago. Your father has quite made up his mind to our going away."

"Oh! Vincenzo, pray, pray do let us stay here," exclaimed Rose, with a piteous look.

"Why do you ask what you know I cannot grant?" answered Vincenzo.

"And why not? we are so happy here," pleaded she.

"Let us hope we shall be happy elsewhere also," returned Vincenzo.

"Oh! nowhere so happy as here — nowhere, nowhere," cried Rose, passionately.

"So long as we love each other as we do now, we shall be happy anywhere, be sure of that. Those who love carry their paradise with them."

"If you loved me truly," said Rose, "you could not find in your heart to thwart me so."

"I might retort your argument," said Vincenzo,

"but I will not. It is exactly because I do love you dearly and truly that I oppose you on this one point."

"But we cannot leave papa alone."

"Your father does not remain alone, dear. He is surrounded by attached dependents; he has a large circle of friends here and at Ibella, who will keep him company and cheer him. The separation must naturally cost him pain, as it does us; but he is ready to sacrifice his pleasure for our good."

"For our good! Not for mine, I protest," exclaimed Rose. "There is nothing but misery for me in this separation."

"I would urge that it is for *my* good," said Vincenzo, "but that all our interests are in common; are they not?"

"I should like you to explain to me what good you expect from scouring through the country at the bidding of the first man in office you chance to come across."

"I expect to secure my own esteem and that of all honest men," returned Vincenzo.

"Really, Vincenzo, it's a mystery to me why you should not attain such ends without making yourself into a Government official."

"On the contrary, the course I adopt seems to me the only one within my reach by which I can make myself useful and respected. Show me any other which holds out the same promise, and I will accept it."

"I have already told you that you could be of use here in many ways, and highly respected as well."

"And on the occasion you allude to I gave you my reasons for thinking the contrary. What I want is real work, and not a mere sham. Listen to me, dear;" and the poor young man went on to repeat all the arguments he had brought forward when they had previously discussed the same matter. He spoke earnestly on the duty incumbent on all men not to leave unproductive the capital of talents and energies bestowed on them by the Creator; the claims a country has on all its citizens; the special obligation, devolving upon him, sprung from so low, to make an honoured name for himself, and thereby justify her father's favours and disarm calumny. He pleaded all this, and much more to no purpose; his passionate eloquence fell dead against what her father, in an angry moment, had once styled her quiet impermeability to reason. Rose was neither touched nor convinced; she said so distinctly in so many words.

"I am sorry for it," was Vincenzo's answer. "All I have to add is, that by the beginning of September I must be at my post at Chambery; otherwise I should lose the appointment."

Vincenzo had needed all his self-control not to say something much more severe. He felt cruelly disappointed and something angry. Was it a perverse predetermination on Rose's part, or was it some peculiar deficiency of judgment, which thus closed her mind to the most obvious and unanswerable truths? He ruminated long on this unpleasant alternative, while instinctively seeking in rapid motion a sedative for his mental disquiet. After rambling far and wide he returned home, softened and tranquillised.

It was five minutes past the dinner hour, and the Signor Avvocato and Rose had already sat down to table.

"At last!" exclaimed the father-in-law. "I began to think that you did not mean to dine with us to-day."

"I beg your pardon," said Vincenzo. "I took a long walk and forgot myself."

"You must not forget yourself," said the Signor Avvocato. The words were emphasized too pointedly for any one to suppose they only referred to the want of punctuality of which Vincenzo had been guilty.

The young man glanced at the speaker, and perceived an awful frown on his brow. He looked at Rose; her eyes were red. The silence during the rest of the meal was unbroken, save by some trivial remark of the father to the daughter, or of the daughter to the father. Neither the one nor the other ever addressed a word to Vincenzo. At dessert, after the servants had left the room, the Signor Avvocato turned to Vincenzo and said, in his severest and most distant manner, "I have arranged with Rose as to the day of your departure. You will start on the 2d of September — that will be quite soon enough. Rose is too sensible a girl not to submit to the conditions agreed upon between us at the time of her marriage. Any little demur she may have made was natural, and does credit to her heart. You had neither right nor reason on your side for treating her harshly."

"Was I harsh to her!" asked Vincenzo. "Does she accuse me of being so?"

"Your business is at this moment with me, and not with her," interrupted the Signor Avvocato, angrily. "Listen to me. When I say you were harsh to her, I affirm what I know to be a fact. Young ladies — women, I mean — do not cry their eyes out because they have been too much petted and humoured. I repeat it. You were very wrong to make her cry; let it be the last time. Remember our agreement — if you should ever cost her a tear —"

"But," here broke in Vincenzo.

"I will hear of no *buts*, sir. I gave you my daughter in order that you should make her happy, and not that you might worry her life out. It seems to me that she and I put ourselves to inconvenience enough for your sake to give us a right to some return. If you have any observations to make," added the old gentleman, rising with difficulty, "I beg you will wait for some other opportunity. I must avoid all emotions after dinner; any agitation interferes with my digestion."

"God is my witness that I have done nothing to deserve your reproaches. That is the only observation I have to make," said Vincenzo, also rising, and following the father and daughter out of the room.

This little domestic *fracas* cut Vincenzo to the heart; he keenly resented the injustice of his wife's complaints of him to her father, and almost as keenly the injustice of the father's lending so willing an ear to those complaints.

There was something besides his sense of the injustice of the accusation which jarred the young husband's feelings; it was that the Signor Avvocato had adopted a tone and manner, both in his reproofs and in his settling the question of their departure, which was not suitable between equal and equal. This misunderstanding threw a shade of coldness over the few remaining days the trio had to spend together, and, contrary to his usual kindly spirit, Vincenzo made no effort to banish this discomfort. But when the actual moment of separation came, when he saw the twist of pain in the old familiar face, and hot tears rolling over his wife's cheeks, his heart melted, and he cast from it the last bitter drop of resentment.

CHAPTER II.

Pitching a Tent.

VINCENZO had taken the precaution of writing beforehand to secure places in the mail, which at that time ran daily between Turin and Chambery. This mode of conveyance, besides being the quickest and safest, had another advantage highly prized by newly married couples; as there were only seats for two inside, they could enjoy each other's society *tête-à-tête.* But there was also a drawback; the mail starting late in the evening crossed the mountain during the night, and, supposing there was no moon, the traveller saw nothing of all the grandeur of the Alpine scenery through which he was passing. As ill luck would have it, Vincenzo and Rose had bad weather for their journey. The sky was as black as pitch, the wind blew chilly and fierce — so tempestuous was it, that it was all the mules, dragging the coach up the ascent, and the men at their heads, could do to stand against the irate gusts which swept along, hissing like so many vipers.

In spite of shawls, and cloaks, and wrappers, Rose complained bitterly of the cold — her feet felt like two balls of ice. Vincenzo, though quite in the same plight, did his best to comfort her, by a promise of procuring some hot water-bottles at Lanslebourg. But he had reckoned without the guard, who, being already behind his time, would not hear of stopping longer than was strictly necessary for changing horses. Nevertheless, Vincenzo made a struggle for the bottles, but all he got for his pains was a thorough wetting, and a threat of being left behind. The rain was falling in torrents as they passed through Lanslebourg. It was by that time broad day, a bleak, lurid day. The Maurienne does not look gay even in the best of weathers, but seen through thick sheets of rain, it is a picture of desolation. Rose felt too intensely miserable even to be out of humour. Shivering and groaning she closed her eyes to shut out the dreary sight. Vincenzo's state of wretchedness was akin to despair. He had no longer enough of courage left to allow of his attempting to cheer her by anticipations of future comfort; the only mark of sympathy he ventured to show was that of silently wrapping about her the shawls and wrappers whenever they slipped off. He had literally the feelings of a criminal — exactly as if all the damp, and dreariness, and forlornness of the situation ought to be laid to his charge. And yet his eyes followed with a sort of automatic interest the mad doings of the waters of the Arc, boiling, tearing, bounding, rushing along by the side of the road, like a troop of wild horses struggling in deadly contest. In fact, his state of mind resembled that of the culprits of whom we read that they speculated upon the cost of the judge's dress-wig, or counted with stolid attention the iron spikes of the rails of the dock, while sentence of death was being passed upon them.

After a time, the aspect of the country improved;

not so the weather. The rain was falling faster than ever when the mail stopped before the Hotel de l'Europe, at Chambery. The landlord and his family fully justified the high character which Onofrio had given of them, when he recommended the house to Vincenzo. The benumbed Signora Candia was carried, rather than shown, to a bedroom on the first floor. As speedily as possible she was put into a comfortably-warmed bed, was persuaded to take something hot, and then left to rest. Madame Ferrolliet, the mistress of the hotel, saw herself to all the arrangements for the young couple's comfort.

Every five minutes during the next two hours, Vincenzo went on tiptoe to listen at his wife's door. Auguring at last, from the uninterrupted quietness within, that Rose must be fairly asleep, and unwilling to run any risk of disturbing her, he had a bed made up for himself on a sofa in the salon adjoining her bedroom. No sooner had his head touched the pillow than he fell into a deep slumber, nor did he awake till early dawn. He rose at once, and went to the window. Alas! no change in the weather — it was pouring as obstinately as it had done the day before. Rather depressed, he stole quietly to Rose's bedside. Her eyes were wide open; she declared that the noise of carriages and carts in the streets had prevented her having a wink of sleep. She had a splitting headache; she was thoroughly unhappy; her room must be changed, or she must give up all hope of ever sleeping again. Vincenzo assured her that she should either have another room, or else they would go to another hotel, though he hoped there would be no occasion to resort to this last measure, for there was little chance of their meeting such kind people as these Ferrolliets were. Did not Rose agree with him in thinking them unusually obliging?

"They seem good-natured enough," said Rose; "but, after all, I am no judge, for not a syllable of their gibberish can I understand — it is dreadfully disagreeable, I assure you — when they speak to me, I feel as if had grown deaf and dumb."

"It is a trial," replied the husband; "but, at the same time, the evil is one that will soon be cured; you'll see that you will learn French in no time"

"Oh! never, never," sighed the wife.

"Oh! yes, yes," said Vincenzo, trying to speak cheerfully; "but first we must try and secure you a good night's rest, and then, when the weather clears, we will hunt out some nice, pretty apartments for you. Once you begin to keep house, you'll soon learn the language"

Rose shook her head in a most disconsolate way, and said, "I wonder if it is ever fine here."

Vincenzo sought out the kind landlady, and told her of Rose's sleepless night, petitioning for another bedroom less exposed to the noise of the streets. Madame Ferrolliet's large eyes grew considerably larger as she listened to this request. She was sorry, doubly sorry that the signora was uncomfortable, because she could see no remedy. The hotel was full from top to bottom. She might, to be sure, inquire if the occupiers of Nos. 27 and 28 (they seemed very good-natured, obliging persons) would object to change rooms with Signora Candia. As soon as she knew that they were up, she would go and ask them. Luckily the negotiation succeeded, and the exchange of rooms was effected.

The second night at the hotel Rose slept like a top; and when she awoke, the sun was shining as brightly as it had ever done at Rumelli, and the mercury of her spirits rose several degrees. But, alas! rooms No. 27 and 28 were not without their drawback, as became too evident in the course of the day. They overlooked the court-yard, and, consequently, were in the close vicinity of the stables, and Rose complained of the unsavoury proximity. Her sensitiveness on this point was that of one who, up to the age of twenty, had passed three-fourths of the year in the pure bracing air of a hill country.

"Reason the more," observed Vincenzo, "for beginning at once to look for apartments;" and so out they sallied in quest of lodgings.

Rose was not so intense a pessimist as she had been the day before; she allowed that Chambery was a pleasant-looking place — she even deigned to approve of its castle, its fountain of "the elephants," its arcades, its well-shaded public walks, and of the vine-covered heights which overhung the little town. The vineyards, arcades, and shaded walls were all familiar objects to Rose, but the Dent de Nivolet and Mont Grenier made scarcely any impression on her.

Few and far between were the notices of apartments to let which they discovered; and, of the three or four sets of rooms they looked at, none were suitable, or even approaching to suitable. Disappointed in their search, they at last thought of applying for advice to the Ferrolliets themselves. These good people left no stone unturned to help the young couple, and Vincenzo spent the whole of the following day in going to all the houses they recommended, without, however, finding anything that answered. One suite of rooms, convenient, of a good size, tolerably well-furnished, seemed just what was required; but Rose, on inspection, discovered that there was no view from the window. This was an insuperable objection. She remained at the hotel, and continued to complain of the stables.

This question of a lodging threatened to become a thorny one. However, whatever its importance, it had to be set aside for the time being. On the morrow, that is, on the fourth day since their reaching Chambery, Vincenzo felt that he neither ought, nor could any longer delay presenting himself at the Intendenza; and, after promising Rose to be back as soon as possible, thither he went. The Intendente had just gone out, but was expected to return every moment. Vincenzo had no choice — he must wait; and so he did — for a whole hour. His interview with his chief, and then the ceremony of his introduction to all the *personnel* of the Intendenza, took up another hour. When he returned to the hotel, Rose exclaimed, "How long you have been; I thought you never intended to come back."

"I am delighted to hear you say so; it proves that you have missed me. At the same time, I cannot help hoping that my little wife will try and accustom herself to my being absent for some hours every day, and, that she may feel her loneliness less, that she will learn to create some occupation for herself at home."

"You should add, when she has a home. I begin to doubt if we ever shall have one as long as we are here," replied Rose. "Other people's troubles are easv to bear, but I can assure you, it is not at all amusing to spend hour after hour alone in this disagreeable atmosphere without the power of interchanging a word with any living soul. Oh! dear, if I had only Marianna here, it would be something."

Marianna was a young peasant-girl, actually one of the housemaids at the Palace, and a great favourite with Rose.

Vincenzo said nothing, but thought to himself that the wish was quite natural in a girl suddenly separated from all she had been used to, and thrown among strangers speaking an unknown language. The more he reflected, the more he became convinced that Marianna would be of infinite comfort to his wife, particularly during the time she was learning French. He wrote at once to the Signor Avvocato, telling him how much it would gratify and console Rose to have Marianna with her. Vincenzo begged his father-in-law not to write to Rose on the subject, for two reasons — to spare her a disappointment should Marianna not be willing to come to Chambery, or, in the event of her agreeing to do so, to leave him, the writer, the merit and pleasure of giving his wife an agreeable surprise.

The Intendente had kindly dispensed with Vincenzo's entering on the duties of his office until he had found himself a lodging. Yet, sadly harassed as he was by his daily unsuccessful hunt, Vincenzo was too conscientious not to show himself at the Intendenza for an hour or two every morning. On the third day of his attendance there, who should come in search of him, but a tall, handsome non-commissioned officer, in whom he instantly recognized Ambrogio, the mayor's son, his companion in his famous expedition to Novara? Ambrogio had seen Vincenzo's appointment and arrival at Chambery mentioned in one of the local papers, and had hastened to find him out. Hearty were the greetings of the two young men, and very complimentary the remarks they made on the changes time had wrought in each other's appearance.

"How tall and strong and martial-looking you have grown, old fellow," said Vincenzo to his friend who towered above him by half a head.

"You knew me again instantly in spite of my height?" said Ambrogio.

"I should have picked you out among ten thousand," said Vincenzo. "We little dreamed, when we lost sight of each other, six years ago, that our next meeting would be at Chambery — you a sergeant in ...."

"And you an Avvocato, and a Consigliere d'Intendenza," interrupted Ambrogio.

"Yes, and more than that, a married man," laughed Vincenzo; "and the happiest and proudest of husbands. Quite a romance, my dear friend. You must come and be introduced to my wife. Will you dine with us today, at six o'clock? We are staying at the Hotel de l'Europe. But tell me, how is your father?"

"Strong and hale as ever, thank God," returned Ambrogio; "and, moreover, as well-satisfied as ever with his scapegrace of a son. True to his word, when my time for the conscription came, he left me free to become a soldier if I chose. I did so, and I don't regret it. The day I win my epaulets — and, if we have a war, as rumour says we shall shortly, win them I shall, or die — the day I get them, and turn my back on this place, I shall have nothing left to wish for."

Vincenzo, surprised by the last remark, said, "I thought Chambery was reckoned one of the pleasantest garrison towns."

"Frenchmen might think so, I dare say," answered Ambrogio, "but not any true Piedmontese. The townsfolk look on all who come from the other side of the mountain, and especially on us soldiers, much as we Italians do on the Austrians. Those who are not Codini — these are the majority — are red Republicans; and the sympathies of both are bestowed on France."

"Well, we cannot much wonder at that, when we remember their geographical position and their language," observed Vincenzo; "nevertheless, I hope there is some exaggeration in your statement."

"You say now exactly what I said when I arrived here a year and a half since. After you have been here twelve months, mark my words, you will sing the same song as I do now."

Signora Candia's reception of Ambrogio was courteous if not cordial. His uniform, and the recollection of how and why he and her husband had become such fast friends, were no great recommendations to her favour. Still, in her present isolation, it was an undeniable consolation to meet with one of her own countrymen, and a spirited, well-informed, obliging man into the bargain. No sooner was Ambrogio told of the dilemma as to lodgings, than he offered his services to the lady, though, as he added, with very faint hopes of being able to find what would please her. A furnished apartment of the style and in the situation she wished, would be almost as difficult to light upon as a prize in the lottery. It was the demand which created the supply, and at Chambery there was no demand for such. Tourists rarely made any lengthened stay at Chambery, and, when they did, always lived at one or other of the hotels. The only persons who ever wanted lodgings were Piedmontese officers and *employés*, and, they had to be satisfied with far inferior accommodation to that which the Signora wished for. Of small cheap lodgings there was no lack.

Ambrogio's prognostications were only too soon verified. At the end of forty-eight hours he went to Vincenzo's office and confessed his failure. "My dear fellow," he concluded, "you must either abate much of your requirements, or give up all idea of living in the town. And, now that I think of it, since your wife makes such a point of having fresh air and a fine view, why not try to find a house somewhere in the outskirts?"

"You are right," said Vincenzo; "that's a capital idea of yours."

"There's a tolerable sprinkling of cozy little country houses all round Chambery," went on Ambrogio; "I saw several to let on the road to 'Les Charmettes.'"

"Les Charmettes — Jean Jacques — delightful!" exclaimed Vincenzo.

"You must take into account, however, that winter is not far off," remarked Ambrogio; "still October and November are beautiful months here, and even in winter there's but a very slight difference of temperature between town and country. The discomfort will be all yours — for you will have to come to your office in all weathers; luckily you are young and strong, and can besides keep a gig if you choose."

"That is — my wife can," said Vincenzo; "let us go and hear what she says to your plan."

Rose caught at Ambrogio's proposal with childlike eagerness; she had a real love for the country.

"Well, then," said Ambrogio, "the sooner we begin the better; my advice is, to hire a carriage and set off instantly on our journey of discovery."

So said, so done; a carriage was easily procured, and away went the trio. The environs of Chambery are always beautiful; they are doubly so, when decked, as was now the case, in the rich tints of autumn. Our party had a charming drive. Rose recovered her happy smile and bird-like chirp. Vincenzo had neither seen the one nor heard the other since their arrival at Chambery. Three or four houses, including the "Charmettes," were examined, all equally tempting. Rose's choice at last fell on one, which had in addition to all the advantages it possessed in common with the others, that of being nearest to the new, pretty little parish church — in fact, within a quarter of a mile. The house itself was a mere band-box of two stories; but it had room enough and to spare for the young couple and for the number of servants they would need; it was simply and freshly furnished and had altogether an inviting air of neatness both inside and out. As to its position, nothing could be more agreeable. It stood on high ground, looking over glorious woods of chesnut and walnut, across an extensive and fertile valley, closed in by the mountains of Dauphiné.

There was also a good-sized garden and orchard, bounded on the side abutting on the road by a high wall; and on the other by a vineyard which sloped down to the woods. The only drawback was the want of a coach-house and stables — but this deficiency was easily to be remedied. The man who showed the house assured Vincenzo that a farmer, living within a stone's throw, would willingly take charge of a horse and gig, besides supplying the family with the best of milk, eggs and poultry. Satisfied with these points, the next thing to do was to drive back to Chambery. Having left Signora Candia at the hotel, the two friends went at once to the owner of the villa; and, as he would not let it for any shorter term, Vincenzo had to agree to take it for six months. This settled, they returned to the hotel, and had a merry dinner with an extra bottle of champagne in honour of Rose's Bower, as Vincenzo named their new residence.

As early as seven of the following morning, Orestes and Pylades were at Rose's Bower. Ambrogio superintended the scrubbing and cleaning of the rooms, saw to the airing of pillows and mattresses, to the trimming of the flower borders, and to the reparations necessary in the tiny greenhouse. Meanwhile Vincenzo was busy taking an exact inventory of the bed and table linen, crockery, china, glass, plate, kitchen utensils; even of the brooms and broom-sticks left in the house. Fabulous the amount of what is required to render a house fit to be inhabited. This was the reflection which passed through Vincenzo's mind as he finished the inventory. When, however, he showed it to Rose, she, with that perspicuity in all pertaining to household matters, which was one of her characteristics, at a glance perceived that whole series of articles of plate and china were wanting, and that, in fact, there was not enough of anything for comfort. Fortunately, she had also the talent of discovering how best to supply the deficiencies. The good folks of the hotel promised to find her a good plain woman cook, who would be willing to assist in the general work of the house, and a man, who should unite the offices of groom, coachman, and gardener. They also undertook the purchase of a gig and horse, if none could be found to hire; but to do either the one or the other would necessarily take a little time. Nor did their active obligingness stop at doing what they were requested to do: innumerable were the little unasked-for services they rendered to the young couple. To quote only one instance; it was through them that Vincenzo heard of an excellent piano, the owner of which, being about to make a long journey, was inclined to hire it out, could he only be sure of his instrument being in good hands. Vincenzo did his utmost so to arrange the interior of the Bower, that Rose should miss, at least, as few as possible of the familiar objects by which she had been surrounded in the Palace; and not a little time and ingenuity did he spend in hunting after some particular sort of work-table and chair to match, and cushions, footstools, and bookstands, such as might remind her in some degree of those she had left behind her. Rose was fond of birds, and had had an aviary at the Palace. Too straitened by time to have one in readiness for her arrival at the Bower, Vincenzo bethought him of a substitute, and, by dint of searching, lighted on a large and elegant cage, in shape like a pagoda; and this he filled with every kind of tame bird which money could procure. Thanks to the Ferrolliets and Ambrogio's indefatigable exertions, a few days sufficed to put Rose's Bower in a fit condition to receive its new inmates; and, in less than a week from their first sight of it, Signor and Signora Candia were installed there. Rose expressed her satisfaction with all the arrangements; and, as she stood in the little balcony, gazing upon the purple-tinted woods (trees were the features in a landscape Rose most admired), she exclaimed —

"Oh! what a relief to rest one's eyes on something else than the walls of houses, and to have some other perfume than that of a stable yard. It is like passing from purgatory to paradise — a comparative paradise, I mean."

"Let us hope that time may change it from comparative to positive," said Vincenzo; "a transformation, believe me, dear, which goodwill can do much to effect."

Vincenzo, it must be owned, had reckoned a little on some acknowledgment, if not on some compliments, on his considerate choice of the several pieces of furniture which he intended should remind her of former familiar objects, and which he hoped might, to a certain extent, console her for the strangeness of a new home — expectations, however, doomed to be disappointed. Rose, indeed, noticed the pretty cage full of birds, and seemed highly pleased with it, but without any more idea of attributing the merit of its being there to any living soul, than if it had fallen from the clouds. So Vincenzo had to rest contented with virtue as its own reward.

Not so, though, when, a few days later, he ushered Marianna into his wife's presence. Rose well remembered having expressed a wish for her favourite maid, and easily traced the link between the utterance of the wish and its accomplishment. Accordingly, she did say on this occasion, "How good Vincenzo was," and actually spontaneously kissed him, and fondly too. Vincenzo felt lifted into the seventh heaven; he had learned to be grateful for the least caress. Rose in her softest mood was chary of such, even of words of endearment. To the best of her husband's recollection, never had she been so demonstrative since the day of his consenting to leave Florence at her request.

CHAPTER III.

Promising Prospects.

On the whole things went on better at Rose's Bower than Vincenzo had anticipated. Rose was daily becoming more accustomed, and also more reconciled to the new life which the requirements of her husband's professional career had imposed on her. Besides, it could not be denied, that she found in her present residence many of the same interests and pleasures which she had had at Rumelli. There was plenty of fresh air, a rich vegetation, fine prospects; here as there she had her birds and flowers. She was at liberty to stroll about when and how she liked in the garden or the surrounding vineyards; she had ample leisure for chit-chats with Marianna; her days were undisturbed by sight-seeing; and, to crown all, she had all the delights of housekeeping. The uncontrolled management devolved on her; and, owing to the distance from Chambery, there was just sufficient difficulty in obtaining provisions and other necessaries, to excite all the young matron's energy, and to tickle her sense of self-importance. Rose was very proud of her management of domestic affairs — and, with reason, for she did it to perfection.

On the day following the Sunday on which Signora Candia had made her first appearance at the neat parish church, the curé called at the Bower. He could speak Italian tolerably, and nothing could be more flattering than his self-gratulations on the acquisition of his new parishioners; he added, how happy his mother would be to make the acquaintance of so charming a neighbour as the Signora. Rose immediately volunteered the first visit, was much prepossessed by the old lady's manner, and, from that moment, a pleasant intercourse was established between the Parsonage and the Bower. This was, indeed, but the beginning of a series of agreeable acquaintances; for Rose, as a matter of course, met at the curé's house the ladies of the principal parishioners — of a country squire, a retired captain, an architect, and a government official. People who live in the country are in general inclined to be sociable, more especially at the approach of winter. Thus it came about that visits were very soon exchanged between the old settlers and the new arrivals. At first the pleasure of these visits had its drop of gall for Rose. There was the difficulty of understanding and being understood; but this inconvenience gradually diminished, and, before the end of the month, Rose knew enough of French to understand all that was said, and to make herself understood, but in so odd a way of her own, that it often severely taxed the politeness of her visitors to suppress a laugh at her expense. Rose was quite conscious of her deficiency; indeed, she made it a plea for positively declining to accompany her husband in any of his town calls. Yet she would take no pains to improve herself. Vincenzo did what he could for her, by reading French aloud every evening, translating as he read; at her own request, he taught her the names of articles in daily use, but to this was limited all her study of the language. She would not hear of learning any rules of grammar, or of reading to herself; in fact, Rose seldom opened a book, and, if urged by her husband to do so, would ask, What was the use? Almost all the books she had ever looked into were dull — and, as for newspapers, it was sheer loss of time to read them, for there was no believing one word in them.

"But, my dear girl," Vincenzo had answered, "among much that may be false, I assure you that, even in the poorest daily paper, you will always find a fund of information; at all events, a French journal would be most valuable to you, as it contains just the phrases which are commonly used in conversation."

Rose tried one, was disgusted by the first difficulty, the first necessity for a dictionary, and never again took up another.

Signora Candia, not having confessed for two months, stood in need of a confessor and spiritual director; she, as was natural, requested that the curé would accept her as one of his penitents. The curé demurred — alleging, as the cause of his hesitation, his doubt whether he should be the right man for that office; accustomed as he was to deal with rustics, he feared he might be too rough a hand for her. He ended by saying,

"I wish you would talk this matter over with my mother. She has a good deal of experience, and a sort of intuition on these subjects. She will single out at a glance the confessor most suitable for you; if she decides on me, I shall be most willing to undertake your spiritual direction."

The old lady, however, judged that her son would not do. The man for Signora Candia, was Père Zacharie, the confessor of the nuns of the Sacré Cœur. He certainly had more to do already than he could well manage; but she would speak to him, and, perhaps, her recommendation might induce him to receive Signora Candia as one of his penitents. Père Zacharie was a Capuchin monk, highly and deservedly renowned for learning, eloquence, and piety; he had the greatest veneration for the mother of the curé, and, out of regard for her, came on certain great occasions to preach in the neat little church. His being a Capuchin was a winning card. If the reader recollects, Rose's first spiritual director, the late Father Terenziano, had been a Capuchin. And then, a confessor chosen by Madame (as the curé's mother was called by Antonomasia) — that is, by a venerable woman whom Rose considered as a saint — could not be otherwise than accepted as a saint.

Rose's natural interest in the doings of the little church and parish waxed warmer and warmer the more she was initiated into the wants of both. The parish church was poor, the curé's salary very small, the services of the church performed in a very modest manner. Seeing this, Rose asked as a favour to be allowed to make some donations which might in some slight degree contribute to the splendour of the display on fête days; for instance, might she present a new stole or cope, an altar cover, or some tall tapers. The permission given, she used it largely. Every Sunday, she regularly sent fresh flowers to adorn the chapel of the Holy Virgin, and on certain Church festivals provided the *pain béni* distributed on such occasions among the congregation. It soon came to be acknowledged throughout the parish that Signora Candia's flowers were the freshest and rarest ever bestowed on the church, her *pain béni* the largest and best made. Competition gave these little triumphs a zest, such as Rose had never known, and could never have known, at Rumelli, where no one ever so much as dreamed of vying with her. Madame openly spoke of her as a benefactress of the church, and, when a few days of biting cold made charitably-inclined people turn their thoughts to the rigours of impending winter, and to the consequent wants of the poor, Madame had her young Italian friend, as she called her, made a member of a local committee of ladies, established for the purpose of supplying food, clothes, and fuel, to the sick and indigent of the vicinity. Signora Candia going on her rounds of charity was a pleasant sight to see — tripping along with blooming cheeks and eyes bright with earnest good-will, from cottage to cottage, into the poorest huts and hovels, making herself acquainted with the necessities of the occupants with the view of having their names put down on the lists for relief. Such was the proud position to which, in scarcely more than two months, our Chatelaine of Rumelli had, through her own merits, attained; a position so satisfactory to her that it prompted the answer she made to Vincenzo, who, as December drew near, asked whether she would not prefer to pass the cold months in Chambery. "No; she preferred remaining where she was unless he found it too inconvenient for his affairs."

Vincenzo was not likely to see any shadow of a shade of inconvenience to himself where his wife's wishes were concerned, and so it was agreed between them that they should spend the winter in their present quarters. Vincenzo would, to say all the truth, have willingly walked through wind and rain all the winters of his life if by so doing he could have secured the continuation of Rose's present happy mood. After the difficulty he had had to separate her from Rumelli, after all the qualms of doubt and despair he had endured during the week of their sojourn at Chambery, to have chanced upon this quiet haven, and to see his wife accommodate herself to the change of home so easily and gracefully, was a piece of good luck for which he could never be thankful enough. He believed that now at last the main obstruction in the road of his future career was definitively removed. Independently of this great benefit, and of the mutual good understanding springing from it, Rose's success in the circle in which she was moving flattered Vincenzo both as a lover and a fervently admiring husband. Not that he nursed the least illusion as to the nature of the influences which were likely to be brought to bear on her. Vincenzo was by this time sufficiently acquainted with the *carte du pays* to be aware that the wind which blew from the Parsonage and the surrounding villas — and he might even add from the houses in Chambery where he visited — was not loaded with over friendly messages to the country from which he came, or to the Government he served. The walls of the little drawing-room of Rose's Bower had too often rung with the wrongs and grievances of Savoy, all imputed to Piedmont, to permit of his ignoring the political bias of his wife's friends. The curé complained that the Government was systematically hostile to religion and its ministers; the half-pay officer loudly asserted that Savoyard blood and money went to further objects antagonistic to Savoyard interests; the country gentleman declared that the weight of taxation had become unbearable, in fact, swallowed up all the rent of the land; the *employé* affirmed that all good places in the Administration were bestowed on Piedmontese; the engineer, that in so poor a country as Savoy the public works ought to be on a large scale, in order to provide work for the labouring classes. What did it matter to Savoyards whether the Austrians were at Milan or not? That which did matter to them was that bread should be cheap! The variety and comprehensiveness of these strictures excuse us from entering into their refutation. None but a blindly insane Government could act in a way to deserve them. Yet that such opinions should be commonly held goes far to prove the breadth and depth of the split between the two countries. It was not any special act or series of acts which was blamed and opposed, but the whole system of government. Nor did this opposition come from the aristocracy or clergy alone — it was pretty general in all classes; nor did it date from yesterday — it was of the same age as the Statuto; at least it found utterance at the birth of the liberty of the press guaranteed by the Statuto.

Savoy, ever since 1848, had been a clog on the wheels of constitutional Piedmont. In spite of the strenuous efforts of a liberal minority, Savoy had sent to Turin, with a few brilliant exceptions, a compact phalanx of ultraconservative deputies — all of them clever, accomplished men, some even unusually gifted with eloquence, but far less solicitous for the interests of liberty than for the privileges of the nuns of the Sacré Cœur and those of the Ecclesiastical Jurisdiction, far less anxious for Italian independence than for economy, far more indifferent to the present than to the past. For this divergence between the aims and feelings of the two countries, many good reasons could be assigned. We prefer to mention only one, which to us appears to comprise them all; and that is, the difference of nationality and, consequently, of centre of attraction. It was in the nature of things that, the more Piedmont gravitated towards Italy — which, ever since 1848 she had been doing with accelerated speed — the more would Savoy incline towards France. How was it possible that the two countries, pulling in contrary directions, should draw the car of Government well together?

All this Vincenzo knew, and much more, which we leave untold; for, together with his public appointment, he had received from his patron, the Minister, a confidential mission. This was to study the state of Savoy, to trace the causes of dissatisfaction to their origin, and, having gained this insight, to propose such remedies as he might deem efficacious, making the whole the subject of a confidential report. To facilitate this task, which he carefully fulfilled, Vincenzo had been furnished with letters of introduction to many notable citizens of all ranks and of every political hue. On these persons we know that he called alone — his wife declining any acquaintances, save those which could not possibly be avoided, on the plea of her ignorance of the French language. The growing disaffection of Savoy was, indeed, one of the most serious pre-occupations of the Turin Cabinet.

Well, then, knowing the ground and its dangers, as he did, Vincenzo could yet do little, in fact, next to nothing, to protect Rose against them. Could he interfere with her choice of a confessor? or could he lay any embargo on her pleasant intercourse with the inmates of the Parsonage? Even had he possessed the right and the power so to do — and he did not feel that he had either — he would assuredly have lacked the inclination for any such interference. After all, this hornet's nest was not of her seeking but of his; and how could he grudge her anything that mitigated a situation which in itself involved a daily self-sacrifice on her part? All that he could or would do, was to place the antidote by the side of the poison, and that he did by invariably upholding what he believed to be the right cause stoutly and fearlessly, whenever it was attacked in Rose's presence. Bearing in mind the intense anti-Piedmontese hue of the opinions of most of the visitors at Rose's Bower, opportunities for Vincenzo's championship were not rare — but latterly, unless forced to do so, he seldom spoke on politics; never *ex professo*, when *tête-à-tête* with his wife, as he had done during the honeymoon.

Under the pressure of what subtle agencies had he thus renounced his first plan of active propagandism with Rose, and adopted a merely defensive line of tactics? This was more than he himself could have explained — he was probably scarcely aware of so complete a change. Men are apt to receive impressions and unconsciously to modify their views accordingly, without being exactly sensible of the fact. It is besides not improbable that a clever fellow like Vincenzo might have come to feel, after six months of marriage, the imperviousness of Rose's mind to any new ideas, and that he should instinctively recoil from perilling a situation, happy beyond all hope, by intruding any such upon her. Add to this, that his leisure for giving private instruction was much circumscribed; he saw much less of his wife now than he had done at any previous time. From ten in the morning till four in the afternoon he was at his office; and in the evening they had often visitors, and, when that was not the case, he had the materials for his private report to arrange. Whatever the cause or causes at work, what is sure is, that Vincenzo no longer practically pursued the project he had once so warmly cherished, of creating between himself and his wife a community of views upon certain cardinal points.

Perhaps also regret upon this head was somewhat neutralised by another disappointment; this was a conviction he could no longer resist of the singular absence of all passion in his wife's nature. That she loved him as much as she was capable of loving, he had not the least doubt; but that *much* was too little for the cravings of his ardent soul. The same smooth brow and placid smile welcomed his return at their usual dinner hour, or at midnight, when he had been detained in town hours later than she had any reason to expect. Rose never showed any of those childlike impatiences or anxieties — shall we venture further? — never had any of those delightfully aosurd fits of jealousy without any cause, which will now and then seize on the heart of a newly-married young woman. She never felt the want of those gently-whispered effusions of the soul, which hallow the twilight, nor of those still more expressive silences to which lovers are prone, as, hand clasped in hand, they watch the moon climbing the heavens. Not that she did not accommodate herself to her husband's moods and whims very graciously. He had only to say, "Come here, my little treasure, and let us have a talk," and she would at once sit down by his side, put her hand in his, and listen by the hour to the oft-repeated tale of the mingled joy and terror which had nearly choked him, when, by a well-meant indiscretion of Barnaby's, he first discovered that he was over head and ears in love with her, or of the agony of despair with which, after confessing his passion to her father, he had turned his back, as he thought, for ever, on the Palace; she would also readily saunter with him on a moonlight evening in the garden, echo his admiration of the gentle luminary, humouring his poetic enthusiasm to the best of her power; but no soul-stirring emotion heaved her bosom, moistened her eye-lids, or trembled in her voice.

This want of responsive feeling in one so beloved, the severance from love's exalted joys which it entailed upon him, could not but clip Vincenzo's happiness, though without reaching its root. Vincenzo possessed one of those buoyant natures which hope against hope, and it was long ere he could or would admit to himself that the case was a desperate one. Rose, he argued, might have within her a mine of passion, which only needed the right circumstance to reveal its riches. He had read of positive wonders worked by a very natural crisis in the lives of young married women. And he already had visions of Rose, the same and yet transformed, Rose bending over a rosy thing in a cozy cradle, looking from the child to the father with eyes full of newly awakened passionate earnestness.

And, even should this picture of the future never be realized, Vincenzo had no lack of arguments wherewith fairly to reconcile himself to his lot, such as it was. Taken altogether, it was surely an enviable one. Was not a calm, steady, always equable affection, better calculated to secure a man's happiness, especially if that man's life was one of study and labour, than the fits and starts of passion? Such were the reasons for contentment with which young Candia's elastic spirits long furnished him. Nature willed it so, that he might the better accomplish the task for which he was destined. It is rarely found that Nature does not force all other claims to yield to the ruling tendency of the individual character. Now, Study had become Vincenzo's ruling tendency, and Politics his favourite study — not politics in their abstract, but in their practical application. His inclination had always pointed that way, though never so decidedly as of late. The ease with which he had mastered the question entrusted to him to elucidate, the keen interest, nay, positive delight with which he worked at it, the ready solutions which seemed to crowd upon him, had given the young Consigliere a revelation of his peculiar and decided aptitude for this branch of study. The sense of his own powers in this respect had awakened a corresponding feeling of self-reliance, heightening his honest ambition to prove of use to his country. Perhaps the ardour of his nature, having been partly checked in love, had turned with redoubled intensity into this other channel.

Piedmont was just emerging from a period of patient preparation and incubation into one of activity. The master-mind of Cavour, which was now presiding over its destinies, had pretty nearly succeeded in inaugurating that policy of action and progress — as he designated it — the aim of which was to win for the little sub-Alpine State the sympathies and confidence of all Italy. The great statesman was now engaged laying the foundations of those foreign alliances without which the achievement of Italian independence was all but hopeless. Two of the Government's boldest measures were yet to come — the one for the suppression of a certain number of convents, and the better distribution by the State of the revenues of the clergy; the second for a treaty of alliance with the Western Powers, and the active participation of Sardinia in the war in the East. To both of these bills — to the first especially — a strenuous opposition was anticipated, in and out of the walls of Parliament; and their being brought forward was confidently looked upon by the leaders of the extreme parties as the signal for the overthrow of the Cavour cabinet. The defeat of either of these bills — being, as they were, cabinet questions — of necessity involved the resignation of the Ministry and the accession to power of the Opposition. Passions ran high, and the issue of the contest appeared doubtful. Cavour, it must be recollected, had not yet attained that preponderance which only a year after carried everything before it.

Vincenzo was a passionate admirer of Cavour and his policy, whose triumph or downfall was, in our hero's eyes, tantamount to the triumph or downfall of the national cause. This being so, we can form an estimate of the keen anxiety with which he watched and weighed the signs of the times, and the chances *pro* and *con*, of the impending struggle. Had Rose's husband drawn an omen from the colour of the opinions of those he habitually associated with, he would have despaired of success; but he relied on the patriotism and good sense of his countrymen on the other side of the Alps, and his torch of hope burned brightly.

Such, then, were the interests, occupations, and tempers of mind of our young couple at the beginning of the month of December.

CHAPTER IV.

The "Great Abomination."

On the First Sunday in Advent the little church of the parish in which Rose's Bower was situated enjoyed the double advantage of Père Zacharie's eloquence in the pulpit, and of Mademoiselle de Pontchartrain's attendance as one of the congregation. The appearance of the former insured that of the latter; Mademoiselle de Pontchartrain was so devoted an admirer and patroness of Père Zacharie, that she made a point of never missing a syllable which fell from the Father's lips in public. To this partisanship, more perhaps than to his individual merits — though they were not few — did Père Zacharie owe his renown as a sacred orator. Mademoiselle was a leader and an oracle in that peculiar world which makes or mars the reputation of a preacher. She was by birth a Belgian, and the descendant of a very ancient and very rich Flemish family; but had long left her native country, residing for the most part in Rome. From the year 1849 to that of 1852, she had travelled a good deal in France and Italy. This year she had taken up her abode in a château in the environs of Chambery.

Signora Candia did not see her confessor and spiritual director mount the pulpit (it was the first time he had preached in the parish since her arrival) without some trepidation lest he should not be properly appreciated by a country congregation. Her flutter of spirits did not last long. The imposing presence, the solemn gesture, the perfect self-possession of the priest, riveted general attention almost before the tones of his deep voice were heard. We are not called upon to give any judgment as to the Father's talents or doctrine; we shall only testify to the incontestable success of his discourse. Probably the only hearer who did not relish it was Vincenzo. It was too highly flavoured for his simple taste, too thickly interlarded with hints and threats and apostrophes against a certain Amalekite, who must have played the preacher some scurvy trick, and Mademoiselle also; for, at every palpable hit, the lady gave most emphatic nods of approbation. Père Zacharie would not have stood so high in Mademoiselle's estimation, had he not been the mouthpiece of the party she favoured.

After the sermon, the curé and the father escorted Mademoiselle to her carriage, into which they handed her amid signs of deferential recognition from the gentry, and the lowest of low bows from the peasants. Mademoiselle was a woman on the wrong side of fifty, tall, fat, of an agreeable though very masculine appearance.

Her moustache might have given many a youth a pang of envy. Judging from the continual use she made of her eyeglass, she must have been extremely short-sighted. She raised it again, after seating herself in the carriage, to take a last survey of the crowd waiting her departure; and then it was that probably she, for the first time, remarked Signora Candia and her husband, who at that moment were just leaving the church.

"Pray, is that Mademoiselle Candia, of whom your mother speaks so well?" asked Mademoiselle.

"That is Madame Candia," replied the curé, with an emphasis on the "*madame*."

"Madame Candia!" cried Mademoiselle, nodding most graciously towards the Italian lady, and at the same time putting out her plump hand — "Madame Candia, allow me the pleasure of making your acquaintance. I have heard a great deal of you; if you are only half as good as you are handsome, you have more than your share. *Au revoir.*"

Mademoiselle's manner was a happy and pleasing combination of aristocratic bluntness and unctuous devoutness. Signora Candia had scarcely time to blush scarlet and stammer forth a polite rejoinder, before the grand equipage drove off. Mademoiselle had vouchsafed no more notice of Vincenzo than if he had not been there.

If the great lady had heard of Rose, Rose had also heard much of the great lady — at the parsonage, and indeed at all the houses where she visited; and what she had heard made praise from such lips precious indeed: heard of her exemplary piety and inexhaustible charity — of the great dangers she had run, by reason of the share she had had in securing Pius the Ninth's personal safety on the occasion of his successful flight to Gaeta in 1848. This last circumstance had invested Mademoiselle in Signora Candia's eyes with an aureole of sanctity.

"I must call on Mademoiselle de Pontchartrain one of these days," said Rose to her husband, as they walked home; "and I hope you will go with me, Vincenzo."

"Thank you," returned Vincenzo; "but I don't see the flimsiest rag of a pretext under which I could shelter my intrusion on that lady. I don't feel sure that she is aware of the existence of a Signor Candia. And indeed, Rose, if you will be advised by me, you will yourself wait for some little more encouragement from her. People of rank have a clear way of making their wishes known. If Mademoiselle de Pontchartrain wants your acquaintance, she will either pay you a visit, or beg you distinctly to come and see her."

"She did express such a wish to Madame, long ago," said Rose; "I don't think we ought to stand on so much ceremony with neighbours."

"Were this lady our neighbour, it would alter the case; but then she is not," returned Vincenzo. "It is a good hour's drive from our house to her château."

Rose looked neither convinced nor pleased.

"After all," resumed Vincenzo, "I only give you my opinion; you can use your own judgment, dear."

"Oh! since you disapprove of my going, of course I shall not; but —"

"I do not disapprove of your calling; only, were I

you, I would delay doing so for a little; that is all I advise."

Independently of his honest desire to guard Rose from taking a hasty step, which might bring upon her some mortification, Vincenzo had plenty of other reasons for wishing to avoid, or, if that were not possible, at least to delay, the making an acquaintance which he rightly considered as a dangerous one for his wife. Mademoiselle was a fanatical partisan, devoted body and soul to the interests of Ultramontanism and reaction; her château was the head-quarters of opposition of every colour. She carried on active correspondence with more than one of the leading cardinals at Rome, and also with the exiled Archbishop of Turin, residing at Lyons — the martyr-prelate, as she always styled him; the same at whose instigation it was that the noble Santa Rosa was, when dying, refused the consolation of the Holy Sacraments. All Mademoiselle's antecedents were perfectly well known at the Intendenza, and there it was that Vincenzo had gathered his knowledge of her. Aware as he was of Rose's predilections, no wonder he felt a decided repugnance to her entering an atmosphere of heated and systematic hostility to the principles he himself warmly cherished, and to the Government he desired faithfully to serve.

Some nine or ten days after the conjugal dialogue related above, the first thing Rose said to her husband on his return to dinner — said in that peevish tone of triumph which so clearly revealed the speaker's sense of her own slighted wisdom — was: "After all, I was right. Mademoiselle de Pontchartrain has been here; she did expect me to call on her, and was surprised at my not having done so. I wish I had followed my own impulse. It is always awkward to disappoint those who mean kindly by us."

Signora Candia rather exaggerated when she spoke of disappointment and expectation. Mademoiselle had merely said that she had hoped they would have met sooner; an empty formula of politeness, by which she meant nothing, and could have meant nothing, but a passing civility — as, were the truth told, she had completely forgotten Signora Candia's existence, until, happening to pay a visit to Madame, that managing old lady had reminded her of the fair inmate of the Bower.

"I am sorry if I led you into a mistake," said Vincenzo; "nevertheless, I am not sorry that Mademoiselle has called on you; it is what all the other ladies of your acquaintance did."

"I hope you will go with me to return the visit," said Rose.

"Did Mademoiselle inquire for me — express any desire to see me?" asked Vincenzo.

"She spoke of you, of course," said Rose, evading any direct answer to the question.

"Ah! my dear Rose," said Vincenzo, with a half-smile, "you are not a good diplomatist — you cannot hide from me that your new friend not only did not ask you to bring your husband with you, when you went to see her, but neglected the common unmeaning courtesy of hoping she should some day know Signor Candia. I, on my side, am as little desirous of Mademoiselle's acquaintance as she is of mine."

"Then you are very unlike everybody else," retorted Rose. "I know of no one who is not anxious to boast of being acquainted with Mademoiselle."

"I will explain my want of ambition," said Vincenzo. "Mademoiselle de Pontchartrain has very strong and decided political convictions, which are the very opposite of mine —"

"What does that matter?" interrupted Rose. "It is the same with the Curé, and Monsieur and Madame Chapron, and the Parmentiers. You differ from almost every person we know, and yet you go to their houses and they come here."

"It is too true," replied Vincenzo, "that a general feeling of dissatisfaction does prevail in this neighbourhood, and that any one who holds to the Government, and yet does not wish to live isolated, must make up his mind to put up with a good deal of contradiction. Still, there are degrees and shades among the opposition. Now, Mademoiselle's is of the deepest dye, the very *ne plus ultra* of reaction. Neither she nor any of her intimates make any secret of their hatred and contempt of the Statuto, and the Government which upholds it. As it happens that I revere the Statuto, and have the honour to be employed by the present Ministry, I do not think that my proper place would be among those who openly revile the Constitution, and would do all they could to overthrow it."

After a pause, Rose said: "To say the least of it, it is unlucky that you should have put yourself, and that without the least necessity, into the awkward position of not being able to associate with most estimable people, solely on account of their political views. However, thank God, *I* am not in the service of the Government."

"True; but you must not forget that you are the wife of one who is."

"Do you mean to say that, because I am your wife, I am to decline the invitations of a lady who is looked up to with reverence by every soul but you?"

"God forbid," said Vincenzo, "that I should ever require you to slight any one who had shown you kindness! only I would caution you against forming any great intimacy in a quarter so decidedly hostile to the institutions of our country. I have too much dependence on the affection and good sense of my little wife to have any fears of her wilfully placing me in a false position."

"Nothing like this would occur if we were quietly where we ought to be," said Rose, with a sigh.

Vincenzo did not follow her on that unsafe ground, but, like a wise man, held his peace.

Why had Signora Candia twice already pressed Vincenzo to accompany her to Mademoiselle de Pontchartrain's, and why had his refusal to do so wounded her to the quick? Simply because she had fixed upon Mademoiselle as a powerful auxiliary in a future, yet hitherto vague, plan for the conversion of her husband. It was the curé and his mother who had first suggested the idea to Signora Candia of forming a close alliance with Mademoiselle for that holy purpose, by remarking to her pretty often that, if any one could cure Signor Candia of his political exaggerations, Mademoiselle was the person. Vincenzo's political and other extravagances were openly discussed and deplored, in Rose's presence, at the parsonage. What a pity that so clever and sensible a young man should have imbibed such extreme and dangerous tenets! What a pity that he, who might live at home in plenty and ease, should choose to drag his wife about the world, and endanger his soul in the service of a Government bent upon Protestantizing Catholic Piedmont!

One clear frosty afternoon, Rose ordered the gig, and drove to Mademoiselle de Pontchartrain's château, to return that lady's visit. As Vincenzo's ill-luck would have it, Rose had hit upon a most unfortunate hour. Mademoiselle had just received the Turin official *Gazette*, in which, at full length, was what Mademoiselle called "The Great Abomination" — namely, the text of the bill for the suppression of certain convents, and for the better distribution of the revenues of the Church, presented to Parliament the previous day.

Mademoiselle, and no wonder, was in a state of great agitation, and the numerous company filling her *salon* no less so. Rose was quite intimidated — first, by unexpectedly seeing so many persons assembled, and then by the disturbed looks of every one. Cut to the heart as the party-woman may be, the woman of the world will never lose her self-possession: her smile will be as easy, her round of phrases flow as gracefully, as though no mischance had occurred.

"I am doubly glad to see you to-day, Signora Candia," said Mademoiselle. "Thank you for this mark of your sympathy. The day of trial teaches us who are our real friends. Ah! we live in sad times." Even the shortsighted spinster could not mistake the look of blank astonishment on her visitor's face. "Is it possible," she asked, "that you are ignorant of the news?" An increasing expression of anxiety on the handsome young face intimated, beyond all doubt, that Signora Candia was quite in the dark as to what Mademoiselle alluded to. "A new persecution," explained the great lady — "a new crusade against religion! All religious orders are suppressed, and their property confiscated— a happy combination of sacrilege and robbery; liberty of prayer in common abolished; thousands of holy men and women torn from the altar, and thrown penniless and houseless on the world — Père Zacharie among the rest. That's the news to-day brings us; there it is — every detail given; you will see I have not misstated anything." And Mademoiselle handed Rose the Turin *Gazette*, adding, "You are aware this is the Government official paper." Rose mechanically accepted the newspaper almost thrust into her hand, and tried to read the article pointed out to her; but the words trembled and danced so before her eyes that she could not make out a syllable. "This will be a finishing-stroke for His Holiness," pursued Mademoiselle. "I am confident it will break his heart. Was there ever, in fact, blacker ingratitude? At the selfsame moment the Supreme Pastor, in his unfailing solicitude for the welfare of souls, defines and publishes the dogma of the Immaculate Conception, thus opening to Catholicity a new fountain of grace, *your* country makes him *this* return!" Poor Signora Candia grew first red, then white, and tears of shame and indignation swelled her eyelids. Mademoiselle, mollified by Rose's irrepressible emotion, added, "No, I am wrong to say *your* country, my sweet child. I know Piedmont well; it is Catholic to the backbone. The authors of this violence are a mere handful of infidels, headed by Count Cavour, and sold to England. But their triumph will not last long; for is it not written in the Scriptures, 'For yet a little while, and the ungodly shall be clean gone; thou shalt look after his place, and he shall be away'?"

Fresh arrivals now called away the attention of the lady of the house; and Signora Candia was left to herself, or rather to the lamentations of her neighbours on her right and left. The one, an elderly lady, declared it to be her firm belief that the time was at hand when they must all prepare for martyrdom; the other, a middle-aged priest, gave her the very words in which Count Cavour had couched his promise to Lord Palmerston, that within two years Piedmont should become Protestant. Rose was horror-stricken; all she now heard chimed in too well with her preconceived notions for her not to imbibe it as if she had been a sponge.

When she rose to take leave, Mademoiselle insisted on her remaining a little longer, that she might have the comfort of seeing that the cause of religion was not entirely deserted — nay, might yet triumph. Little doubt of victory to the cause Mademoiselle upheld, had all the owners of those angry, gloomy, excited faces wielded swords instead of tongues for it. Visitors poured in — the first had to withdraw to make room for the last comers. Mademoiselle had a nod or a word, a shake of the hand or a smile, for every one. A general, reviewing his troops on the eve of battle, could not have displayed more energy or tact. Rose's heart overflowed with admiration for the heroic lady, and with hatred for her adversaries. It never occurred to her that, in a country where such gatherings could take place in broad day, and such manifestations of feeling be indulged in without danger, martyrdom could not be so near at hand as the elderly lady at her side had been predicting.

Rose was at last permitted to say adieu; and the

reader will be better able to imagine than we describe her state of mind during her drive home. It was fortunate that the distance between the Château and the Bower was considerable, thus giving her time to cool down sufficiently to put some method in her passion; otherwise a domestic storm would have been inevitable. Shall we also turn to account a few minutes of this interval, and try to free the "Great Abomination" from the clouds of exaggeration wrapt round it by party-feeling, doing our best to reduce it to its real proportions?

The bill in question, be it fully understood, cast no one penniless on the world, nor did it confiscate any property whatever. It suppressed, it is true, a certain number of useless religious communities, but allotted to each of their members a pension sufficient to live upon. It claimed for the State the administration of all conventual property, yet strictly maintained the application of all ecclesiastical revenues to exclusively ecclesiastical purposes — such, for instance, as the payment of those pensions above mentioned, the redemption of the ecclesiastical tithes in Sardinia, and the raising of the stipend of poor parish-priests to a minimum of twenty-four pounds per annum. Be it known that, up to that period, between two and three thousand parish-priests (*parrochi*) in Piedmont had incomes under twenty pounds a year. The bill, further, imposed a tax on the revenues of the convents which were not abolished; also on those of the colleges conducted by ecclesiastics, as well as on the annual rents of archbishoprics and bishoprics. The bill was guilty of no greater enormities than these.

Signora Candia was just stepping out of the gig

when, from the opposite direction, Vincenzo appeared, bringing with him two guests to dinner, instead of only the one (Ambrogio) who was expected. The second, a nephew of the Intendente of Chambery and just arrived from Turin, had been a fellow-student of Candia's. Vincenzo made no scruple of now and then bringing home with him a friend, or even two, without any previous notice; for he knew that Rose rather liked than not the being taken unawares, that she might prove the extent of her foresight and the fertility of her resources. This afternoon, however, he perceived that something was amiss; but he abstained from making any inquiry. He introduced his old acquaintance, and was glad to see that he was courteously received; his coming, then, had not caused the cloud on Rose's brow. The dinner went off well, even cheerfully; for the Signora's reserve melted under the warm and unanimous praises given to the cookery and to the perfection of the way in which every dish was served. How had Signora Candia managed to train her servants so admirably? No mistress of a house, let her causes of vexation be what they may, is proof against this sort of flattery.

The three men, after smoking a cigar, had scarcely joined the Signora in the drawing-room, when the curé came in. Since the days had grown so short, instead of a morning visit, he occasionally dropped in of an evening to enjoy a sociable talk. The curé was a very hardworking, very meritorious, labourer in the vineyard of the Lord; a simple, sober-minded, sensible sort of man in all respects, and in all subjects, save one — viz.: what he called the prerogative of Rome, and by which he meant the prerogative of all wearers of a cassock, from the Sovereign Pontiff down to the seminarist in minor orders. On this topic the curé was passionate, one-sided, fanatical, intractable. He was on this particular evening full of the news of the day, and had purposely come to the Bower to vent his spleen. He thus began:

"Good evening, gentlemen, good evening. I am not surprised to see you in such good spirits. I have come to congratulate you on the courage of your masters at Turin. The Protestantizing scheme begins at last to assume both colour and shape."

"Most ungrateful of curés," said Vincenzo, good-humouredly, "how can you be wroth with a measure which rescues three thousand brother-priests from starvation?"

"A drop of honey in a cup of poison," retorted the curé. "For my part, I spurn the bribe, *Danaos et dona ferentes*. And besides, what right have you to take from one to give to another?"

"But we are not taking anything from anybody," here put in Ambrogio. "We are simply administering that well which you have administered ill — first of all, making it yield more, and then distributing the produce more justly and humanely; that is what we are going to do."

"Say, if you are allowed the opportunity," cried the curé; "do not cry out victory before the battle is ended. You may live to learn what it is to cope with Rome."

"It is Rome which insists on coping with the spirit of the age," cried Vincenzo. "Why does she compel us to take, by force, that which we were disposed to ask as a favour — that which we begged for with humility?"

"Ah! but what if you ask for things which Rome cannot consistently grant?" said the curé.

"*Was* it impossible to grant us the abolition of ecclesiastical jurisdiction, which we on our knees implored?" asked Vincenzo.

"Don't mention that subject," exclaimed the curé, chafing; "that was your declaration of war to the clergy — a spoliation and an insult."

"Exactly so," burst out Rose; "those are Don Natale's very words."

This sudden profession of faith by the hostess took every one by surprise, and was followed by a perfect blank of silence. Vincenzo was the first to recover his presence of mind.

"If," said he, turning to the curé — "if it was a spoliation and an insult, why did the Church take it so meekly from France, Austria, and Naples? — why resent it alone from Piedmont?"

"I do not admit your right to put the question. Rome lies under no obligation to explain her course of action. One of two things: either you believe that the Holy Spirit abides with her, or you deny it. If you believe, then you must be persuaded that whatever she does is right; if you deny it, then you are a heretic, and I shall avoid all discussion with you."

"*Distinguo*," said Vincenzo; "in all that regards dogma, I submit to Rome; as regards discipline, I reserve my right of examination."

"Then are you no true Catholic, and I will not argue with you any more," cried the curé, rising and moving towards the door. "Only I warn you," he added (and he paused on the threshold), "if you imagine that Savoy will passively follow in the wake of your Protestant movement, you never were more mistaken in your life. Let this abominable law pass, and the last bond between us and Piedmont is loosened. Our natural leaning towards France — which up to this day has been counterbalanced by reason and traditional attachment to a dynasty — will then be transformed into an imperative duty, a necessity of self-defence: Catholic France from that moment will be our chosen country."

"Why not rather at once choose Rome, the model Government?" asked Ambrogio.

"Her Government is incomparably better than yours," sneered the curé; "if you had any right feeling, you would be ashamed of it."

"Not a bit," said Ambrogio.

"I am, for one," retorted the curé, and went away.

"And I, for another," said Rose, rising and leaving the room.

Vincenzo flushed scarlet to the very roots of his hair, then grew deadly pale, but said nothing. A minute or two of awkward silence ensued. Ambrogio was the first to break it, by a sonorous peal of laughter.

"Great asses that we are," he exclaimed, "to be arguing and quarrelling with a curé on such topics! It is like pounding water in a mortar. The Church in our country has so long lorded it over the State that the least attempt on the part of the Government at independence, even in the most trifling matter of discipline, is *bonâ fide* regarded and resented as an intolerable interference and usurpation."

The stranger followed Ambrogio's lead, and after a little Vincenzo roused himself to take a share in the argument; but so pre-occupied were all three speakers with their own private thoughts that every effort to keep up the ball of conversation failed. Ambrogio saw that the kindest thing to do was to say "Good night." Begging Candia to present their farewell compliments to the Signora, the two gentlemen rose to depart. The night was dark and tempestuous, snow was beginning to fall; yet Vincenzo put on his hat, and announced his intention of seeing his guests part of their way home. Ambrogio remonstrated in vain.

"I have a headache," urged Vincenzo, "and the cold air will do me good." And so, one step after another, he went with them almost to the entrance of Chambery; he then said "Good night," and turned back. Rose's husband felt angry, very angry — more angry than he had ever fancied it possible he could be — with his wife; he wanted to give himself time to cool, and walked leisurely, heedless of snow and wind. Many were the wise counsels he gave himself during his solitary walk; and these, combined with the beneficial effect of air and physical exertion, enabled him to re-enter his own dwelling in an even frame of mind.

He found Rose sitting in her usual place on the left of the fireside, her work-table before her. She neither spoke nor looked at him when he went in. Vincenzo walked up to her, and, without speaking, took her hand, raised her gently from her seat, and, with a little tender compulsion, made her sit down by his side on the sofa. Still retaining her hand in his, he said: "Rose dear, I hope, nay I am sure, you are now sorry for having been so hasty. You know to what I allude?"

"Yes, I understand you perfectly," said Rose; "but, to tell the truth, I do not regret either what I said or did, nor do I think I ought to feel any regret."

"I am sorry, more than sorry, to hear you say so. I still hope you will alter your mind, when you come to reflect on how painful it must be to me — how unbecoming it must appear to my friends and visitors — to find you siding so openly and vehemently with my opponents."

"I took the side of truth," said Rose.

"Rather of what you believe to be the truth," answered her husband. "Still, even the cause of truth should not be rashly or injudiciously defended. Your whole manner, the remark you made during the unlucky debate, pointed out clearly enough the opinion which had your sympathy. You were not called upon to indorse the curé's last taunt — a most unjustifiable one — against the Government."

"Unjustifiable, perhaps, in your eyes, but not in mine," said Rose, quietly disengaging her hand from Vincenzo's clasp.

"We'll come to that point by-and-by. I now appeal to your heart, not to your reason. Dear Rose, how have you the courage not only to inflict real pain on me, but also to place me in such a false position, by making a display of feelings diametrically opposed to mine, and without, I again repeat it, any necessity for so doing?"

"Some years ago," returned Rose, "it was in 1850, I believe — in order to prevent disagreeable scenes, I begged you to humour certain of my father's opinions; you then said — his views being contrary to truth, how could you humour them without being guilty of equivocation? That is my answer to you now. I will not equivocate."

"But to humour your father's ideas, in the sense you meant, would have been my acquiescing in that which I held to be false — I must have made a positive sacrifice of truth. Do I ask anything of the kind from you? I merely beg you to be silent."

"My silence would be misconstrued," observed Rose.

"Little danger of that. You have taken very good care that your way of thinking should be known; and then your memory is good, but mine is not bad, and I can complete your recollections of the incident to which you have just alluded. Our conversation did not stop at the phrase you quoted against me. After a while you asked me, you may remember, whether I was sure of being on the side of truth, and I replied that I was sure of being on the side of what I conscientiously believed to be truth."

"Well, what difference does that make?"

"It makes this difference, that the convictions which I supported, in contradiction to those of your father, were the result of time and reflection, of much honest searching and conscientious study. Now, put your hand on your heart, and tell me truly, can you say as much in behalf of the opinions which divide you from your husband?"

"It is not necessary to be learned in order to have

decided opinions as to right or wrong, in certain matters: Conscience is often our surest guide."

"Yes, when the conscience is an enlightened one."

"Many a child knows more as to faith than the subtlest philosopher," said Rose.

"Allowed; but the point at issue is not one of faith, but of legality. It is simply this — Has the Government a right to interfere with the civil existence of corporate bodies? Yes or no?

"Certainly not with corporate religious bodies, unless with the consent of the Pope."

"And, supposing he withholds his consent, what then?"

"Then they cannot be meddled with."

"That is a monstrous doctrine, my dear Rose, which has no foundation but in your prejudice. If such were the general belief, the Pope would be master everywhere."

"So he undoubtedly is, in all spiritual concerns."

"But convents, inasmuch as they are corporate bodies, are not spiritual concerns, my dear."

"Yes, they are," said Rose, doggedly.

"Why, dear love, a positive proof that they are not so is that, by the law of Piedmont, no convent can be established, as a corporate body, anywhere in the limits of the kingdom, without the authority of the Government, in whose hands naturally remains the power equally to withdraw as to grant an authorization."

Rose was silent for a moment — then said, "You may outargue me, but you will not bring me over to your opinion for all that."

"Really, Rose," said Vincenzo, losing patience, "this is being too absurd."

"Of course, I know that to differ from you must be absurd."

Vincenzo was about to reply, but suddenly checked himself — sitting by her side with the compressed lips, the clenched hands, the tightly-closed eyes of one undergoing a spasm of intolerable pain. At last he said, in a subdued voice, "Rose, we may hold different opinions and yet live in peace, if we only resolve to bear and forbear."

Rose answered, "You told me at Florence that either of us who thought the other wrong was bound to try and put that other right."

"True, and so it ought to be; but . . . ."

"You mean me to understand that you have given up the hope of making me adopt your views?"

"I begin to despair of making you understand me."

"Well, I don't give up the hope of some day converting *you*," said Rose with animation.

"I don't say nay," replied Vincenzo, somewhat sadly. "In the meantime, let us live in peace."

"I ask for nothing better," said his wife.

"Then, if that be the case," continued Vincenzo, "promise to offer no pointed opposition to my political creed in the presence of others."

"That I cannot promise," said Rose, quietly.

"You cannot promise that!" repeated Vincenzo, in a sort of blank amazement. "Are we come to such a pass that, after only eight months of marriage, you can coolly tell me, your chosen husband, that you cannot promise to impose a slight check on yourself, for the sake of our mutual peace?"

"It is written, 'He that loves father or mother better than me is not worthy of me,'" quoted Rose.

"And you believe that, in conducting yourself as you do, you are acting up to the spirit of the Gospel? Oh! poor Gospel!" and Vincenzo covered his face with his hands.

Rose, after a little while, said, "There is one way of securing a good understanding between us; let us go back to Rumelli."

"And resign my appointment? — never!"

"Then, it is not my fault if we do not live in peace," wound up Rose, rising and leaving the room.

Vincenzo did not close his eyes the whole night for thinking and commenting upon that prophetic question, addressed to him years before by Onofrio: "Can you not foresee a day when this young lady (alluding to Rose) will take one side and you the other of a question, and when to do your duty will cost you a severe struggle?" And he, Vincenzo, had answered, without hesitation, "No!"

CHAPTER V.

Sundry Conjugal Dialogues.

THIS is perhaps the place to clear away a doubt which may possibly have crossed the mind of the reader. Was Vincenzo a freethinker, or was he only a Protestant sympathizer? Neither the one nor the other. Vincenzo was a sincere Catholic, and earnestly wished to remain so. No one, indeed, had hailed with more enthusiasm than he the marriage between Religion and Liberty which 1848 had inaugurated; no one had acclaimed with more tender reverence the name of the Pontiff Reformer. Even the desertion of the national cause by Pius IX. had not succeeded in alienating from him the young enthusiast's heart. Vincenzo, a mere lad at the time, had nevertheless felt the full force, and allowed to the Head of the Church the benefit of, the provocation received; and, though the day on which Pius IX. re-entered his capital, more like a conqueror than like a father (and a conqueror, too, by foreign arms), had been to our hero a day of infinite sadness, yet that sadness had not been unmixed with hope. Yes, he still retained a confident hope that the fountain of mercy and of wise improvements, checked awhile by the pressure of the storm, would again flow abundantly when tranquillity was restored.

We give the impressions and feelings of one whose education had been entirely clerical, and of whose belief one of the fundamental tenets consequently was, the absolute infallibility of the Pope. But, when he beheld reaction enthroned in the Vatican, and persevered in wantonly, in spite of the calming effects of time and the pressing counsels of France; when he beheld Piedmont, the only plank still floating of the total wreck of Italian independence and freedom, made the target of a systematic and passionate hostility by the Holy See — then Vincenzo's conscience was sorely troubled — then began a painful struggle between his reason and his faith, his duty to his country and his duty to Rome. Who was wrong? — who was right? — the Pius IX. of 1848, the initiator of Reform, the champion of Italian Independence; or the Pius IX. of 1850, the despotic ruler, the bitter opponent of the only remaining representation of National Independence in Italy? This contention of mind was long and severe — volumes could not describe its phases; its issue we already know. This was chiefly brought about by two circumstances: first, by those parliamentary debates on the Bill for the Abolition of Ecclesiastical Jurisdiction which we saw him so assiduously follow; and, secondly, by the subsequent denial of the last Sacraments to the dying Rossi di Santa Rosa, by reason of the share he had had in the passing of that bill. Vincenzo came out of the struggle, he honestly hoped, a sincere Catholic and a firm believer in the Papal prerogative, so far as it did not interfere with the Civil Independence of the State. It was a limitation forced on many a wellwisher to their country at that period — a limitation without which Italy would be still in her limbo. This point cleared, we pursue our narrative.

The ill-omened discussion with the curé, which had led to that deplorable one between husband and wife closing our last chapter, was destined to have a long train of disagreeables for all parties. The curé did not show his face at the Bower during the next three days; thereupon Rose went to the parsonage to inquire the reason. The curé pleaded want of leisure, having had more to do than usual, and also that the severity of the weather had deterred him from venturing out, except on a call of duty. Madame was more explicit, though not, of course, in her son's presence.

"The truth was," said the old lady, "that the curé had been obliged to listen the other evening, at the Signora's house, to declarations of principles, to professions of faith, to arguments coupled with taunts, which no ecclesiastic who respected himself would run the risk of enduring a second time. It was sad, very sad indeed, that a lady of Signora Candia's sterling piety should, in a degree, countenance by her presence the use of irreverent, irreligious language."

"But what can I do?" asked Signora Candia, in very real distress; and then she made a clear breast of her troubles, told of her late difference with Vincenzo, of the sort of persecution she suffered at his hands, &c. &c.

The old lady, who was undoubtedly well-meaning, and who would not for the world have wilfully run the risk of sowing discord between husband and wife, did not, for all that, spare her young friend either advice or exhortations as to her conduct for the future — advice easier to give than to follow, Signora Candia must, at the same time, be firm and yielding — conciliating, yet very careful as to what or how far she conceded; in short, it was a case of how to do and not to do. Above all, Signora Candia was to pray, to be for ever praying, never to be tired of praying, for her husband's conversion — yes, Madame said, for his conversion, just as though he had been a heathen. To such a pitch can party-feeling pervert the ideas and confuse the language of some of the worthiest of human beings!

As Rose was leaving the rectory, she met the curé coming in, and she could not resist telling him that she now knew the reason why he stayed away from the Bower — adding that, however much she regretted it, she could not say she thought him wrong. The curé was too conscientious a man not to strive, to the best of his power, to diminish the force of the impressions which he instantly discerned his young parishioner had received. With much candour he declared that he considered himself as the cause of the scene of the other evening; for he it was who had given the first provocation, by broaching the vexed question. If he no longer went to the Bower, he begged her to believe that he refrained, not from resentment for what had occurred, but rather from fear of what might happen. He confessed that he distrusted his power of self-control when certain topics were discussed; he was easily stung, and apt to sting in return. Better for all parties that, for the present, he should make himself scarce. He was bound in justice to say that Signor Candia was always moderate and becoming in argument. Every one, however, could not boast of Signor Candia's tact and good-breeding. The curé concluded, as he had begun, by affirming that he had blamed, and ought to blame, no one but himself: he was too irritable, especially considering the cloth he wore; but, as so it was, the more advisable it became that he should shun occasions for exhibiting his bad temper. The curé's allusion to Ambrogio's want of respect and politeness was not lost on the Signora. She had never liked the young soldier, and had always looked upon him as a pernicious and dangerous associate for her husband; from this moment she began to detest him.

Vincenzo had not been blind to the discontinuance of the curé's visits, and had easily guessed the cause; but had thought it most prudent to seem as though he had not noticed the change. This silence did not suit Rose. On the evening of the day she had been to see Madame, she said, "So long as you have your everlasting Ambrogio, you don't care a straw who comes to see us or not."

"Why do you speak of Ambrogio as everlasting?"

asked Vincenzo. "Such an epithet implies, either that you think him tiresome, or that his visits here are indiscreetly frequent. I must say, however, that I see no ground for one or the other imputation. Ambrogio is, in my opinion, lively and entertaining; and I have not perceived that he takes undue advantage of your hospitality."

"How you blaze up in defence of this dear bosom-friend of yours!" retorted Rose. "Had I said twice as much against Monsieur Parmentier or the curé, you wouldn't have had a word to offer in their defence."

"I cannot say — probably not," was Vincenzo's reply. He went on: "Ambrogio is an old and very dear friend of mine. I both esteem and like him; besides, I am very thankful to him for all the trouble he has taken to make himself useful and agreeable to us."

"I don't deny that he has been obliging, but you seem to me to overrate his services."

"Perhaps; and, if I do, I don't regret it: as regards gratitude, better err by too much than by too little. However, that has nothing to do with what we were discussing. You said, I think, that I did not care who came to see us or not?"

"Well, and isn't it true? For instance, the curé has not been here for an age, and you have never vouchsafed an observation on the subject."

"An age would be indeed a long period. If I am right in my reckoning, only four days have elapsed since the curé's last visit, and that supposing he does not look in on us this evening."

"As to that," interrupted Rose, quickly, "you may make quite sure he will not come."

"Besides, my dear Rose," continued Vincenzo, "my

not mentioning a subject is no proof that I have overlooked it. I had my reasons for abstaining from any remarks. I now see, and grieve to see, by the certainty you express as to the curé's not calling this evening, that my conjectures as to the motive of his unusual absence were too well founded. He has taken offence where none was given."

"None given!" exclaimed Rose. "Do you think it can be a matter of indifference to any ecclesiastic to hear religion and its ministers attacked in his presence?"

"Not a word, Rose, my dear, was uttered against religion or its ministers the other evening. Pray, don't *you* get into the habit of confounding ideas and words. Religion is too holy a thing for its name to be taken in vain."

"What is the good of affecting respect for the name, when none is felt for the reality?"

"Your speech is very uncharitable, Rose; but let us keep to the curé. He was himself the originator of the dispute, and he certainly gave more blows than he received — two excellent reasons for his not taking offence."

"He is offended, though, and he will never call here again; our house will soon be shunned like a lazzaretto."

"Oh! no danger of that; you will always have plenty of visitors; they will come for your sake, to be edified by your piety."

"My piety is, of course, a matter of ridicule to you."

"Not of ridicule; rather of surprise that it should steer so clear of charity. Since the other evening's ill-fated discussion, every word you have said to me, every look you have given me, has been that of a bitter enemy."

Rose did not repel the charge; probably she felt it had in it some truth. Rose closely resembled her father: easy and good-natured, so long as everything went smoothly with her — that is to say, so long as she had her own way; the moment she was crossed, she became all pricks and thorns. The absence of any early check — nay, the system of over-indulgence pursued by her father with regard to her — had increased her natural tendency to domineer, and sharpened her impatience of all contradiction.

After this conjugal dialogue, Vincenzo made a point of seeking the curé and expressing his regret that so long a time had elapsed since they had seen one another — adding a hope that the change was not in consequence of what had occurred at their last meeting. The curé denied having taken any offence; but admitted, as he had done when similarly challenged by Rose, that there were certain topics highly unpalatable to him, and which he wished to avoid hearing discussed.

"Come and see us, as you used to do," replied Vincenzo, "and the disagreeable subjects you allude to shall be entirely banished from our conversation. Now then, when may we expect to see you?"

The curé promised that he would go to the Bower as soon as the pressure of business attendant on the solemnities of Christmas and New Year's-day should be over.

Christmas and New Year's-day went off tamely enough at the Bower. Ambrogio was the only guest, and to his hostess not one of the most welcome. His Christmas-gift to the Signora — a bouquet of beautiful hothouse flowers, which had cost him a month's pay — was frigidly received, and left to wither in a corner. Vincenzo after a while took up the flowers, and, placing them in a vase full of water, called his wife's attention to how charmingly the red-and-white camellias, with their glossy-green leaves, represented the national colours of Italy. Nor was the slight to the nosegay the only one Ambrogio had to put up with from the Signora. Women, no doubt, have at their command a thousand delicate ways of showing their sympathies; they also have at least as many of making evident their antipathies without laying themselves open to the charge of being ill-bred. In short, Ambrogio had quite enough of it; and, once his *visite de digestion* paid, Rose's Bower saw him no more.

Vincenzo had now to hunt up his friend. "What has become of you, my good fellow? I began to fear you were ill."

"Not ill, but uncommonly busy," answered Ambrogio.

"Nonsense!" said Vincenzo; "not all the business in the world could or would prevent you seeing your friends, were there no other reason. The truth is, you are offended with my wife?"

"Not offended," protested Ambrogio. "Signora Candia is an excellent woman, but she does not like me, and takes good care to let me know that she does not. What, therefore, can I do in such a case but stay away?"

"You ought to do something better still; put up with my wife's whims for my sake, and come and see us as usual. She has taken it into her head that what passed in our last fencing-match with the curé has scared him from our house; *inde iræ.* She holds to this curé and his mother more than I could wish. Yet how object to the intimacy? However, what I have to ask you is this — the curé has agreed once more to favour us with his company; I will get him to fix an evening; will you come and meet him?"

Ambrogio assented.

"Thank you. I will send you word what evening he fixes; and only remember this, my friend," wound up Vincenzo, "we'll keep clear of politics. No possibility of living in peace in this blessed country unless we banish politics from our talk."

"Ha! ha!" cried Ambrogio; "what did I tell you? I gave you a year, and, behold, within four months you are singing my song."

Bent on making peace, Vincenzo, on leaving Ambrogio, went direct to the curé, and, reminding him of his promise, pressed him to say what evening he would spend at Rose's Bower. The curé did his utmost to parry the attack; however, after a stout defence, he had to yield, and named seven o'clock of the evening of the day after but one. Vincenzo informed Ambrogio of the arrangement, and begged him to be punctual. The young man was to the minute, and so was the curé; and, if hand-shakings can be accepted as honest witnesses, a full reconciliation then and there was effected between the priest and the soldier. The difficulty in such ticklish circumstances is at once to find some subject of general interest, so that there should be no pause between the first preliminaries and the subsequent conversation. On this occasion there was ready at hand a topic of public, though melancholy, interest.

On the previous day, the 20th January, the Queen Dowager, Maria Teresa, widow of Charles Albert and mother of Victor Emmanuel, had died at Turin. This sad event had excited universal regret. It was commented on and deplored everywhere, and it was natural enough that it should be discussed in Signora Candia's drawing-room. The species and length of the Queen's malady, her age, her lineage, and suchlike particulars, were all sifted and ascertained. Her Majesty's unfailing benevolence was also dwelt upon with enthusiastic and well-deserved praise. The curé especially enlarged with warmth upon this point, going so far as to hint that even by her death she might confer a lasting and great boon on her country. It is next to an impossibility for persons of passionate temperaments not to colour facts, more or less, according to their own feelings or prejudices. The curé's insinuation was something obscure, at least to Signor Candia, who asked, "In what way?"

Avoiding a direct answer, the curé said, "Is it not written that afflictions are sent from on high to deter the powerful from their wicked purposes?"

The allusion was transparent enough now; the wicked purpose was evidently the suppression of the convents, and the heart to be softened was that of the King.

Ambrogio was nettled, and observed that, in his poor opinion, it was far more Christian to bow one's head simply and submissively to God's decrees, than to presume to interpret them according to our own shortsighted views and passions. Vincenzo had to interfere at this critical juncture, and succeeded, not without difficulty, in preventing an angry retort from the priest, and in launching the conversation into another and less dangerous channel. Vexed with himself for his want of caution, Ambrogio, in a praiseworthy spirit of conciliation, spoke to the curé of those things most likely to please him — admired his little church, inquiring whether Father Zacharie would preach there soon again. Ambrogio had never heard the eloquent monk, and was very desirous of enjoying that pleasure. The curé answered civilly, but laconically. Rose was mute. The curé rose to go away early, and Vincenzo and Ambrogio saw him safe home; Vincenzo then walked on to Chambery with his friend. We pass over their conversation.

Rose had retired to rest before her husband's return. He betook himself to his little study, his haven of peace; and there, amidst his notes and speculations, he for a time forgot all his worries. But for the real enthusiasm with which he pursued the particular kind of avocation he had taken in hand, such a life as he had been leading for now nearly a month would have been unbearable. The report he was drawing up for the Minister was his great consolation. The first part, that which embodied the political and social state of Savoy, was all but finished; indeed, he meant to forward it within a week to Turin.

From that evening Ambrogio adopted the habit of seeing Vincenzo at his office; his visits to the Bower were made at rare intervals, while those of the curé ceased altogether. Vincenzo was not sorry for this. Political and religious partisanship waxed so hot and bitter all round that it was vain to hope that people of different opinions should meet without quarrelling. Various causes, besides the chief and permanent one — we mean the stormy debate in the House of Deputies on the vexed question of the convents — various causes, we say, contributed to this recrudescence of hostile feelings. First, in chronologic order, was the death of the Queen, the wife of Victor Emmanuel, which followed close on that of the Queen Dowager; scarcely a week separating the two melancholy events, which were represented, by those whose interest it was to do so, as signs of celestial wrath, provoked by the bringing forward of the obnoxious bill. Next was the Encyclic of the 22d of January, in which the Head of the Church reproved and condemned the proposed law as to convents, demanded its withdrawal, together with the repeal of all laws and ordinances tending to infringe upon the authority, or to limit the rights, of the Holy See and the Church; in short, summing up by declaring all such null and void. Simultaneously with the issue of this Encyclic arose rumours of impending excommunication. The Bishops of Savoy were convened, and recorded a public and violent protest against the law. On the 26th of the same month, Cavour laid before Parliament the treaty of alliance between France, England, Turkey, and Piedmont, by which Piedmont bound herself to send twenty thousand soldiers to the Crimea. This master-stroke of policy was met, both on this and the other side of the Alps, by an outburst of opposition. Measures which entail on the country a sacrifice of blood and money are rarely, if ever, popular.

Such were the facts which, skilfully dressed and coloured for party purposes, brought in their train a fresh crop of fears and irritations. Not one of these incidents, not one of the comments to which they gave rise, but in its rebound struck Signora Candia's mind, and through her, alas! murdered Vincenzo's peace. Religion in jeopardy, the country on the eve of destruction! — such was the burden, varied in form, never in substance, of the conversation current in Rose's little world. She heard it everywhere. At the parsonage, it was asserted by Madame in biblical style; at the other houses where she visited, passages from the local clerical papers were paraphrased; even in her own household the panic was shown by clumsy queries from the cook and gardener, as to whether it was true that the King had turned Protestant, and that mass was no longer to be said. If so, what was to become of them all?

On the 11th of February, Vincenzo came home at his usual hour, looking very pale and sad; he found Rose sitting, or rather crouching, before the fire. He went to her, and pressed his lips to her forehead, as he had taken to doing since she had left off meeting him with a kiss. He said, "Have you been calling anywhere to-day, Rose?"

"Yes."

"Then you know the bad news?"

"Yes, I do," she answered.

"Did you hear it at the parsonage?"

"Yes; from Madame."

"What a terrible fatality!" exclaimed Vincenzo. Rose made no reply, but sat looking vacantly at the fire. "You say nothing?" observed Vincenzo, after a pause.

"Of what use speaking?" asked she in a forlorn manner.

"Are you ill, Rose?"

"Not ill, but stunned," she said.

The news alluded to by Vincenzo was enough to stun any one. For the third time within the space of a month had the Angel of Death knocked at the gate of the royal palace. The Duke of Genoa, the King's brother, was dead! He died on the 10th of February, at the early age of thirty-two.

Dinner that day at Rose's Bower was a mere ceremony. Vincenzo tried to eat, tried to converse; Rose neither ate nor spoke. The meal was short and gloomy as a funeral feast. When it was over, Rose resumed her crouching attitude before the fire, staring intently at the burning wood. Vincenzo took up a newspaper, held it before his eyes for a few minutes; in vain; he could not read. Throwing it down, he drew near to his wife, took both her hands in his, and said, caressingly, "Rose, my darling, talk to me."

"I have nothing to say," was the reply.

"Oh! yes, you have; tell me your thoughts at this moment."

"Indeed, I scarcely know if I am thinking. I feel so heavy and giddy."

"Then you must be ill, dear; let me go and fetch a doctor."

"No, no, pray don't. I am not in need of a doctor: what I want is rest. I have had a shock, a great shock; the best thing for me at this moment is to go to bed and try to sleep."

Rose accordingly went to bed, had a cup of hot tea, which she said had so greatly relieved her head that she was sure she should be able to sleep. Vincenzo sat by the bed until he had seen her drop into a quiet slumber; then he left her, in obedience to the wish she had expressed, that he should leave her as soon as she was fairly asleep.

It was still early in the evening, not yet eight o'clock; Vincenzo, therefore, determined to devote two or three hours to his favourite task. It was some time before he could enter into it with his accustomed interest, but he did so at last. The first portion of his report had been sent to Turin at the end of January; the second and last part, on which he was now engaged, was devoted to the consideration of the measures best calculated to stem disaffection. To point out practical ways and means to accomplish this desirable end, taxed all the young politician's powers; the very feeling of difficulty added a keener relish to the labour. Vincenzo believed, rightly or wrongly, that he had hit upon a plan, which would reconcile the claims and interests of Savoy with the claims and interests of Piedmont. Plunged in his speculations, Vincenzo had for some hours completely forgotten the external world, even to his fire, which no longer retained a spark of heat. Suddenly the door opened, and on the threshold stood Rose, robed in white, her face as white as her dress, her eyes sparkling ominously in her pale face. She began thus, in a solemn voice:

"Vincenzo, you asked me this evening to tell you what I was thinking of. I told you then I scarcely knew; now I do, and I have come to answer your question."

"Not here, not here," cried Vincenzo, folding her in his arms; "it is too cold, the fire is out; your hands, my poor darling, are like ice, your forehead burning; you must not stay here."

She paid no attention to his entreaties, but went on, in the somewhat inspired tone in which the curé's mother generally spoke —

"Vincenzo, the finger of God is plainly to be discerned in all these startling deaths. Woe to those who will not see the Hand that strikes! Let us leave this Tower of Babel, before it be laid low in the dust; let us abandon the doomed vessel ere it sinks. I am come now to warn you, to implore you."

"Not here, not here," exclaimed the half-distracted young man, trying to draw her gently from the room. "You are not well, my precious one—you are feverish: come, come away — to-morrow. . . ."

Rose broke in: "To-morrow will be too late. Hear me — nay, you must and shall, even to the very last word I have to say. Vincenzo, you are on the high road to perdition. God Himself calls on me to save you. Zeal for your salvation has eaten up my heart from my very childhood upwards. From the day you left the seminary, I have never ceased to tremble for you. Turin and what you learned there have been so much poison. I tried to the best of my power to counteract the effect. My conscience is heavy with self-reproach, for not having done all that I might have done. When God made me the instrument to save your life, I felt that He had also chosen me to save your more precious soul. I accepted the mission, and, in order to fulfil it, I married you."

"Oh! Rose," expostulated Vincenzo, with a groan, "only for that."

"Chiefly for that," returned she. "I liked you, without ever thinking of you as a husband. My real wishes turned towards the cloister. The first time I ever thought of you as my husband was in connexion with the mission confided to me. When, later, Barnaby told me how unhappy you were on my account, I felt for you also in another way. I won't deny it; but my mission stood foremost — to accomplish it, my first object. Now, I come and say to you, Will you help me to fulfil the will of God as regards you?"

"Certainly, with all my heart," said Vincenzo, soothingly; "only you must allow me a little time for consideration, my dear Rose."

"For consideration of what? There is but one way."

"Be it so, dear; yet this is neither the time nor the place for coming to so serious a resolution. You are shaking with cold, and so am I. Let us go to bed. Night is the mother of good counsels, you know; and we shall resume the argument whenever you please."

Rose, whose feverish energy was nearly spent, suffered herself to be led back to her room, and to her bed. She was restless, and for some time went on speaking incoherently; at last, however, she fell into a profound sleep. Vincenzo was completely bewildered. Rose had saved his life (through the infallible scapulary he supposed)! Rose had a mandate from on High to save his soul! Rose had married him not for love, but from Christian charity! All these statements had taken him by surprise, the last most of all. Though uttered in a moment of feverish excitement, though contradicted to some extent by his own previous observations and experience, still this last declaration had cut him to the heart — one must be in love to understand how deeply. After all, how few really had been his opportunities for observation; how limited his communication with Rose, during what may be termed the period of his courtship! The poor young husband was swimming in a sea of perplexities. Another and appalling contingency presented itself: what if the fit of morbid excitement which had all at once seized on one so passionless, should be only the beginning of a series of such? What if her religious fanaticism should react on her constitution? What if, one of these days, he should have to choose between his appointment and his wife's health — perhaps her reason?

Rose got up at her usual hour the next morning, and went about her domestic operations as usual. She said, in answer to Vincenzo's inquiries, that she felt quite well, only a little tired. She supposed she had had a slight attack of fever, which had, however, now entirely disappeared. Vincenzo was unwilling to go to his office that day and leave her alone, but ended by yielding to her pressing solicitations that he should not stay at home for such a trifle. When he came back, she kissed him affectionately, quite a novelty; she looked grave, but her manner to him was sensibly improved from what it had been previous to her nocturnal visit to his study. Withal, as she made no allusion to it, Vincenzo began to hope that she had retained no consciousness of it. He was shortly to be undeceived; for on the evening of the third day, Rose said calmly, "Vincenzo, you have now had plenty of time for consideration. What is your answer?"

"My answer?" repeated Vincenzo, startled as by an electric shock.

"Yes, your answer? Are you going to resign your appointment or not?"

"Listen to me, Rose."

"Not before you have answered my question."

"Well, then, I have no intention of giving up my appointment." She rose to leave the room. "Stop," he said; "you promised to listen to me." She sat down again. Vincenzo gave her his reasons for resisting her suggestion; spoke firmly, but with great moderation. He said that, before flinging away an advantageous opening in life, and one on which he had set his heart, a young man in his position must have peremptory reasons indeed, and he had none. The motive which she put forward, of a kind of judgment of God, was merely a groundless and very uncharitable assumption. Neither the King nor the Government had done anything to justify the supposition; it was rash and impious in man, to distort into signs of celestial wrath events which were in the ordinary course of nature. "Judge not that ye be not judged." The three successive blows which had fallen upon the King ought to serve rather to augment the sympathy and loyalty of his subjects, than be made the starting-point for disloyal attacks and sweeping condemnations. He had a conscience as sensitive as that of other people, and his conscience was tranquil. He claimed for himself the independence of opinion and action which he readily granted to her. He besought her, in the name of all that was holy, in the name of their future peace, to moderate her zeal in his behalf. In short, all that a sensible, a loving and conciliatory husband could say under the circumstances, Vincenzo said.

"Is that your final determination?" asked Rose, when he stopped speaking.

"It is."

"Well, then, I will tell you what I am going to do. I shall write to papa to come and take me back with him."

"Do so."

"You said that when papa came to see us, I might return with him if I felt inclined."

"Yes, I said so."

"Then we understand one another?" wound up Rose, as she was leaving the room.

"Perfectly."

Her unfeelingness had raised a storm of indignation within Vincenzo's breast. It burst forth in this cry, "Why, her heart is as dry as a pumice-stone."

CHAPTER VI.

Coup de Grace.

The beginning of the month brought with it welcome and unwelcome tidings for Vincenzo. The glad ones were conveyed in a letter from Onofrio, written by the desire of his chief. The Minister, so wrote Onofrio, had read with interest and pleasure the first part of the report sent in by the young Consigliere. It had afterwards been laid before the President of the Council, who had been pleased to express his approbation, and had asked sundry questions as to the author. As a proof of his satisfaction, and as an encouragement, the Minister had promoted Vincenzo to the rank of paid Consigliere, his pay to begin from the 1st of March. Onofrio added from himself, privately, that this favour was almost unprecedented, after only six months' service; and Vincenzo's fortune was made, if the second and last part of his report confirmed the expectations raised by the first. Vincenzo must strike while the iron was hot; that is, work hard, and send in the complement of his memoranda as early as possible. Then followed affectionate congratulations and assurances of friendship.

Enclosed in the letter was an order upon the Treasury for four hundred francs — a hundred for the emoluments of the current month; the remainder as an indemnity for travelling expenses and for those on first taking possession of his office. Four hundred francs! — an enormous sum in the eyes of one who had never yet possessed a farthing of his own — gained too by his own exertions; the money was fairly his. Vincenzo, be it known, was as poor after his rich marriage as before; he had shrunk from any present or future pecuniary benefit to himself, to be derived from that source. Without entering into tedious particulars, it may be as well to state here that the settlements had been so arranged, at his express desire and instigation, as to give him no legal claim to a penny of his wife's fortune. Well! this money, and the far more valued approbation of his services, which, but a few months ago, would have made him leap for joy, left him unmoved now; nay, even added to his depression. Both as coming from the Government which stood condemned without appeal in Rose's eyes, and as creating further obstacles in the way of her fervent wishes, these rewards could not but widen the chasm between her and him, a chasm wide enough as it was. From the day of that final explanation which closes our last chapter, Rose had given up all voluntary communication with her husband. She never spoke to him unless he spoke to her first, and then her answer was restricted to the words absolutely indispensable; even in the presence of a third person she never addressed him. They had now, to be sure, few evening visitors; but during the day the lady received and returned calls pretty often. For all this, Rose's attitude towards her husband had no shadow of provocation in it; still less was it indicative of anger; it was more like that of a resigned victim. She had taken the habit of withdrawing for the night very early, sometimes almost immediately after dinner. Vincenzo, on his side, never interfered with her movements. We must, in fairness, allow that his efforts at conciliation were neither many nor very energetic; he was too full of resentment for that — resentment at the unjust treatment he received at her hands — resentment at her threat of making her father a party in their difference.

That threat was realized. Rose had written to her father; which had procured for Vincenzo a letter from his father-in-law that had in it the germ of a rich crop of worries. This is the unwelcome news to which reference was made above. The Signor Avvocato mentioned that he had received a letter from his daughter, pressing him to keep his promise of coming to see her, and begging that he would allow her to return with him to Rumelli. The present precarious state of his health made his undertaking any journey at that season of the year difficult, but one across the Mont Cenis an absolute impossibility. March and April were the months when the mountain was most unsafe on account of the avalanches. Still, if, as he feared, the climate of Chambery did not agree with his daughter, some way must be found of meeting her wishes. All other considerations must yield to the important one of her health. His principal motive for writing to Vincenzo was to know all the truth about this most interesting point. Rose's letters had for some time been sad and depressed. He took it for granted, of course, that Vincenzo had nothing to do in causing this dejection, and that he remembered and fulfilled his promise, never to cost his wife a tear. The Signor Avvocato begged that he might be relieved from the state of anxiety in which he was, by a speedy answer. The last page of this epistle was covered with high-flown declamations against Cavour's insensate policy in the Oriental Question.

Vincenzo wrote back without delay, that, in fact, Rose had lately expressed a wish that her father would make out his promised visit to Chambery, that she might avail herself of his return to Rumelli, to accompany him and spend some time there. This wish had a natural explanation in her love for her father, and her attachment to her native place. Impaired health, he was glad to say, had no share in it. Rose bore the severe climate of Chambery very well; and, except a slight touch of fever, which had lasted only a few hours, she had been perfectly well ever since her arrival. He assured the Signor Avvocato that he quite agreed with him, that all other considerations were as nothing compared to that of Rose's health. That her letters should be sad and depressed he very much regretted, though it did not surprise him. Rose had very decided views as to religious matters, and objected strongly to certain measures lately brought before Parliament. Most of the persons of her acquaintance entertained the same opinions, and confirmed her in them. At this moment religious party passions ran very high in Savoy, and Rose carried her opposition to the Government so far as to consider holding office under it as a disgrace, and one she would fain spare her husband. He, on his side, saw the points in question in quite another light, and naturally this dissonance occasionally caused some discomfort between them. But Rose had too much good sense not, sooner or later, to feel that the same liberty of judgment and action which she claimed for herself her husband was also entitled to. Leaving this topic, Vincenzo gave a summary of Onofrio's letter containing the Minister's golden opinions of his report, and mentioned the high token of favour he had received. The son-in-law then ended his letter by a spirited vindication of Cavour's policy with regard to the East, expatiating on the bright prospects it opened to the nation.

With a deep sigh, half of sorrow, half of vexation, Vincenzo sealed his long explanation, and took it himself to the post; for he had received both Onofrio's and the Signor Avvocato's letters at his office. All the way to the Bower he was busy revolving in his mind how he could best break the news from Turin to his wife, so as to run the least possible risk of a disagreeable ebullition of feeling from her. The result of his reflections was, that he kept the knowledge of his good fortune to himself until the next morning after breakfast, when he placed the letter open before Rose, saying she would oblige him very much by reading it, and fled. This Parthian method is that, alas! to which more husbands than one have resort. Did she read it or not? Probably she did, though she made neither remark nor allusion to prove that she had; nor did Vincenzo proceed to any interrogations. The letter when he sat down to table was lying by his plate; he took it up and thrust it into his pocket-book. He made no mention of the Signor Avvocato's despatch; but the recollection of the new hornet's nest she was bringing about his ears did not tend much to sweeten his temper towards her.

The month of March of the year 1855 was one of great rejoicing throughout the Catholic world. Pope Pius IX. had, to use Mademoiselle de Pontchartrain's words, conferred an everlasting benefit on all Christians, by the definition and promulgation of the Dogma of the Immaculate Conception. Bells were tinkling, torches blazing, incense smoking, sermons spouting, congregations swimming in and rushing out of all the churches in Christendom night and day. Nowhere was the movement taken up with more fervour than in orthodox Savoy. Great religious excitement prevailed there, and not alone of an unmixed religious character. The Glorification of the Holy Virgin could not be complete, it seems, unless enhanced by an increased feeling of bitterness. Indeed, the *enfants terribles* in the Ultramontane camp turned it into a political counter-demonstration. Through their newspapers, from their pulpits, they called to the Government, "See the faithful who flock to us; count their numbers, and grow wise while it is yet time. Rome is all-powerful, and no force on earth can prevail against her. Be warned."

It was from no fault of the young benefactress of

the parish, as Madame was wont to style Signora Candia, if the display at the neat little church fell short of the grandeur of the occasion. Signora Candia had grudged neither money nor time nor personal exertions for that purpose; and she had the consolation of hearing it said on all sides, that not in the memory of the oldest inhabitant of the village had any *fête* ever gone off with so much *éclat*. The weather was beautiful on both Sundays; a circumstance almost miraculous, considering that it had done nothing but rain in the interval; and, further, on both Sundays, Father Zacharie was in the pulpit, giving it soundly to the Amalekite. Mademoiselle de Pontchartrain, who had been absent for a fortnight in Lyons, could only be present on the second Sunday. Her graciousness to Signora Candia was extreme. She regretted more than she could express having missed the Signora's last two visits — she had been much occupied; she had a great deal to say, and would soon do herself the pleasure of calling. To have done with the *fête*, Chambery and its environs were splendidly illuminated on the *fête*-days mentioned above: as for Rose's Bower, it was in a blaze. Perhaps Vincenzo would rather have had it otherwise; but, in the state of incandescence which mistress and maid, cook and gardener, had reached, a word of opposition might have cost the master dear — supposing even that he had intended to hazard anything of the kind. He refrained, and shut himself up in his study.

Not long after this Signora Candia went again to call on Mademoiselle de Pontchartrain. The two ladies had not had a *tête-à-tête* for months; they now indulged in a long and confidential talk.

"I am sorry," said Mademoiselle, "to hear from Madame that your husband favours all these abominations."

A look of intense deprecation, addressed to the ceiling, was the young wife's only answer.

"But that must not be," continued Mademoiselle. "You must convert him. My dear, what are husbands good for, except to be converted by their wives?"

"I have tried," said the Signora, with a despairing shake of the head.

"You must try again, my dear; if a pious and charming wife like you does not carry every point with her husband, it is her own fault."

"Perhaps," said the Signora. "But, you know, it is possible to feel the full evidence of a truth, and still lack the power of persuasion, so as to impress it upon others."

"True; but, if that is your only difficulty, I can easily remove it. I will give you some of the newspapers which are on our side, and in them you will find plenty of unanswerable reasons ready-made."

"He will find an answer, though," said Rose. "He is clever, and somehow or other he always gets the better of me in every argument."

"Then send him to me," said Mademoiselle.

"I thought of that long ago, and I have begged him more than once to come with me to call on you. I am ashamed to say he would not."

"Ah! he would not," repeated Mademoiselle; "I suppose he is afraid of me." The great lady fell into a fit of musing. Presently she asked, "Do you think your husband is such a determined sinner as not to take the sacrament at Easter?"

"I don't think so."

"In that case, my dear, he must go to confession first; persuade him to choose Father Zacharie as his confessor; if you succeed, your husband is saved."

"I will try; I will do my best," said Rose; "but I doubt...."

"That is exactly what you must not do, my dear. What? doubt, with that pretty face and sweet voice of yours! Why, my dear child, they would coax the Grand Turk himself into becoming a good Catholic."

From this date, there was a partial thaw of Rose's icy manner to her husband. The drooping mouth of the victim drooped no longer; the lips even curved into a smile now and then. She condescended occasionally to speak to him without being first spoken to, and even asked after Ambrogio, and how it was he had been so long in calling. She still persisted in the habit she had lately adopted of going early to her own room, but she no longer left Vincenzo alone immediately after dinner. They had rarely any callers of an evening, since Ambrogio had ceased coming — once or so, perhaps, in the week; but, during the day, Rose received visits as usual from her neighbours, principally from the ladies, and at dinner she regularly told Vincenzo whom she had seen. Vincenzo was at a loss what to make of this unexpected rainbow in the heaven of his home. Was he to see in it a token and a covenant of renewed peace? He knew not; nevertheless he welcomed it, as though he were certain of its bringing him nought but good. Forbearing and generous as it was in his nature to be, Vincenzo had nearly forgotten his late great cause of irritation against Rose — that letter which she had brought upon him from his godfather. The wound it had inflicted was healing fast under the influence of time. A month had nearly elapsed, and there had been no fresh communication from Ibella. Vincenzo gave his wife the credit of this peaceable result; and his gratitude towards her disposed him the more to hail, and encourage, and meet in a kindly spirit, her conciliatory advances.

One evening, during the whole of which Rose had been unusually talkative and lively, she suddenly said, "By-the-bye, here's Easter close at hand already; how time does go! We ought to be thinking of preparing ourselves for taking the sacrament, Vincenzo."

"We ought, indeed," replied Vincenzo.

"I should be so glad," said Rose, "if we could take the Communion together."

"With all my heart; nothing to prevent us," said Vincenzo.

"And also confess together," she went on.

"We can do so on the same day, but not together, since we have different confessors."

"Why, you have none, have you?" asked she.

"Yes, I have; the chaplain of Ambrogio's regiment."

"But you have not been to him yet?"

"Not yet; but I know him well."

"Why should we not have the same confessor? Try mine instead, will you?"

"Father Zacharie!" exclaimed Vincenzo.

"Yes, Father Zacharie. Do, pray do, go to him, if only for this once," urged she, coaxingly.

Vincenzo turned pale, as if he had been stabbed;

he had had an instantaneous revelation that his wife's late sweetness had been part and parcel of a scheme.

"I am sorry to refuse you," said Vincenzo; "but I have a prejudice against Father Zacharie."

"Oh!" protested Rose.

"Yes," he went on, "a prejudice which excludes the chief requisites for a good confession — implicit confidence, and entire giving-up of self on the part of the penitent."

"But what is the reason you can't have confidence in him?" asked Rose, deprecatingly.

"Because, right or wrong, I look upon him as a party-man, and therefore likely to call me to account not only for my sins, but for my political opinions."

"Well, and, suppose he does, you can defend your opinions?"

"Ay, and change the confessional into an arena of political controversy. To argue and contradict is essentially destructive of that spirit of unlimited submission which a penitent ought to bring to the feet of a confessor."

"How can you be sure that Father Zacharie will lead you into a controversy?"

"I don't say that I am sure; I have my doubts that he may, and, doubting, I abstain. Father Zacharie is not the only man, is he, to whom power is given from above to bind and to loose?"

"Certainly not; but he is a man of superior piety and learning; everybody allows that. What sacrifice could it be to you to go to him?"

"Penitence, my dear, is a sacrament, and ought not to be made a matter for experiments. My conscience says, No."

"Your conscience! your conscience!" cried Rose, in a burst of passion; "say rather your obduracy in sin, which shrinks from the remedy."

"To listen to you, Rose dear," said Vincenzo, resentfully, "one would suppose your husband to be the blackest sinner under the canopy of heaven."

"Oh, no! that you are not; don't mind what I said. I know you are not that; but even the righteous sin seven times a day; and it would be such a consolation to you, such a consolation to me, to know, and to know it from so holy a quarter, that you are in the right path."

"Such a consolation you shall have, I hope, from lips as authoritative. I promise you, before communing, to bring my confessor to you — a pious and enlightened man — that you may hear from him whether I am in a fit condition for communing."

"Oh! But how can I make sure from any one else — from a person I don't know? If you were to commit a sacrilege!"

"Yours is a perverse predetermination to drive me mad!" cried Vincenzo, springing to his feet with a jerk of desperate impatience. He strode distractedly across the room, and bending forward, leaned his head against the window. The moon was shining beautifully: he did not see it. His whole frame was vibrating with contending emotions. He stood with his head against the cold glass for a few minutes; then turned round, his face pale as death; went to his wife, and, kneeling down before her, put both her hands on his head, and said — said with tears in his voice — "On my knees, I implore peace. I am weary and spent. This perpetual warfare is killing me by inches. For pity's sake, let us be good friends again: lately we have been such good friends. Why shouldn't we be so now, and for ever? I am not exacting — that I am sure of; I shall become even less so in future. I wish to content you — only, oh! . . . . let us have peace." And with both hands he pressed the hands he held in his convulsive grasp upon his head.

"If your longing for peace were as earnest as you say," observed Rose, freeing her hands, "you would do something for its sake."

"Is there anything that I have not done, that I do not daily do, to secure it?"

"Indeed! as your ready acquiescence to the prayer I made you a moment ago testifies!"

"Implacable!" cried Vincenzo, starting to his feet, and striking his forehead with his clenched hand. "It is not enough, then, that I have sacrificed for her my best friend, my very self-respect; I must also sacrifice my conscience, endanger my soul, risk the committing a sacrilege, to please her. Never! never! never!" And in a paroxysm of uncontrollable passion he flung himself upon the sofa, and buried his head in the cushions. Rose mused a while; then, rising, lighted a candle, and said —

"I shall start for home to-morrow. Good night."

"Good night!" After such a scene, the words sounded like a mockery. Vincenzo spent the greater part of this night in wishing that he was dead. As the hours went by, the cold became intolerable in the drawing-room; so he stole, with chattering teeth, to his little study, made a great fire there, and sat gazing into it. Whichever way his mind's eye turned, it could see no outlet to the magic circle which encompassed him; or rather, no outlet but one — to resign his appointment, renounce all chance of usefulness, of independence here below, to wrench from himself the best part of himself, return to Rumelli, to live and die there. A terrible sacrifice, the mere prospect of which made his hair stand on end, and drops of cold perspiration start on his brow; still one a man might make to purchase his own peace and that of his wife! But would it accomplish that end? That was the awful question. Would not the causes of antagonism survive the sacrifice, and infallibly beget fresh strife? Would not passing events at Rumelli, as well as at Chambery, strike out of the incompatibilities of two such opposed minds sparks which would burst into a blaze? And, if so, would it not be a fool's bargain to throw away his occupation, his last consolation — for what? For a respite of a few months, perhaps — for a little enlargement of the magic circle in which he turned.

Amid this conflict of thoughts, Vincenzo fell into a heavy and uneasy sleep, sitting in his chair. When he awoke it was broad day — a grey, misty, rainy day, well suited to the colour of his thoughts. Somebody was stirring in the adjoining drawing-room. It was Marianna putting things in order. Vincenzo asked if the Signora was up.

"Up and gone," said Marianna.

A qualm of terror chilled Vincenzo's heart.

"Gone! And where, pray, in such weather?"

Marianna could not tell.

"Had the Signora taken the gig?"

"No; the Signora had gone out on foot."

There was an undercurrent of anger in the tone of Marianna's answer. She belonged to that species of uneducated hirelings whom the favour of a master or mistress disposes to be insolent. Vincenzo had more than once repented having placed this girl near his wife. His regret would have been greater, could he have guessed the baneful influence she exercised over her mistress. She detested Savoy, longing after Rumelli where she had a sweetheart. The only idea in her wooden head, on which she enlarged continually when alone with the Signora, was this: "What could induce a man who might live in peace and plenty at the Palace to choose instead to stay at Chambery, and work like a slave?"

In order to account well for Rose's infatuation, we must keep in mind the variety and continuity of action brought to bear upon her, and which, from whatever side exercised, always came to the same practical conclusion — the giving up his situation by her husband, and their return to Rumelli. Vincenzo went to his wife's room. Everything was in its place; not the least trace of the disorder incident to the preparations for a journey: he breathed more freely. Rose appeared at the usual hour for breakfast. She was quite collected; there was even a tinge of solemnity in her look, but no hostility. She spoke more than was her wont during the meal, but on indifferent subjects; spoke with a new addition of condescending unctuosity in her voice, just in the tone of a kind superior to an erring inferior. When breakfast was over, she made the remark to her husband that he was not dressed for going out. Vincenzo said that the weather was so bad, he was not sure whether he should go out or not.

"I know what detains you," said Rose; "you may, however, go in all security to your office, without any fear of a rash step on my part during your absence. I forgot last night, for a moment, that this was Passion Week, the season of all others for meek behaviour and forgiveness. Fortunately, I have some good friends who have reminded me of my duty."

Vincenzo guessed perfectly well that Rose had gone to the parsonage to consult about the flight she meditated, and had been advised against it. He said, "I am happy to find you in such a truly Christian frame of mind, more happy than I can say. In so far as I can, I shall make it my study so to act as to secure its continuance."

"I have no doubt you will. Thank you. Now you had better go. Adieu!"

He went, but came back the next instant with his hat on, and said, "If you will tell me on what day you mean to take the sacrament, I shall so arrange that we may be able to do so together."

"No, thank you. I can fix no day; and then, upon second thoughts, I think it best that we should fulfil that duty separately."

Vincenzo went away much disappointed. What he had believed to be a living fire was only an *ignis fatuus;* the spirit of meekness and forgiveness which was on Rose's lips had not penetrated to her heart. He had not gone far before he met Ambrogio striding along most vigorously. Since Ambrogio had given up calling at Rose's Bower, it was by no means unusual for him to meet his friend halfway to town, or to accompany him part of the way home. As soon as they now came in sight of each other, Ambrogio shouted, "I have got them," and cut a caper.

"What is it you have got?" asked Vincenzo.

"My epaulettes, my dear friend. I am sure of them now; I am going to the Crimea."

Ambrogio's regiment forming no part of the expedition to the East, he had volunteered for the service, and the Minister of War had been pleased to grant his petition. This was the news he had received that very morning, and which had caused his elation. He was to start from Chambery at three in the afternoon of that same day. Vincenzo, as he listened, felt as if he could cry like a girl. Instead of that he took his friend with him to the Intendenza, and, having asked and easily obtained leave for the day, accompanied Ambrogio on his several errands, saw him take a hasty meal, and at last went with him to the coach-office. The two friends formed a striking contrast — the one so buoyant, so sanguine, so full of life; the other so dejected, so spiritless, so worn-looking.

"I wish I could take you to Sebastopol; it would be a fine cure for all the blue-devils," said Ambrogio, observing Vincenzo's depression.

"I wish to God you could!" said Vincenzo, with a sigh.

Ambrogio was too discreet to put any direct questions, and too clear-sighted also; he well knew where Vincenzo's shoe pinched. Solemn promises of writing were interchanged; a last squeeze of the hand, and ... there was poor Vincenzo wending his solitary way home.

Ambrogio's departure was a heavy blow, heavier still than he had at first imagined. He knew not, until he missed it, all the comfort he had derived from that friendly presence, that lively talk, that silent sympathy. Vincenzo strove manfully to conquer the despondency which was daily stealing more and more upon him, but with little or no success. The temperature he found at home had nothing in it to raise drooping spirits. Rose, looking down upon him benignantly from her cloud of saintly forbearance; Rose, communicative out of duty, with about as much spontaneity as an automaton or a parrot, chilled him far more than Rose scowling or scolding. In the latter mood she was, at least, true to nature; while in the former she was — should he avow it? — artificial. For that she played a part, consciously or unconsciously, in opposition to her real feelings, Vincenzo had ample proof in the flashes of anger which not unfrequently darted from her cloud.

To add to his discomfort, a letter came from the Palace, containing the sad intelligence that Don Natale had breathed his last. Vincenzo was desired to break the news to Rose as gently as possible. The Signor Avvocato wrote that he missed his daughter much in this moment of sorrow. Could not Vincenzo ask leave of absence for a month or so, and bring his wife home? The Signor Avvocato added that "he felt he was breaking fast, all his friends were going one after the other. It would soon be his turn. Don Natale's death was a warning." A more mournful letter could not be. The shadow of death lay on every line. A postscript, probably written a little later, lauded to the skies the devotion and unremitting attention shown by Don Pio to Don Natale up to the very last. Don Pio was the young priest, Don Natale's assistant, whose acquaintance we have already made.

Had they been on the best terms, Vincenzo could not have used more care and tenderness in telling Rose of Don Natale's death. She was greatly affected, moved even to shedding abundant tears. Vincenzo's answer to his godfather was one full of heartfelt condolence, full of sympathy. Yet he did not dissemble his repugnance to apply for a holiday after so short a period of service, and scarcely six weeks after being promoted to the paid list. He promised, however, to write to Onofrio, leaving it to his friend's discretion to forward the request or not, according to precedents, and to Onofrio's own impression of the likelihood of its being granted or not. At all events, if it was necessary, could not Rose, entrusted to the care of the guard and accompanied by Marianna, undertake the journey without him?

Onofrio wrote back at once that leave of absence, as a rule, was never granted under a year's full service, except in cases of the death of very near relatives. Onofrio felt sure that, much as the Minister might wish to oblige Vincenzo, he would not feel himself justified in acceding to his request under the circumstances. This being so, Onofrio had come to the conclusion that what there was no hope of obtaining it was safer not to ask for, the more so as a petition of this kind might create in the Minister's mind a prejudice far from favourable to his *protégé*. Vincenzo inclosed Onofrio's letter to the Signor Avvocato, and waited with a beating heart for the result. He could not but apprehend fresh and disagreeable complications. The opportunity seemed too good for the Signor Avvocato not to use it as a battering-ram against that appointment which was in everybody's way. Rose's appearance also caused him some uneasiness. Surely, her colour was not so brilliant as hitherto it had been, and, at times, she looked wan and dejected. His anxious inquiries on the subject elicited the invariable answer, "that she was very well — that she had never been better;" an assertion, so evidently exaggerated as not at all to reassure him. What with misgivings about Rose's health, and what with anticipations of some disagreeable communication from Rumelli, Vincenzo had not a moment's peace of mind. Even the solace he had constantly found in applying himself to the report failed him now. Care sat beside him at his writing-desk, and interfered with his work.

About the middle of May arrived the dreaded letter from the Palace. Vincenzo opened it with trembling fingers. The contents surpassed his worst expectations. An ultimatum, diluted in a sea of phrases, was given him. The Signor Avvocato put an absolute veto on Rose's travelling, as Vincenzo had proposed, with her maid, and in charge of the guard; at the same time the old gentleman insisted on it, as a matter of urgent necessity, that his daughter should go to him without delay. Thus, he said, there remained no alternative but for Vincenzo himself to accompany her. If Vincenzo could do so with the consent of his superiors, so much the better; if not, so much the worse for his appointment, for do so he must. After all, there was little profit or honour in serving a Government which did its utmost to disturb the conscience of the nation, and made itself the blind tool of the ambition of England and France. Rose's health ought to be the first consideration, to which all others should yield — especially so in her present interesting situation. . . . .

Vincenzo bounded from his chair, as though a thunderbolt had fallen on the desk before him. A stab through his heart would have left more colour in his face. What! Rose was .... and had told him nothing..... Impossible! She could not have been so unnatural as that. It was a delusion of fatherly fondness. It could not be .... Out he dashes, speeds through the streets like mad, reaches home, lays her father's letter before Rose, his finger on the momentous passage, "Is that true?"

Rose changes colour, and falters a "Yes."

"And you did not tell me!" came in a cry of anguish from his heart, with a storm of tears and sobs. "And you did not tell me! You withheld that blessed announcement, which I would have fain received on my knees, which was mine by right; you withheld it from me, your husband, the father of your child — kept it from me, deliberately, as from your worst enemy!"

"Don't be so hard," stammered Rose, hanging her head. "I was wrong ..... didn't think ..... then you were so cross."

"I cross," groans Vincenzo; "I cross, who implored peace at your feet!"

"I mean before that — when I begged you so hard to give up your appointment."

"Confound the appointment!" thundered the young man, striking his forehead in a new burst of passion; and out of the house he rushes, and down the hill like a dart.

Where can he be gone? thought Rose, recovering from her surprise: to send in his resignation, perhaps. From the curse fulminated against his appointment, this was no improbable hypothesis. At the end of another hour she recollected having heard of volunteering for the Crimea, and she took a sudden panic that he had gone to enlist, and would never come back. Enlistment for the Crimea was the utmost stretch to which her imagination could reach. That he might possibly have gone to throw himself into the first well in his way, or to buy a pistol and blow his brains out, never crossed her mind for an instant.

He had done neither, thank God; for here he comes at last, reeling with emotion and fatigue, and as blanched as if he had been his own ghost. He sank upon a sofa, and said, "I have sent in my resignation."

"Have you, indeed?" cried Rose.

There was in her voice (unconsciously so, probably), a ring of exultation too naively selfish not to be offensive. All the sediment of gall which had been gathering at the bottom of his heart for months now rose to his lips.

"Yes," said he, with concentrated bitterness; "I have; it is written and signed by my own hand, and in the post by this time, all safe. The King himself could not get it back again. So you may set your heart at rest, and so may your father also. You have, both of you, your wish. Be happy. And, if what makes your happiness breaks the heart of a poor wretch, what matters it? It is only your husband's."

Nature will assert itself. After all, Vincenzo was only made of flesh and blood.

CHAPTER VII.

Welcome Home.

Once the first shock of uncontrollable anguish over, Vincenzo set himself to consummate his sacrifice with dignity — to put as much method as he could in his wreck. It was, above all, urgent that he should communicate to his godfather the decided step he had taken and to communicate it so as to keep to the truth, and yet spare his wife. He accordingly wrote a few plain lines to the following effect: —

"I hasten to inform you that I have done what you implicitly advised me to do in your last letter — that is, sent in my resignation. And yet I must disclaim all credit for a docility which is only apparent, the motive impelling me to take so extreme a resolution having nothing in common with the reasons put forth by you in support of your views. The fact is that, simultaneously with the receipt of your letter, I acquired the certainty that my continuance in office in this country injured far more important and precious interests than those involved in the office itself. Inexpressibly painful as was the sacrifice, I could not and did not hesitate to make it. May it not be a barren one, at least! Do not, I pray you, take it unkindly if I have referred the determination to which I have come to a motive quite distinct from any of those suggested in your letter. I should have been better pleased to say nothing on this head, did I not fear to give you, by my very silence, the erroneous impression, were it only for a moment, that I shared in your unfavourable opinion of the Government; which emphatically, do I not. There may be, as you urge, little profit, but there is plenty of honour to be earned in its service; and it is a great consolation to me, in my present trial, to think that I am still young enough to make some of that crop of honour mine, when this transitory cloud has passed away. On this point I reserve my full liberty of action. Believe me, in the meantime, &c."

There was also another danger to be guarded against — namely, the possible, nay probable, misinterpretation which his wife's acquaintances would give to his sudden retirement from office. To prevent all ambiguity on this subject, next morning, at breakfast, he handed to Rose his letter to her father, adding by way of comment, "I wish you to read what I have written, as I am anxious there should be no mistake as to the spirit by which I am actuated, and that you may undeceive such of your friends as might be disposed to see, in the course I take, either a recantation, or a desertion, or a conversion, — anything, in short, little respectful to the Government, or honourable to myself. There is nothing of the kind. What I was yesterday I am to-day. What I do I do *you* know why; but I cannot let the public into the confidence of our domestic squabbles: and yet the step I have taken must be accounted for somehow or other; first of all to the Intendente, and that, too, this very day. As far as I can see, there's no better way of saving appearances — supposing they can be saved — than to plead your health and your present situation as calling for a change of air, and my natural unwillingness, under the circumstances, to be separated from you for any length of time."

Rose promised to abide faithfully by the version he proposed — one, she said, more founded on fact than he was aware of, considering how often she had felt more poorly, of late, than she had chosen to say. She spoke submissively — nay, humbly. Her tones and looks were those of one who, sensible of having offended, seeks to propitiate. The sin of omission, of which she had been guilty towards her husband, weighed heavily on her conscience. The more so, as it was the first of which she believed herself to be guilty — yes; the first and the only one. She, *bonâ fide*, gave herself credit for having been, up to this day, a dutiful and an exemplary wife. Had she not left father and home for her husband's sake? Had she not zealously and assiduously watched over his salvation? Repulsed, had she not returned repeatedly to the charge, and wrested him at last out of the road to evil-doing? We beg the reader's attention to what we would fain call the young woman's conscientious infatuation, if the words were not at such direct odds with one another. Rose was persuaded that she was not only perfectly justified in what she had done, but bound to do it. She laid the flattering unction to her soul, that whatever pain she had inflicted on her husband she had inflicted for his ultimate good. She had well deserved of him, and this, thank God! he would some day himself acknowledge. Did not the end — and what an end! his salvation — justify the means? It was only because unnecessary to that end that Rose condemned herself for the reticence which had so upset her husband.

Vincenzo went to Chambery to fulfil his disagreeable task of making known his resignation of his office to the Intendente. The interview was as trying a one to his feelings as can be imagined. He returned at his usual hour for dinner, which was nearly over, when a messenger arrived with a telegraphic message. It was addressed to Vincenzo, and was couched in these terms: — "Are you mad? You are throwing away a position the like of which you will never find again. Reflect once more. I have intercepted your letter to the minister, and shall keep it back until I hear again from you. Onofrio." The poor young man was not prepared for this. When he believed that all was fairly over, to have this chance of escape opened to him, to have again to go through the agonizing process of closing, one after the other, all the doors of hope behind him! — it was really too hard. A mist swam before his eyes, and his hands trembled as if with palsy, as he presented the telegram to his wife. O that she might have a generous impulse — that she would only say, Let it be as you wish, Vincenzo! And how he would press her to his bosom, and thank her and bless her, and weep for joy at her feet! It seemed so natural that she should yield; he yearned so much that she should do so, that, for a moment, he actually began to believe that she would.

Rose ran her eyes over the message, and immediately a twist of disappointment contracted the corners of her mouth; and, as she returned the paper to him, she asked, "And what answer do you mean to send?"

"Whatever you wish," replied Vincenzo, in a faltering voice.

"After writing as you have done to papa," said Rose, "I don't see how you can draw back."

Vincenzo's heart seemed to turn into a lump of ice. "You are right," he said; "I'll be off to Chambery this minute, and telegraph to Turin."

A few hours later, Onofrio received the following: — "I am not mad, though I am compelled to act as if I were. Thank you for your kindness; but let my letter of resignation take its course. I'll explain *vivâ voce*. — Vincenzo."

That night there were tears of rage, and gnashing of teeth, in the little study in Rose's Bower. Another six-and-thirty hours later, and a ministerial despatch came to hand. "Your resignation of the office of Consigliere to the Intendenza of Chambery, in date of the 16th May, is accepted." This, with the signature of the minister, was all the contents. The laconism of the communication spoke volumes. Vincenzo had estranged his powerful patron for ever.

There remained nothing now to be done, but to take leave and go. Always an unpalatable task, that of leave-taking; but more peculiarly so when it has to be accomplished, as in Vincenzo's case, under a necessity for a certain amount of dissimulation, which added not a little to the real pain it gave him to part with acquaintances, some of whom had ripened into real friends, and by whom — political adversaries as most of them were — he had always been treated with the utmost kindness and cordiality. With these, Vincenzo's more particular friends in town, as well as with his neighbours in the village, hearty and sincere was the exchange of goodwill and kindly regret. The Curé and Madame even, in spite of politico-religious differences and their consequent coolness, now thawed altogether, and from their hearts wished him all manner of happiness. A singularly gifted, warm-hearted race, these Savoyards; and with whom it is impossible to come in contact without, whatever their crotchets, liking and respecting them.

Happy those who have never had to enter upon a course of action so glaringly in contradiction with the dictates of reason and their own inclinations as to be startled by, and almost to doubt, the unnatural results which nevertheless have been brought about by their own exertions. Such persons will not understand the mixed feelings of bewilderment and alarm with which Vincenzo, a few days after the acceptance of his resignation, stared from the inside of the mail at the rapid flight of the poplars skirting the road to Turin, with half a mind to protest against the flagrant breach of logic which forced him away from the natural field of his labour; just as if his being in the Turin Mail was not the consequence of acts of his own extending over nearly a week, and the last of the series of which had been to secure three places in this same coach, and to pay for them beforehand. Had the weather only been a little more in unison with his gloomy mood, he thought his regrets would have been less harrowing. But no; the day was beautiful, the sky clear, the air bracing: the sun, near its setting, cast a golden halo around the wooded hills; the birds chirped their evening farewell to the waning light. All in nature betokened joy and repose, while all within him was sad and restless. He leaned long out of the window in fond and silent contemplation of a particular point in the long ridge of chestnut trees on the right of the road, the top of a steeple gilt by the sun peering above the foliage. There was the quiet haven where he had thought, poor fool! the bark of his hopes seemed secure; and there it was his hopes had gone to wreck. It was a last, bitter pleasure to him to look at the spot where he might so easily have been happy, where he felt he had deserved to be so. Presently a turning of the road robbed him of the view, and he drew in his head, pulling his cap over his eyes.

It was once more broad day when they entered the pass of the mountain. The grandeur of the Alpine scenery, to him quite a new spectacle, revived his spirits for a moment; but even that failed to kindle any lasting enthusiasm: his soul was too much out of tune to take in the sublime harmonies of nature. His poetic vein, usually so excitable, was now as though it were muffled. Marianna's screams of terror, her cries to stop, her ejaculations and invocations to the Madonna, whenever the coach swept swiftly round the corners of the zig-zags forming the descent, were enough, to say the truth, to conjure away all poetic associations. There was nothing for it, to prevent her growing frantic, but for Vincenzo to give her his place in the inside, and climb up himself to her elevated situation near the guard outside — an exchange which was not effected without difficulty, and an immense deal of blubbering on Marianna's part, and reproaches from Signora Candia at her making such a goose of herself. Signora Candia had steel nerves, and could look into any depth without wincing.

She was not, however, proof against the fatigues of the journey, as she perceived to her mortification when they reached Turin. Her strength so completely failed her that she was forced to give up her original plan of going straight on to Ibella without stopping, and had, instead, to put up at the nearest hotel, and submit to stay in her bed till the next day. Hence the necessity, in order to avoid inflicting anxiety and disappointment, of sending a telegram to Rumelli, *viâ* Ibella, to make known this change of programme. Vincenzo's first business in Turin took him to the telegraph-office — the second, to Onofrio's office. He had promised to explain, and explain he must. He must do so, under the penalty of writing himself down an ungrateful ass, unworthy of the interest his friend had taken in him. And yet how explain, we do not say satisfactorily, but at all intelligibly, without drawing up a formal and terrible case against his wife? Seen in the light of a confession to a friend, his wife's conduct assumed a character of heinousness quite new to himself, such as he shrunk with horror from imparting to any living soul. There is a treatment which, received from a deadly foe, can be acknowledged, but not when suffered at the hands of a wife, and a wife still dear.

Fortunately, he was spared alike the distress of an avowal repugnant to the delicacy of his nature, or the remorse of an intentionally ambiguous statement. Onofrio was a man of the world; and we may guess, from the query he put to Vincenzo long ago as to Rose — "are you sure that this young lady will never become a clog in the path of a political man?" — we may guess, from this query, that he had had some experience of cases in which the wife had proved a shackle to her husband. He was, besides, a shrewd man; and even the little he had seen of Signora Candia before her marriage, at Rumelli and afterwards, when she passed through Turin, had left the impression that the lady had none of the largeness of views which characterized her husband — a want of equilibrium always fraught with danger. This was sufficient to put him on the right track the instant the unexpected news of the resignation exploded like a bomb about his ears; and when, in answer to his question, "Are you mad?" Vincenzo telegraphed back, "I am not mad, but compelled to act as if I were," it was just as if he had said in so many words (at least in Signor Onofrio's opinion), "I am the victim of my wife's religious scruples."

"And so here you are, my poor friend," said Onofrio, warmly grasping in his both Vincenzo's hands. "I was just thinking of you. Bless me, how you are altered!"

"No wonder. I have suffered cruelly," said Vincenzo, turning away his face. He fought hard against his emotion. When one's heart is full, nothing so sure to make it overflow as a word of sympathy.

"That I can easily believe," resumed Onofrio. "No wounds so cruel as those dealt by a dear hand, and in mistaken kindness. Is *your* wife well, at least?"

"Yes — that is, not altogether so. She has been rather poorly of late; there is, however, a natural reason for her not being strong. That will help you to understand my having yielded. It was not without a struggle, I can assure you. You may imagine what it cost me. But there are situations in which a man, worthy of the name, is completely disarmed. We lived in an atmosphere of fanaticism; she caught the infection; contradiction injured her health; she became every day more estranged; her father wished her to return to him — in short, I could not help myself."

"Of that I have no doubt. There's no tyranny like that of weakness. Well, I wish it could have been otherwise; that is all I can say. With such an opening — and Cavour to push you on! ah! it's a thousand pities. However, we'll say no more about it."

"Why not? Let us hope that what is deferred is not lost. You are to understand that I have not renounced public life for ever. As soon as Rose's health is re-established, I shall resume my liberty of action. I have taken care to make a formal reservation of all my rights on this head; and, when the propitious moment arrives, I rely on you, my dear friend, to assist me."

"You may do so with confidence; but I must candidly tell you beforehand, that it will be next to impossible to reinstate you in a position only half as promising as that you have thrown away."

"Never mind that," said Vincenzo; "I shall rest contented with an inferior one, with anything. Young as I am — only twenty-four — and possessed by a very demon of study, it will go hard with me but that I make up for lost time. Ah! one thing I must not forget to say — the first half of the second part of my report is ready, and I have by me all the materials necessary for the second half. Shall I finish it and send it to you?"

"Yes, do," said Onofrio.

"Could you obtain for me a five minutes' audience of the Minister?"

"I think I could, but I would not advise you to seek to see him. The Minister, I need scarcely say, is extremely annoyed with you, and I believe that time will serve you better with him than an interview just now. Such extenuating circumstances as you would, in your innocence, plead, would only make matters worse, by further lowering you in his estimation; it being one of his crotchets — a pardonable one in a bachelor — that men should be masters at home."

Vincenzo, when, after a long visit, he left his friend, was a little less wretched than when he had come to him. That which had done him most good, next to those marks of affection so precious to one in his predicament, was the contract he had entered into with himself taking his friend as a witness of the same (and from which he could not draw back without disgracing himself in that friend's eyes), to re-assert his liberty of action within a short period of that time, and Onofrio's acquiescing in his so doing as a matter of course. Onofrio perhaps entertained some doubts as to Vincenzo's being able to carry out his present intentions; but he did not choose to express any. Suppose the young man was deceiving himself, where was the use of throwing cold water on a hope which did him who harboured it good? Vincenzo's case was an incurable one in Onofrio's eyes; and he felt in charity bound to act the part of a humane physician, who humours the harmless whims of a patient past recovery.

Rose was greatly disappointed, and not a little alarmed, when on reaching the Ibella station she saw the familiar faces of Don Pio, Barnaby, and Giuseppe, but not that of her father. Don Pio hastened to reassure her. He was there, he said, for that purpose, at the desire of her father. Nothing serious was the matter with the Signor Avvocato — only a slight, and, as Don Pio hoped, a temporary increase of the former weakness in the old gentleman's left side, from which, as the Signora was aware, he had suffered more or less for years. The Signor Avvocato had gone through more exertion last week than it was perhaps prudent for him to do, on the fête day of St. Urban, the patron saint of Rumelli, and had complained of fatigue ever since. And therefore Don Pio had taken the liberty of advising him against a drive which could do no good, and might do some harm; and the Signor Avvocato, with the practical good sense which distinguished him, had seen fit to act upon the suggestion, though it was at the expense of his feelings.

Rose thanked Don Pio with warmth, and insisted on his taking a seat in the close carriage which Giuseppe had brought for the travellers. This arrangement increased to its maximum of intensity the cloud of annoyance which had gathered on Vincenzo's brow at the very sight of Don Pio, and which the slight dash of premiership in the young Reverend's harangue had not tended to dissipate; but, like the well-bred man he was, he showed as little of his vexation as he could. To make room for Don Pio, Marianna was consigned to the care of Barnaby, who had been bribed to drive Don Pio in the gig by the prospect of being among the first to welcome the young couple back — a task, this last, of which we must say he acquitted himself but indifferently. His mind was caught in a cobweb of doubt whether the event was really one for rejoicing or for condolence. From some words occasionally dropped by the Signor Avvocato Barnaby had imbibed a sort of notion that there was some one who was being unfairly dealt by.

Giuseppe, guessing his mistress's impatience to reach home, kept his horses at the full trot. Don Pio, on his side, turned the time to account by giving Signora Candia a graphic and touching description of what he styled Don Natale's enviable end, a description which repeatedly filled the Signora's eyes with tears. He then glided into a glowing picture of the splendour of St. Urban's fête. Altogether, Don Pio's conversational powers certainly helped to abridge the drive to Rose. Vincenzo had expected that Don Pio would alight at his own parsonage door, and had even ventured on the sufficiently broad hint that the reverend gentleman need not put himself to further inconvenience by accompanying them to the palace; but to no purpose. Don Pio jocosely pleaded the engagement he had taken to see the daughter bodily into the arms of her father, and his firm determination not to be debarred his share of pleasure in the happy meeting.

The palace, as we said before, stood on a raised terrace, accessible from the avenue by a short flight of steps. The Signor Avvocato, who had been sitting at the door, at the sound of wheels hurried to the top of the steps, crying — "Is that you at last?" Rose, in her impatience, did not wait for the carriage to stop, and, in trying to get out while it was still in motion, fell heavily to the ground; but the echo of the four cries of horror elicited by the accident had not quite died away before she was on her feet again, and hanging on her father's neck. With what a passionate embrace they clung to each other! Rose especially — undemonstrative, cold-mannered Rose — vibrating with emotion from head to foot, and transfigured by it, was quite a new sight to Vincenzo. He could not help thinking, with a feeling akin to envy, "If she loved me only half as well!" Certainly, whatever their shortcomings in other respects, no one could deny to this father and daughter that great redeeming point of filial and parental love. Rose was not hurt — so she said in answer to her father's repeated inquiries — she was sure she was not a bit hurt; but the ill-dissembled difficulty with which she walked, leaning on her father's arm, towards the house, and her instantly sinking into a seat on entering the dining-room, told a different tale to Vincenzo.

"How pale and thin you look, my poor child!" exclaimed the Signor Avvocato, gazing tenderly on his daughter; "you are not half the woman you were. And you" — turning round to Vincenzo — "and you had the assurance to tell me that she was well!"

It was by this gracious address that the Signor Avvocato first showed that he was aware of the presence of his son-in-law. Had he received a blow in the face Vincenzo could not have crimsoned more deeply. He said, "There was no great stock of assurance needed to tell the simple truth. I have never, that I know of, given you any reason to doubt my veracity."

"Plenty of reason to doubt your clearness of vision henceforth," retorted the Signor Avvocato. "No eyes like those of a father, that's certain. Isn't she sadly changed, Don Pio?"

Don Pio admitted that Signora Candia did not look so well as she did formerly, but this might arise merely from the fatigue of a long journey; "nor," added the priest, in corroboration of this view of the matter, "nor does Signor Candia look half so well as he used to do, and probably from the same cause."

"In fact, he does not look well," assented the Signor Avvocato, after a lengthened survey of Vincenzo.

"The climate of Savoy agreed with neither the one nor the other. Thank God, they are quit of it at last."

It being now close upon eight o'clock, supper was served — but, in spite of the most pressing invitations from father and daughter to stay, Don Pio took his leave, though not without first going through a round of queries about the present state of each and all the limbs composing the ponderous body of the Signor Avvocato, winding up by pointing out Signora Candia as the panacea for all her father's evils. This interrogatory served as an opening for the Signor Avvocato (as soon as the priest had departed) to enumerate all his bodily ailments, which were legion; and also to confess how much he owed to Don Pio's kind care and excellent advice, by both of which his sufferings had been much alleviated. Don Pio had more than a superficial knowledge of medicine, and excelled in all that related to Hygiene. Notwithstanding all his maladies, the Signor Avvocato had a healthy mien and a capital appetite; indeed, he was the only one of the party who did much honour to the meal. His old enemy alone, obesity, had gained any advantage over him. Such desultory conversation as took place during supper — Savoy, the appointment, and the resignation were three topics carefully avoided — passed chiefly between the father and daughter. Few and far between were the opportunities given to Vincenzo to join in what was being said; and, as for seeking to do so of his own accord, Vincenzo was far too exasperated for any such thing: so that there he sat, between his wife and father-in-law, in the uncomfortable predicament of one who feels himself *de trop*. What could there be at the bottom of this seeming predetermination first to provoke and then to slight him thus?

Nothing but the embarrassment arising from a troubled conscience. That of the Signor Avvoçato reproached him loudly enough with having done all in his power to evade and annul, under false pretences, an engagement freely entered into with Vincenzo. Now, embarrassment, especially that of a superior towards an inferior, rarely exists without a tinge of resentment. One does not acknowledge oneself in the wrong without feeling a little bitterness against him who is in the right. Then, resentment helps us to put a good face on the matter, and also excuses us from making inconvenient admissions. Vincenzo's letter from Chambery added to the stock of the Signor Avvocato's embarrassment and resentment. What the deuce did the boy mean by his airs and reservations? Was it his place, forsooth, to propose conditions? To a man in such a quandary the alteration in Rose's looks was a perfect godsend. It afforded him a ready-made, plausible *casus belli.* The occasion was too good not to be snapped at, and made the most of; and the first shot was fired.

Supper was soon over, and then Rose and her father left the room together. Vincenzo, loath to be in their way, went out in search of air: he was suffocating, less from heat than from inward rage. His blood was boiling with indignation. This, then, was the return that was to be made him for all he had endured, for all he had sacrificed! An unjust rebuke in the presence of a stranger — cold indifference and disdain. A pariah would have been treated with more respect. If it were his godfather's intention to drive him to some extremity, let him try it. Vincenzo felt ready to confront any attack — nay, even any scandal. Under the lash of such ireful thoughts, he strode for some time hurriedly up and down the terrace, until, wearied out, he seated himself on the top of the balustrade running round it, and fell into a brown study.

"What art thou so deep in thought about?" asked a voice by his side.

"Is that you, Barnaby?" said Vincenzo. "You wish to know my thoughts, do you? Well, I was thinking how much better it would be for me to be dead."

"That's an unnatural thought for a youngster like thee," said Barnaby. "What ails thee?"

"Disappointment, my old friend. I wanted to make myself a credit to them and to myself, and — they will not let me; that is what ails me."

"I don't understand thee. Thou art an Avvocato, ar'n't thou?"

"Yes."

"Pray, then, what canst thou wish for more? Is not being an Avvocato all that a man can be?"

"Yes, so far as knowledge and social position are concerned. But, Barnaby, what is knowledge worth if it is not to be made use of? Of no more value than a purse of gold which may not be spent."

"I don't understand you a bit better now than before," answered Barnaby, with a shake of his head.

"I'll try and make you understand," said Vincenzo. "You are a gardener — that is to say, you are acquainted with everything which concerns gardening. Now, of what use would your knowledge be to yourself or others if you had not a garden to which you could apply it?"

"I see now," returned Barnaby.

"Well, then," went on Vincenzo, "what the garden is to you, the situation I have just left in Savoy was to me — a means of applying, honourably for me and usefully for others, the knowledge I acquired by studying to become an Avvocato."

"But," objected Barnaby, after a pause employed in scratching his bald pate — "but the Signor Avvocato never had any place under Government, and yet has been a useful and honourable man."

"But the times were very different when the Signor Avvocato was in his prime; the priests and the nobles were then all in all; but now we have the Statuto, and every citizen counts for something. It is, therefore, every citizen's duty who values the rights it gives to support it and defend it; and that's best done by using in its service all the talent God may have bestowed."

"That seems to me well said," remarked Barnaby.

"Then you must remember," pursued Vincenzo, "that the Signor Avvocato was rich, and rich people can find ways of being useful and honourable without following any particular profession; while I am a poor devil, with nothing in the world but my brains by which to earn myself a name and an honest independence."

"As for independence," said Barnaby — "your wife is rich enough for two."

"Were she rich enough for ten," burst out Vincenzo, "is that a reason why I should not try and suffice for myself? I shall never feel like a man until I do. Do you think it is pleasant or praiseworthy to go on till one's grey asking one's wife or one's father-in-law for a pair of shoes or a coat, or a hat?"

"There I must say you are right again," cried the old man, emphatically. "What an old donkey I am never to have seen all this before! It's clear enough to me now that thou must have some situation which will give thee both credit and money. Now, how long dost thou think it will take thee to make a name and a fortune?"

"How long? Why, all my life."

"But thou canst not keep the father and daughter always asunder — that's impossible."

"Who speaks or thinks of keeping them asunder? Cannot the daughter go to the father and stay for a while with him; cannot the father come to the daughter and remain with her, as he said he would?"

"Ah, that he never will — he's too heavy and sluggish to move."

"Why, then, did he promise to do so?" asked Vincenzo, impatiently. "Why did he agree to my accepting an office under Government? Am I to rot in idleness and uselessness all my life because he is heavy and lazy?"

"Thou art forgetting, my dear boy," said Barnaby, in a tone of mild remonstrance, "that the Signor Avvocato is getting oldish and shaky."

"I see he isn't what he used to be," replied Vincenzo, "but not to the extent of being unable for a four or five hours' journey — it isn't more from Rumelli to Turin; and the odds are that, in a year or two, I should have been promoted to Turin. Ask any medical man you like, and I'll bet you what you please he says that a little moving about would be beneficial to the Signor Avvocato's health."

"I make no doubt of it; still he would never do it: habit is too strong for him; just the same with me. I would rather die here than live elsewhere."

"Rose, at all events, could come to him, couldn't she, and spend half the year with him?"

"Ay, but six months out of the twelve would be too much for you, and too little for him. It won't do."

"I see what will," cried Vincenzo, impatiently, and rising to go back to the house. "Nothing short of my being sacrificed will do. What does it matter that such an insignificant creature as Vincenzo Candia should die of a broken heart? Well, so be it, that others may have their ease."

"Those are foolish and wicked words," said Barnaby; "the first that have ever passed thy lips in my hearing. Thou must be indeed wretched to speak thus, and to thy oldest friend."

"That you are! my oldest and truest friend — forgive me," said penitent Vincenzo, catching hold of Barnaby's hand and pressing it forcibly to his breast. "Ah! Barnaby, you don't know through how many gaps this poor heart of mine bleeds — that's my excuse. Good night."

Vincenzo had remained out of doors until he saw a faint glimmer of light peeping through the blinds of his godfather's bedroom windows. He felt pretty sure then of finding his wife alone. He hurried up to her room, and found her already in bed.

"You hurt yourself when you fell," said Vincenzo.

"No such thing," said Rose, hurriedly.

"It's no use denying it," insisted Vincenzo. "I saw from your way of walking that you were hurt."

"Only slightly, very slightly, I assure you," replied Rose. "I shan't feel anything of it to-morrow."

"I hope it may be so," said Vincenzo; "still, in your situation, a hurt, however trifling, should not be neglected. I shall sleep more tranquilly, if you will allow me to go for a doctor."

"For God's sake," exclaimed Rose, sitting up in her bed, terrified — "for God's sake, don't. Papa would be so uneasy — he is enough so already."

"To spare your father a little uneasiness, you have no right to run the risk of inflicting a serious injury on yourself, and not on yourself alone. This is a matter in which I ought to be allowed a voice. Really, I must go."

"Don't, I implore you. I give you my word, there's not the least cause for alarm. All I require is repose; and how could I rest if I thought papa was alarmed?"

"Yield, Rose, if only to screen me from undeserved reproach. This is the last consideration I would urge, if I could think of any other. Your father is prone, too prone, to hold me responsible for your altered looks. You heard how harshly he attacked me on that point. Suppose you were really ill to-morrow, how furious he will be with me!"

"Set your heart at rest on that score," said Rose. "I promise you, whatever happens, that he shall not blame you. Now do, I beg of you, say no more on the subject; you really do me harm by insisting; let me go to sleep. Good-night."

As Vincenzo laid his aching head on the pillow, he

could not help muttering to himself, "Yes, she, too, has got her share of the divine element of self-sacrifice — only, as it seems, exclusively for the benefit of her father. As for me, whether I sleep or not — break my heart or not — it is a matter of supreme indifference to her, so that her father has a quiet night. What a consoling thought for a husband!"

Rose felt too tired and bruised next day to get up; it was only the effect of the journey, she declared, and that in all other respects she was well, and greatly disposed to enjoy her breakfast. All this show of buoyancy and high spirits did not go far to re-assure Vincenzo. If she chose to stay in bed, with so many reasons as she had for rising, it was evident that she could not do otherwise; in other words, that she was suffering. He accordingly pressed her again and again to have medical advice — which she might very naturally have, without mentioning to her father that it was on account of her fall. He even threatened to fetch a physician, whether she wished it or not. Whereupon, Rose threatened him in her turn, that, if he did, she would get up, and refuse to see the doctor. Reasonings, entreaties, and threats, were shattered to pieces by her rock-like determination.

Vincenzo was more vexed at this issue of the contest than he dared to show; and a little of the vexation — unreasonably, to be sure, yet naturally — could not but be added to the stock of resentment which he entertained against the Signor Avvocato. The old gentleman, on his side, when he heard of his daughter's indisposition, was no less vexed than Vincenzo; and nine tenths of his vexation went to swell the amount of resentment which rankled in his breast against his son-in-law. For had he not here a tangible and unanswerable evidence that his unworthy son-in-law had wittingly and designedly played with his godfather's feelings, by constantly representing Rose's health as excellent? All the assurances which Rose, faithful to her word, gave, that Vincenzo had not used any deception, went for nothing with her father; and the promise she forced from him, not to call her husband to account for an imaginary offence, only served to make the Signor Avvocato set down all she said as dictated by a blind fondness, which was endeavouring to screen the culprit.

It was in these dispositions that father and son-in-law met at dinner, *tête-à-tête* for the first time. Frowning, swelling, swaggering, the one wore his wrath on his sleeve with provocation; natural, self-collected, unobtrusive, the other held his in abeyance. Sham force and real force in presence for a duel. For a while the clatter of knives and forks alone broke the ominous silence. At last the elder gentleman said —

"Have you lost your tongue?"

"I was waiting for your pleasure to speak," said Vincenzo, quietly.

A pause.

"There are some passages in your last letter from Chambery," resumed the Signor Avvocato, "as to which I shall be obliged to you for an explanation at your leisure."

"With all my heart," said Vincenzo, taking up the gauntlet with a will. "I am at your orders."

Had he stumbled on a long-coveted treasure, the sudden flash of his eye could not have conveyed a keener delight. The Signor Avvocato felt cowed, and attempted to beat a retreat.

"Not now, not now," said he, in his most dignified tone. "We had better avoid all irritating topics for the present. I am provoked enough as it is."

"I am sorry for that," said Vincenzo. "I am at a loss, however, to understand how my letter can afford matter for an irritating discussion, or, indeed, for discussion at all."

"But I do, and that's sufficient," said the Signor Avvocato, curtly.

"So be it. Allow me, then, to say that I maintain every word in my letter."

"We'll see about that by-and-by. All your airs of braggadocio won't succeed in goading me into a quarrel. My poor girl shall not have her sufferings increased by the recoil of her father's agitation. I know the regard which is due to her state, if others don't."

"On what occasion, at what time, or in what manner, have I failed in the regard I owe to my wife, either ailing or in health?" asked Vincenzo, in a quiet voice, his eyes rivetted on the Signor Avvocato.

"I have mentioned no name, have I? Why should you take what I said to yourself?"

"Because in that phrase, if *others* don't, the word others can apply to no one but me. Dare to say you didn't mean me?"

"Dare!" repeated the Signor Avvocato, looking very big indeed. "You might, I think, use a more respectful mode of asking an explanation."

"You see that you dare not deny it," continued Vincenzo, reckless of his godfather's pompous looks or words. "You hurl injurious insinuations at me, and, when called upon to substantiate, them, you extricate yourself by a *qui pro quo*. I leave it to yourself to give a name to such tactics. Last night, too, the first words you addressed to me, your son-in-law, after an absence of ten months, was to accuse me, before a stranger, of deceit. Was it just? Was it decorous? Was it manly?"

The Signor Avvocato rose, saying, "I see what it is — nothing short of a quarrel will satisfy you, and I will not quarrel. One of these days I shall be at liberty to speak, and then you will have to listen to me. For the present I leave you master of the field."

It is provoking to be beaten when one has the best will in the world to beat. The Signor Avvocato felt as if he could have made a mouthful of that indomitable son-in-law of his, who, somehow or other, always got the better of him. Vincenzo was no less incensed by the conviction he had acquired that his resumption of office would be furiously opposed by his father-in-law. The split between the two had widened considerably.

CHAPTER VIII.

Heavy Hours.

Rose was well enough on the morrow to take her usual place at the dinner table and for some time there was no further occasion for the two belligerents to meet *tête-à-tête*. When the necessity again presented itself, Don Pio infallibly occupied her place, serving as a buffer to prevent collisions between the father and son-in-law. From the moment of her reaching Rumelli,

Rose was, without being positively ill, never quite well. She was a constant sufferer from all the ailments and inconveniences incidental to her situation. It seemed as if it happened so, on purpose to confirm her father's suspicions of insincerity or worse on Vincenzo's part.

Don Pio made sunshine or rain at the Palace. When he did not call during the day, which was seldom, the Signor Avvocato was sure to send for him. It needed no long observation on Vincenzo's part, to get at the root of Don Pio's influence. What the adroit attentions and winning ways of Don Natale's assistant had begun, Don Natale's demise achieved. The sad event, though far from unexpected, had forcibly struck the Signor Avvocato's imagination, and ever since a terror of approaching death had never ceased to haunt him. Fear of death had given birth to other fears. He was the more accessible to all sorts of alarms, from having lived all his life more as a philosopher than a Christian. He had certainly gone to Mass on Sundays, and abstained from meat in Lent, and received the Sacrament at Easter, but only because others did so, and that the not doing so might involve him in a scrape with the powers that were. As was the case with many others of the generation to which he belonged, a reaction took place in his mind against a religion lowered by an ill-inspired policy to being a means of government and a tool of oppression.

It is easy to see at a glance all the advantages which the Signor Avvocato's new phase of feeling afforded to an intelligent man of the world, and a priest into the bargain. While in the former character he soothed with his sympathy, and by the suggestion of common-place expedients for the ailments of the body — which were Legion, if the invalid's fancy were to be trusted — in the latter, he probed the wounds of the soul, pouring into them the oil of hope, the balm of mercy. The old gentleman was soon like wax in Don Pio's hands, and readily abjured all the errors of his past life, the political ones included. Could old Del Palmetto have risen from his grave, he would have willingly saluted and acknoledged, as a brother Codino of the first water, his once political antagonist. A few months under the influence of Don Pio had changed the old sceptic into a believer, an edification for all the village; the *ci-devant* liberal into a most ardent opponent of Cavour and the Statuto; the writer of the famous epistle to the Principal of the Seminary into a fanatic partisan of monks and nuns of all colours and denominations. Better late than never.

His external habits also had undergone a great alteration. All the little activity which he had still possessed before Rose's departure for Chambery, was now gone. He never went out for a morning's walk, as had been his wont, seldom indeed left his room before one o'clock, which was the dinner hour. In the afternoon he had an armchair placed in front of the house•door, and there he enjoyed a nap. Since his return to Rumelli in the end of March, he had not been once to Ibella, and talked of remaining all the year round at the Palace. He had renounced his musical studies altogether — the legal consultations were few and far between. His only occupation was to search for and discover fresh maladies in himself, and to brood and groan over the old and the new ones. This was taking the proportions of a mania — he could speak of nothing else but his distempers. He carried about him a pocket looking-glass, and watched the changes in his physiognomy with childish anxiety. His terror of sitting in a draught was unceasing. This perpetual pre-occupation about himself rendered him exacting, peevish, querulous, irritable, often to a degree which few could stand. Don Pio alone could at all times manage him — his very presence, the mere sound of his voice, had, like David's harp on Saul, an instantaneous soothing effect on the old gentleman's disturbance of body or mind.

Don Pio knew his power and used it for his own ends, but never made a parade of it; quite the contrary, he studiously dissembled it — dissembled it most studiously from him over whom he exercised it, and who, while not so much as moving his little finger independently of the impulse given, yet thought himself a free agent, and gave himself the airs of being such; so gentle and skilful was the hand by which he was managed. Not the keenest eye nor ear could have detected, in the bearing or speech of Don Pio, the least particle of the self-consciousness of a man aware of his own importance. Deferential, without servility, to the master of the house, affable and companionable, without familiarity, to Vincenzo, paternally condescending to Rose, full of grave amenity towards the household, such as he had been on his first setting foot in the Palace, a perfect stranger, such he was now, when he found himself always welcomed there, an honoured guest of nearly twelve months' standing.

We said that Don Pio knew his power and used it for his own ends. We would have none imagine that these were sordid ones. The glorification of the

Church, that is, the realization of the universal acknowledgment of the supremacy of Rome and the autocracy of the order to which he belonged — Don Pio aspired to no lesser aim; an ambition a little out of date, perhaps you will say, but lofty at all events. The grinding to dust of all that came in the way of this consummation, formed, of course, a natural corollary to the above premises.

Rose was poorly two days out of three; yet she never showed any impatience. The physicians, repeatedly summoned at her father's request, declared one and all that there were no symptoms about her to cause any anxiety. Hers was by no means an uncommon case — repose, a mind kept unruffled, tepid baths, they prescribed nothing further. Rose spent the greater part of the day with her father and Don Pio. Her husband was relegated to the back-ground — not that she showed any ill-humour or unkindness to him; on the contrary, now that that perpetual cause of irritation, his appointment under Government, no longer stood between them, her easy-going nature had taken the upper hand again; only she did not evince, nor indeed feel, any want of intimate communication with her husband. Nay, the frequent fits of tenderness which would seize on Vincenzo's heart, impelling him towards the mother of his hoped-for child, found no response from her. Their intercourse was that of two well-bred and not sympathizing persons in a boarding-house — polite, good-natured, but devoid of cordiality.

Barnaby, lost in the solution of the insolvable problem, how to reconcile claims so contradictory, so exclusive of each other, looked more like a fish out of water, than the old fire-eater of former days. Often of an afternoon, when father, daughter, and son-in-law had chairs in the front of the house, Barnaby would make one of the mournful party, and from the top of the marble balustrade, where he usually seated himself, speculate long and intently upon the countenances opposite to him, as if to single out the most forlorn of them, and that consequently of the person most entitled to consideration. Failing to do which, he would rise up, turn round and round, dog-like, and then depart in high dudgeon; or, suppose his inspection had succeeded, which might be the case now and then, he would turn a cold shoulder for days and days to the one momentarily condemned, whether it was his master or Vincenzo. Barnaby was now past eighty.

As dull and melancholy an interior as a Trappist could wish for; enough to damp the highest spirits — and those of Vincenzo, we know, could not but be at a low ebb! Debarred of all congenial or intellectual intercourse, incessantly haunted by the sense of his virtual usefulness and his actual uselessness, wounded in his self-respect, his affections, and his convictions at every moment, Vincenzo, worried and harassed, dragged on his burden, day after day, with about the same readiness or willingness with which the galley-slave drags his chain behind him. *Ennui*, heavy, poignant deadly *ennui*, was gnawing at his heart's core, from morning till night, with perhaps occasionally the diversion of a fit of rage, which made him tear his hair and knock his head against the first wall in his way. His Report, at which he worked steadily, had lost the charm it formerly possessed, of making him forget the disagreeables that beset him on all sides; nor had he any longer that entire confidence in the soundness of the ideas he was developing, which had at Chambery given to his task somewhat of the zest of a good action. Indeed, he was not now sure that all his lucubrations were not downright nonsense; still, the only bearable ones of the twenty-four were those hours — those long hours — of the night which he spent at his desk in the solitude of the garret. For, to avoid disturbing the slumber of his wife, whose bedroom on the second floor adjoined his, he had made the attic he occupied as a boy his nocturnal study, to which he withdrew immediately after supper, there to remain till midnight. Barnaby, indeed, who slept on the same story, would pretty often creep into this den of Vincenzo's; but his presence scarcely interfered with its quiet: the old man rarely spoke, though he would sit for hours together watching, as a faithful dog might do, the quaint evolutions of his favourite in the heat of composition, who, by turns, urged his pen at full gallop, stopped it, bit it, twisted his moustache and whiskers as though determined to screw out of them what he wanted, or, suddenly rising with an impatient jerk, began to stride up and down the room.

Nearly three months had crawled on in this deadly monotony when, one night in early September, Signora Candia was suddenly taken ill. For thirty hours she suffered terribly, and then, alas! received no compensation — the poor little baby was born only to die. This grievous issue took none more by surprise than the medical men who had been in attendance from the first — they were at a loss how to reconcile the mishap with the strong constitution of Signora Candia; unless, indeed, there had been some accident, such as a fall, or some imprudence. Rose faintly denied having met with any accident or committed any imprudence. Vincenzo, however, when the subject was talked over in his presence, at once mentioned that his wife had fallen on the day of her arrival at the palace, as she was alighting from the carriage; nor did he dissemble the misgivings that he had felt at the time and afterwards. These misgivings the Signor Avvocato pooh-poohed as sheer nonsense, stoutly asserting that Rose's fall scarcely deserved to be called such; it was not then she had been hurt; no, the cause of the misfortune, whatever it was, must be sought for in something that had occurred anterior to her arrival at home. The Signor Avvocato upheld this opinion of his with a sharpness, and a peremptoriness of tone, quite unaccountable to the men of medicine, yet which warned them that it would be better to avoid all further questions on the subject.

Rose's state of prostration bordered on annihilation. One of the doctors remained at the palace in anxious expectation of what the night might bring. It brought nothing good — violent fever accompanied by delirium. By break of day, however, entire consciousness returned, but the patient was in a most precarious condition. She felt this herself, and succeeded in forcing from the doctor an acknowledgment of the fact. She begged for and obtained a promise that her father should not be made aware of her danger so long as any, the least hope remained, and then asked for the Sacraments, which were administered to her by Don Pio. Her composure and serenity did not forsake her for a moment. But her father did not reap any benefit from her kind thoughtfulness, for he no sooner heard of the Sacraments, than he guessed the truth and became frantic with despair. Vincenzo, all heart-broken as he was, found strength enough to comfort the weak old man; and, for the first time since his arrival, a mutual overpowering feeling, setting aside for a while past and present feuds, threw father and son into each other's arms, and mingled their tears.

After more than a fortnight of awful suspense, Rose's strong constitution turned the scale on the side of life; yet, before she had rallied sufficiently to bear the fatigue of removal to Ibella, another month had to elapse. As a long medical treatment was considered indispensable to her complete recovery, it had been decided that she must be taken to the town, so as to be within easier and speedier reach of the faculty. Rose improved slowly but steadily. The winter happened to be mild and dry, another circumstance in her favour. With the same admirable patience with which she had borne her bodily discomforts prior to her illness, did she now bear the inconveniences of her convalescence. Forbidden as she was to walk, even so much as to put her foot to the ground, and that for weeks and weeks together, no complaint ever passed her lips. Her father and husband were unremitting in their care. Vincenzo read to her, held her skeins of worsted while she wound them, entertained her with amusing stories and lively talk, carried her from her bed to her sofa, from her sofa to her bed, supported her when she was first allowed to take a few steps, and had the satisfaction of perceiving that his attentions were received with a show of pleasure, to which, since their honey-moon, he had been little accustomed. The shadow of death which had passed over her, the foretaste she had had of maternity, evidently had softened some of the sharp angles of her character, and disposed her to look upon her husband with more of forbearance and gentleness. The thought that she had been so nearly snatched away from him exercised an equally wholesome influence upon the husband; his tenderness for her revived, and much of the past was thrown into the shade.

Other causes coincided to make him less despondent and gloomy. The change from the palace to Ibella was of itself a great mitigation of his situation. Ibella, though more than sufficiently dull, was not half so dull as the palace. There he did not feel so entirely out of the current of the rest of the world: he had within his reach newspapers, which told him that there was life yet stirring in the country; and, if he did not meet with lofty intellects, a rare item everywhere, he at least found congenial spirits and warm hearts, with ideas, and hopes, and aspirations in common with his own. Then, Don Pio's disagreeable shadow no longer everlastingly crossed his path. Don Pio, indeed, called oftener than Vincenzo deemed necessary, for he made his appearance once or twice a week — but that was nothing to his daily visits at Rumelli. Is it needful to say that time had not abated Vincenzo's strong aversion to the young priest? Vincenzo in his heart held him responsible for the deplorable state of subjection and quasi-imbecility to which the Signor Avvocato was reduced. Vincenzo was further convinced — and in that he was not mistaken — that Don Pio had done anything but serve him in the past with his godfather, and that he would do anything but serve him in the future.

The better feeling which pervaded the intercourse

between husband and wife did not, unluckily, extend to that between father and son-in-law. On the contrary, each day, especially since they had been in the town, seemed to add to their mutual estrangement. That, indeed, on the part of the old gentleman, assumed every now and then the character of a confirmed hatred. By what new offence had Vincenzo drawn upon himself this recrudescence of wrath? By the most unpardonable one which a disappointed old man's fancy could create. The Signor Avvocato had longed for a grandchild with all the obstinacy and intensity of a senile passion. At first, his regrets at the failure of his hopes were swallowed up by his all-absorbing anxiety about his daughter; but, when all danger ceased, those regrets broke forth afresh and with renewed vigour, and along with them a sort of mania to ascertain the cause which had deprived him of the coveted treasure. Now, this cause was easily to be found, more particularly by an infatuated old man bent on finding one, and one, too, exclusive of that ridiculous fall, on which Vincenzo, probably not without his reasons, had laid such a stress. An insalubrious climate, vain yearnings after home, contention of mind arising from perpetual quarrels, Rose had gone through all these; and such were surely enough and to spare, to occasion the mishap. One of the physicians in attendance on Rose, hard pressed on the point, had ended by allowing that all these circumstances combined might have produced an agitation of mind in the mother, which had reacted fatally on the unborn child. This admission was eagerly laid hold of by the Signor Avvocato. It had a threefold advantage in his eyes. Instead of an unseizable irresponsible agency to speculate upon, it gave into his hands a concrete reality on which to hammer away, if need was; it set aside once for all, that ridiculous allegation of the fall; and, lastly, it afforded him a precious weapon wherewith to parry all possible future attempts to separate him from his daughter.

Had these advantages had any share in the putting together of the case presented to the physician? any weight in the conclusion drawn from the physician's admission? If he was biassed, the Signor Avvocato was unconscious of being so. Of this only was he dimly conscious — that perhaps he had treated Rose's fall too lightly, considering that she had been obliged to keep her bed the following day; hence some of his eagerness to persuade himself and others that that fall could not have had, and had not had, any injurious effects on her.

Vincenzo, on his side — who naturally enough had longed for a child to the full as much as the Signor Avvocato for a grandchild, and who had moreover his own special reasons for desiring such an event — Vincenzo, we say, was cut to the quick by the overthrow of all his hopes, and felt more than reasonably embittered against him who had been the occasion of this mortification. For, without Rose's scruples as to alarming her father, ten to one but that which had happened would not have happened. Vincenzo, truth to say, had too much sense to make his father-in-law formally answerable for a result to which he had unknowingly been instrumental; still, he could not overcome a feeling of irritation against the man without whom that result in all likelihood would not have been brought about. Great or small, we have all of us this in common with children — we are ready to blame the stone which makes us stumble. Vincenzo, accordingly, was far too exasperated to put up with the Signor Avvocato's airs of superiority and more open provocations; skirmishes were frequent and sharp — generally, however, in Rose's absence; they mostly occurred at dinner-time, as for many weeks she did not come to table.

The mildness of the winter had proved an excellent auxiliary to the physician's prescriptions. By the middle of February, 1856, Rose was all but well; fresh air and exercise were all she now required to bring back her strength and colour; in short, to complete her cure. The weather was enchanting, the sun genially warm. Why should they not hasten, by a month or so, their return to the palace? asked the Signor Avvocato. Ibella had become odious to him: his temporary alliance with the late Del Palmetto had rendered him unpopular with the ultra-liberal youths of the rising generation; his present apostasy had alienated from him the whole of the moderate party; even many of his old friends had entirely dropped him. And then he missed Don Pio, his favourite physician for mind and body. The physicians made no objections to the proposal; Rose was delighted; Vincenzo said nothing, but looked anything but pleased. And so, *nem. con.*, the quarters of the family were shifted to Rumelli.

Rose's first care, once there, was, after having duly confessed and communed, to present a votive offering of a large swaddled babe in massive silver to the altar of the Madonna, to whose particular intercession she attributed her recovery; the ex-voto accompanied by the gift of a rich set of sacerdotal vestments from her, and a pair of silver candlesticks from her father. The presentation was made with great pomp, all the bells ringing; it gave occasion for a little extra fête in the village; old and young flocking to witness the proceedings, and to see the young lady of the palace once more restored to health. Rose was sincerely loved and respected by her poorer neighbours; nor had the partial loss of popularity which her father had sustained in consequence of his retired habits, peevish humour, and almost total withdrawal of his legal advice to the needy, in any way lowered the tone of general good will to the daughter.

The change of abode worked no perceptible change in the dispositions or relations of our three chief actors to one another; only that Vincenzo, owing to the frequent presence of Don Pio, was far more separated from his wife than at Ibella. Her father or Don Pio was constantly between them. Don Pio had become Rose's confessor, a circumstance which had not diminished his hold upon her; her religious fervour was evidently on the increase; she took the Sacrament almost every Sunday, and, by preference, made the parish church the goal of the daily walks prescribed to her, and remained there to hear a mass. Her husband accompanied her to Rumelli and back, and these were the only moments of privacy which he had with her. In this manner week after week passed away rather drearily and monotonously.

By the end of March, Rose had completely regained her youthful bloom and spirits, and every one she saw complimented her on her good looks. Now or never was the moment for Vincenzo to strike a blow for his emancipation. He had waited until his wife's recovery of strength should be a matter of public notoriety, in order to meet all objections founded on the plea of her delicate health. Should he delay longer, he felt that his continued inaction might be later claimed as a right by prescription. To spur himself on, he sent to Onofrio the last part of his Report, finished long ago, explaining the cause of its not having sooner been forwarded, and announcing his return to Turin *within two months at furthest.* Then he watched for an opportunity to broach the subject first to his wife. There was an undefined something about her looks and in her manners, a something of new-born warmth and softness, which made him hope.

CHAPTER IX.

A Stag at Bay.

One fine morning in early April, Vincenzo said to Rose, "Let us go and see if the honey-suckle in your arbour is going to blossom soon." Rose having graciously assented, they took their way thither. The sun shone bright and warm, the birds called amorously to each other, the trees and shrubs quivered under the tepid breath of spring. It was on just such a day as this, at the same season, almost at the same hour, that exactly two years ago they had walked hand in hand, a happy affianced couple, along this very alley of old chestnut trees on their way to this very same bower. His heart full of these memories, Vincenzo felt encouraged to speak out his mind; taking one of Rose's dimpled hands in his, he said — and said it in a voice grave yet slightly tremulous with contending emotions

— "It is hardly twenty-two months since you consented to be mine, and to share the weal or woe of life with me, dear." A light gleamed in Rose's eyes which seemed to the speaker vaguely responsive to the softening influences at work in his own soul. Vincenzo went on, "Am I right in thinking, Rose, that you have not become utterly indifferent to me?"

"You are quite right," said Rose; "only you might have worded your question less modestly."

"I must be of a very sanguine nature indeed to have worded it otherwise. However, that is not the subject I have in hand. I may then take it for granted that you still feel a little interest in me — enough, for instance, to prompt you to make a small sacrifice in order to avert a danger from me."

"No doubt," said Rose, "always supposing the danger be a real one."

"I leave you to judge of that. Look at my face, Rose. Do I look like a man in good health? And mark this; the havoc on the surface is nothing to the havoc within. I am growing sickly — growing wicked; this is the double danger from which I call on you to save me."

"With all my heart, if I can," said Rose, suddenly alive, for the first time, to the precociously care-worn appearance of the young man's features. "What is it you wish me to do?"

"Help me out of a situation injurious both to body and mind; help me to substitute for the paralyzing incubus of forced idleness the healthy stimulus of congenial occupation."

"In other words," said Rose, "you ask me to renew

an experiment which failed most miserably, and which, in all probability, would fail again most miserably."

"Not if we tried it wisely and in a spirit of conciliation — failure always brings with it a little wisdom. For my part, I have grown wise enough to make every concession that is compatible with the end I have in view. I am ready to accept work, I declare, on almost any terms."

"Why not accept it here, then?" hastened to say Rose.

"Not here; for I could have none that would answer the requirements of my nature. I must have real work homogeneous to my bent of mind and to my profession."

"And where's the difficulty of finding that here?" persisted Rose. "Why shouldn't you do what papa used to do, give legal advice to all the people round about? You could have a room all to yourself to see your clients in; and, as soon as it is known that you are ready to be consulted, I am sure you will not want for business."

"Ah! to be sure, plenty of business — but of what sort? the trespass of a pig or cow into a neighbour's orchard; a disputed right of way across a meadow, or of drawing water from some well; and such like. You don't expect that my mind should be satisfied with such pabulum. And, then, why should I not have my honest labour properly requited; which is entirely out of the question here?"

"I see," said Rose, with a grimace of disappointment, "that nothing will content you but an office under Government."

"You don't do justice, Rose, to the ultra-conciliatory spirit I show. I have just been saying that I was ready to accept work on almost any terms. A situation under Government, I confess, would best suit my capabilities and my tastes; but I am not blind to the dangers such a situation would have for our future good understanding; and, if you still object to it..."

"I do," interrupted Rose.

"Well, if you do, I make no difficulties in setting aside my wishes."

"That is very kind," said Rose, "and I thank you very much."

"But it is a concession," continued Vincenzo, "which costs me a great effort, and for which I have a right to expect some more substantial return than your thanks, however agreeable they are."

"How self-interested you have grown!" said Rose, jokingly.

"A little so, but for your sake also," answered Vincenzo, following her lead; "because, after all, it is you who would have to bear the burden of a sickly or a wicked husband." Then, changing his tone to one of sober earnest, he said impressively, "Believe me, Rose, there is more at stake on the issue of our present conversation than you, or perhaps even I, wot of."

"What is your proposal?" asked Rose.

"To do at Turin what you pressed me just now to do here — to establish myself there as a barrister."

"Of course you can do that if you choose; for my part I neither make nor shall make any objections to your doing so; only I hope you do not expect me to go with you, and to leave papa."

"Persuade your father to go with us, and then

every difficulty will be smoothed away — the Gordian knot cut. You know that he likes Turin, and so do you."

"True, but we both like this place best."

"I asked of you a concession, and the word implies a little sacrifice."

"And then," continued Rose, "papa must change his habits; and it is not safe, at his time of life, to change anything in his mode of living."

"It may be so; I'll not insist on that point. I will limit my request to this; get your father to agree to spend henceforth, at Turin, the three months or so of the winter which he passes at Ibella. It will be a clear gain for him; his body and mind will equally benefit by the movement and the change. As far as I could judge while there, Ibella has lost all its attractions for him."

"He certainly does not like it as well as he used to do," said Rose; "well, now, supposing that I am able to induce papa to spend the three winter months at Turin, what is to come of him during the remaining nine months of the year?"

"Say during the remaining seven; for the vacation months of August and September we shall be together here. As to those seven months, I give you *carte blanche*, Rose. If your heart prompts you to pass them all with your father, I shall not complain; if it inclines you to bestow on me a half, or a third, or any part whatever, I shall be thankful. Perhaps your father might be easily prevailed on to come with you to see me occasionally for a fortnight or so; however, in one word, manage it as you best like. At any rate I shall always come to see you every Sunday while our separation lasts. Tell me, can I be more reasonable, or more accommodating?"

"Accommodating with a vengeance," said Rose, piqued in a manner that never would have been the case six months before. "So long as you can have your hobby, you care little for anything or any one else — your wife included."

"How can you say that, when I have just told you that I should see you once at least in every week that God makes? If you were a man, Rose, you would understand the perfect compatibility of what you call my hobby with fond and deep-rooted affections. You would indeed."

"As I am not a man, I have no choice but to try and believe you," said Rose. "You don't think me so ridiculous, I hope, as to be . . . what shall I call it — over-exacting?"

"Jealous was the word you had on the tip of your tongue," said Vincenzo. "Would to God you were — that would be a proof that you loved me — but it isn't in your nature; to be jealous, I mean."

"I dare say not, and I am not sorry for it," said Rose, with a blush. "However, to return to the point; I will think over your plan, and give you my answer to-morrow."

"Why not now?" urged Vincenzo, putting his arm gently round her waist, and drawing her close to his bosom. They were by this time seated side by side in the belvedere.

"No, not now," said Rose; "I must sleep upon it, ere I give my decision: if my comfort alone were concerned in the change you propose, I would not hesitate to say, yes; but, where papa's well-being is also at stake, I must act with caution."

Nothing that Vincenzo could say had the least effect in altering her determination. Of this he might rest assured, that she had the greatest wish in the world to do what was agreeable to him, if possible. He had made, to please her, far too great a concession in giving up all idea of any appointment under Government, for her not to be desirous of showing her sense of his considerateness to the best of her power.

Vincenzo had an obvious reason for pressing for an answer on the spot; he apprehended Don Pio's interference during any delay, and he had it twenty times on his lips to beseech her not to take the priest into her confidence. However, he refrained from doing so, on reflecting that, if she had made up her mind that way, his request would be useless; if she had not, then it might be dangerous, inasmuch as it would prompt that which he most wished avoided. As it was, he had every reason to be satisfied with the reception his overture had met with. True that, to give it some chance of acceptance, he had had to reduce his pretensions to the lowest figure; and it was with a cruel struggle that he had pronounced those fatal words which consummated his divorce from a career which, from the taste he had already had of it, he knew to be so well suited to his powers and inclinations. But the unceasing reflections of now nearly a twelvemonth had brought him gradually to feel the utter hopelessness of obtaining his wife's acquiescence in any compromise which had not as its basis the renunciation of all official employment.

The book-worm, sedentary life of a barrister, which

for some time must necessarily be a briefless one, had little attraction for a young man of Vincenzo's broad sympathies and active spirit. His mind was too keenly engrossed by the political questions of the day to find congenial food in the respectable, though comparatively narrow, interests of *meum et tuum*. Still there were points on which the practice of the bar commingled with politics, when forensic eloquence became the surest safeguard of all liberties; and these particular points it was Vincenzo's intention most sedulously to cultivate and make his special walk. Not a few Turinese advocates had gained fame and popularity by their defence of Journalism, prosecuted by the Crown, as also in the seeking of legal redress for abuses of power committed by responsible agents. Then, there was that platform, to which every one was at liberty to bring all questions, and from which the cause of truth and progress might still be modestly, but usefully advocated, viz. the Daily Press; with frequent recurrence to which Vincenzo had promised himself to fill the gap between one brief and the other. Next to drawing up reports of the nature of that which had been entrusted to him in Savoy, furnishing articles to a newspaper was the task which, perhaps, was best suited to the young man's talents and likings. By these means Vincenzo trusted he should be able to create for himself an amount of intellectual excitement and interest, sufficient, if not to make his life a happy one, to prevent, at least, existence being a burden to him.

Unluckily for him, all his calculations were destined to come to nothing. Rose had been already long gone to the village, when he went in search of her next morning — an unpromising sign to begin with; and a worse one still was the confusion she showed at seeing him when he met her coming out of the church. He offered her his arm, remarking that she must have got up unusually early. She said yes, for that it was one of her days of confession.

"And," continued Vincenzo, with an appearance of perfect calm, "have you nothing to say to me?"

"Indeed I have, and I wish it were something more agreeable for you," said Rose; "but really, upon consideration, I cannot agree to your yesterday's proposal."

Rose felt the arm on which she was leaning shake as though struck with palsy.

"And why not?" asked he, clenching his teeth to keep in his passion.

Rose said hurriedly, "For several reasons. I will tell you by-and-bye."

"You need not. I know the real one. Don Pio has forbidden you to do so."

"You go too far, Vincenzo," cried Rose.

"Not a bit. He did not make use of the word — he is too wily for that — but he gave you to understand what to do, and you do it. Everybody orders you about, everybody is listened to, except your husband. Blind, blind, blind that you are. But what's the use of appealing to you? You are the tool, and his the hand which wields it. It is he whom I ought, and shall call to account." And, suddenly disengaging his wife's arm from his, Vincenzo took his way back to the church. Rose ran after him —

"Pray, pray don't. You can't expect Don Pio to change his mind."

"I shall curse him, at all events, for the injury he inflicts upon me; and there will be some comfort in doing that."

"If you do, it is all over between us," cried Rose, now also in a passion.

"It is long since it was all over between us," retorted Vincenzo. "I am prepared for all consequences. I am tired of being for ever trampled in the dust, tired of for ever playing the part of a worm — once more I lift up my head, assert the dignity of a man. Accept, purely and simply, my yesterday's proposal, or —"

Rose made no answer, but turned towards the palace. Vincenzo, one minute after, stood in the well-known parlour of the parsonage.

Don Pio was reading his breviary: as he raised his eyes from his book, and fixed them on Vincenzo's agitated countenance, he perceived the signs of a forthcoming stormy interview, and at once buckled on his armour. With bland composure of mien and manner, he rose, uttered a polite welcome, and with a courteous wave of the hand motioned to a chair. There is for the gently-bred a positive spell in forms. Heated to a white heat as he was, and far more disposed to break than to pour out the phial of his wrath on the tonsured head bowing so civilly to him, Vincenzo felt the charm, and the ex abrupto address which quivered on his lips was replaced almost unconsciously by a dry,

"I wish for a few moments' conversation with you, Sir, if it may suit your convenience."

"I am quite at your service, Signor Candia," returned Don Pio. "Pray be seated."

Vincenzo sat down, and began: "I desire to state

to you, Reverendo, that I had occasion yesterday to communicate to my wife a decision on which I have long meditated, and which I have so arranged as to conciliate my duties and feelings with her feelings and inclinations. To satisfy her wishes, I made great sacrifices in my own plans. My wife understood this, and was disposed to yield me a graceful acquiescence. In this reasonable frame of mind she went to rest last night. This morning, a moment ago, I met her returning from a conference with you, and received from her a decided refusal to my proposals — a refusal for which I hold you responsible, and have come to call you to account. How dare you, sir, meddle in my domestic affairs, and thwart my arrangements?"

"Allow me to observe, Signor Candia, that your manner of speaking is somewhat intemperate," replied the priest, a shade of pallor alone betraying his emotion, his voice remaining composed and paternally grave. "Having made this remark, I shall now reply to your accusation, that, in point of fact, I had so little intention to meddle, as you call it, in your domestic concerns, and thwart your arrangements, that until this very moment I had not the least idea of your being the originator of this scheme of removal to Turin. Signora Candia mentioned it to me without the least allusion to the quarter from whence it came."

"Which did not, however, prevent your instantly guessing that it came from me," interrupted Vincenzo.

"She mentioned it to me," pursued the priest, without heeding the interruption, "and then asked my advice, which I gave —"

"With more zeal than discretion," broke in Vincenzo.

"Permit me to be of a different opinion," returned Don Pio with a sort of haughty serenity; "as to my right to counsel Signora Candia, I don't suppose you mean to question that. You are not ignorant that I am her spiritual adviser, and that, as such, I have charge of her soul."

"Direct her soul as much as you like, but don't presume to hamper my movements."

"Not even if your movements endanger her soul? —"

"No reservations. I don't admit that they can ever have that effect, and I resent the mere supposition as an insult. I am neither an infidel nor a madman. I am of that age at which the law gives every man authority over himself; and under no pretext, I warn you, will I suffer you to interfere with my liberty of action."

"And I warn you that no threats shall make me swerve from my duty to my penitent."

"Does it form part of your duty to your penitent to teach her to disobey her husband?"

"It forms part of my duty to my penitent to deter her from whatever may mar her spiritual welfare, from whatever quarter the temptation comes."

"In other words, you maintain your right of interference, of censure, and of a final veto against me. Your monstrous theory does nothing less than annul the authority of fathers and husbands."

"Not at all. It corrects it where it is wrong. The authority of father or husband must be subordinate to that of God."

"Certainly; but not to yours — a poor fallible man, as liable to error as I am, priest though you be."

"You forget, young man," returned Don Pio, with a slight modulation of his voice, indicating rising irritation, "that the priest, all unworthy as he may be, is the representative upon earth of the authority of God."

"In the exercise of his ministry, I bow to him as such; out of it, I look upon him as my equal."

"I do not admit the distinction. The sacred character conferred by the imposition of the Bishop's hands is indelible, continuous, indivisible. Perhaps," wound up the Priest with a sneer, "in Protestant Turin they may think otherwise."

"Whatever may be thought or not in Turin," retorted Candia, speaking with concentrated energy, "let me tell you this, Don Pio, much as I wish to live and die as a good Catholic, rather than submit to the yoke of your autocracy, rather than be the bondsman of my wife's confessor, rather than that I would —"

The keen eager glance of his listener, the glance of a duellist intent on a false move of his antagonist, and prepared to profit by it, cautioned the speaker in time that he had better say no more. He stopped short accordingly, and after a silence resumed in a tone the calm of which contrasted strongly with the vehemence of the minute before, "Listen to me, Don Pio. You will do me this justice, that I have done my best, in spite of provocation, to live at peace with you?"

"Why, what provocation have I given you?" asked Don Pio, haughtily.

"I am not ignorant, Don Pio, of how much I owe to your good offices with my father-in-law," said Vincenzo bitterly. "However, let bygones be bygones. Let us mend the present if possible. Help me to do so, help me to avoid a scandal, for otherwise a scandal there will be, and a great one; for it is my fixed determination to go to Turin; with my wife, if she will accompany me, without her, if she refuses. You have only one word to say to bring about this happy result. Say it. Withdraw your opposition to my plan."

"Never!" exclaimed the priest; "in matters of conscience there can be no possible compromise, and I wonder at you for proposing such to me."

"Consider, Reverendo," urged Rose's husband, much excited, "that some of the scandal which must infallibly ensue will lie at your door. People will say, After all, he only wanted to take his wife with him to Turin, and Don Pio would not let her go."

"Turin is a den of perdition," shouted the Priest. "Never, while I live, will I consent to Signora Candia's going there."

"Consider, Sir," went on the young man, "before it is too late, for your sake as well as for mine, whether it would not be advisable not to drive things to extremities."

"Do you threaten me, Signor Candia?"

"By no means," replied Vincenzo. "I only plead with warmth such considerations as should, and ought to, incline you to moderation. I am not so utterly powerless as you, perhaps, deem me. I have some influential friends who will stand by me. I have my pen, and the public press is a formidable engine. If you push me to the wall, you may repent it one of these days."

"Young man!" cried the Priest, starting to his feet,

"I am as indifferent to your menaces as to the buzz of the flies round me. In the exercise of my ministry, I am ready to endure any persecution."

"It is easy to brave persecution when there is no danger of any," retorted Vincenzo.

He also had risen, and the two stood facing each other — Don Pio with the imperious bearing of offended priestly pride; Vincenzo with the frank defiance of honest, unrepressed resentment.

"Do you doubt that in defence of the interests of religion I would willingly go to the stake?" asked the Priest, crossing his arms, and drawing himself up to his full height.

Vincenzo fixed his penetrating eyes upon the questioner, and answered, "No, Don Pio, I do not doubt your capabilities for martyrdom: only it is not the interests of religion you have at heart, but those of your caste. You are an excellent partisan, Sir, but a bad priest."

Don Pio shrugged his shoulders scornfully. Vincenzo went on: "Remember the words of Christ, 'The tree is known by his fruit.' Now, what fruit have you borne? A ministry of peace and love you have turned into one of strife and hatred. Not a day of your sojourn among us but you have marked it by some new mischief. You have estranged from me the heart of my father-in-law; you have made it a case of conscience for my wife to disobey me; you have sown the seeds of mistrust and rebellion among your parishioners. Yes, the traditional reverence for their King, which, before you came, formed the sole political creed of these simple, ignorant villagers, you have shaken to the root; you have covertly hinted to them from the pulpit that their King was a son of Belial, a persecutor of religion. . . . . And the Signor Avvocato, the good, kindly old man, full of gentle sympathies, both public and private, beaming with benevolence for all — what have you made of him? You have transformed him into a selfish, morose hypochondriac, having no thought but for his own ailments, haunted day and night by the terrors, not of religion, but of a miserable superstition. He is become *ut cadaver* in your hands."

"If it is convenient to you, Sir," said Don Pio, "I should not be sorry to be alone."

"I am going," said Vincenzo, moving away, "but you shall have yet a last word from me. Don Pio, I adjourn you to that tribunal where cold-bloodedness and arrogance are of no avail." So saying he turned, and left the house.

He was back at the palace in a twinkling. Rose, behind the curtains of one of the ground-floor windows, was on the watch for him. The moment she saw him enter the house she ran into the passage, and met him, seemingly by accident, with the exclamation, "Oh, here you are! was Don Pio at home?"

"He was," answered Vincenzo.

"And how — did you part?" Rose looked perplexed and disturbed.

"Come, and you shall hear," returned he, taking her by the hand and leading her upstairs to the first floor. The door of what had formerly been the Signor Avvocato's musical retreat stood open, and exhibited the old man, wrapped in a flannel dressing gown, lying down full length on a sofa. Vincenzo walked in, took off his hat, and said, "Sir, I have come, as in duty bound, to inform you of a resolution which I have taken." His tone was calm, nay subdued, but every word came forth with the sharp distinctness of the note of a clarion. "I have made up my mind, Sir," continued Vincenzo, "to go and set up as a barrister in Turin."

"Have you, indeed?" said the Signor Avvocato, lifting himself up a little. The inflection of the voice had a strong infusion of sneer in it, but the look of the speaker was anything but confident; it was rather that of a man more than half frightened. Vincenzo, as he stood there, white to his very lips, his hair flying in disorder about his temples, his eyes flashing like carbuncles, was not a person to trifle with.

"Yes, Sir," resumed the young man, "I need not annoy you with the repetition of the motives which dictate this course. You know them already: you have admitted their cogency, given them the sanction of your approbation. To these existing motives a new one is now added, which alone would suffice to decide me to leave this place. I have, this very day, had proof that there is an influence here to which my wife pays more deference than to mine — a power above my power with her. Under these circumstances it becomes imperative on me to free myself from this degrading situation, and to take my wife out of so baneful an atmosphere, subversive and destructive of the very essence of marriage —"

"Make your meaning clear, sir," gasped the Signor Avvocato, half-choking with anxiety.

"Therefore," pursued Vincenzo, "here in your presence, I adjure my wife, for the sake of the affection I bear her; I order my wife (if necessary) in the name of the obedience she owes her husband, to follow me to Turin."

"Never!" shouted the old man, springing from the couch with an agility of which he would not have given proof had the palace been on fire. "I forbid her: speak out, Rose; you will not go, will you?"

"He knows that I will not," stammered Rosė, in great distress: "I have already told him so."

"There — you have heard her — that settles the matter!" cried the old man, exultingly.

"Sir, I beseech you, I warn you most respectfully, not to encourage my wife in disobedience. You are too good a lawyer, Sir, not to know that the authority of a father goes for nothing against the authority of a husband."

"But I know, as a lawyer, that there are such things as separations on the ground of cruelty."

"Cruelty!" repeated Vincenzo, looking about him as if to make sure he was not dreaming. "If you can make out a case of cruelty against me, I shall give you credit for being the first lawyer in the world."

"Not so difficult as you seem to believe. We shall plead, sir."

"In that case I will have no other advocate than my wife. Be frank, Rose — have I ever treated you with cruelty?"

"I never complained of your having done so," said Rose.

"If your wife chooses to forget or to forgive, I have done neither. I recollect only too well the deplorable condition in which you brought her back to me. If my daughter was delivered of a still-born child — if she was within a hair's-breadth of her grave — it is you she may thank for it; it was your bad treatment brought about the catastrophe."

"Oh, father!" cried Rose, standing before him in earnest deprecation of such a charge. Vincenzo reeled back as if he had received a blow from a club; grasping his hair with both hands, he stood for a while like one stupefied. His face had become livid, his eyes haggard. At last he said, in a low whisper, "May God forgive you, for I cannot." Then, with a sudden burst of fury, "And it is you who bring this monstrous accusation against me, you who —"

Rose rushed to him, clung to his arm with one hand, tried to stop his mouth with the other, exclaiming, "Oh don't, pray don't speak another word, Vincenzo."

"Stand back! let me alone. I shall and will speak," shouted Vincenzo, frantic with passion. "There are charges which a man cannot bear, which he must resent and repel were they made by his own father;" and, turning to the Signor Avvocato — "Is it you who arraign me for the murder of my child — for the danger of my wife? you, who did it all, if any one did — yes, you who were blind enough not to perceive that your daughter had hurt herself in her fall — you, who were the cause of her despising my entreaties to send for a physician, lest you should be alarmed."

It was the Signor Avvocato's turn to look blank and stunned. His eyes wandered mechanically from Rose to Vincenzo, from Vincenzo to Rose, like one bewildered by fear. "Is what he says true?" asked he of his daughter at last. Rose, for all answer, wrung her hands.

"Is it true?" again asked the old man, with a forlorn air.

"No, no, it is not," faltered Rose; "but indeed he was never cruel to me."

The old man's face grew purple. "Get out of my sight," thundered he, stamping his foot, "you liar, slanderer, calumniator! get out of my sight, villain, or by Jove —"

Rose's false testimony against him had sobered her husband so far as to make him feel the utter uselessness of any further remonstrance. He now answered composedly: "I obey your command, sir. It agrees with my own intentions, as you know. I free you from my presence. Rose, you know where to find me, if you wish it. Farewell." And he was gone.

He went up to his attic, made his papers into a bundle, put it under his arm, ran down the stairs again, out of the house, through the terrace, along the avenue, without meeting a soul, and so into the high road. It being midday, the general dinner hour, there was nobody out of doors at Rumelli. After having walked at least three miles at a prodigious pace, the great hubbub in his head and heart subsided a little, and then he recollected Barnaby, whom he had for the nonce entirely forgotten; and he blamed himself severely for not having said good-bye to old Barnaby, his trusty, and indeed sole friend at the palace. However, it was now too late; not for the world would he have gone back. He reached Ibella in time for the last train; and by eight in the evening he was in Turin.

CHAPTER X.

"Libertà va cercando ch'è sì cara."

VINCENZO's long experience of Turin enabled him soon to find a very cheap lodging, a vile hole, in a vile court; he paid a week in advance, left there his bundle of papers, which was indeed all his luggage, and then sallied out in quest of Onofrio. Thorough as was his confidence in Onofrio's willingness to serve him at all times, he could not prevail on himself to go to him without warning, and, as it were, to take his friend's hospitality by storm. His letter, in which, if the reader recollects, he announced his probable return to town *within two months*, was not yet a week old, and here he already was. We must not forget to mention *en passant*, that Vincenzo was still possessed of the greater part, in fact, of three hundred and fifty of those memorable four hundred francs, which he had received from the Minister full a year ago.

Great was Onofrio's surprise, and greater still his pity, at sight of the familiar face, so strikingly changed for the worse, grown so wan and aged. Vincenzo had come resolved to unbosom himself; and at the first word of heartfelt sympathy, elicited by his altered appearance, forth gushed, like lava, the sad tale of his sorrows and grievances, old and new, from first to last, this time without reservation. The young man was too excited, too full of the injustice he had suffered, he stood in too great need of giving vent to his long pent up misery, to think of hiding any of the wounds from which he was bleeding. On the contrary, it was a relief to exhibit them in their complete nudity, to probe them to their full depth. The unfeigned emotion of the listener was scarcely second to that of the narrator. Onofrio declared that never, in all his experience of family feuds, had he heard of a case more painfully complicated and of a more aggravated character than that of his friend.

"Better that it should be so," said Vincenzo, emphatically; "better that I should have been so driven by the force of irresistible circumstances, for, had the situation been less extreme, less untenable, I should not feel so entirely justified as I do, for having extricated myself from it, at any cost. It is a serious step, my dear friend — I can speak of it with knowledge; I thought of it for months and months, till my head was ready to burst — it is a serious step to abandon one's wife, to part with one's father-in-law, when that father-in-law (here Vincenzo's voice grew husky) is also one's benefactor, and was to all intents and purposes like one's own father — it is a serious step, and which nothing can make legitimate except an absolute necessity. But I am so far satisfied," continued Vincenzo, his voice once more clear and steady, "that I did my duty to the last, and that, consistently with what a man owes to himself, I could do no more. So there's an end of it. My conscience is at ease, thank God; and here I am a new and unfettered man, with plenty of good will and work in me, which I shall be too happy to give in payment for my daily bread."

The topic of ways and means being thus broached, Signor Onofrio expressed himself very sanguinely as to Vincenzo's finding the means of supporting himself, more sanguinely probably than the good gentleman felt. Like the good Samaritan that he was, he felt that this was not the moment for starting difficulties, but for comforting and encouraging where there was so much need of encouragement and comfort.

"Don't trouble thyself about the crust of bread," said Onofrio; "with God's help we'll find thee that, and a bit of cheese too. In the meantime thou wilt come and stay with me."

To this Vincenzo would not consent; not at least until he had earned enough to pay for his board, as formerly.

"I'll give thee credit," said Onofrio, smiling. "Proud, stupid fellow that thou art, canst thou not see that by becoming my debtor thou makest sure of my finding something for thee to do in order that I may reimburse myself?"

Pressed in so gracious a manner, it was impossible to resist. Vincenzo yielded with eyes far from dry; only he stipulated for leave to sleep that night in the room he had hired. It was past midnight when he took his way thither, comforted and soothed to a degree at which he was himself the first to wonder.

Let us now explain why Signor Onofrio was far less confident of his ability to serve his young friend than he chose to appear. We forbore to mention at the time, because we were aware it could be more usefully done at this place, that Vincenzo's untimely resignation, just after receiving such marked proofs of his patron the Minister's satisfaction, had piqued this personage more than was reasonable — the best of men, we know, will be touchy sometimes — and had been the occasion of an hour's misunderstanding between the Minister and Onofrio.

"I beg of you," had said the Minister, "not in future to waste your interest on fools."

"Wait until I recommend somebody to you again," had retorted Onofrio.

So that there was an end to any opening in that quarter, Onofrio being a man to suffer a thousand deaths rather than eat his own words. He also had his weak point, as we see. When Vincenzo's letter came, bringing the news of his speedy return to Turin, Onofrio began at once to look sharply about him for something suitable, and, to his great mortification, found nothing but a supernumerary clerkship or two, with no work, no emolument, and no prospects; upon which he said to himself, "I have more than half a mind to take my protégé straight to Cavour — short of that I see no chance for the young man. But, before doing this, supposing I do it, I must be satisfied, I must make doubly sure, that he will not bolt off the course again. One failure is more than enough."

Vincenzo's unexpected arrival, precipitated as it had been by such exciting circumstances, while changing nothing in Onofrio's inclinations to befriend him, yet confirmed him in his plan of prudent delay. Not until time had tested the temper of Vincenzo's resolution, would Onofrio play his trump card in his behalf.

But in the meanwhile — that is, during this period of probation — Vincenzo could not remain idle to chew the cud of his misery; he must have plenty to do, and earn money for his labour. Here was the difficulty. Requited occupation at twenty-four hours' notice is not to be had for the wishing. After ransacking all the cells in his brain for half the night without finding the clue to what he sought, Onofrio with a sudden jerk sat up in his bed, gave his head a great thump and exclaimed, "What an ass I am! And my statistics? What should hinder me from making over that task to him, and paying him as from the Government?" Whereupon Onofrio laid himself down again and slept soundly.

Next morning Vincenzo, after a frugal breakfast, a cup of chocolate and a slice of bread, putting his bundle of papers under his arm, went to take possession, as agreed upon overnight, of his old room at Onofrio's. It was a cheerful little room, commanding, as we already know, a fine view of the hills on the other side of the Po. As Vincenzo stood at the window and gazed at the familiar features of the beautiful landscape, and evoked the memories connected with it, a whiff of his bachelor days, a whiff of hopefulness and confidence in the future swept over him. Presently he sat himself down near the window, untied his bundle of papers and began a survey of them. There was, besides his Report to the Minister, much miscellaneous matter; extracts from various books, notes for an Essay — the Duties of a Priest — two chapters of a novel, sundry poetical effusions, thoughts on politics, translations from Byron, and what not. To beguile a heavy hour or two, Vincenzo had begun many things, but finished, or indeed even pursued steadily, none.

About two in the afternoon, Onofrio came in apparently in a hurry. "Bless me!" cried he, with a scared look at the heap of papers scattered about, "you seem to have got work enough already to last you your life."

"Mere sham-work!" said Vincenzo, "and which

shall be cast into limbo the moment I light on some that is real."

"Poetry! into the bargain," continued Onofrio, taking up one of the scattered sheets of paper. "The mere sight freezes on my lips a prosaic proposal, I had come to make."

"Make it nevertheless, my friend," said Vincenzo. "What may it be about?"

"About a tedious, dry and badly-paid task, which has only two points in its favour — one, that it is at your service immediately; the other, that it is likely to last for a few months."

"Accepted!" said Vincenzo.

"Wait a moment; first of all, I must premise that of course I only propose it to you provisionally, and without hampering you, should something better and more permanent offer — a something which I hope to find for you within a short time."

"Thank you, thank you!" said Vincenzo, pressing his friend's hand affectionately; "now, then, what is this task?"

"It is a statistical work, and, consequently, bristling with figures, every one of which must be verified. Now, I don't think that arithmetic is your *forte*."

"I beg your pardon," protested Vincenzo, warmly; "I am not quick at figures, but sure —"

"Well, then, the matter in question is a detailed account, intended for publication, of the present state of public instruction throughout the kingdom. All the facts, most carefully collected, are ready; they only require to be coordinated according to a certain method which I shall explain to you at leisure."

"Capital!" exclaimed the delighted Vincenzo, "I am your man."

"But listen to this," said Onofrio; "the minister who commissioned me to superintend the drawing up of these statistics, grants me, for such mechanical help as might be required, only a sum of three hundred francs. It is very little."

"It is Potosi, California, and Australia put together," cried Vincenzo. "When shall we begin?"

"When I have had time to put together the pile of indispensable documents relating to the subject, and to send them here for your use. This can't be before two or three days. Now, good-bye, till dinner time. Reconsider my proposal, and, if you change your mind —"

"No danger of that," put in Vincenzo.

"Well, if you should," continued Onofrio, "don't stand on ceremony to say so; we would search for something else."

Let us hasten to add, within a parenthesis, that Onofrio's statement was true in all its particulars, save in that of the grant of a sum of money. The minister had allotted and could have allotted no extraordinary funds for a task which came under the head of ordinary business.

Vincenzo did not alter his mind, and some of the promised documents began to flow in on the morrow. Truth to say, Onofrio was as impatient to see Vincenzo at work, as Vincenzo was to be at it. By the morning of the third day, all the materials were at hand; and Vincenzo, in high spirits, was in the very act of making his first numeral, when Brigida, the old servant, handed him a letter. It was in the Signor Avvocato's well-known writing, and addressed to Signor Avvocato V. Candia, care of Signor Onofrio, at whose office it had been delivered, and who had considerately sent it by one of the messengers belonging to the bureaux. Candia expected this letter, had counted upon it, and received it with a chuckle of satisfaction; less, indeed, at the implicit proof it conveyed of all being well at the palace, than at the eagerness it betrayed of entering into communication with him. His self-love was more tickled than his heart touched by it. The contents were such as he had anticipated; only far more moderate in tone, and specious in argument, than accorded with the habits or with the powers of the writer. "That wily priest has been meddling here;" thought Vincenzo; and, looked at through this preconception, every word had a suspicious air about it.

The Signor Avvocato began by expressing his and his daughter's utter amazement and grief at Vincenzo's unaccountable disappearance; unaccountable, because no man in his right senses could have construed into an order of departure — such hasty words as might have passed the writer's lips in a moment of passion. The Signor Avvocato felt sure that Vincenzo, better advised, would go back immediately to Rumelli. It was his absolute duty as a Christian and as a husband so to do — a full page, with quotations from the seventh chapter of St. Paul's first epistle to the Corinthians, was devoted to proving the above proposition. The Signor Avvocato's old age and growing infirmities were next touched upon and skilfully pleaded. The conclusion was this. Vincenzo's speedy return was a preliminary *sine qua non* to a renewed good understanding between him and his wife, and his wife's father. Failing this, he would henceforth be considered as a stranger, and treated as such. This letter, as it was the first, so it would be the last that would be written on the subject.

Vincenzo shrugged his shoulders at this threat, too much at variance with the argumentative habits of his correspondent to be believed, and forthwith penned an answer. He said how much he regretted having caused the Signor Avvocato and his daughter any uneasiness by his departure, though he was at a loss to understand how it could have taken either of them by surprise, as he had previously announced it in sufficiently positive terms, and had only hastened it by a few days in consequence of the scene which had taken place. He regretted also that his notions of the duty of a Christian and of a husband should differ *toto cœlo* from those put forward in the letter he was answering. Then followed a full page, interspersed with counter-quotations, wherein the arguments of the adverse party were grasped, crushed, and ground to nothing with a zest which made his hand tremble with pleasurable excitement. Let us plead in exoneration of Vincenzo, that, in thought, he addressed himself less to him who had written, than to him who had inspired the letter from Rumelli. He ended by maintaining his resolution, and his right and duty to maintain it, irrespective of all consequences, and expressing his hope that his wife would, on reflection, see the propriety of joining her husband, who was ready to receive her with open arms.

Vincenzo was so pleased with his performance that he delayed posting it to the last moment, in the hope that Onofrio might come home in time to hear it. Disappointed in this, he repeated from memory to his friend, during dinner, the spiciest phrases of his answer. Onofrio laughed and said, "You are in for a regular theological controversy. Don't expect that your black-robed antagonist will give in so easily."

"I dare say he won't," said Vincenzo. "I should be disappointed if he did. I confess that a little pass of arms with his reverence, once a fortnight, let us say, tickles my fancy amazingly."

Vincenzo now attacked his work in earnest. With the exception of an hour or so given to the daily papers early in the day, and a couple of hours spent in walking in the evening, his time was devoted to his task. Without being exactly that which he could have desired, it was not devoid of a certain interest for one who had so keenly at heart the improvement of his country, and who, from the insight given by the documents before him, received ample assurance of the superiority of the new methods over the old, and evidence of the progress, both in quality and quantity, that public instruction had made in a few years. Even-tempered and cheerful, as a rule, Vincenzo had occasionally fits of high spirits, when he would sing himself hoarse while at work, or talk Onofrio deaf, by the hour. But sociableness with him began and ended at home. Abroad, he sought to be alone, and studiously avoided frequented thoroughfares and places of resort where he might meet acquaintances. He had not even been able to bring himself to go to a café to read the newspapers, necessary to him as his daily bread.

"Could you not procure some for me at home?" had Vincenzo asked of Onofrio on the scecond day after his arrival.

"Surely; as many as you like; but why not go to a café and read them — you would have a greater variety."

"Because," had answered Vincenzo, "friends are to be met with at cafés, and friends ask questions about folks' wives and fathers-in-law, which are better avoided just now."

Onofrio brought home with him from that day loads of newspapers.

Three weeks passed away, and no second letter from Rumelli. Vincenzo was not uneasy, but he was piqued, and could not help showing it.

"In all likelihood," said Onofrio, "Don Pio is concocting an epistle, which is to be your *coup de grâce*, a sort of thunderbolt which it takes some time to forge."

"Probably," assented Vincenzo laughing, but he remained thoughtful.

Another couple of weeks passed and no thunderbolt. Vincenzo felt uneasy, and said, "If I could only be sure they are not ill."

"It would be strange indeed if they were both ill," said Onofrio, sharply; "it is not very likely at all events." Then he added after a pause, "You must be on your guard, my friend, against your imagination, or it will play you some sorry trick."

"You are right; I am a great goose," replied Vincenzo; "what a blessing it is to have a wise friend by one's side."

The wise friend from that moment augured ill of the issue of Vincenzo's coming to Turin.

One evening, not long after, Onofrio happened to mention, incidentally, the great loss of life from disease which the Piedmontese had sustained in the Crimea. This remark sent a painful thrill through Vincenzo's heart, to explain which it is only necessary to know that he had never heard from his soldier friend Ambrogio. At first he had taken it for granted that Ambrogio's letters had miscarried through the carelessness of the post-office clerks at Chambery, who had probably forgotten his directions to forward all letters for Signor Candia to Rumelli. Vincenzo, we must recollect, had quitted Chambery for Rumelli shortly after Ambrogio's departure. But, as time wore on and the expeditionary corps returned, and the ominous silence still continued, Vincenzo began to fear the worst and purposed to write to Ambrogio's father — an unpleasant undertaking, however, from which he shrunk, and which he consequently put off from day to day, from week to week, from month to month — in fact, until the present instant. This dilatoriness would have been inexplicable in any one but Vincenzo, who had had, as we are aware, to go through, during this period, such a series of worries and trials, as might and indeed must have distracted the steadiest mind.

Vincenzo briefly explained to Onofrio the preceding circumstances, and ended by begging him to help to ascertain Ambrogio's fate.

"Nothing easier," replied Onofrio; "they will be sure to know at the War Office; but I warn you not to be sanguine of good news."

The advice was not mistimed, as the event too well proved. The following day Onofrio brought home, alas! the sad intelligence that Ambrogio had fallen one of the first victims to the cholera, almost directly after landing at Balaclava. Vincenzo staggered under the blow; then, with a flood of tears, he bitterly upbraided himself for his heartless neglect of one of his best friends. Never should he forgive himself for not having written, as though thousands of the kindest words could have averted the sad catastrophe.

The deep sadness which now fell upon him laid him open to depressing influences of all kinds. The old misgiving consequent upon the unnatural silence maintained by those at Rumelli preyed upon his mind with daily increasing poignancy. Day and night he was haunted by the one desire, "to be made sure that they were not ill." At last he could bear it no longer, and he wrote a short and affectionate letter to his wife, expressive of his wish and hope, that the novel and rather strange situation in which he stood towards her and his father-in-law, should not deprive him of the comfort of hearing now and then how they were, and begging for a speedy answer. Onofrio made a very wry face on hearing in the evening what Vincenzo had done; but, out of pity for the embarrassment of the young man, said nothing. Vincenzo made it a point of honour to hide none of his weaknesses from Onofrio.

The letter to Rose brought no reply, and Vincenzo's anxiety had reached such a climax, that, had he dared, he would have gone and ascertained the truth with his own eyes. But Onofrio's steady glance nailed him to the spot. Instead, then, of going, he wrote to Barnaby, his last anchor of hope — "Was any body ill?" Barnaby's answer came by return of post. Such a scrawl as, at any other time, would have thrown Vincenzo into convulsions of laughter! As it was, it was opened and deciphered — no easy matter this last — with the religious awe befitting a message from heaven. The contents of the letter were as follows: "Nobody was ill, thank God, though nobody looked well; the Sr. Padrone especially did not, he did nothing but groan and complain of pains and aches. The Signora Padrona went regularly every day to mass as she used to do. None ever called at the house, save Don Pio, who oftener came twice than once a day. The gloom of the place, since Vincenzo went away, passed all conception; the churchyard was a gay spot in comparison. The father and daughter sat like ghosts for hours, without exchanging a word; they seemed to have forgotten how to smile. Barnaby had no doubt that Vincenzo had acted for the best, though all he could say was, that he wished his old carcass had been put under the ground before things had come to the pass they had." The scales of the old gardener's sympathy, according to precedent, inclined towards the side which alone fell under his observation, and therefore seemed to him, of the two, that most to be pitied.

This letter produced a momentary reaction in Vincenzo. Assured that nobody was ill at the palace — the only statement in Barnaby's letter which allaying as it did his predominant fears made any impression at first on him — Vincenzo felt a little ashamed of the extravagance of alarm to which he had given way. Onofrio availed himself of this state of his friend's feelings, to read him a little lecture. "I told you to beware of your imagination, my good fellow. If you do not take care you will be the dupe of it sooner or later. Let the present experience be of use to you for the future. It ought by this time to be as clear to you as it is to me, that you are the butt of an artfully-contrived plot, at the bottom of which is your Don Pio. He it is who has prevailed on your wife and father-in-law to keep this dead silence. Don Pio knows perfectly the imaginative turn of your mind, and he relies upon your power of forging all sorts of visionary alarms, to drag you back bound hand and foot.

Vincenzo could not help being struck by the justness of Onofrio's guess; and his indignation at the base attempt to play on his best feelings in order to get the better of him, steeled him afresh in his resolution. His anger, truth to say, was less against his wife and father-in-law, than against Don Pio. Don Pio was evidently the originator and instigator of the plot; but for him they would never have dreamed of it, though it was offence enough that they countenanced it. Let them wait till he went back.

This impression, however, softened before long — softened as he thought of the solitude and gloom he had left behind — of the old man and young woman, "sitting like ghosts for hours, without exchanging a word, having forgotten to smile." Sad, indeed, must be the plight of things up there, soliloquized Vincenzo, to wrench from poor Barnaby the wish that he was dead. Poor Barnaby! He who had invariably been so kind and affectionate; he who was so innocent of all these troubles; it was painful to think that he suffered for the faults of others — that he suffered on account of him, who would willingly sacrifice himself over and over again, to make the old man happy. As for the master and mistress, if they were uncomfortable, they had nobody to thank for it but themselves. Vincenzo asked himself, Could he have carried the spirit of conciliation further than he had done? Could he have reduced his legitimate claims to smaller proportions? No, his hand upon his heart! No, only nothing would satisfy them but to trample him under their feet! Well, then, now they must reap what they had sown: not that he rejoiced in their mortification! God forbid — he had enough of the Christian in him to render good for evil! He wished he knew how, without self-abasement, to make them contented; but of what avail his wishes; he must be thankful that no self-reproach mingled with his regrets!

It was towards the end of June that Vincenzo was indulging in these not very cheerful or coherent scraps of soliloquy. He had, by this time, been at his task for two months and a half; and the statistics had made great strides towards completion. Vincenzo was a conscientious worker; and, whatever his causes of affliction or disquiet, he allowed nothing to interfere with the discharge of his duty.

CHAPTER XI.

"I can't get out," said the Starling.

THERE was a revival of sensibility in Vincenzo, brought about by Barnaby's letter, and which was attended by a curious mental phenomenon. Hitherto the image of Rose and that of her father had come to him, as he had seen them during the painful circumstances which preceded his departure. There was a scowl on their brows, a curl on their lips, defiance in their eyes. But from the moment he had received Barnaby's scrawl, as if by a spell, Vincenzo's mind began to reflect the reverse of the medal. The Rose of yesterday gradually faded from his thoughts, and instead there stood, as though on a pedestal, the Rose of former days — the gentle patroness, friend and peacemaker; the discontented, irritable, father-in-law, in his turn, lost his scowl in a smile, and was replaced by the stanch protector and benefactor, grumbling now and then *pro formâ*, but beaming with benevolence and good humour. The effect of these sweet besetting recollections may easily be guessed. As the memory of past kindness obliterated that of recent harshness, as sentiment grew preponderant over reason, so Vincenzo began to doubt the legitimacy of his revolt. Not on the ground of insufficiency of provocation — as to that, Vincenzo's conviction was unalterable — but on the ground of the peculiar situation in which he stood towards the givers of the provocation. Was he, considering his antecedents, entitled to resent any thing from that quarter? This misgiving did not arise all of a sudden, nor was it uncombated; we have compressed within a few lines the work of weeks and weeks; but, once born, it rankled in his bosom, and gave him no truce. Vincenzo turned to Onofrio for succour against himself. He said one day —

"Can you conceive a state of relations between two individuals which places one of them morally at the mercy of the other?"

"I can't say I do between two civilized and rational individuals," returned Onofrio. "I see nothing at all approaching to this problem of yours, except the relation of a son to a father; and even then, you know, there are limits to the duties of a son, as there are to the authority of a father."

"In my opinion," said Vincenzo. "there are ties

more binding, more deeply enchaining the conscience, than even the natural ones between son and father. I mean those between the recipient of voluntarily-bestowed benefits and the benefactor; when, for instance, a man on whom you have no claim, to whom you are a stranger, takes you by the hand, and, from boyhood upwards gives you not only your daily bread, but also the far more precious food of the mind; treats you, in fact, to all intents and purposes like a beloved son, even to the extent of giving you his only daughter; — I say that your duty to that man is unlimited."

"The case in itself is strong, and you have put it strongly," said Onofrio; "and your conclusion?"

"And my conclusion," replied Vincenzo, "is, that I am not justifiable in thwarting that man's will, whatever it may be."

"Even if his will were to throw himself out of window?" asked Onofrio.

"His will in reference to me," explained Vincenzo, fretfully.

"Even," urged Onofrio, "if his will should be to roast you alive?"

"The moment is ill-chosen for indulging in jests."

"My dear boy, one may be roasted alive morally as well as physically," said Onofrio, gravely, "and a jest may be opportune in the most serious moment, when it conveys a sober truth — the truth that there are and must be limits to self-abnegation. The present question is one which must be tested by reason and not by sentiment. Now reason clearly shows you that you have duties of many kinds, and a theory which sacrifices to one all the others cannot but be fallacious and dangerous. The clergy do not proceed otherwise, when they subordinate all their obligations as citizens to their allegiance to Rome. It too often happens, it is true, that duties clash, and render a painful choice necessary; but that, thank God, is not your case. Nothing new of any consequence has altered your position from what it was three months ago. I understand what your shake of the head means — that there is sadness at Rumelli. Sadness, mind, and not broken hearts, as your imagination represents it! Well, if they are sad, for my part I am glad of it; sadness will inspire them with wise reflections, and do them good, and you too. In conclusion, I see no shadow of a reason why you should abandon the experiment on which you were so bent. The question as to who is to be master in your family, you or Don Pio, seems to me worth pursuing to a solution."

Onofrio's plain logic went home to Vincenzo's reason, who felt so much strengthened and comforted by it that he believed himself proof against any recurrence of his late misgivings; but he soon found out that what he had mistaken for a radical cure was a mere respite. The intellect may be convinced, and yet the heart doubt. A fortnight had scarcely elapsed, and here was poor Vincenzo once more plunged in the same sea of perplexities, once more arguing against himself with an ingenuity that an advocate for the adverse party might have envied him.

"The situation in which I stand," reasoned Vincenzo, "is one of my own seeking, the fruit of my own blindness; and I cannot, without injustice, call anybody but myself to account for the disagreeables I find in it. Least of all Rose, who has sacrificed for me the prospect, nay the certainty, of a far more advantageous establishment. If she has spoiled my life, I have spoiled hers, and we are quits. She is not naturally ill-tempered, quite the contrary; and — had she married, instead of me, a blockhead, such as there are plenty of, fearing God and the curé, very abstemious in politics, and disposed to enjoy the good things of the earth, which her fortune would procure him — there's every chance she would have made him an excellent and pleasant wife. What right, then, have I to complain, and to talk big and act big? Far more manly and rational to accept the situation which I myself sought, with all the good and bad and indifferent inherent in it."

"Not, at least, until you have satisfied your own mind that no efforts of yours can improve that situation," retorted Onofrio.

"What means have I for ever arriving at any satisfactory conclusion on that score?" asked Vincenzo.

"A little longer perseverance in your present course, and the judgment of your friend."

Onofrio, from the first, had entertained but little confidence in the firmness of Vincenzo's angry determination, and that little had vanished long ago. The only object of his present opposition was to gain time, in the faint hope that each succeeding day might bring from Rumelli some overtures for a compromise, which would spare his young friend the humiliation and the danger of a surrender at discretion. For all that was come and gone, Onofrio's estimation of Vincenzo's character remained unaltered; and exactly in that which many would have scoffed at as weakness he only saw and respected the working of a rare conscientiousness, excited to morbidness by what were truly exceptional antecedents. And when, in answer to his arguments, Vincenzo would say, as he often would, "You speak at your ease, because you are not me," Onofrio, in his heart of hearts, was ready to admit the full force of the objection. Like most men who have seen and suffered much, Onofrio was indulgent to others — severe only to himself.

June dragged on heavily, July was passed, and August was at hand, and still no signs of life came from Rumelli. Vincenzo's task was verging towards its close; and the moment of its completion, according to all probability, would also be that of the resumption of his chain. Onofrio was at his wit's end how to avert that calamity, were it only for a period. He tried (in military parlance) a desperate diversion. He said one day, "I have this morning seen Count Cavour." (Count Cavour, but lately returned from the congress in Paris, was at the zenith of his power and popularity.) "He was in high spirits, as he well may be, and very talkative and friendly. I have scarcely a doubt that, if I were to recommend you to him, he would find some suitable employment for you."

Vincenzo's face brightened at these words.

Onofrio went on: "I am sure he has not forgotten your report; he forgets nothing. That is the man to give you scope for the full play of your talents, to satisfy your ambition to be of use to your country. Shall I speak to him — what do you say?"

In the interim Vincenzo's features had fallen, and now intense dejection was their only expression.

"No, thank you, my good, my dear, my true friend. I will not repay your kind interest by making you commit yourself a second time for me. If I had not this gnawing vulture within me, I should be proud and happy to sweep the office of such a man as Cavour; as it is, I am useless even for that. I feel that, sooner or later, my destiny will force me back."

The figure of Don Pio triumphant alone stood between Vincenzo and Rumelli; and, as things turned out, even that was no longer an obstacle.

He dreamed, one night, that the Signor Avvocato had been taken suddenly ill, and was dying. We must premise that the thought of such a contingency, suggested by the old man's growing obesity and sedentary habits, had intruded itself more than once into Vincenzo's mind, both during his last stay at Rumelli and since. The dream had all the vividness of reality. The scene of it was the dining-room on the ground-floor of the Palace. On a mattress on the floor lay stretched, at full length, the Signor Avvocato's powerful frame, to all appearance a corpse. The eyes were shut, the teeth clenched, the nostrils pinched, the rigid countenance of a cadaverous hue. Bending over the motionless form in deadly suspense, were Rose, Barnaby, and Giuseppe, all three on their knees, so as to be nearer to watch it. At the head of the mattress stood Don Pio, breviary in hand, reciting the prayers for the dying. Farther back were grouped all the household, with blanched faces. Vincenzo himself was wondering how no one thought of fetching old Geronimo, an old man belonging to Rumelli, who knew how to bleed.

After a while the closed eyes opened, and stared slowly at each of the bystanders in succession, then pryed restlessly into all the corners of the room.

"He is looking for Vincenzo," whispered Rose.

Vincenzo, as is usual in dreams, could see and hear all this, though not there.

Presently the lips of the dying man moved as if he were speaking, but no sound issued from them. He shook his head forlornly, and shut his eyes again. All was over.

"*Requiescat in pace*," said Don Pio.

Vincenzo awoke in an agony of terror, and it took some time and the testimony of his senses to force the certainty upon him that he had been the dupe of a dream. Yes, thank God, it was a dream; but one which might become a terrible reality any day. How stupid of him never to have thought of the possibility — rather, how heartless! Only imagine his benefactor, his second father, breathing his last, and he not there — he, the son, the creature of that dying man, not by his side to receive his farewell blessing! Unnatural, horrible, monstrous, impossible! And his hair rose on end as in fancy he put himself face to face with the Irreparable; as he pictured to himself his own feelings on the morrow of such a day — the feelings of Cain in his heart — the curse of heaven and earth on his head — remorse and despair everlasting. Oh! rather than *that* should be, he was ready to do anything; to crawl in the dust and entreat forgiveness. Yes, rather than *that* should be, he would willingly be the slave of Don Pio all his life long. What would Don Pio's triumph matter to him, so long as he felt himself guiltless? Provided only that he was in time — that this awful dream was not the shadow cast by a dread reality! Truly, he must have been out of his mind to give to such contingencies the fearful odds of five months. Five months! when a day, an hour, a moment, would suffice to bring to pass the Irretrievable!

This whirlwind of passion lasted the whole night: one of those nights which turn black hair grey. With the light of day the feverish organism calmed, and was followed by complete prostration; but his resolve remained immutable. Few and solemn were the words in which he communicated his determination, and the occasion of it, to Onofrio.

"I must go, dear friend," wound up Vincenzo; "the past claims me; the past is my Prometheus' rock; I am chained to it indissolubly. Be kind to me to the last, even to sparing me your remonstrances. They can change nothing in my resolution; they can only pain and weaken me, and I need all the little energy I have left to meet my fate decently. A hard fate — I cherish no illusions as to that; I descend into my tomb with my eyes open. I know what awaits me out there, and I shudder in thinking of it. But it must be. I have no choice, but of unhappiness; I choose, therefore, to be unhappy at Rumelli with a clear conscience, rather than be so here with my conscience troubled — *sotto l'asbergo del sentirsi puro*, you know. As to you, my stanch, my noble, my indulgent friend, what can I say to you . . . . that —"

The rest was lost in a sudden burst of tears. And Onofrio, old as he was, and hardened to trials, and well accustomed to control himself — well, Onofrio did exactly what he saw Vincenzo do, sobbed and cried like a child. Such was the parting between the elderly and the young man.

And now, before accompanying Vincenzo to Rumelli, we must take a trip thither on our own account, and try to ascertain the frame of mind in which were father and daughter, and the sort of reception which their state of feeling forebodes the fugitive — a reception, we apprehend, different from that which he had met with after his first escapade and wanderings with Colonel Roganti. The Signor Avvocato had so little expected Vincenzo to put into execution his threat of going away, that he doubted the fact long after it was publicly patent; and, when he could no longer doubt it, he flew into a frantic rage. It was the bursting forth of a fire which had been smouldering for upwards of a year. The circumstance that the offender had just been convicted of a lie and of a calumny against his father-in-law lent to the act of rebellion a peculiarly heinous character.

Well, the furious old gentleman gave vent to his anger in a letter, the tenor of which frightened even Rose, incensed as she was. Don Pio intervened and remonstrated. The letter was given up; a great concession, and obtained with the greatest difficulty. Another epistle was concocted between the Signor Avvocato and Don Pio — another, which, though sharp and peremptory enough, was to the first what whey is to vinegar. The answer reached Rumelli by return of post. We saw Vincenzo pen it with great care, and an inward chuckle at the prospect of the effect it would produce. All that he could have expected was far surpassed. A shell falling into a barrel of gunpowder could not have produced a greater explosion than did Vincenzo's letter. The violence of the old man's passion was truly terrific; he stormed and raged and foamed at the mouth like one possessed; he loaded his son-in-law, that viper that he had warmed in his bosom, with the vilest abuse; he yearned, he prayed for revenge, and revenge he would have; he would institute a law-suit for a legal separation, and, if his daughter ever dared to do as much as look at that abominable wretch again, he would disown her, consign her to beggary. None like feeble characters, when once they have broken bounds, for rushing into the maddest extremes.

Again Don Pio had to interfere, and remonstrate against the sending of a letter to Vincenzo, far worse than the first, and of another to an old lawyer in Ibella, directing him to take legal steps for his daughter's separation from her husband. "What was the use," argued Don Pio, "of giving publicity to family differences, which had far better be hushed up?" Again, however just the Signor Avvocato's resentment, it did not justify the addressing unchristian and ungentlemanly language to his son-in-law. Why write at all? The Signor Avvocato would consult his dignity far more by remaining silent. Absolute and persevering silence could alone, if anything could, reclaim Vincenzo and bring him home. (We see from this how exactly Onofrio had hit the mark when he attributed to Don Pio the plot of keeping silence.) Don Pio's last argument it was which made the strongest impression upon the old gentleman, who asked eagerly, "Do you really believe that, if he hears from none of us, he will return?"

"That is my opinion," said Don Pio.

"Well, then, I shall not write; nobody shall. Not for the world will I miss the chance of having him here," — (Is he softening already? thought the priest) "were it only for a minute," went on the old man with a sudden burst of savage energy, "to trample him under my feet — to spit in his face — to —"; he lacked images and expressions strong enough for his feelings.

Henceforth revenge became a ruling passion, a fixed idea with him — revenge on the monster of ingratitude on whom he had lavished every good thing, even to his daughter, and who, in return, had broken his and his child's heart! Of the provocations given, of altered circumstances — no passing thought. Vincenzo was still, in his godfather's eyes, the humble boy in fustian of other days, whose only duty and business in life was to be submissive. Time did not take off the rage of this craving for vengeance; it rather sharpened it, by the increasing fear it brought lest the craving should go unsatisfied. And those were gloomy days indeed, when this dread got the upper hand, when, rousing himself from a long meditation, the father would say to the daughter with a despairing shake of the head, "Ah! he won't come after all."

Rose's feelings with regard to her husband were scarcely less acute than her father's. She acknowledged to herself that Vincenzo had received great provocation; but not the less did she hold him responsible for all the injury he was doing her father. The old man's health could not but suffer from the troubled condition of his mind; his digestion was bad, his nights often sleepless, and the old pains in his left side were more frequent and keener than of old; indeed, the weakness of the whole of that side of his body had increased to such an extent that, even when actually exempt from pain, he was unable to walk without a stick.

But, of the three persons whom Vincenzo had

offended, the least embittered against him was Don Pio. Why so? Because Don Pio had too much character himself not to esteem character in others; and, prepared as he was to keep his own against Vincenzo to the last, he could not help respecting him for the spirit and independence shown in the fact and manner of his departure. Such was the mined ground on which Vincenzo was about to venture. Was it a presentiment of its danger that made him so weary of limb, so faint of heart? It could not have been so; for, let him have given the reins to the sombrest fancy, he never could have imagined a state of things at all approaching the reality which lay in wait for him. He was weary of limb and faint of heart, because he knew that by the mere act of setting foot again in the Palace he would consummate his abdication of all independence throughout life; and, though resolved to do it, he felt sinking under the sacrifice.

The bells of all the churches of Ibella were striking noon when he entered the little town — a most propitious hour for passing through it with the least chance of awkward meetings, every one being then at dinner. He stole through the streets quietly, and without accident, and soon found himself on the high road to Rumelli. It was one of the last days of August, when the splendour of the sun is most dazzling, the heat oppressive; and the dust, that plague of dry climates, lay five inches thick on the ground. Vincenzo went on a little way, then looked about him for a shady spot, and laid himself down in it. That elasticity of foot and of spirits which had once enabled him to fly over the distance between Rumelli and Ibella in an hour and a half, was no longer his. True, his present errand was widely different from that which had at that time lent wings to his feet — he was then going to recover Rose's purse — while now . . . . He had yet another reason for wasting as much time as he could on the road: he wished to arrive at his destination when all this glare around him should have subsided. The mere idea of standing before his wife and his father-in-law in that strong light, harassed him. And then, the later he arrived, the less chance he had of finding Don Pio at the Palace; not for the world would he have had him present at the meeting. Accordingly, he proceeded leisurely by short stages, with long rests between. Presently he came to a part of the country where the gathering of the grapes, everywhere else at an end, was still going on in the vineyards skirting the road. It was a busy, a gay, a most picturesque scene; merry sights and merry sounds met the ear and eye on all sides. Every one seemed happy. Vincenzo could not help drawing a comparison between his joylessness and the light-heartedness of these peasants. He thought, with a sigh, "How far better for me had I remained, as I was born, one of them."

It was near five o'clock when he approached Rumelli; and oh! how his heart beat at sight of the well-known Belvedere, topping the gentle slope, and of the Palace towering beyond. He shrunk from traversing the village in a state of emotion which gave him the aspect of a criminal; so, diving into the nearest bushes to the right, he made his way as best he could, through fields and fences and ditches, in an upward direction towards the Castle. One glance at that awkward building had satisfied him beforehand that it was not inhabited. All the windows were closed, and everything on the face of it, as well as the neglect of the grounds, spoke of absenteeism and decay. For the first time for many years Vincenzo thought of young Del Palmetto, and, with a sort of compunction for having so completely erased him from his recollection, wondered what had become of him. Perhaps he was dead; soldiers died young — poor Ambrogio was an instance.

While thus thinking, Vincenzo emerged, after a long circuit, into the road below Rose's Belvedere, almost on the spot where young Del Palmetto on horseback had stopped to bid her adieu, and had snatched from the summer-house window the purse she was then working. Here lay the most perilous part of Vincenzo's journey; from thence to the gate of the avenue the highway lay between two walls, so as to allow of no escape from any one coming from the Palace. Now, to meet Don Pio, or indeed any member of the household, would have been to Vincenzo, in his present mood, something intolerable. Accordingly, faint with fatigue, emotion and heat as he was, he ran on at a quick pace until past the gate; then, being in comparative safety, he lay down on the ground to take breath. So near, why not go in at once? Because that odious garish glare of day was not yet subdued, and then he wanted still a little respite to get composed; he felt so out of joint. At the end of a good half hour, however, there was a sound of steps and voices from up the hill. Vincenzo did not stay to see who or how many were the new comers, but got up in a hurry, and walked on to the gate, went through and up the avenue. The sobered light which pervaded the shaded walk was most welcome. As far as his eye could reach, no living soul to be seen; that was another comfort. The Palace, as we know, stood upon a raised terrace, accessible from the avenue by a short flight of steps. At the foot of these Vincenzo stopped a few seconds, pressed both hands on his heart, which felt ready to burst, then tottered up the steps.

Seated in front of the door, or rather sunk in an arm chair, was the master of the Palace — his head drooping forward on his chest, his arms hanging down heavily on either side of the chair, his eyes rivetted to the ground — a very image of desolation. The sight was too much for Vincenzo, a mist came over his eyes, his legs gave way under him, and he would have fallen had he not grasped the balustrade, which ran breast high on both sides of the flight of steps. At the same instant the old gentleman looked up, and, as his glance fell upon the unexpected apparition, his eyes dilated frightfully; in a twinkling the pale face grew purple, and a fiendish grin lighted it up. He got on his feet after a struggle, and by the help of a cane placed by his chair, limped stealthily towards Vincenzo; when within reach of him, he balanced himself so as to be able to stand without support, and then, lifting up the cane, dealt a blow with it at the young man's head, which sent his hat flying. Up went the cane and down again it would have come, God knows with what possible effect, on the now bare head, but for Barnaby's timely interposition. Barnaby (we have hitherto lacked the opportunity to mention the fact) was at work within a few paces of his master at the moment of Vincenzo's arrival; only the work he was at, the training of some creeping plants about the windows of the great hall, necessitated his turning his back to the quarter from whence Vincenzo had come, and thus it was that he had not seen him. The rest needs no further explanation.

"Are you going to take up the trade of a negro-driver?" cried Barnaby, as he arrested the raised hand and hurled away the cane. Then, turning to Vincenzo, "Art thou hurt, my poor boy? — not much, only a scratch. Come along with me; this is no place for thee; it is a madhouse," and, putting his arm within Vincenzo's, he dragged the young man down the steps and along the avenue. Dragged is the word, for Vincenzo was shaking from head to foot, and staggering like a drunken man. "Why didst thou not write that thou wert coming? Why come at all? Weren't thy friends down there kind to thee? Wert thou short of money? And, if so, why not write and say so?"

To this avalanche of questions, Vincenzo gave no answer — probably he had not heard them.

Barnaby went on — "Thou shalt never want money again. I have found a capital investment for my savings — eight per cent., eight per cent. on twenty-four thousand francs; there's enough and to spare for living like a gentleman, isn't there? Thou sayest nothing?"

"Where are we going?" asked Vincenzo, startled by the sight of the gate.

"To Rumelli, for the present," replied Barnaby.

"No, no, I am not going away from this — I will not go," exclaimed Vincenzo, looking scared. "Take me to some quiet place, some dark corner where I can rest, and think — I must think .... long."

A quiet out of the way corner was not difficult to find.

Once there, Vincenzo sat down and said, "Now let me think, but don't leave me." He clasped his head with both hands, and thought — thought on, and on, and on, even until Barnaby could scarcely see his face for the growing obscurity, and yet Vincenzo went on still thinking. The instinct of self-preservation and the spirit of self-immolation were waging a great battle within Vincenzo's bosom. In the face of the extreme pass to which things had come at the Palace, did what he had considered his duty hold good, or cease? Was he to go, or was he to stay? These were the questions, the solution of which he sought in an agony of body and mind. He found it at last, and said aloud, "I remain."

"A downright piece of folly," said Barnaby; "he's capable of murdering you."

"Let him," replied Vincenzo; "better die with the sense of having done right, than live with a troubled conscience. Listen to me, Barnaby;" and he related to the old man his dream of the night before, described the horror and despair which had seized on him at the mere thought of the possible realization of that dream — told it all so vividly and forcibly that Barnaby began to tremble like an aspen leaf. "And now," wound up Vincenzo, "you can understand why I choose to remain."

"I do," was Barnaby's concise answer.

"Well, then, let us return to the house," said Vincenzo, rising. "Are we likely, do you think, to find.... anybody in our way?"

"I should say not," replied Barnaby; "it has struck

nine, and the Signor Avvocato goes to his own room very early. At all events, I can go on before hand, and see if the coast is clear."

"No, my good friend, no attempts at concealment. I am ready for anything, resigned to everything that can happen. Only I would fain avoid any further scene this evening. I am fairly worn out and faint."

They took their way towards the house. There were lights in the Signor Avvocato's apartment. All was safe. They stole in, as they thought unperceived, and went up to the third story in the dark. Vincenzo had so long slept in a room in the attics before last leaving the Palace that he now returned thither from mere habit. Barnaby wished him good-night, but lurked about in the corridor until he heard the bolt fastened inside, which gave him the assurance that his earnest recommendation had been acted upon.

But Vincenzo had not stolen in unperceived as he had imagined. Rose had been on the watch for him. She had heard from her father of her husband's arrival, and of the sort of reception he had met with, and she was burning with curiosity to ascertain whether he had set off again, which seemed to her most probable, or whether he was going to remain. The moment she saw him from her window coming towards the house, she ran on tiptoe to the door of her chamber which opened on the stairs, and listened, listened in mortal suspense, lest he should seek access to her. Not for the world would she have had him do so; principally, it must be allowed, because she had the moral certainty that her father was on the look-out, and would immediately interfere. And yet, at the sound of the well-known footstep passing the landing without a moment's hesitation, Rose felt — shall we say disappointed? No, but slighted, and piqued in proportion. Had Vincenzo sought her, ten to one but that he had been sent about his business pretty sharply; he had not done so, and he was equally in fault. Poor Vincenzo! he had a hopeless game to play.

CHAPTER XII.

Sweets of Home.

Early next morning Signora Candia hastened to the parsonage, and made Don Pio acquainted with her husband's arrival, her father's assault upon him, and her own distress of mind at the possible repetition of so disgraceful a scene. Rose, like most women, had a thorough abhorrence of violence. Don Pio, with praiseworthy alacrity, returned with her to the Palace, and read her father a severe lecture on his conduct of the previous afternoon. The priest felt really indignant, and did not mince his words. He said that the Signor Avvocato ought to be ashamed of himself; that the act of brutality of which he had been guilty, scarcely excusable in an uneducated unreflecting boor, was unpardonable in a gentleman and a scholar, let alone in a Christian. How could he claim respect from others, when he showed so little self-respect? Having right on his side, he had wilfully put himself in the wrong; for if, in consequence of the indignity inflicted on him, Signor Vincenzo had gone away for ever, who would not acquit him — who would not condemn the Signor Avvocato? He (the curé) would for one.

The old gentleman admitted that he had given

way to an uncontrollable fury of passion, and promised that such a thing should not again occur; that is, supposing that the . . . . the person in question, should choose to stay at the Palace. Well, if he chose to remain, the Signor Avvocato had no objection to his doing so — no objection to supplying him with his daily bread, as he had done up to that very moment, but on condition that that bread should be eaten elsewhere than at his (the Signor Avvocato's) table. After what had passed, he and the person in question could not possibly sit at the same board. Don Pio urged plenty of obvious reasons against this unnatural exclusion; but the Signor Avvocato would listen to none, and stuck sturdily to his point. "After all," said the curé to Rose, as she accompanied him down stairs, "it is a difficulty of form, and not of substance, which I hope we shall be able to remove in a few days. You must, however, let Signor Vincenzo know of the Signor Avvocato's resolve, in order that all possible disagreeable complications may be avoided. He has good sense enough, I hope, to make a virtue of necessity."

Rose perfectly understood how urgent it was to have Vincenzo warned in time, and at once hit upon Barnaby as the fittest ambassador for the occasion. As to going herself to her husband's room, in her present temper of mind, she would as soon have thought of entering a lion's den, had there been such a thing at Rumelli; and, even had her heart inclined her to seek Vincenzo, which it did not, the fear of her father would have held her back. The Signor Avvocato was full of suspicions, was on the *qui vive* whenever he heard her step on the stair, calling out to know where she had been or was going, not omitting to caution her by hints against siding with his enemies. Rose, therefore, had, as it were, to lie in wait for Barnaby; and, to give herself a chance of catching him unseen by the Signor Avvocato, she kept wandering from her room to the kitchen, and from the kitchen to her room, taking care to tread heavily in going up and down stairs, and humming one air after the other, that her father, from his room, might be sure of her whereabouts.

Barnaby, in the meanwhile, had been to listen at Vincenzo's door a score of times or more, until at last, seeing that it was nearly ten o'clock, and his patience being quite exhausted, he had knocked and obtained admittance. Vincenzo had slept soundly all night, and felt much better, only very weak.

"Thou art in want of something to eat; that's what is the matter," said Barnaby.

Vincenzo agreed, the more so as he now recollected that he had not tasted any food since leaving Turin.

"Give me some bread, Barnaby — I say bread, only bread, do you hear? If you bring anything else, I shall not touch it."

Barnaby, in going to fetch the bread, met Signora Candia, who gave him the message for Vincenzo. Barnaby received it with the most expressive grimace of disapproval at his command; he said nothing, however, but went on his errand. Vincenzo ate the bread, and the bunch of grapes Barnaby had ventured, in spite of orders, also to bring, with an appetite growing keener with every mouthful, and felt wonderfully revived. While Vincenzo was eating, the old gardener seemed lost in a brown study. "By-the-bye," said he all at once, "I think you are too weak to go down to dinner."

"Not at all," said Vincenzo; "I feel quite strong now."

"I tell you, you look horridly pale and worn out, and unfit for any exertion," insisted Barnaby; "take my advice, stay quietly in your own room, and I'll bring you up something at dinner-time."

"No such thing," protested Vincenzo. "I shall go down to dinner. I have made up my mind to do so."

Barnaby, in great distress, scratched his bald pate. At last he mumbled out, "Better not expose yourself to be insulted . . . ."

"If any affront is offered to me, I shall not resent it," replied Vincenzo; "but I shall not act as if I expected and deserved such treatment. My place is at the same table with my father-in-law and my wife, and that place I shall seek. If it is refused me, I shall submit. Understand this, Barnaby, I have no intention of defending any of the rights or privileges of my position, should they be contested; but it is as little my purpose to surrender one tittle of them voluntarily."

"You are right; you are a true man," cried the old gardener with naïve admiration; "there's more spirit in one of your little fingers than in the whole carcass of such a downright old coward as I am." And, to give greater emphasis to this sentiment, Barnaby took the striped cotton cap off his head and threw it on the floor.

A quarter of an hour before the dinner was served,

Barnaby slipped into the dining-room, added a third cover to the two already on the table, and stood sentinel over it with the look, we can imagine, of the dragon watching the golden apples of the garden of the Hesperides. Presently the Signor Avvocato came in. His first glance took in the addition made by Barnaby. "Who is that third knife and fork and plate for?" asked the old gentleman with a frown.

"For Signor Vincenzo," answered Barnaby, quite gently.

"The devil take him," growled the Signor Avvocato; "clear those things away."

"They are for your daughter's husband," said Barnaby, warming.

"The devil take him, I say. Do you hear me?—clear away those things," was the peremptory answer.

"They are for the son of that Angelo Candia who lost his life in your service; do *you* hear?" cried Barnaby, exasperated.

Whatever was the retort which rose to the tip of his tongue, this time the Signor Avvocato choked it back, and said instead, "I see what it is; I shall have to give up my place to that person. I shall have to go and dine in my room."

"If you do, you must first walk over the body of your father's old servant," shouted Barnaby; and, sure enough, the old fellow deliberately flung himself down across the threshold.

To pass over the prostrate figure without doing it some injury, was, for one so bulky and infirm as the Signor Avvocato, a matter of physical impossibility. Was it that which made him desist, or was his energy spent for the moment, or his heart touched by Barnaby's allusion to Signor Pietro? Whatever the cause or causes, the Signor Avvocato, without further remonstrance, limped sulkily to the table, and sulkily took his usual seat. Barnaby was scarcely on his feet again when Vincenzo entered the room. He was dreadfully pale, but to all appearance composed; he bowed low to his father-in-law, who looked another way, and nodded to his wife, who slightly nodded in return, and then sat down. That day Barnaby chose to wait at table; and, between one dish and the other, gave the company a history of what was going on in the parish — beginning with Martha who had got twins, and Peter's son, who had been caught stealing grapes, and ending with the great rumour of the day — viz. that *it was said* the Marquis del Palmetto had just made a rich marriage, and was soon expected at the Castle. Barnaby's monologue, for he addressed no one in particular, and seemed to rattle on for his own exclusive benefit, met with no other interruption than sundry snarling sounds proceeding from the Signor Avvocato, which the orator did not deign to notice.

The dinner was short, though it seemed long to all parties; the master of the house made it shorter still by rising at dessert and taking himself away, in evident high dudgeon. Rose followed him immediately. Vincenzo, thus left alone, with the instinct of a wounded animal went out to seek some lonely spot, where he might lie unmolested on the grass, and meditate on his sad plight. He had plenty of leisure to do this, and to doze and yawn to his heart's content. At eight o'clock he went in to supper, which, as regarded any interchange of sympathy, or any agreeable intercourse, was the exact counterpart of the dinner, with the exception of Barnaby's chatter. By nine, again in his own bed-chamber, and a few minutes later in his bed.

The morrow brought no change in the mode of proceeding adopted by the Signor Avvocato and his daughter; and, to make a long story short, Vincenzo's pittance of the first day became his daily diet. With some slight variations, though; one of which was, that the icy silence during meal-time was occasionally superseded by a blustering volley of abuse levelled at the young man, under the shelter of another name. One day, the theme of the discourse would be the son of a chemist at Ibella, who had broken open his father's desk, and gone off with the money nobody knew where. The Signor Avvocato had always predicted that he would turn out ill; for what good could be expected of a proud-stomached, conceited fellow, without feeling, as without fear of God, &c. &c. and so on for a quarter of an hour. Or it was a tirade against that penniless adventurer, the singing master, who had so long made love to the daughter of the Commandant of Ibella, and had at last managed to marry her. And what had been the result? Why, that he had grown as arrogant, and imperious after, as he had been humble and honey-tongued before — playing the fine gentleman, never having money enough for his wants, and in a fair way to break his wife's and his father-in-law's hearts.

"And served them right," said the Signor Avvocato; "for how could they be so blind as not to see that he only cared for their money, the vile snivelling good-for-nothing scamp that he was."

These instances were not very appropriate to Vincenzo's case; but they were excellent pegs on which to hang invective, and that was what the Signor Avvocato desired. Sometimes it would be Vincenzo's dearest political feelings and preferences that the Signor Avvocato would fall upon and lash till the blood came, on the back of Count Cavour or some other statesman of note.

"What," would he thunder forth — "what has been the final result of their policy? — The kingdom impoverished and on the brink of bankruptcy, taxation swollen to unbearable proportions, the country divided against itself, all respect for religion gone," &c. &c.

But these ebullitions grew rarer, and in course of time ceased altogether — the distemper lost its acute character, and lapsed into a chronic disease. The keen eagerness to wound and trample under foot subsided into the quiet indulgence of slighting and ignoring. Father and daughter took to discussing their interests and affairs at their meals, with no more reference to the third person sitting at table with them than if he had not been present. But for Don Pio, who dined twice a week at the Palace, and never failed to inquire after Signor Candia's health, and otherwise now and then address his conversation to him — but for Don Pio, we say, and Barnaby, Vincenzo might easily have forgotten how to speak. To be impartial, we must here note that Vincenzo on his side did nothing to mend this uncomfortable state of affairs. After the sacrifice of self which he had made, Rose's husband felt entitled to a better treatment than he received; and thus, though submitting to it, he did not accept it as his due. Accordingly, if he carefully avoided in his manner and bearing whatever might in the least look like defiance, he was equally guarded against doing anything which could be interpreted as a wish to propitiate.

Except at meal times, Vincenzo kept out of sight all day long. There were two or three sheltered nooks in the park which were his favourite resorts; there he lay on the sward, and spent the long hours in doing nothing. As for his old haunt, once so dear — Rose's Belvedere — he never now went near it; it had too many associations not to be instinctively shunned. If he carried a book with him, it soon dropped from his hand, and lay forgotten by his side. If, bored by inaction, he got up to walk, he presently sat down again bored by exertion. His mental and bodily faculties were gradually sinking into a state of stagnation. Books once so prized, nature once so loved and enjoyed, were now regarded with indifference. Even politics had ceased to excite him. Of all earthly things that had once an interest in his eyes, only one retained a value — one never likely to be his again — liberty; to be again his own master — the forbidden fruit. Ennui devoured him — ennui without hope of release; his one cheering thought was that with which at night he laid his head on the pillow.

"Another day gone!"

And, when winter set in (all idea of removing to Ibella had been long given up by the Signor Avvocato), which fortunately was late in the year, and the long dreary hours had to be got through within four bare walls, instead of in the open air, beguiled by a multitude of half-unheeded diversions of sound, and colour and form, filling park, or wood, or glade — then, indeed, Vincenzo's lot became almost intolerable; and, had it not been for Barnaby, his sole friend and companion, whose sympathy, especially when silent, was a balm of unspeakable comfort to the recluse, Vincenzo, as he often himself declared, would have gone mad, or done worse.

He never set his foot beyond the precincts of the Palace, except on Sundays, when he attended mass at the parish church — an extremely painful duty for one whose sociable inclinations were not likely to be increased by the life of solitary confinement he was leading, and who moreover felt himself to be the butt of an embarrassing and often of an offensive curiosity. The Rumellians, who, so long as his good fortune lasted, had taken it for granted that it was deserved, no sooner discovered that a cloud hung over him, than they began to entertain doubts as to his having merited his prosperity, and to show pretty plainly that opinion. Fortunately the necessity of appearing in public ceased at the coming of the new year; and here was how it happened: —

For some time previous to Vincenzo's return, the Signor Avvocato, to his own and his daughter's infinite sorrow, had been obliged to give up going to church. His increasing obesity, and the pain and weakness of his left side, made it too difficult and painful for him to get in and out of a carriage. Don Pio had immediately suggested the propriety of sending a petition to Rome to ask permission for the erection and consecration of a chapel in the Palace, where the family might hear mass said. No one can doubt that the suggestion was eagerly caught at by Rose and her father. Don Pio wrote the petition, had it backed by the Bishop of the diocese, and despatched it. In a little less than four months there came an answer from the authorities at Rome granting the request; and, a couple of days later, several skilful workmen, brought for the purpose from Ibella, were busy partitioning off, by means of large fixed panels with folding doors in the centre, a good portion of the great dining hall on the ground floor, and raising an altar in this kind of alcove. When this little impromptu chapel was finished and properly provided with all the articles necessary for Divine worship, the Bishop came in state to consecrate it — our old acquaintance of Ibella, that very dignitary whose absence on St. Urban's fête, in 1848, had sealed the defeat of the Castle, and the triumph of the Palace. We need scarcely add that there was a great dinner on the occasion, the first there had been for many a day at the Palace, and that a good deal of edifying talk seasoned the courses, more than half the guests belonging to the clergy. The upshot of all this was, that, beginning from the next Sunday, the first of the year 1857, mass was said in the chapel, and Vincenzo could thus attend on all holy days in comfort and peace. The service was performed by an old priest belonging to Ibella, whom Giuseppe went regularly to fetch in the gig, and drove back after dinner.

Rose's untiring activity had greatly contributed towards the rapid completion of the chapel. She spared neither time nor trouble for that end; she was the first on the spot in the morning, and the last to quit it in the evening. Every thing was done under her eyes, and by her orders: she fitted it up *con amore;* we know she had a knack, (and was proud of it) for that sort of thing.

Not one of the many items requisite for Divine service — candlesticks, artificial flowers, surplices, chasubles, chalices, etc. — but she chose herself, and all of the best and costliest.

Rose, in all respects, was the ruling spirit of the Palace. From the age of fourteen she had had the management of the household; and now that of the estate, or rather estates, had, little by little, devolved upon her. She kept all the accounts, received the rents, paid the wages, directed the tilling of the land, directed the sales, invested the proceeds, wrote all the letters, did every thing with a clearness of head, a method, a spirit of order, which were quite astonishing in so young a woman. The daily communications which took place between father and daughter on these and such like matters in presence of Vincenzo, afforded him ample opportunities for testing and admiring her singular aptitude for business. And often and often did he repeat to himself what he had said to Onofrio on a certain occasion, "What a blessing this woman would have been to a blockhead, who feared God and still more the curé, who did not care a fig for politics, but a great deal for a good table, and the *dolce far niente!*"

CHAPTER XIII.

The Blade wears out the Scabbard.

In what way does the mind so affect the body as even to trouble the vital functions? Science can well account, by the decomposition of the blood, or the disorganization of the tissues, for the ravages attending the introduction of a poisonous agent into the animal economy; but Science has little to say when called upon to explain the damages occasioned to the human organism by a mental corrosive. And yet the latter eats its way through the frame as steadily and as surely as any arsenic or strychnine. Witness our poor Vincenzo. The vulture within him, though there was no beak visible, was not the less devouring the very principle of his life. Without being actually ill, without, in fact, any special or precise ailment, he was dying — a little and a little every day. The deprivation of fresh air and exercise, entailed on him by the winter, further helped to undermine his constitution. He had lost his appetite, and with it had disappeared all the scanty portion of flesh he had about him; his strength was so reduced, that walking fifty paces put him out of breath. It seemed as though the vital flame was gradually narrowing previous to going out altogether. Withal he did not suffer; physically, not at all; morally, far less keenly than he had done at the beginning of winter. Vincenzo was becoming apathetic.

It was a day in early March. Here and there feeble indications of the coming spring gladdened the eye. The tops of the tall poplars of the avenue were speckled with green dots; a green cobweb seemed to envelop the lilac-bushes shooting up from the outer side of the terrace; through the mist of the valley peered a bright ray of sun, lustily cheered by the first warblings of birds. Attracted by the genial feeling of the air, Vincenzo had just crawled out of the house after dinner, and was standing, speculating which way he should go, when the sound of some one running quickly up the flight of stone steps, as if in a hurry, and humming a tune energetically notwithstanding, decided him immediately to turn in the opposite direction from that in which the new comer was approaching. But he had not gone ten paces, when a voice from behind him said:

"Can you tell me whether your mistress is at home?"

Vincenzo turned round and answered that Signora Candia was in the house.

"Then," pursued the stranger, a tall commanding-looking young woman, dressed all in black, "will you be so good as to announce the Marchioness del Palmetto?"

Vincenzo showed the visitor into a parlour on the ground floor, and then went up to his wife's room. The door was ajar; he knocked, and, on being answered from within, said:

"The Marchioness del Palmetto has come to pay you a visit; she is in the parlour down stairs."

"Say that I am coming directly," said Rose.

Vincenzo gave the message, slipped away quietly, and went as far out of reach of any summons as his legs would carry him. This trivial incident had quite upset him; in his morbid mood of shyness, and nervous weakness, nothing disturbed him so much as change. The bare idea of having to meet new faces, of visits to pay and to receive, of the thousand complications which intercourse between the two families could not but bring with it for one whose situation at home was so degraded as his was — the bare idea of all this and much else threw him into a state of much agitation, hardly conceivable to any one in strong health. He comforted himself as best he could with the hope — a very faint one, to be sure — that this might prove a mere passing visit. The fact of the Marchioness having called alone gave some colour to this view. Had the Marquis been at the Castle, surely he would have come himself to introduce his wife — *ergo*, he was not there. Alas! the open windows of the Castle, the moment Vincenzo, emerging from the young plantations, could get a sight of them, gave quite another impression; yet it was still possible that the Marchioness had only come to stay for a day or two.

Vincenzo's presentiment of fresh annoyances had a beginning of realization that very evening. He had no sooner taken his seat at supper, than his wife, for the first time addressing him directly since his return, said:

"Where did you bury yourself after dinner, that nobody could find you?"

"I never supposed that I should be wanted," said Vincenzo; "I was up in the nursery-garden."

"The very last place one would have thought of in this damp weather," said Rose. "The Marchioness del Palmetto inquired for you, and it was very awkward that you could not be found, when I had just told her I had seen you the minute before."

The search for him could not have been a very earnest one, thought Vincenzo; for, had his name been only once shouted, he must infallibly have heard it, at the short distance he was from the house. Bitter-sweet favours were poured upon him this evening. The Signor Avvocato also condescended to speak to him; for the first time breaking the silence he had hitherto persevered in, he said:

"You have taken to a system of skulking and sulking, which, to say the least of it, is liable to misinterpretation. So long as we were *en famille*, well and good; but now that we have near neighbours, who are likely to call often, as the Marchioness was so good as to say they would, I advise you to change your habits."

This was nothing to what the next day had in store for Vincenzo. He was in his own room, about eleven o'clock in the forenoon, looking out disconsolately at the rain which was falling fast, when a great commotion down stairs gave him an intimation of fresh danger. The stirring and dragging about of chairs in the apartment below, accompanied by a cross-fire of Ohs! and Ahs! unmistakeably announced an important visitor; and what visitor would call at that hour but Del Palmetto? Presently the sound of the well-known voice left no doubt as to the person. The Marquis seemed in high spirits, rattling away with such hearty bursts of laughter as proved he was relating something very droll. Vincenzo counted the minutes in painful expectation of a summons down stairs, from which there seemed no chance of escape, unless some happy inspiration should prompt Federico to come to him in his attic, which would be a lesser evil. Or could it be that he was going away without asking for Vincenzo? That which inclined Vincenzo to think this was a short lull of the voices, followed by a fresh stirring of chairs, then an interchange of some more phrases, probably of leave-taking, and finally by a jingling of spurs on the landing-place. Vincenzo held his breath. The jingling of the spurs ceased, and from the foot of the stairs Federico called out at the top of his voice —

"I say, Signor Avvocato, junior, art thou coming down to greet an old friend? or must the old friend ascend and force himself on thy notice?"

Vincenzo had it on the tip of his tongue to say, "Come up;" but then he reflected that by so saying he might give offence, and also that to avoid a general meeting, sooner or later, would be impossible; so he said instead, feebly, "I am coming," and, putting on his most decent coat, went down to the Signor Avvocato's sitting-room.

Del Palmetto embraced and hugged Vincenzo with all the demonstrativeness of the most demonstrative Italian.

"There's a lucky dog, and of my making; isn't he, Signora Candia?"

Signora Candia smiled an embarrassed smile, and said nothing.

"But for me," went on the Marquis, "and my naughty trick of running away with a certain purse, and all that ensued in consequence, the odds are that this gentleman would be now wearing a cassock and saying mass, instead of whispering pretty things to the prettiest of wives: now, wouldn't he?" and he laughed merrily at his own sally.

Civility wrung from father and daughter a responsive grim smile.

"As thin as a grasshopper," went on Del Palmetto, taking a survey of Vincenzo, "but hale and healthy."

Vincenzo was red as a brick with annoyance.

"And now for my business," resumed Del Palmetto. "My wife is as impatient as a woman can be, which is saying a good deal, to make honourable amends for her yesterday's awkward mistake."

"Not worth thinking of," interrupted Vincenzo, who as yet had not had an opportunity to say one word; "I dare say I looked as shabby as any man-of-all-work."

"And pray, who is to blame for that but yourself?" asked the Signor Avvocato, tartly. "No one, that I know of, grudges you clothes or anything else."

"Did I say that anybody did?" retorted Vincenzo.

Del Palmetto perceived the expediency of forcing the conversation back into the channel from which it had diverged. "I maintain," said he, "that the mistake was awkward for a firstrate physiognomist, such as my wife has the pretensions to be; in her defence, I must allow that the blunder was only that of a moment. I was telling the Signor Avvocato and Signora Candia, before you came in, that the truth had already flashed upon Teresa's mind, when you brought her word that the Signora would be with her directly, but you gave her no time for a question. However, you are to understand that I am sent here, commissioned to carry you off, dead or alive, to my wife, who will best make her own explanations and apologies. And, as I would rather have you alive than dead, be so good as to put on your hat, and give up for to-day the excellent dinner that awaits you here, for pot-luck at our house."

"Not to-day, thank you, pray excuse me," said Vincenzo, with as much earnestness as if he were pleading for his life.

"I am sorry I cannot excuse you," returned the other with mock gravity; "I am a soldier, and must obey orders; I must take you to the castle, alive or dead — which shall it be?"

"Indeed, you must let me off . . ."

"I wish I could; but my duty prevents me. All

the proper authorities have been duly consulted and have kindly acquiesced. The Signor Avvocato, to oblige my wife, agrees to want your company for a few hours; and so does Signora Candia, who promised, moreover, not to be jealous."

"Pray, Signor Federico," interrupted Rose, "don't make me say anything so ridiculous."

"Is it ridiculous, then," was the quick repartee, "not to be jealous?"

"Nonsense!" exclaimed Rôse, and, turning to her husband, she said, "It is extremely ungracious of you to require so much pressing."

The Signor Avvocato, in his turn, observed with sharpness, "I wish you would be done with all this shilly-shallying; when Signor Federico is so kind and does you the honour to invite you, the least you can do in return is to accept his invitation gratefully."

"Everybody is against you, you see," said Del Palmetto, laughing; "so the sooner you get ready the better."

Vincenzo, without further demur, went up stairs for his hat, and was down again in a minute. Del Palmetto took leave of father and daughter, and withdrew arm-in-arm with his conquest. When they reached the outer door, Vincenzo perceived that it was still raining — a fact which in his bewilderment he had forgotten; and he now inwardly called himself a ninny for not having urged in time that which his wishes made appear to him an unanswerable argument against going out. However, he made an effort at release by saying, "Don't you see that it is raining?"

"Ah, to be sure," said Del Palmetto; "luckily I have an umbrella," taking it out of a corner as he spoke, and thus overruling the objection. He opened the umbrella, put his arm again within Vincenzo's and then they went down the steps into the avenue.

"Between you and me," began Federico, "your father-in-law is looking very ill, he is sadly altered. The last time I saw him — when was it? — in 1854 I think — yes, towards the end of '54 — you were then in Savoy — he looked like a young man, he did indeed . . ."

"It is raining heavier than ever," observed Vincenzo.

"No; it is the drops from the trees makes you think so. At that time," continued Del Palmetto, pursuing his subject, "he was full of humour, and chatty as possible. That in little more than two years he should have become what he is, a decrepit old man, does surprise me. What is his age — do you know?"

"Whose age?" asked Vincenzo.

"Why, the Signor Avvocato's — art thou dreaming?"

"He is about sixty-four."

"He looks twenty years older than that," said Del Palmetto. "But what a beauty Signora Rose has become. As a matron she surpasses even the bright promise of her girlhood. Lucky dog that thou art! If I were not Teresa's husband I should envy thee."

They were now close to the gate.

"Don't you think," said Vincenzo, suddenly, "that it would be more agreeable to all parties if I were to call and pay my respects to the Marchioness on some finer day than this?"

"Heyday! what's the matter now?" exclaimed Del

Palmetto, coming to a standstill, and facing round upon Vincenzo. "Here have I been doing my best to talk and be agreeable, and all the while thou hast been thinking of nothing; but how to give me the slip. If it is really against thy will to come, I don't mean to force thee;" and he let go Vincenzo's arm.

"I beg of you," said Vincenzo, gently, "not to take offence where none is intended."

"Why do you always call me *you*, when I use only the *thou?*" asked Del Palmetto. "I should never have suspected you of bearing me a grudge for such a length of time."

"Why should I bear you a grudge, my dear friend?"

"How can I tell? Perhaps for having, once upon a time, played you stupid, boyish tricks, or sneered at the Statuto, or for having been a fool and a codino."

"Thou art welcome to be a codino, so long as thou art so conscientiously," said Vincenzo, in a conciliatory tone.

"But I am so no longer, I tell you; I am a radical, and a thorough-going Cavourist; I am for the Statuto and all its consequences; I am for the unity of Italy — ask my wife," cried Del Palmetto, in a perfect ferment.

"I am glad to hear it," gasped Vincenzo; "though, I give you my word, the recollection of your former political opinions had nothing whatever to do with my wish to put off going to the Castle. The truth is, that I am not quite well; besides, I have grown shy and misanthropic — there, give me thy arm; we'll go on presently; emotion and walking have taken away my breath." And, unable to go on speaking, he stood panting for breath, trying, in the meanwhile, to reassure his friend by signs. Del Palmetto looked anything but reassured.

"Really, thou art very far from well," said Del Palmetto; "and I am grieved to the heart to have so insisted on thy coming. But how could I guess? — I will go back with thee, and..." Vincenzo shook his head. "Well, it shall be as thou likest."

At the end of a few minutes, Vincenzo was better, and able to move on.

"We must go on little by little," he said; "thou must have patience with me, for I am far from strong."

"Suppose we give up the introduction to Teresa for this morning," suggested Del Palmetto, "and to-morrow I will drive over to fetch you."

"No, no," said Vincenzo, who now made it a point always to use the familiar *thou* in speaking to his friend — a mode of address too inconvenient in English for us not to discontinue it. "No, I hold to going, and making up as far as I can for my late unfriendly shuffling; besides, to tell the truth, I am beginning to be extremely anxious to be introduced to the Marchioness Del Palmetto, who, if she has been your converter, as I guess, must indeed be no ordinary woman."

Del Palmetto's features brightened as he answered, "No, indeed; I can vouch for her not being one of the common run, and that without fear of your being disappointed. She is a..." He sought for a word adequate to his enthusiasm, and, not finding it, wound up with, "Never mind what; she is a wonderful creature, that's all I can say. You will soon see, and judge for yourself."

Thus discoursing, with every now and then a halt, they reached the Castle; "his hereditary brick pie," as Del Palmetto called it. Vincenzo, well-nigh spent with the exertion, was ushered into a small room on the ground floor, where Del Palmetto made him ensconce himself in an easy chair by the side of a cheerful fire, and swallow a glass of Malaga. His host then left him alone to rest a while and recover his breath and spirits. By and bye, Del Palmetto returned with the Marchioness, who, hastening to Vincenzo, shook hands cordially with him, saying, "I am delighted to welcome you to our house, Signor Candia; we mean to try to make ourselves so agreeable that you will be induced to come and see us very often; I am sorry to hear you are an invalid; we shall be able to sympathise with one another, for I am not very well, and the doctors have sent me here, with orders to eat and drink, take plenty of fresh air and exercise, and — be idle."

"And, in obedience to the last recommendation," observed her husband, "I believe you were beginning your eighth letter when I went to find you just now."

"That's telling tales out of school. Signor Candia will fancy I want to set up as an opposition Madame de Sevigné — however, that, I assure you, is not the case, Signor Candia; my correspondence is of a far graver and sadder nature. I am a native of Brescia, and my letters are from old friends or dependents; and how can I refuse to write a word of kindness or condolence to some poor old father, whose only son has been sent to prison, or some wretched mother who has hers taken from her to be sent as a soldier to Bohemia? Ah! the amount of bodily and mental affliction in this unfortunate country of ours is incredible. But this is not the way to cheer you. I won't touch on these grievous topics again; and now, will you excuse my leaving you till dinner time?..."

"To go and finish my eighth letter?" said Del Palmetto, concluding the sentence for her.

"No, indeed, Mr. Faultfinder; but to go and see that dinner be ready in time and eatable; for" — here she turned with a pleasant smile to Vincenzo — "for, you must know, we are very far from being in order yet, as to servants or anything else. Besides, you will like to have a quiet *tête-à-tête* with an old friend; but, if Federico bores you, send him away. There are plenty of newspapers and books about to amuse you."

She was gone, without Vincenzo's having had the opportunity, or indeed the wish, to open his lips. If it were his fancy which had evoked that stately figure, and made it look at him with such gentle eyes, speak to him so kindly and considerately, behave to him as if he were a friend, and not a stranger — if it were all a delusion which one word could dispel — better that such a word remain unsaid. One must have been weaned from the milk of human kindness, and treated like a pariah for months, to understand the kind of bewilderment which a sudden shower of sympathy and cordiality can produce on the recipient. Vincenzo gazed about him as if he were trying to discover whether he was awake or asleep.

"What art thou staring at?" asked Federico, laying down the newspaper he had just taken up.

"I want to make sure that I am not dreaming," said Vincenzo.

"Ah! I was right, wasn't I, when I said she was a wonderful woman?" said Del Palmetto, enraptured.

"Ay, and thou — a wonderful man," returned Vincenzo, gravely.

"Ah! that is rather *trop fort*," cried Del Palmetto, roaring with laughter.

"A wonderful man to me," repeated Vincenzo gravely; "so friendly, so affectionate, so brother-like. What have I done to deserve all this from thee?"

"Thou wert in the right, while I was in the wrong, and I am making amends for having wronged Truth in thy person; and then," added the marquis, with a burst of feeling he could not control, "and then — I must tell it, because it really is so — since I have known her, my heart is grown bigger and warmer towards my fellow-creatures. There, now, you have it!" After this outburst, Federico plunged into his newspaper with such determination that nothing was left for Vincenzo but to follow his example, and read, or pretend to read.

In about an hour the Signora Del Palmetto peeped in, saying, "Will it shock Signor Candia too much if I confess that I have come to announce that dinner is on the table?"

"On the contrary, I am charmed," said Candia rising.

"Just at present," exclaimed the lady, "I am positively the only person available for that office. My maid is laid up with her *migraine*; Luigi is nowhere to be found; and the cook declares she has some mysterious dish on the fire, which she would not lose sight of for a kingdom."

"*À la guerre, comme à la guerre*," said Federico; "Candia, will you give my wife your arm?"

Vincenzo obeyed, and led the marchioness to the

dining-room, where the truant Luigi, just fresh from the cellar, was already on duty, napkin in hand.

"All this time," said the hostess, motioning Vincenzo to a seat on her right, "I have not apologized for my yesterday's blunder."

"I do beg you will not mention it," said Vincenzo, colouring.

"I can only say in extenuation," continued the marchioness, "that I was rather nervous. I had taken it into my head that I would introduce myself to your family and give my husband a surprise ..."

"I had had to stop at Ibella till the evening," said Del Palmetto.

"Well," resumed the marchioness, "the idea that had tickled my fancy as being original, when I came to put it into execution, seemed only eccentric. So, as I said, I was rather nervous at the moment I met you."

"I'll tell you what, Vincenzo," interrupted Del Palmetto, "Teresa was in truth dying with curiosity to see my first love."

"Why not say at once that I was jealous?" said Teresa.

"Who knows?" replied Del Palmetto, ready to laugh, and with a significant glance to Vincenzo. "Men are such vain coxcombs. I beg your Pardon, Signor Candia; I ought to have said soldiers."

The playful turn of this conversation between husband and wife did much to dissipate Vincenzo's shyness; their cordiality to him, and the perfect *sans façon* of an excellent dinner, ended by making him feel quite at his ease. He ate and drank more heartily than was his wont, and talked certainly more within a couple of hours than he had done during the last six months. In answer to Del Palmetto's friendly inquiries, he gave a summary account of what had chanced to him since their last meeting, and, in so doing, naturally touched upon his experiences in Savoy, and spoke of the difficulties there were for the administration in so disaffected a province. The marchioness observed that, "if the Savoyards had come at last to perceive that nature meant them to be French, nobody was entitled to thwart their wish to become such, and the sooner they were given up to France the better. If we are to make good our rights to nationality, if we expect and look to having our claims acknowledged, we must set the example of acknowledging and respecting those of others. I know that Count de Cavour, whatever his personal feelings may be in the matter, as a statesman, thinks as I do with respect to Savoy; and the day is, perhaps, not so distant when he may be called on to turn his theory into practice. When this happens, sooner or later, I cannot help wishing you, Signor Candia, a pleasanter field for your activity than disaffected Savoy. When I say pleasanter, it is merely politically speaking; for, in natural beauties and agreeableness of social intercourse, I know few cities that can compete with Chambery. You still hold the appointment there, do you not?"

"I hold none, either there or anywhere else," said Vincenzo. "I have renounced the administrative career."

"What a pity!" cried the marchioness, "so young, so talented, and after such a brilliant *débût* too; I give you fair warning that I for one shall never cease to oppose such a resolution."

"Alas! Madam, I have fought against it myself, and suffered defeat; there are circumstances too strong even for an iron will. My wife cannot bear to leave her home — suffers, really suffers from home-sickness — in short, is never well anywhere but at the Palace. My father-in-law is getting old and infirm ..."

"That I can answer for," broke in Del Palmetto; "had you seen him only two years ago, Teresa, you would not recognise him now as the same man."

"I could not take it upon myself," resumed Vincenzo, "to keep a father and his only child asunder; could I? nor could I go about the world by myself and leave them alone. There are situations out of which there is no possible issue. All that I am, I owe to this father and daughter."

"I understand," said Signor Del Palmetto, musing.

There was a minute of awkward silence, which Federico hastened to break. "By the bye, Vincenzo, you must give us the *carte du pays*. What sort of fish is this new Curé, Don Pio?"

"A very rough sort of fish, my dear friend. A man, however, deficient in neither education nor talent; a fanatic to the very marrow of his bones, professing the most unbounded contempt for the civil power; a martinet in a cassock, and who lords it over the parish with a strong hand."

"But the Signor Avvocato keeps him in order, I suppose," said Del Palmetto.

"The Signor Avvocato is his firmest supporter and friend, and one of his penitents to boot," was the answer.

"Is it possible?" exclaimed Del Palmetto. "I remember a time, and that not very long ago, when the

Signor Avvocato was the Mirabeau of Rumelli, and the Palace — a stronghold of liberalism."

"It is now a *succursale* of the parsonage," said Vincenzo; "old age, bodily infirmity, the death of Don Natale, the influence of Don Pio, have worked the change."

"Then we'll make the Castle a centre of opposition; we'll cut out some work for this Reverend Gessler; won't we, Teresa?"

"If he dares to speak a word, in the pulpit, against the King and Statuto, I'll take him to task in the church itself; that I will," said Teresa, with the look of a woman who could and would do it. "*A propos*, tell me," added she, "how does the Curé manage on the fête day of the Statuto?"

"Just lets it pass as if there existed no Statuto to celebrate."

"And his parishioners bear it; and the town-council keep silence?"

"Yes, indeed — they are all mute — in fact, the council is composed of Don Pio's creatures; and, as for the people of the village, they also bear the omission with perfect composure; peasantry are pretty much the same all over the world — they know of and care for no other Statuto than the weather and the crops."

"I remember there was a miller, though I forget his name, who had made money, and who played the patriot; what of him?" asked Del Palmetto.

"Ah! yes, his patriotism was to be elected Syndic," replied Vincenzo; "he is now Don Pio's right hand."

"And that other who kept the Post-office?"

"You mean Peter the chandler, who made a parade

of radical opinions that he might be named officer in the National Guard; he is Don Pio's *left* hand. No, no; seek where you will, you will find but one liberal in the parish, and that's old Barnaby; and his liberalism, honest old soul, consists in wishing every one hanged who does not hold the same creed as he himself does."

"And what of the National Guard?"

"Dead and buried."

It being too wet to allow of strolling in the park after dinner, they all three went to an adjoining drawing-room, where they had coffee, and Del Palmetto his cigar.

"I have given you an account of myself," said Vincenzo; "but you have told me nothing of your doings since we parted."

"My tale is short," said Federico. "I had been fooling, if not worse, to my heart's content, when my good angel bid me volunteer for the Crimea."

"Bravo!" cried Vincenzo; "that was like you; it was nobly done."

"Don't give me more credit than I deserve," said Federico. "I have no claims to any merit but one — obedience; obedience to the commands of a real angel in human form, and but for whom I should have stayed tranquilly at home."

"Don't believe him, Signor Candia," said the marchioness; "he was wild to go."

"Very true," returned Del Palmetto; "but I should not have gone for all that unless my regiment had been ordered out, which it was not, because I had taken it into my wooden head, like many other wiseacres in and out of Parliament, that the war was not for the good of the country."

"A mistake which I was clever enough to get out of your head," said the wife; "and you went and did your duty gallantly, and came back a captain and a knight of St. Maurice and Lazare."

"And you have forgotten my best reward," wound up Del Palmetto — "and, the accepted husband of the loveliest, dearest . . ."

"Old maid of five-and-twenty," interrupted the marchioness, blushing; "and who, among her other perfections, has that of a good sprinkling of grey in her hair."

"A good sprinkling!" repeated Del Palmetto; "half a dozen silver lines, perhaps — just enough to set off the brilliant black of the rest. I maintain that it is a beauty."

"Well, well, be it so for you; but I don't think these are the details to interest Signor Candia; tell him, instead, of the Crimea and the war."

Del Palmetto complied, and gave some spirited sketches of camp life, and of a sortie of the besieged in the dead of night.

From the war in the Crimea to the advantages likely to accrue to Italy from the alliance of Piedmont with the Western Powers, the transition was natural; and upon this subject Signora del Palmetto expatiated at length, with a vigour of deduction, an abundance of evidence, and an energy of conviction, quite irresistible. Her anticipations for the future were as sanguine as passionate desire could make them; and that the cause she debated was the great passion of her life, the vibration in her voice, the flush on her cheeks, the sparkle of her eyes, could leave no doubt. The amount of information about men and things which her demonstrations implied was truly wonderful. Not an Italian of note, either at home or abroad, but she knew, personally or by correspondence; no foreign question, however remote, but she was familiar with, and with its bearing upon the interests she had most at heart. Most of the anticipations, which sounded almost like wild prophecies as she spoke them, are by this time either accomplished facts, or in a fair way of becoming so; and to recapitulate them here would be worse than lost labour. But, in 1857, these facts were anxious problems, the mere discussion of which quickened men's and women's pulses, and took away their breath. Vincenzo was in a thrill from head to foot.

The marchioness perceived this, and, checking herself, said —

"But these are exciting topics, and excitement is good neither for you nor for me; so, if you please, we will have a game of chess, by way of a sedative."

Chess, a little music — the Signora del Palmetto played well on the piano—and some quiet talk, agreeably filled up the rest of the afternoon. At a little past seven, Vincenzo rose to go. Del Palmetto pressed him to stay yet a while, but at last yielded the point, on seeing that Vincenzo was really anxious to be back at the Palace in time for supper. The weather had cleared, the sky was studded with stars; so Vincenzo would not hear of being driven home; he assured his friends that he much preferred walking, and, after taking a cordial leave of the Signora, went away arm-in-arm with Del Palmetto.

"My dear Federico," began Vincenzo at once, "you called me a lucky dog this morning; allow me to return the compliment with interest — to say that you are the luckiest fellow under heaven."

"Ain't I?" exclaimed Federico, with the most naïve sincerity. "Isn't she a wonderful creature?"

"She is incomparable; but what guardian angel placed this phœnix in your way?"

"My folly. It is as romantic a story as any that was ever written. Yes, it is to my folly that I owe the inestimable discovery of this treasure. So goes it in this strange world of ours. A good father of a family walks out on an errand of charity, and breaks his leg or his neck; a scatter-brained, harum-scarum fellow sallies forth, bent on mischief, and — stumbles on the Koh-i-nor. But moralizing does not tell my tale. Perhaps you still recollect that brother-officer of mine, with whom I was playing billiards, the day you came to Ibella in search of the purse; an excellent fellow in the main, but devilish touchy, and sharp-tongued. Well, one day, when we were again playing billiards, we had some dispute about the balls, in the course of which some disagreeable words were exchanged — in short, a challenge ensued. This happened at Turin, in 1854, in the month of November. On the day following, we accordingly met in a solitary avenue behind the Valentino; and, after a useless attempt at conciliation, made by our seconds, we crossed swords. We had not been at it a minute when, lo and behold! a lady, who suddenly seemed to start out of the earth — for we had taken care to be sure that no one was in sight — a tall lady in a black habit, a riding-whip in her hand, an utter stranger to all of us, thrust herself between our swords, and had an uncommon narrow escape of being hurt."

"Gentlemen," she cried, "I beg of you, I command you to desist." It was all she could say, she was so out of breath with running. After a time she recovered, and made us a beautiful speech, I assure you, which I should only spoil if I tried to repeat it. But this was the sense of what she said — That it was our mania for quarrelling with one another which had too long been the custom and the bane of Italians, and that it was high time that such an evil should cease. She bid us remember that our blood did not belong to us, but to our country; and that that man robbed his country, who, instead of shedding his blood in her defence, wasted it for the gratification of his own private feuds. It was for the enemies of Italy that we ought to reserve our wrath and our blows. It could not be, it should not be, that two fellow-countrymen, two brother-officers, probably two excellent friends only yesterday, should to-day cut each other's throats — and for what? Some trifle; she was sure there was nothing but a trifle at the bottom of our quarrel. Her large black eyes were riveted upon me as she said this, and I was obliged to look away in order not to confess that she was quite right. It was of course the duty of our seconds to speak. One of my antagonist's friends came forward, and, bowing to the lady, said that it was impossible to refuse anything to such a charming peace-maker; and then he bid us return our swords to the scabbards. The lady's face brightened as she saw us do this. "Now then," said she, addressing us, "Now then, shake hands heartily, to seal the peace." My adversary and I remained as we were, without moving, looking on the ground — for we had both noticed the wink which the second who answered the lady had given us before he spoke — a wink which we understood to signify we must make believe. As if she had divined this, she turned upon him and exclaimed, "What does this mean? You were not in earnest then in what you said — you deceived me. Oh, sir! a gentleman and an officer ought not to trifle with a lady." Her cheeks grew scarlet as she said this; she threw back her head with the gesture of a queen. "Excuse me, madam," said the officer; "I intended no offence, I assure you. I own I made an attempt to evade your request, which appeared inadmissible under the circumstances. I will now try to atone to the best of my ability by striving to meet your wishes." He beckoned the other seconds aside, and, after a moment's consultation with them, came back and said that they were unanimously of opinion that we had done all that was requisite for our honour, and that we were to shake hands. This we immediately did with right good will. "Thank you, gentlemen," said the lady; "and, if at any time Teresa Ombelli can be of use to any of you, you will not remind her of this day in vain." Saying this, she bowed and hurried away to the end of the avenue, where a groom on horseback was holding her horse.

"The rest," said Del Palmetto, "may be told in a few words. Teresa Ombelli from that moment became a fixture in heart and head. I sought her everywhere, and at last met her in one of our aristocratic salons, and was allowed to visit at her father's house. Her political opinions and those of her surroundings were too widely at variance with those I had imbibed from my father not to shock me a little at first; but, in a few months, love aiding and abetting, I was in a fair way of being converted. Teresa had told me frankly, on the occasion of my proposing to her, that she would never marry a man holding a political creed different from her own: and this knowledge perhaps hastened my conversion. It was, notwithstanding, not yet complete at the time of the expedition to the Crimea, as my repugnance to join it as a volunteer showed. This repugnance, however, she somehow overcame. My obedience, together with a rather narrow escape I had at the Tchernaia, of which I told her in a letter, made her relent so far as to overlook my deficiencies, and consent to our union as soon as I should return. Thus it was that the beginning of 1856 saw me the happiest and proudest of husbands and men."

By this time the two friends had reached the door of the Palace. They shook hands warmly, and bid each other good night.

CHAPTER XIV.

Currents and Under-Currents.

THE Marchioness Del Palmetto was one of those noble devotees of a fixed idea, whom Providence scatters among a nation when its destinies are ripe — moral engines of an incalculable power, and without which the task even of a Cavour would be relatively lingering and thankless. He who has not seen one of these exceptional beings at work can form no conception of the vastness and the importance of results which the devouring activity of a single individual can effect. The independence of her country was the focus to which all Signora Del Palmetto's energy of thought and action converged; and that day was lost for her which had not secured to Italy a new friend, to Austria a new foe.

She belonged to a heroic family of heroic Brescia, in which love of Italy, abhorrence of Austria, were hereditary. She had turned her father's house into a hospital for the sick and wounded of the Piedmontese army in 1848; she had, in 1849, loaded and handed muskets to her father and brothers defending Brescia inch by inch against the soldiers of Haynau; she had, on the cold corpse of her eldest brother, killed by an Austrian ball, sworn the oath of Hannibal. Teresa Ombelli was then only seventeen. At Turin, where she and the other survivors of her family had to seek a refuge from the vengeance of the flogger of women, her name, her youth, her beauty, her very eccentric style of dressing, constantly in mourning for her country, surrounded her with a halo of sympathy and respect which gradually extended from the Lombard emigrants, to which it was at first limited, to that of the Turinese society at large, until in a few years the name of Teresa Ombelli — a name ever associated with all benevolent acts and progressive undertakings — became familiar and dear to the whole liberal party. Her interest and favour with the official and parliamentary world, especially of late days, had considerably and deservedly increased; for it is no exaggeration to say that her indefatigable propagandism had counted for something in the successful cutting of the two hardest knots which the Cavour administration had had to deal with — we mean the suppression of the convents, and the participation of Sardinia in the Crimean War. And persons were hinted at — not a few of them senators and deputies, professedly adverse to both measures — whose conversion she had worked, and whose votes she had sent to swell the ministerial majority. All this, of course, had nothing to do with the hearty reception she met at Rumelli. Who she was, or what she was, the Rumellians knew as little of as they did of Sanscrit; nor would the knowledge have at all helped her popularity. All that the good folks knew, or cared to know, concerning her was, that she was the marchioness, the wife of the representative of a family which had knocked them about for generations, and in whom they consequently put their pride and reverence. Being the marchioness, they would have welcomed and cheered her even had she been old and ugly, haughty and cross — they welcomed and cheered more loudly, perhaps, because she was young and handsome, smiling and affable. This display of good will took place on the Sunday after their arrival; and certainly the explosion of enthusiasm which greeted the young couple on their way to and from Church was remarkable. Not even on the memorable occasion of the Signor Avvocato's return from Turin a cavaliere, was the popular commotion so great and universal. The good people of Rumelli had a vast arrear of unsatisfied excitement to give vent to — an arrear which dated so far back as the end of 1854, that being the epoch at which the palace began to put on its cap of dulness.

After vespers the whole village, headed by the town council, and preceded by the band, flocked to the castle. We spare the reader the mayor's official address, as well as the other speeches and the programme of the music performed; the finale of the ceremony was the presentation of an enormous bouquet to her ladyship. The national guard shone by its absence, as Captain Del Palmetto was heard to remark sarcastically. The gates of the castle were thrown wide open, and any one who chose might enter — whoever came was graciously received and hospitably entertained. Nor were the more discreet majority, who were contented with staring in at the windows, or strolling in the park, overlooked. The marquis sent them out tables and chairs, and plenty of wine, and mixed among them, shaking hands and drinking healths with all the zeal of a new convert.

Among the magnates who went in *de jure* and were received with due honour, was Don Pio: the reverend gentleman made a neat little oration, expressing his appreciation of the singular good fortune which had befallen him in the acquisition, were it only for a time, of two such distinguished parishioners, whose presence alone was the cause of such rejoicing among his flock. The marchioness thanked him, and said how touched she was by the cordial welcome the Rumellians had given her.

"A truly excellent and conservative population is ours hereabouts," said Don Pio. "They hold to old associations, and also to old habits and ways."

"Not too much of that, I hope," returned the Marchioness, smiling.

"May I ask," said Don Pio, in his most persuasive voice, "how one can hold too much to that which is good?"

"Gently," said the Signora; "your question implies

that you think all was good in the past. Now, that I do not admit. The past has its good and its bad; and true conservatism, to my mind, consists in preserving the former and getting rid of the latter."

"Even admitting this," replied the Curé, "it still remains to be determined what is the good to be kept and what the bad to be removed; and that is a matter of opinion . . . but," he added, in a tone of self-reproach — "but I am ashamed to catch myself arguing when I ought only to think of greeting and congratulating."

Don Pio had only intended to sound the ground; he had every interest not to prepossess against him his newly-arrived and powerful neighbours. The Marchioness, on her side, had neither reason nor wish to offend the most influential person in the parish; her sole motive in saying as much as she had said was to prove to him that she was not the woman to hide her colours. So the discussion ended there.

The pleasurable excitement created by the young Marquis's return with a bride to the castle of his ancestors, did not die away with the demonstrations made on that Sunday. The Del Palmettos themselves, all unwittingly, kept it alive by their daily rounds through the village, and the easy familiarity they displayed on these occasions. They were really grateful for the goodwill shown them, and returned it in kind. By the end of a few days there was no cottage at the door of which they had not stood in friendly converse with the inmates; no old man or woman of whose exact age they were not cognisant; no young candidate for the first communion they had not congratulated; no babe whose gamut of screams they did not know by heart — not that the babies of Rumelli had a greater disposition to scream than to laugh; but, if they had begun by laughing at the Marchioness's pretty face bending over them, it was rare that they did not end by screaming at the hirsute appearance of that of the Marquis. Del Palmetto had been repeatedly told, and took a pride in believing it, that he was very like the King; and, to render the likeness still more striking, he had allowed the tuft on his chin and his moustachios to grow to the fabulous length of those of his royal menechme.

But democratic bias, and study of popularity with the common herd, did not make the young pair forget the claims of the bigwigs of the land. Del Palmetto had his head full of plans of reform, and he knew full well that the influential few could help him far more effectually to carry them out than the many who had no finger in the pie. The curé, the mayor, the ex-mayor, the town councillors, the officers of the defunct national guard, were accordingly called upon, and such among them as could best forward his views, in proper time, asked to dine at the Castle, and carefully catechized *inter pocula*... But we must not anticipate.

As to the inmates of the Palace, there was no end to the friendly advances made to them by the Marquis and his wife — advances persevered in, in spite of the passiveness, not to say coolness, with which they were received. The Palace was far from ungracious, but stood on the defensive.

"Really you are too good," would Signora Candia observe at the Marchioness's every fresh call, "and I am heartily ashamed of myself when I think of what a poor return I make you for all your kind visits. But

I hope you will forgive me — I have had so very much to do; and then papa is far from well, and I cannot leave him, you understand."

"Reason the more that I, who have nothing to keep me at home, should come and enjoy your society here," would the lady of the Castle answer. "There can be no question of etiquette between us."

Or it was the Signor Avvocato, who, as soon as he caught sight of the Marquis, would cry out, "Here you come, my poor Del Palmetto, to do penance. This is a dull place, and I am but dull company for a spirited young fellow like you."

"I suspect I am not so spirited as you would make me out," was the Marquis's laughing rejoinder, "for I confess that such dulness as I find here pleases me wonderfully well, as my frequent appearance proves. Now, what can you say to that, eh?"

If there were ever people in the world likely to disagree and to keep as far apart as they could, surely it was the master of the Palace and his daughter, and the Marquis and Marchioness Del Palmetto. Fire and water have as much affinity. The two last were the bold assertion of all that whereof the two first were the negation. What, then, was at the bottom of this seeming predetermination on the part of the latter to force themselves on the former? There was nothing more mysterious in it than regard for Vincenzo and a wish to be useful to him. The Marchioness was not so absorbed by politics as to have neither eyes nor ears for other matters. Within a very short time, the Palace had no longer any secrets for her. The split between Vincenzo and the Signor Avvocato, and the siding of Rose with her father, the causes which had engendered it, and the deplorable consequences which it entailed upon Vincenzo — the Marchioness understood it all. To see an evil and to look for the remedy was for her ardent nature one and the same thing. Now, of remedies there was but one — a reconciliation on reasonable terms. She was sure that Vincenzo was too sensible a man not to acquiesce, were any such offered to him; but she was far from having the same confidence in the good sense of Signora Candia and her father. The Marchioness's conclusion — we give it in her own words — to her husband, was this: "We must lay regular siege to the hearts of this father and daughter, and try to acquire an influence over them, which we shall use in behalf of your friend. If we succeed, well and good; if not, we shall always have gained this point — that Signor Vincenzo's daily intercourse with us will be looked upon as a natural return for our unremitting civilities to his family, and thus nobody will take umbrage at it." For by this time — the middle of March — Vincenzo was a daily visitor at the Castle — nay, regularly spent his afternoons there, from three o'clock to seven in the evening. He drank largely, we see, from the fresh source of kindness and affection which had gushed up from under his feet, as it were; but he was so thirsty, poor soul! and then his warm-hearted neighbours made him such a golden bridge. Vincenzo had even his little sanctum at the Castle, that same small parlour into which Del Palmetto had taken him to rest on his first visit. "You are to consider this as your own private room," had the Marquis said to him. "In case we are out, or have visitors you don't care to meet, or in case you choose to sulk, here you will find newspapers and books, and perfect solitude, to suit your humour. Recollect, it is entirely your own, and you can come in and out without reporting yourself to anybody." It is useless to say that Vincenzo profited but sparingly by the permission to remain alone — only, in fact, when there were callers upstairs. His morbid shyness and horror of company, or, worse still, of appearing in public, had outlived his isolation. He never went by the high-road to the Castle, but took the bypath more than once already mentioned. To return: Vincenzo, after availing himself of the opportunity to read the papers, which he did with a zest enhanced by long deprivation (the only paper received at the Palace was a clerical one, and even that rarely came in his way) — Vincenzo, after reading the papers, would seek his friends, and pass the rest of the afternoon with them, indoors, when the weather was bad, but more often in the pleasant shades of the park. Political news and speculations thereon usually formed the staple of the conversation. Signora Del Palmetto had correspondents in all parts of Italy, and consequently had plenty to tell about the blunders of the rulers, and the humours of the ruled, and the almost universal disposition to adhere to and support Piedmont. Politics did not exclude lighter topics. The Marchioness was quite at home in contemporary literature and art. No distinguished writer of the liberal school, from Leopardi to Giusti, that she had not at her fingers' ends. All Berchet's ballads and Giusti's satires she knew by heart. No renowned painter and sculptor with whose productions she was not familiar, more especially those of the artists who had devoted their talents to the service of the Italian Idea. And, having been, or being personally acquainted with all the men of note, dead or alive, of whom she spoke, she seasoned her conversation about them with the most interesting traits and anecdotes. She laid a great stress on music as a means of inoculating the masses with a national feeling, and used to say that in this point of view Italy was much indebted to the eminent composer and patriot Verdi.

The reader must not infer, from our exclusive mention of the Marchioness's sayings, that she played the lecturer, and had all the talk to herself. No such thing. She courted discussion, even contradiction; and such opinions and preferences as we have had occasion to mention came forth impromptu in the course of friendly chats, in which her husband, and particularly Vincenzo, took a good share. Vincenzo possessed a good store of general information, and had decided opinions on most subjects; and, when these differed from those of the lady, he was not backward in saying so, or to support his own views, though gently and discreetly. The Marchioness did not easily yield; he was tenacious of his point; hence courteous passes of arms, in which the advantage was not always on the Signora's side. She was never so well pleased as when she had succeeded in putting him into a passion — an argumentative passion, that is; Vincenzo needed only just a touch of excitement to grow eloquent. "Did you notice how I set Signor Vincenzo off? What a pity he is too young to be a member!" was what she would often remark to her husband when he came back from convoying his friend home. "With a little practice, what a debater he would make! It is positively a treason to one's country to condemn such powers of mind as he has to such total and cruel inactivity." But the least approach to this subject with Candia himself, the remotest hint as to the possibility for him of a career of usefulness, was invariably met by the same sad shake of the head, the same hopeless answer, "It is vain to think of such a thing." Nevertheless these earnest friends of his did continue to think of it, and to try their utmost to work the thought into a reality. Their conspiracy of kindness towards their neighbours was pushed on with unabated vigour. Not a day passed without either the Marquis or his wife calling at the Palace — if only to inquire for the Signor Avvocato's health after their usual morning ride or walk. The Del Palmettos were early risers, and loved to saunter about on foot, or ride, in the cool of the morning; they generally, however, went to the Palace towards noon, to make sure of seeing the Signor Avvocato, who was seldom visible before twelve. Not unfrequently, when he was confined to his room by his attacks of pain, the Marchioness would go and sit with him by the hour, talk to him about Turin and Brescia, tell him of Haynau and Austrian rule in Lombardy. The Signor Avvocato's political conversion had not been so thorough as to have cured him of his life-long aversion to Austria. The old gentleman was amused by his visitor's spirit and liveliness, and very soon began to miss her when she did not come — signs which, perceived and noted with feminine perspicacity, gave her the measure of the ground she was gaining in the father's heart.

It was otherwise with the daughter's; there was no way to it, or, if there were, the Marchioness could not find it. She might carry her work as much as she pleased to the Palace, and spend whole afternoons *tête-à-tête* with her fair neighbour, and yet, when she rose to go away, feel herself as much a stranger as when she had sat down three hours before. All the Marchioness's efforts to thaw Rose's coldness, to gain her confidence, to establish that sort of companionship so natural between young women, were neutralized by a *vis inertiæ*, which might arise from an absence of personal sympathy, or from a studied reserve.

"Signora Candia," at last said Teresa to her husband, "is like a smooth surface, off which everything glides; none of my grappling hooks of friendliness can find one point in her on which to fix themselves. Do you know that lately I have begun to suspect she might be jealous?"

"What an idea!" exclaimed Del Palmetto; "jealousy presupposes love, and does she look as if she loved her husband? I should say quite the contrary."

"Certainly, as far as appearances go, I must say you are right; and yet I cannot get rid of the impression that she is jealous. Why should her heart be so shut against me, unless . . ."

"Her heart is shut against you, and me, and her husband, because we are all of us liberals, and she is a furious *codina*. I declare to heavens, my hair stands on end when I think that I once proposed to her; it does, upon my honour."

The Del Palmettos' assiduity at the Palace could not but place them in frequent contact with another equally assiduous, and possibly even more welcome visitor, namely, Don Pio.

These meetings, if devoid of cordiality, were not

at all wanting in that washy substitute for it, good-natured civility. It formed part of the policy pursued by the Del Palmettos towards the Palace to keep well with a personage so influential in that quarter as Don Pio; and the priest, on his side, had obvious reasons also for being on good terms with the first family of the neighbourhood. With a view towards maintaining this good understanding, each party had made tacit concessions to the other. For instance, Del Palmetto had given up the turning the Castle into a stronghold of opposition, as he had at first intended; and, in order to divest his favourite plan — the reorganization of the National Guard — of all aggressive character, he had repeatedly mentioned it to Don Pio, asking him for his co-operation — a co-operation, however, which the priest had declined to give, on the plea that military matters were alien to his calling. The curé had been as courteous on his part. He abstained, in the presence of the Marquis and Marchioness, from all such subjects as might hurt their feelings, or be displeasing to them; more than that, he had entirely given up those broad political allusions and denunciations of men and things with which, like too many of his clerical brethren of that time, he had hitherto richly seasoned his Sunday sermons. We must not forget that the Marchioness, immediately after her arrival, and when as yet she had no good reason for temporising with the curé, had proclaimed everywhere, and loudly enough to reach his ears, her determination to call him publicly to account if he indulged in diatribes against the Government.

Such was the posture of affairs on the 5th of April, the day which was to inaugurate the formation anew of the National, or Civic, Guard, as thereabouts it was more commonly called. The rank and file of the defunct body were to assemble, by appointment, in the Town Hall, and there proceed to the election of fresh officers, the period of the commission of the former ones having long since expired. It had not cost Del Palmetto any extraordinary efforts to bring about this issue; the Civic Guard virtually existed; it was a mere matter of form to call it into activity, so long as its members were willing. And this the immense majority were, who felt it would be no trifling honour to be commanded by their Marquis, a real captain to boot, with three medals on his breast; for it was already preconcerted that the captaincy should devolve upon Del Palmetto.

Well, out of delicacy, and that it might not be said that he had sought to influence the poll, the Marquis had not budged from home, where he waited for the result with undoubting confidence. To his amazement John the Miller and Peter the Chandler, the lieutenant and sub-lieutenant in expectancy, came to seek him, much discomposed; and not without cause, for the news they brought wore a very disastrous look. There had been no election for want of electors — only six out of twenty-seven had attended the meeting — of the remainder eight had already had their names struck off the rolls, and many more were spoken of as having expressed their intention to do the same; it had very much the appearance of a general *sauve qui peut.*

"But there must be a cause for all this," cried Del Palmetto; "what is it?"

The cause was a very prevalent rumour, a terrible

rumour — nothing less than that Don Pio had declared that not a single man of the new National Guard should be allowed to receive the sacrament on Easter-Day. Now Easter was close at hand. We spare the reader the polite little appellative which Del Palmetto, on hearing this, hurled at the head of Don Pio.

"And you, what do you think of doing?" asked he of the messengers. John the Miller and Peter the Chandler protested their entire devotion to the Marquis; at the same time they were Christians, they were fathers of families, they had souls to save; in short, for nothing in the world would they miss fulfilling their Paschal duty. Vexed to the heart as he was, Del Palmetto felt and admitted the full force of their reasons, and upon this there was an end of the interview.

The Marchioness took the infection of her husband's wrath, and they both did nothing, during dinner, but fret and fume, and devise measures of retaliation.

"Since war he chooses, war he shall have," said Del Palmetto, as he rose from table. "I shall go this very instant, and give this Don Pio a piece of my mind."

"Yes, do," said the Marchioness, going down-stairs with him.

Fortunately, as they passed the small parlour they called Vincenzo's study, they thought of looking in and telling their friend of their grievance. Vincenzo, after listening attentively, strongly dissuaded their acting upon so flimsy a foundation as a vague rumour.

"As for me," went on Candia, "I take it for granted that Don Pio is the prime cause of this morning's defeat, but I know the man too well not to be sure that he has managed the matter so adroitly as to keep himself clear of all responsibility. Depend upon it, Don Pio is too clever to commit himself so clumsily as by a threat of the kind alleged. At all events, let us first get proofs that he has, and I shall not be the one to bid you restrain your just indignation — only in the meanwhile obey the saying of the sage, 'In doubt abstain.'"

Vincenzo's advice, supported by the Marchioness, won the day, and Del Palmetto, conquered if not convinced, consented to wait for more reliable information before risking an *éclat*. This more reliable information was not long in being obtained; it came through our old friend Barnaby. That Barnaby was a great partizan of the Castle, and a great favourite at the Castle — that he had at all times his *grandes* and *petites entrées* at the Castle — is what the reader does not need to be told. Barnaby had had all the particulars of the case from Lucangelo, who had every right to be believed, as he was art and part in the whole affair from beginning to end. This was that same Lucangelo who had been dairy-lad at the Palace in 1848, and who had then brought back from Ibella the first news of Vincenzo's escapade. He was now a full-grown man of twenty-two or twenty-three, and farmed a little bit of land of his own, the dowry of his wife. Being by far the tallest and handsomest young fellow of the village, Lucangelo was a very desirable acquisition for the National Guard; bethinking himself of which, Barnaby, who had continued on good terms with the ex-dairy lad, gave him no peace until he had got him to put his name down on the rolls — an acquiescence which, by the way, had cost Lucangelo many and many a peevish remonstrance from his wife, who, like most wives, and mothers, and women in general, was against the National Guard. Now, then, to come to the gist of the business — Lucangelo, on this very morning of the 5th of April, had gone early to confession. Don Pio being the only confessor at hand, had nine-tenths of the custom of the village. Don Pio, on his way to the confessional, stopped a while, as was his wont, to count over the number of applicants for confession, and, probably, having satisfied himself that he had not time for the whole, singled out of the number Lucangelo and two of his comrades, and told them they need not wait, as he should not be able to attend to them. This exclusion, not unprecedented on occasions of large attendance, looked the more ominous to the objects of it, that on that morning there were only a scanty few waiting. However, there was nothing for it but to obey, and, much discomfited, they accordingly retired; but meeting the Sacristan, Lucangelo stopped and asked him whether the Curé would be in the confessional that afternoon, and at what hour. This Sacristan — a gruff, tyrannical old man — was the *âme damnée* of the Curé. He replied,

"You belong to the Civic Guard, do you not?"

They said that they did.

"Well, then," resumed the Sacristan, "you may spare yourself the time and trouble of coming back here. Not one of the Civic Guard shall receive the Sacrament on Easter Day."

At this terrible fiat, only too well confirmed by the Curé's refusal to hear their confession, the three rustics were seized with a panic — they had a vision of their names ignominiously placarded, as is still the custom in small villages, over the door of the church. They ran in hot haste to such of their friends as they knew to be in a similar predicament to their own; and, before an hour was over, all Rumelli was full of the news that Don Pio had declared — Don Pio, mark, and not the Sacristan — that none of those who belonged to the National Guard should be allowed to take the Sacrament on Easter Sunday. Such was the substance of the statement made by Lucangelo to Barnaby. We withhold the old gardener's wrathful comments, on account both of their quality and quantity.

"You see how lucky it was that you did not act on your first angry impulse," said Vincenzo to Del Palmetto. "It would, as we now see, have put you quite in the wrong. If Don Pio has thrown the stone — which, for my part, I don't in the least doubt — he has taken good care that the hand from which it came should remain concealed. It is likely, too, that he has been served beyond his hopes by the gooseishness of Lucangelo and Co. Be this as it may, all we have heard has not given us a tittle of evidence against him. The putting off the confession of three penitents to another time is a course perfectly justifiable by precedent. This indiscreet zeal of that old dotard the Sacristan may be easily disavowed. And then what remains? Zero."

The defeated were the more galled the less they saw any means of reprisal. The natural corollary of this state of feeling was the growing coldness of the Castle towards the Parsonage, which the Parsonage was not slack in reciprocating, and that more markedly after the incident we are now about to relate. On

Easter Eve the Del Palmettos and Vincenzo went to confession at a Convent of Capuchins not far off — the same where Rose's deceased spiritual director, Father Terenziano, had lived; and on the morrow they took the Communion at the parish church of Rumelli. Their having sought a confessor elsewhere was so little a measure of retaliation that husband and wife had determined upon doing so long before the late broils — in fact, from the moment they had learned what a fanatic Don Pio was, and what a liberal-minded confessor Vincenzo had found at the Convent above mentioned; but such a step was not the less resented by absolute Don Pio as an intentional slight. Materials for an explosion were thus accumulating on both sides.

CHAPTER XV.

A Tempest in a Tea-pot.

To perpetuate the memory of the granting of a free constitution, the Subalpine Legislature of 1851 passed a law which instituted a national holiday, under the title of *Festa dello Statuto*, to be kept annually on the second Sunday in May. The putting of this law into execution met with many difficulties from the clergy, who, especially since the abolition of ecclesiastical jurisdiction, were anything but friendly to the Statuto. Indeed, except in towns of first and second-rate importance, where public opinion exercised a wholesome pressure on the reluctant ecclesiastical authorities, the honours paid to the national holiday were everywhere null or incomplete — null, where the local clergy had influence enough with the municipal body to deter them from any public demonstration; incomplete, where the municipal body had spirit enough to take the initiative as to the rejoicings, the local clergy, as a rule, abstaining. In saying this, we do not mean to allege that there were no exceptions to this rule. They were few, indeed, but there were some; as, for instance, Don Natale.

Thanks to his easy-going nature, and to his friendship for the Signor Avvocato — at that time still a Constitutionalist, at least in name — things had gone on smoothly at Rumelli on the second Sunday in May. Don Natale had arranged that, while he was taking off his robes in the vestry, the singers should begin the *Te Deum* — not the slow and pompous *Te Deum* reserved for great solemnities, but the quick and less imposing one used for minor occasions — in the middle of which Don Natale would, perhaps, show himself, but not in canonicals, and, standing by the singers' bench, join his voice now and then to theirs; and there was an end of the matter. This very lukewarm performance had been persevered in down to 1854; but in 1855 (Don Natale had just died, and Don Pio had been surrogated to his place) the new curé had judged fit, with the Signor Avvocato's full approbation, to put an end even to that pretence of thanksgiving. It was very easily done. The choir received a peremptory injunction — to which they conformed, nothing loth — to leave their bench immediately after mass, and go about their business. The congregation loitered a little, stared at the empty bench, whispered, "It seems we are to have no *Te Deum* to-day," and took their departure. Two or three of the most daring, who ventured to ask Don Pio the cause of this novelty, received for answer that the Church could have no thanksgiving for the granting of a fundamental law under the rule of which holy monks and nuns might be robbed and despoiled, even of the right of prayer in common. This reply shut the mouth of the questioners, and of all who might be inclined to become such; and for that year and the one ensuing (Vincenzo was absent on both occasions) the anniversary of the Statuto was no more commemorated at Rumelli than at Vienna or Timbuctoo.

But it was utterly impossible that this sort of shuffling should succeed in the present year, 1857, while the Del Palmettos were actually at the Castle. They neither could nor would remain quiescent, thus appearing to give their sanction to an act of omission which implied disparagement of that which they respected with all their hearts. They accordingly decided that, with or without Don Pio's concurrence, they would celebrate the second Sunday in May as a day of thanksgiving and rejoicing for the Statuto. Don Pio, when applied to, and respectfully requested by the Marquis to have a *Te Deum* sung, returned a flat refusal. Short of receiving an order to that effect from his ecclesiastical superior — an order which he had not received, and which he had every reason to believe he would not receive — Don Pio would abide by the precedent he had established. Del Palmetto urged the contrary precedent established by Don Natale.

"Don Natale acted according to his conscience, and I according to mine," replied the priest.

"Then," said the Marquis, "you will not take it amiss if we go by ours, and if we do the little we can to honour an event which we consider a most happy and beneficial one."

The conciliatory tone of the young nobleman's language was belied by none of the acts which followed. While resolved to accomplish what they looked upon as a duty, the Del Palmettos were equally resolved to accomplish it in the way most calculated to spare, as far as possible, the feelings of the Curé, and, consequently, also those of the Signor Avvocato and his daughter. They made it a point, therefore, to say nothing of Don Pio's having refused his cooperation, and even abstained altogether from pronouncing his name in connexion with the approaching fête; for that there was to be a little family fête at the Castle on the anniversary of the Statuto, of this they made no secret; nor could they, even had they desired it, there being several men actually employed in erecting a scaffolding in front of the Castle for the display of fireworks. There were also preparations being made for an illumination. The Del Palmettos wished it so clearly to be understood that their fête was a family one, that they apologized to their habitual guests of Rumelli for not inviting any of them to dinner, on the plea that their party on that day was to be exclusively composed of relatives.

However modestly announced — or perhaps because so modestly announced — the Del Palmettos' forthcoming fête had put the whole village on the tiptoe of expectation; and the approaches to the Castle on the important morning were besieged betimes by a large crowd eager to have the first view of the expected visitors. As nine o'clock was striking three carriages drove up, out of which got nine persons, three ladies and six gentlemen — four of these last officers. Was this only a beginning, or was it all? Opinions were divided. A quarter after nine struck, then the half hour, then the three quarters, and no further arrivals. Alas! it was all — a conclusion which made the funds of the Castle fall ten per cent. in the estimation of the lookers-on; but there was a proportionate rise the moment the party, issuing forth to Church, afforded the by-standers the opportunity for a nearer inspection. The *personnel* was scanty, it was true; but then it was uncommonly good-looking, and quality made up for quantity. Could there be a finer specimen of an old gentleman than the one who walked in front with the Marchioness, evidently her father? — or a more prepossessing young fellow than that lieutenant of the Bersaglieri, whose lithe erect figure, expressive olive countenance, and jet-black eyes and hair, allowed of no mistake as to his being the Marchioness's brother? And that fair lady in the blue silk, leaning on the Marquis's arm — had she not the air and the step of a queen? — and this, and that, and the other, was it not a pleasure to behold them? By the time the party from the Castle had taken their seats in the Del Palmettos' side chapel, the funds of the Castle had jumped up to par again; and when, after mass, the Marquis and Marchioness did the honours of the village to their guests, introducing to their notice, as they went along, the inhabitants *en masse*, and the notabilities one by one, the rise in the said funds reached to quotations unprecedented.

The least the village could do, under the circumstances, was to go after vespers and return the compliment to the Castle, and this it accordingly did, accompanied by the band as a matter of course; even the Town Council thought fit to send a deputation. This last demonstration, made on such a day, was the more indicative of the actual temper of popular feeling, that it came from a body notoriously composed of partisans of Don Pio. What added piquancy to the affair was, that this deputation were ushered into the dining-hall just at the moment of the toast to the Statuto, and, whether they would or no, they had to drink it.

We have no time to spare for either the official or unofficial proceedings that followed; they differed in nothing from those we have repeatedly seen take place at the Palace. Suffice it to say that they were now gone through to the perfect satisfaction of all parties. The hospitality of the Castle, great as it was, proved only second to its graciousness. The Marquis and Marchioness went out frequently into the grounds to make sure that no one was forgotten or over-looked, and their guests mixed freely with the villagers. These latter looked pleased and animated, but as little actuated by any political feeling as if they were wholly ignorant of the cause and purport of the festival they were sharing in. There were lusty cheers for the inmates of the Castle as they passed to and fro among them, but as yet not one single voice had raised one single hurrah for the Statuto. Was this indifference, or was it fear of Don Pio? Whatever the cause, it gave way before one of those irresistible impulses which seize upon a crowd with the instantaneousness of an electric shock. It was *à propos* of a numerous cavalcade of Del Palmetto's brother officers, a dozen of them at least, who came rattling up to the Castle about six in the evening. Both the sight and the sound were inspiriting; and when, before dismounting, the cavaliers waved their shakoes and cried, "Viva lo Statuto!" off went all the rural hats and caps present in joyous sympathy, and every rustic throat joined in a hearty shout for the Statuto.

We must not omit to note that there was by this time, mixed with the local population assembled in the Castle grounds, a good sprinkling of mechanics from Ibella, who had come to see the fête, and contribute to the success of such a novelty in Rumelli as the commemoration of the granting of the Statuto. It was, most likely, with these that the above responsive shouts had originated, but the cry being taken up so quickly and lustily, abundantly showed that it answered to a desire generally felt. Certain it is that, from this moment, the fête assumed a decided political colour; witness the toasts to the Statuto which went off like crackers from one table after the other, and the snatches of patriotic songs, which every now and then swelled into a chorus. The band caught the infection and struck up "*L'Italia si desta*," an attempt which at first proved abortive, none of the performers knowing by heart beyond the first three or four bars of the tune. Seeing which, they had to send for the music, and in fact wholly retrieved their honour by playing nothing else as long as it was light. As is generally the case, the darker it grew the louder waxed the clamour and the mirth; until the whizz of the first rocket came to act as a stopper on the hubbub. The fireworks went off admirably amid alternations of dead silence and of deafening cheers; and, when, after the dazzling splendours of the "bouquet," the *façade* of the Castle, pitch-dark for one moment, blazed up, as if by magic, with *Viva lo Statuto*, traced in flaming characters of gas, then one immense joyous cry rent the air, and the Statuto was acclaimed for some minutes with a sort of frenzy. Fancy how agreeably tickled by such sounds must have been Don Pio's acoustic nerves; set on edge already as they were by the patriotic performance of the band. The illumination of the Castle was the climax of the entertainment; the good folks loitered yet awhile to enjoy the *coup d'œil*, to admire and to criticise — there's never any lack of critics, be the assemblage large or small — and then the grounds began slowly to empty. Most of the Rumellians went to their homes and their beds; a few of the youths of the place, and the majority of the Ibellians, roamed through the village in search of fresh sport, and fresh sport they soon found.

A squad of urchins, determined to have their illumination also, were busily engaged opposite to the church square, heaping up materials, brought from the adjoining fields and hedges, for a bonfire. You need not ask whether or not the new comers lent a willing hand; and, the pile having soon reached — thanks to their active assistance — to respectable proportions, it was set fire to amidst a perfect volley of merry shouts. Now, the spot for this harmless *auto-da-fé*, being isolated from all habitations, was judiciously chosen in so far as the safety of the village from conflagration was concerned, but it had the serious disadvantage of being overlooked by one of the back-windows of the parsonage. Presently this window was opened, and Don Pio's voice was heard asking, in its harshest tones, What was going on down below there, and if they meant to set the place on fire. This interrogation was answered by a burst of hisses and groans; and a threat which followed of coming out to punish the offenders, was received with a renewed cry of "Viva lo Statuto! Down with the Codini!" whereupon the window was noisily shut to an accompaniment of crowing, barking, mewing, grunting, squeaking, and what not. Don Pio had the prudence not to commit himself any further, and let the bonfire and the excitement spend themselves unopposed, which came to pass in good time. The party from Ibella marched off the ground in military order; and, with a parting salutation to Don Pio in the shape of another hearty "Down with the Codini! down with Don Pio!" bellowed beneath his very windows, they left Rumelli to finish its slumbers in peace. The young men of the town had, in truth, a crow to pick with Don Pio, for having suppressed the fête of the Statuto, and also for having so changed and enfeebled that old favourite of theirs, the Signor Avvocato.

The Marquis and Marchioness knew nothing of this episode until the morrow. The Marchioness first heard all the particulars from Signora Candia, who had had them fresh from no less an authority than Don Pio. Don Pio, entirely silent as to any provocation having been given, represented the whole affair as a premeditated insult to himself; the violence of the assailants might be easily conjectured from the insolent sentences chalked over the parsonage door, "Down with the Codini! down with Don Pio!" Signora Candia had seen this with her own eyes. She felt strongly on the subject and expressed herself strongly, and so did the Signor Avvocato, who could not sufficiently regret that the Castle, by the demonstration it had made, should have set an example which had led to such excesses. The Marchioness, with much warmth, disclaimed any such responsibility, and threw it back upon those who opposed the general feeling of the community. The Castle had simply exercised a right, and fulfilled a duty, with all due moderation. In fact, the only example the Castle had given was that of respect to the laws of the country. If others had done the contrary, they had done so at their risk and peril; if there had been excesses — which, however, she was not inclined to believe — let the proper authorities prosecute the offenders; there was justice for every one in the land, thank God!"

"Except for Ecclesiastics," quoth the old gentleman.

"Indeed, Signor Avvocato, you calumniate your country," was the quick retort.

It made her lose in one instant the place she had secured in his good graces by the attentions of months. But the Marchioness's blood was up.

To widen the split, there came a flaming article in *The Citizen*, the Radical paper of Ibella. It was headed, "*Post tenebras Lux.*" It gave an extravagant description, through three columns and a half, of the fête at the Castle; every item of which — hospitality, illuminations, fireworks, concourse of people, and enthusiasm — was on an unparalleled scale. The conclusion ran thus: —

"Are we to consider this as a mere *ignis fatuus?* "We can answer emphatically, No. We are able to "give all friends of liberty the glad tidings that "Rumelli is definitively gained over to the cause of "progress. We can ask no better voucher of the fact "than the name of Captain Del Palmetto and his "worthy lady, née Signora Ombelli, who have put "themselves frankly at the head of the Liberal party "there. The blighting influences which for the last "two years have preponderated in the village and its "environs have now received their death-blow. We are "happy and proud to be the first to record this fresh "victory of the spirit of the age, a spirit so worthily "represented at Rumelli by the accomplished givers of "a fête which marks a new era in the annals of "that little and interesting community. *Post tenebras* "*Lux*."

Copies of the paper containing this rhapsody were liberally disseminated through the parish. The barber's shop, the chandler's shop, each received one by the post, and so did Don Pio, and the mayor, and the councillors, and all the principal inhabitants; all except the Signor Avvocato, an exception which proved beyond all doubt that the distribution of this number of *The Citizen* must have taken place under the superintendence of the Castle, for the Castle naturally wished to spare the feelings of the Palace. And the fact of the superintendence, once ascertained, of necessity implied the other fact, that the article had been inspired, if not actually composed and written, by the Del Palmettos. The feeling of Rumelli was unanimous on this point, and the earnest denials of the master and mistress of the Castle, who regretted the incident more than anybody, only served to confirm and root more deeply the common sentiment. The only person who dissented was Don Pio, too clear-sighted not to perceive at a glance the flagrant contradiction which existed between this act of open defiance, and the temperate behaviour of the Castle throughout the whole affair. However, it mattered little who had, or who had not, thrown down the gauntlet — it sufficed that it had been thrown, that public opinion indicated a certain party as having thrown it for him to lift it; he must do so, or farewell his authority — and so he did lift it.

Don Pio, on the next Sunday, addressed his flock from the pulpit on the events that had taken place on the preceding Lord's Day. He said he much regretted to have to state that serious disorderly conduct had marked a day especially intended for rest and prayer. Their pastor, in the privacy of his domestic abode, had been made the butt of much coarse abuse and invective, nay, had even been threatened. A furious gang, in the dead of night, had laid a sort of siege to the parsonage, and left on its door, amid vociferations and imprecations worthy of savages — testimonies of the fiendish passions by which they were animated — expressions of hatred and contempt too disgusting to be repeated in a holy place. Don Pio hoped and trusted that none of his parishioners had taken any part in this disgraceful scene; if any of them had, so little was he prompted by resentment that he did not wish to know: he pardoned them from the bottom of his heart. His motive for at all referring to the painful subject was the opportunity it afforded him of deducing from it a practical moral, of pressing upon his hearers a sound piece of advice. Don Pio's piece of advice to his flock was from henceforth not to let themselves be prevailed upon, under any circumstances, to keep any other festivals than those instituted by "our holy mother, the Church." The dangers of a contrary course were too clearly illustrated by the incidents of the Sunday before. In the Church alone was vested the power to establish obligatory fêtes; those imposed by the State were not binding on the conscience. The Church, assisted by the Holy Ghost, was an infallible guide, and as such was to be blindly and implicitly trusted in; whereas the State, with no safer beacon than that Will-o'-the-wisp, called human wisdom, was liable to err, and to lead others into error. Nobody, for instance, was ignorant that under the very shadow of that Statuto (the recurrence of the anniversary of which many would fain make an occasion of rejoicing) unpardonable acts of oppression and spoliation had been committed against both the secular and the regular clergy. . . .

At this point of Don Pio's harangue the Marchioness Del Palmetto rose from her seat, and, followed by her husband, walked out of the church. The sensation created by their sudden exit may be more easily imagined than described. The Curé had to abridge the explanation of the Gospel, and to go through the second part of the Mass in a hurry, so palpable was the impatience of the congregation to be at liberty to discuss the great event. Indeed, it was the talk of all Rumelli, and nowhere was it commented upon and discussed more thoroughly, or with more spirit, than at the Castle itself, where there happened to be on that very day a large dinner-party, exclusively composed of Rumellians, to whom the noble hosts thought themselves bound in common civility to explain the motives of their behaviour that morning. They had gone to church, they said, to be edified, and not to listen to political lucubrations, still less to hear the fundamental law of the land reviled and traduced. Don Pio had no more right to attack the Statuto from the pulpit than a deputy to fall foul of a dogma, or to preach a schism from his seat in Parliament. It was much against the grain that they had left so abruptly, but on no account would they even for a moment seem to countenance by their presence, language against which their consciences protested. No, never again would they set foot in a church, where party spirit instead of the spirit of the Gospel, inspired the language held in the pulpit. This, and much more that they added, the Marquis and Marchioness knew full well would be reported to Don Pio by some of those present, and they were not sorry for it; nor did they in the least shrink from saying it all to Don Pio's face on the very first opportunity that occurred.

From this day the rupture between the Castle and the Parsonage was complete. Faithful to their word, the Del Palmettos never again set foot in the parish church, but went regularly to Ibella to hear mass on all succeeding Sundays and fête-days. Del Palmetto again took up, and with renewed vigour, his lately abandoned scheme of the National Guard — this time with perfect success. Next Easter was too far off as yet to serve as a scarecrow, and Don Pio had the mortification of seeing his noble antagonist — who of course had been elected captain — drilling his men in the Church Square on every Saturday afternoon. An active canvass was also begun, and vigorously pursued, the avowed object of which was the ousting of the *Piani* (the adherents of Don Pio) from the Town Council, and filling their places by *Marchesotti* (as the partisans of the Castle had been nicknamed), at the next election of 1858. By this time those Piani who had still continued to visit at the Castle after the rupture, had gradually withdrawn, and the Castle had become what the Marquis had meant to make it from the beginning, the head-quarters of the Opposition.

Meanwhile the intercourse between the Castle and the Palace lived on as well as it could, or rather, as well as the Castle's firm determination not to let it die, could keep it alive. The visits of the Del Palmettos, those especially of the Marchioness, met, indeed, with little encouragement in a region so devoted to Don Pio; but so long as they lasted they accounted for, and, so to speak, justified the daily ones paid by Vincenzo to the Castle, and which were positive life to him. Vincenzo had necessarily experienced at home the recoil of the passions which were rending peaceful Rumelli in twain — dividing it into two hostile camps. What did he care? What did a few pin-pricks matter to him, the spoiled child of a friendship as pure as it was elevated? The Castle was his real home — there, he felt among his own, in that sympathetic atmosphere alone did his intellectual and affective lungs — we, each of us have a pair somewhere — breathe and expand freely; his looks were less wan, his breath less short, his step less heavy, than some months before had been the case. The very excitement of the strife going on around him did him good; he could not help taking some interest in it, though convinced it would burst like a bubble the moment those who had produced it should be gone. Were they, then, about to go? Alas! yes. Del Palmetto's five months' leave of absence expired with the month of August. The time for their departure drew nearer and nearer — it came at last.

The Marchioness would not go away without making a last effort in Vincenzo's behalf, or rather without accomplishing what she considered a duty. One day that she found Rose alone, she gave her, with the utmost prudence and gentleness, some hints as to the delicate state of Vincenzo's health. She was sure, that Signora Candia must have remarked how little he ate, and how easily he was put out of breath. Did she not think that a change of air and scene, and perhaps some agreeable and regular occupation, might prove beneficial to him? There were certain organizations, certain temperaments — the Marchioness had known of such — for which work of some kind or other was a condition, *sine qua non*, of good health.

Signora Candia answered that her husband had always been more or less delicate, nor had she noticed any change in him for the worse, though, truth to say, she had seen so little of him lately that, of the two, the Marchioness must be a better judge than herself of how he was. If Signor Candia wished for change of air, no one detained him at home — he was free to go; and why should he not avail himself of the present opportunity to do so, in such excellent company?

The Marchioness chose not to perceive the palpable irony of the suggestion, and replied, with great coolness, "Had Signor Candia expressed any wish to accompany us, we should be only too happy to have his society; but he has said nothing of the kind; we are only his friends, and do not consider ourselves entitled to interfere in so delicate a matter, or to give advice which by right ought to come from those nearer and dearer to him. After all, since you feel no uneasiness on Signor Candia's account, I take it for granted that you know best, and that there is no ground for anxiety. All I have to do is to beg you to forgive me for having broached so disagreeable a subject."

This interview impressed upon the Marchioness's mind the double conviction, that Signora Candia loved her husband enough to be jealous of him, and that the hint she had thrown out in reference to Vincenzo's health was not likely to be lost. And thus she was a little re-assured as to Vincenzo's future welfare. We pass over the parting hour; it was painful to those who went; to him who remained, it was awful. The offers of service which the Del Palmettos pressed on their friend were as unlimited as they were cordial and sincere.

"If ever you alter your mind, and feel inclined to give your country the benefit of your labour, remember you have only a line to write, and a place worthy of your talents will be ready for you at any moment." Such were the parting words of the Marchioness to Candia.

CHAPTER XVI.

The Great Peacemaker.

On the morrow, when the usual hour for his going to the Castle arrived, Vincenzo. . . . But what is the use of entering into any detailed account of his misery? The task is too sickening for us to undertake it. Suffice it to say that Vincenzo felt as if he had never before known what it was to be alone and miserable and hopeless. For the following three months his mind and body were in a continuous state of collapse. He was perfectly conscious of the fact, and anything but sorry for it.

On a wet day in early December, it might be four o'clock in the afternoon, Vincenzo was lying on his bed, dreaming wide awake, as usual, when he was startled out of his reverie by a succession of piercing screams from Rose. He hurried down stairs, went into his wife's apartment — it was empty — rushed to that of the Signor Avvocato; ran through the two first rooms, and in the third and last, he came upon a sight which for an instant made his tongue cleave to the roof of his mouth. Stretched at full length on the floor, near the foot of the bed, lay the ponderous form of the Signor Avvocato, to all appearance lifeless; Rose was kneeling by his side trying to lift up his head. "Quick, for Don Pio, somebody, run directly for Don Pio." Such were her first words at the sound of approaching footsteps; she could not see who had come, her back being turned to the door. The excitement of the moment supplied Vincenzo with energies, of which five seconds before he would not have believed himself capable. He snatched the pillows off the bed, pushed them under the prostrate head, flew into the next room, opened the window, shouted for help, and in a twinkling was again standing by his godfather.

"How did it happen?" he asked.

"I don't know," was Rose's answer. "It might have been three o'clock when I left Papa; he begged me to go away, as he felt so heavy and drowsy, and inclined to sleep. I went down stairs to count over some linen, which took me rather a long time. I was listening all the while though, for any noise overhead. I heard none whatever. When I came up about an hour after . . . . ." sobs here stopped her utterance. The household were now flocking in one after the other — the cook, the housemaid, Marianna, Giuseppe, were all there. "Quick, quick, go for Don Pio," Rose kept on repeating; but not one of the servants stirred; they seemed spell-bound, the women already beginning to wail.

"Hush!" cried Vincenzo; "instead of weeping, make yourselves useful; bring me some cold water and some vinegar. You, Giuseppe, look sharp, take the carriage and drive to Ibella, as if for your life, and bring back with you Doctor B. or Doctor N.; or stay, better bring them both. You, Carlo, take the gig to Rumelli; go first to the Parsonage, and tell Don Pio he is wanted at the Palace in a hurry; tell him why, but don't stop for him — make all haste to old Geronimo, and bring him and his lancet-case here at full gallop. The quicker you are, the greater the chances of saving your master's life." Then turning to Barnaby, who might think himself ill-used if he had nothing to do (only that poor Barnaby was too terror-stricken to think of anything but his master), Vincenzo added, "Come by me, Barnaby, we want your help;" and, Barnaby was made to assist prominently in the application of the usual restoratives in such cases — too familiar for us to spend any words in describing them. They proved fruitless. The old gentleman's teeth being tightly locked, there was no possibility of forcing any cordial down his throat.

The first of all the persons sent for who made his

appearance was naturally old Geronimo. Why so called, considering he was old neither in age nor looks, we cannot say, unless it were on account of his proverbial taciturnity.

Old Geronimo was a retired army surgeon of that inferior class — now, we believe, done away with — which went under the name of phlebotomists, and whose only business was to bleed and apply leeches. He asked no questions, but, going straight to the unconscious Signor Avvocato, knelt down by him, and began with a large pair of scissors to slit up the left-arm sleeve of his dressing-gown and those of his shirt and flannel waistcoat.

"Are you going to bleed him?" asked Rose, in some alarm. Old Geronimo turned his eyes on her, as much as to say, "For what else was I brought here?" and then coolly proceeded with his preparations; which being finished, he opened a vein, and let the blood flow freely. At this juncture, Don Pio stole in on tiptoe. Rose went up to him, and, drawing him into a corner, said something to him in a whisper, and then resumed her place by her father. Don Pio followed her; inspected the patient closely, felt his pulse, his hands and feet, and nodded affirmatively to her. She had asked him whether he thought it had been right to bleed her father. The taking away of blood had, however, worked no change for the better; the Signor Avvocato lay motionless as before, to all appearance dead or dying. Don Pio, after repeatedly leaning over his face, put on his stole and began reciting the prayers for those in the agony of death. Rose, on her knees to the right of her father, tried in vain to repress her sobs; near her was old Geronimo, his eyes fixed on the Signor Avvocato. Vincenzo and Barnaby stood on the left; they were scarcely less moved than the sobbing daughter. Grouped in the background were the servants, some terrified, some loudly weeping. The scene was the exact reproduction of Vincenzo's dream at Turin; with this difference, however, that he was at the Palace — and oh! what a comfort it was to him to be there!

At the end of twenty interminable minutes of this awful suspense, the pale lips began to quiver — a pin might have been heard to drop — but there issued forth no sound. Old Geronimo speedily forced a spoon, full of some cordial, between the half-opened teeth — this was swallowed, thank God; then the eyes half-opened, but only to close again and then again; at last they remained wide open, and stared slowly round. They had a distracted look as they travelled from face to face; the moment they fell upon that of Vincenzo, the wildness in them softened, the rigidity of the countenance relaxed by degrees, especially about the mouth, and melted into a sweet smile. Had the expression of intense agony convulsing his son-in-law's features gone straight to the old man's heart and conquered it anew? or had his apoplexy struck off the tablets of his memory a whole set of relatively recent disagreeable impressions, leaving associations of a far older date, and far more agreeable also, intact and fresh? just as lightning will strike dead some young branches, leaving alive some old ones on the same tree.

Vincenzo, who was not prepared for this change, in a transport of tenderness leaned forward over his father-in-law, threw both arms round his neck, and kissed him on the forehead. At sight of this act a murmur of pleasure ran through the room, and all eyes moistened. Rose spoke cheerfully to her father, and so did Don Pio. The Signor Avvocato listened to them, nodded his head, would fain have spoken, as was evident from the motion of his lips, but could form no articulate sound — nothing save that bubbling noise which persons shuddering with cold are apt to make.

All this time the old gentleman was lying on the bare ground — too uncomfortable a position for him to be left in; and yet to lift so ponderous a body as the Signor Avvocato's on to the bed not only offered serious difficulties of accomplishment, but might be fatally injurious to one still labouring under such an alarming attack. Old Geronimo, in this dilemma, brought his experience of similar cases into play; he suggested that a couple of mattresses should be laid on the floor, and then the patient slipped gently upon them — an operation which required the united exertions of all present, but which was safely managed. They then proceeded to make this temporary couch as comfortable as circumstances would permit; and then Rose dismissed the servants, with the exception of Barnaby, and she and Don Pio, Geronimo, Vincenzo, and the old gardener, brought chairs and sat round the shake-down, keeping silent watch over the old gentleman, who lay very quiet; giving no indication whatever of being in pain. Indeed, he dozed almost constantly, awoke from time to time with a slight start, his eyes wandering with a restless expression, which vanished whenever his glance fell on Vincenzo. He would then again drop off to sleep.

At nine in the evening Giuseppe returned from Ibella with one of the doctors sent for, who immediately proceeded to a careful examination of the patient, in the course of which he put several questions to him, which met with no more articulate answer than the bubbling sound mentioned above. The doctor, in reply to Rose's anxious inquiries, said that she need not be so much alarmed by this symptom, which, nine times out of ten, was only temporary; it was rare that, in cases of congestion, the nerves presiding over the functions of speech should not be more or less affected. The doctor, on the whole, seemed tolerably easy about the old gentleman; his having been so promptly bled had been of the greatest service — had, indeed, probably saved his life. There was nothing more to be done for the present — absolute abstinence from food, although drink might be given in moderation if asked for; this was all. Should any new symptoms be observed during the night, he begged he might be immediately called; otherwise there was no necessity for his seeing the patient before the morning; and then the doctor said good night, and retired to the room which had been prepared for him. Don Pio and old Geronimo took their leave. Vincenzo and Barnaby each put a mattress on the floor, and lay down dressed as they were. Vincenzo was dead tired. Rose had a bed made up for herself in the adjoining room, and half an hour afterwards the house was as silent as if it were uninhabited.

The Signor Avvocato passed a good night. The doctor was very early by the sick-bed, and this time subjected his patient to a far more minute and close examination than that of the previous night. Vincenzo observed, among other things, that the doctor, keeping his eyes firmly rivetted all the while on the Signor Avvocato's countenance, pinched and stroked his legs and arms very hard; not a muscle of the sick man's face moved. The doctor's fiat, nevertheless, was, or at least sounded, altogether reassuring. No fever, no plethora, no coma, no difficulty of respiration. The nervous centres, it was true, had not yet recovered from the shock that they had sustained, nor would do so, in all likelihood, yet a while. Science might do a little to hasten the salutary action of time, and to this effect he recommended the immediate application of a blister to the nape of the neck, and frictions with flannel along the spine thrice a day, each friction to last a quarter of an hour. Light food was to be given occasionally, always in small quantities; no wine or other stimulant at all. Should the Signor Avvocato (it was better to be prepared for all contingencies) grow suddenly restless, and also become red in the face, with red streaks in the eye-balls, the lancet must be had recourse to without delay. But he hoped there would be no necessity for that. If everything went on well, he saw no objection to the old gentleman being lifted — of course, as gently as possible — and placed in his bed towards the afternoon; and, winding up with the promise of returning on the morrow, the doctor made his bow. Vincenzo and Rose accompanied him, with many thanks, down the stairs. While doing this, Vincenzo felt a light tap on his shoulder from the doctor, who was behind him, which he interpreted at once as a sign that the medical man wished to speak to him in private. The doctor, in fact, desired Giuseppe, who was already at the bottom of the perron with the carriage, to go and wait for him at the gate of the avenue. "I feel rather stiff," he added, "and I shall be better for a little walk." Vincenzo insisted on accompanying him, and Rose left them.

As soon as they had cleared the flight of steps leading into the avenue, the doctor, passing his arm under Vincenzo's, said, "Do you know whether your father-in-law has made any arrangements — I mean, made his will?"

"Indeed, I have not the least idea," gasped Vincenzo, horrified. "Why do you ask?"

"In case he has not done so, to impress upon you the urgency of getting him to do it the moment he recovers his speech, if he ever should."

"Is he, then, in danger?" exclaimed Vincenzo.

"For the moment, no more than you or I — but — you are a man, and I may speak frankly to you — but I do not believe he will survive a second attack, and I am sorry to say a second attack is inevitable."

"Inevitable?" repeated Vincenzo; "can you, then, do nothing to avert it?"

"Alas! I could martyrize him to no purpose, and that is what I will not do. He is paralyzed from head to foot, his nervous system is shattered — don't you see that his intelligence is already obscured, and will grow more so every day. I am grieved to be obliged to distress you, but .... forewarned is forearmed. It is in your interest that I speak."

"I have only one interest — that he should live," returned Vincenzo.

"In that case, recommend him to God Almighty,

who alone can work a miracle. Hullo! what's the matter with you?"

Vincenzo, what with emotion and the exertion of walking, was nearly exhausted, and had to stop to recover his breath.

"You are yourself ill, my dear sir," exclaimed the Doctor; "I can scarcely find your pulse. Take my advice; turn back and go to your bed at once."

"I don't feel ill, only weak; it's of no consequence," said Vincenzo.

"I beg your pardon; weakness, when it reaches this degree, constitutes an illness of itself. Go to your bed, I say."

"That's impossible just now."

"Well, at least, do not over-exert yourself; above all, don't sit up late at night; I positively forbid it. There are people enough at the Palace to nurse your father-in-law without you. Follow my advice, I beg of you; and good-bye for the present."

The Doctor jumped into the carriage, and Vincenzo went up the Avenue again, with heavy tottering steps, and a still heavier heart. He might have been absent half an hour. Rose met him at the door of the sick-room:

"How long you have been, Vincenzo! Papa has been fretting after you all this time."

It was quite a novelty for Vincenzo to hear himself addressed by his christian name, and in so gentle a tone. The Signor Avvocato's face was slightly flushed; there was a frown on his brow and anger in his eyes. Vincenzo hurried forwards, and, leaning over him, stroked his forehead, speaking at the same time cheerfully and kindly: as if by magic, the wrinkled brow grew smooth again, and the eyes and mouth smiled. Don Pio called early and stayed for some hours, now and then addressing words of encouragement, or pious exhortations, to the sick man, who, truth to say, hardly seemed to heed the Curé at all. The Signor Avvocato ate with evident pleasure the little that was given him; Vincenzo it was who had to put the food into his mouth, and, so long as he could see Vincenzo, he lay quiet, with a look of contentment — save, indeed, when the operation of transferring to the bed the mattress, with him on it, was undertaken, a change of which he expressed his disapprobation as explicitly as a dumb man might, and to which all Vincenzo's caressing words and smiles could scarcely reconcile him. Vincenzo, Rose, and Barnaby, took their meals on a small table placed close to the bed. That Barnaby should so easily be prevailed upon to sit at table with his young mistress — he who had resisted the entreaties to do so of two generations of his masters — was another decisive proof that the good old fellow had fairly broken down.

Days swelled into weeks without bringing any amendment in the patient's power of speech, or of understanding. The doctor from Ibella called regularly three times a week, professed himself satisfied with the Signor Avvocato's state, and for the rest, inculcated patience and a reliance on the action of time. Dr. Moreri, who had been telegraphed for, came from Turin, approved of all that had been done by his medical brother of Ibella, delivered a sort of lecture upon the sluggishness of the nervous centres, once interfered with, to resume their functions, and further spoke of the mud-baths at Acqui as worth trying in the spring. "But it was a long while yet to spring," observed Rose; "in the meantime, might her father leave his bed?" Certainly, he not only might but ought to do so, always provided he was properly attended to, and care was taken not to shake or fatigue him. Signora Candia must not anticipate the possibility of her father being able to stand; but he might be able to sit in a half-recumbent position, less fatiguing than always lying at length. At Turin, under the Portici of la Fiera, there were to be had couches on castors, a new invention for invalids, which, by a very gentle pressure, could be raised or lowered at will. Perhaps, the Signor Avvocato being uncommonly bulky, it might not be easy to find one of these couches to suit him ready made, but one could be ordered.

Signora Candia had all the requisite measurements taken, went to Turin herself, and ordered one of these invalid chairs, which, thanks to the extra price she volunteered to give, was finished in a relatively short time and sent to Rumelli. It was wheeled in triumph into the sick-room, shown to the Signor Avvocato, and its use and intention explained to him — the comfort it would be to him to change his position by sitting in it enlarged upon, all to his seeming satisfaction, so long as the demonstration was confined to theory; but, when the moment arrived for putting the theory into practice, and the first step to that end was taken by dressing the old gentleman, such was the horror he betrayed at the novelty, he grew so cross and excited and red in the face, that, from fear of consequences, the attempt had to be given up; nor could he be restored to his usual tranquillity and serenity, until the obnoxious piece of furniture was removed out of his sight.

It must be here noted that full three weeks had now elapsed since the Signor Avvocato's seizure, and communication with him — such communication, at least, as could be had with a speechless person — had become somewhat more easy to those in constant attendance upon him. Rose, Vincenzo, and Don Pio — (Barnaby was too deaf and too stunned to have much perception of anything) — had come by dint of habit to fix a precise meaning to each of the inarticulate sounds emitted by the sick man. They knew, for instance, by the peculiar intonation, when it was his daughter or Vincenzo that he wanted, when he wished for food or drink, when he meant yes or no, enough or more, &c. As to how far his comprehension went of what others said, there was a great difference of opinion. Vincenzo thought that he understood very little; Don Pio, that he understood a good deal, especially on certain days; and Rose, that he comprehended everything and always; but with her the wish was probably father to the belief. Rose was most anxious that her father should receive the Sacrament; but this he could not do without having first confessed, and confess he could not, unless he was in the full enjoyment of his understanding. The terror lest he should die without having taken the Sacrament had been haunting her, day and night, ever since his illness.

One thing was certain, that Don Pio, in his character of the Signor Avvocato's spiritual guide, was the most competent judge as to whether his penitent was in a befitting condition or not for confession; and Don Pio, one morning, declared his penitent to be lucid enough for that purpose. Accordingly, Vincenzo was requested to leave the room, which he did; not, however, without observing that the Signor Avvocato's medical man ought first to have been consulted as to the safety of the step. Rose answered this objection by affirming that she had asked and obtained the physician's authorization long ago. There was nothing more to say, and so the confession was proceeded with. When, after the interval of a good half-hour, Vincenzo was again admitted, he found his godfather dreadfully excited, and he had to use all his influence to soothe him into calmness again. Seeing this, he urged the expediency of putting off the Communion to the morrow. Rose explained that this could not be done, Don Pio having already gone to fetch the Host. Vincenzo then entreated her to go, and herself see that there was no ringing of the bell within hearing of the sick room, and also to give orders that no one should enter it, not even the house; no one, in fact, except Don Pio. Rose willingly agreed to follow his advice. Owing to these precautions, and, probably, yet more to Vincenzo's presence and gentle encouragement, the Sacrament was administered without any impediment — indeed, without the Signor Avvocato betraying any special uneasiness. We need hardly mention that all Rumelli had accompanied the Host to the Palace — those of the inhabitants who happened to be at work in the fields hastening, at the sound of the Communion-bell, to join the impromptu procession. It required all Don Pio's authority, and Signora Rose's popularity, to keep the crowd from entering the house; the feminine portion being almost frantic with disappointment at this deprivation of what they considered their right. In small rural places, it is, in fact, a sort of right, based on custom, for neighbours to go and have a peep at the dying persons on the occasion of their receiving the Eucharist.

Up to this day the godfather's predilection for his godson had made the latter somewhat of a slave; from this day he literally and altogether became the old man's victim. No respite for Vincenzo by day or by night — the Signor Avvocato could not bear to lose sight of him for a moment. There was the waywardness of a child to manage, and the wants of an infirm old man to minister to. The Signor Avvocato generally slept from nine or ten in the evening to three or four o'clock in the morning; and, as he could not bear to remain alone, the moment he awoke he summoned Vincenzo to his side. He was not difficult, it is true, as to the diversions chosen for his amusement. Vincenzo had only to show him the pictures in a book, or to read aloud to him, or even merely to sit by the bed, and speak to him from time to time, to make the old gentleman look quite contented. But even this entailed on Vincenzo an almost total loss of sleep; for, in his state of nervous excitement, the result of anxiety and exhaustion, it was seldom that he fell asleep before midnight, or even one in the morning. Indeed he never, any night, laid himself down on his mattress, without asking himself, with terror, whether he should be equal to getting up on the morrow, and praying God that it might be so. Rose, with the best will in the world, could do nothing to relieve her husband; if she went, instead of him, to answer her father's call, an angry jerk of the sick man's head warned her that she was not the one he wanted. Rose was evidently uneasy about Vincenzo's health. Supposing that the Marchioness's broad hints on that score had produced no effect, the doctor's reiterated warnings to Vincenzo against sitting up late at night at all events had.

Rose was now thoroughly awake to the dangers of over-exertion for her husband, and more than once lately he had caught her eye fixed on him full of a tender anxiety. Could it be that the Marchioness's conjectures were well-founded, and that the partiality shown for him by a young and handsome woman had awakened Signora Candia to a sense of her husband's merits? Or was it the revival of her father's fondness for his godson, and the rich return it met with, which had pleaded in his favour and touched her heart? Whatever the cause, or causes — and each of those we have enumerated had, probably, its share in the result — the fact is that Rose's feelings were singularly softened towards her husband.

As to poor Barnaby, his part in the sick room was more that of an incumbrance than a help. It seemed as if the same stroke which had rendered his master speechless and motionless, had done the same to him. He would sit for hours, his hands on his knees, looking about him vacantly, like a man in a dream. When he got up from his seat, which he did with difficulty, it was to shuffle along, bent double, here and there, without any apparent object but that of making himself believe that he was of some use, and then he would sit down again and relapse into listlessness. Perhaps if Rose, or Vincenzo, or Don Pio, or indeed any one belonging to the household, came in his way, he would whisper a question, always the same — "Do you think he will ever come round?" immediately adding, "I don't." These were the only words that had passed his lips since the fatal evening; at the same time he kept his watch faithfully, even to the last, like a *sentinel perdu.* Vincenzo could not help a tear at sight of the good old man, his own faithful friend, so sadly broken down.

One very stormy night, late in January, that Vincenzo could not sleep, less from the noise of the incessant peals of thunder than from the effects on his shattered nerves of the electricity in the air, he saw, by the glare of a flash of lightning, the Signor Avvocato start up with a sudden jerk, as though he strove to assume a sitting posture. Vincenzo sprang to the bed, and found his godfather with his head hanging over the side, and quite black in the face. In an instant he had given the alarm, and the whole house was on foot. Old Geronimo and Don Pio were sent for; and, in the meanwhile, water and cordials, and strong scents were tried, in the desperate hope of restoring the old gentleman's consciousness. This time Geronimo's lancet was of no avail. The Signor Avvocato was dead.

Don Pio and Rose remained the whole night in prayer by the corpse. Vincenzo, who would fain have done the same, before long fell into a deep sleep, and was removed to a bed in the adjoining room. Amid the general bewilderment caused by the fatal event, nobody had thought of Barnaby, who continued to lie quietly on his mattress. At break of day Rose went and called him. No answer. She then touched him on the shoulder. Barnaby was stiff dead. God in His mercy had spared the affectionate old servant the trial he had most dreaded — that of seeing his master die first.

CHAPTER XVII.

Rose seen to Advantage.

BARNABY shared in all the honours paid to his master. The two bodies lay in state in the same room, open to the public, and there was a never-ceasing flock of visitors on the next day, and the one following up to ten in the forenoon, the hour appointed for the double interment at the parish church. Vincenzo, though scarcely able to stand, could not be dissuaded from attending, and drove to Rumelli with his wife. The funeral was on the most splendid scale. The whole church was hung with black, and masses for the souls of the departed, succeeded each other without intermission at all the altars. The concourse of people — not counting the Rumellians, who were there to a man — was very great, especially from Ibella. The Del Palmettos had come on purpose from Turin. Rose was the more overcome by this mark of respect and interest from them, that she did not expect it, that indeed she had done nothing to incite it, not even sent any announcement of her father's death, and it was a touching episode of this sad drama, and which left few eyes dry, when the bereaved daughter, in her deep mourning, threw herself on the neck of the Marchioness and, in default of speech, sobbed aloud on her bosom.

Another and still more painful incident threw an increased gloom on a ceremony, lugubrious enough in itself. Vincenzo had presumed too much on his strength, and it had failed him. He fainted away, and had to be conveyed home and consigned to his bed. Fortunately, the Ibella physician, who had been in attendance at the Palace, was present, and could render immediate assistance. "It was a case of marasmus," said the doctor, "and he regretted to have to add, of confirmed marasmus. He had warned Signor Candia already more than once, but his advice had been unheeded, and here was the consequence. None of the vital organs, so far as he could judge, seemed in any way damaged; it was their action, languid in the extreme, which was faulty; the lamp was whole, but the oil was wanting. The doctor wound up by saying, he apprehended no danger just at present, but . . . ." That *but* was pregnant with a frightful significancy. Rose threw herself at the doctor's feet in a paroxysm of terror. "For God's sake, Doctor, save him! oh! save him — take my fortune — all I have; but don't let him die, so young, so — Oh! it's too horrible — I cannot bear it." The doctor answered that no doubt he would do all he could for the invalid; the first step was to put him in a state that would enable him to bear a journey to the sea-side, without danger. Sea-air alone, if anything, could restore his stamina. Sea-air, yes, and unremitting care; without this last desideratum the other would be insufficient — Signor Candia needed devoted, persevering care — not a minute relaxed in — the care of a mother for a sick babe. The physician had apparently his own reasons for insisting on this point. Rose said simply — such care her husband should have.

Within a couple of weeks the doctor pronounced that, with due precautions and with several rests on the road, Vincenzo was able to undertake the journey, not a long one after all; as to go from Rumelli to Genoa was not over twelve hours by railway. But Vincenzo did not wish to go, could not bear the thought of moving. A benumbed traveller, who has dropped by the side of the road in a snow-storm, has not a greater horror of exertion than had Vincenzo. His wife had to beg the Marchioness to help her to overcome his resistance, which was successfully effected. The Marchioness, unwilling to leave the neighbourhood while Signora Candia was in the first bitterness of her grief, had stayed all this time at the Castle; duty had obliged Del Palmetto to return to Turin the day after the funeral. The Marchioness watched for every opportunity to make herself useful, and she could be so in many ways, among others, by writing and securing an eligible house by the sea-side, as well as the services of a trusty hospital attendant, who had much experience in the management of invalids. And when the time came for the move, she preceded the travellers to Turin, and was at the terminus on their arrival to take them in her carriage to the nearest hotel, where rooms had been bespoken, and beds prepared, and fires lighted, in short every possible arrangement for comfort made. And when they started for Genoa on the next day but one, the Marchioness accompanied them to the railway, and obtained their immediate admission into the coupé purposely arranged with pillows and wrappers and furs; small attentions not much thought of by the strong and healthy, but of which those ailing or those attending some dear invalid, know the full value. Rose's heart overflowed with gratitude, unmixed gratitude; she felt towards this Good Samaritan very differently from what she had done at their last interview in August, and she expressed what she felt. As to Candia himself, he was too weak to notice, or if he noticed, to heed, what was passing round him.

The husband and wife, with the attendant, reached their destination on one of the last days of February. The weather was as mild and lovely as if it had been May, the air embalmed with the fragrance of orange-flowers. Nobody will wonder at this who knows Nervi, and its sheltered position on the eastern Riviera of Genoa. The little casino hired for them by the Marchioness was situated to the east of the small town, at the distance of a quarter of an hour's walk; on a diminutive promontory overhanging the sea. It had a small garden and an open lobby or gallery on the side next to the sea, with a short flight of steps leading down to the beach. Short of choosing a vessel afloat for an abode, no situation could be more exposed to the strengthening emanations of the sea.

We have just left one sick room, and have no intention of detaining the reader long in another; we will tarry in Vincenzo's only the time indispensable for the ascertaining a few facts essential to the comprehension of the little that remains of our story. Rose, to begin with, performed the mission she had taken on herself with admirable skill and devotion; no mother could have been more assiduous, more tender in her care of a dear fragile babe, nor more full of contrivances to soothe, nor more anxious to comfort, than Rose was to comfort and soothe this big husband of hers, who in many respects was as helpless as an infant. Nor was this unremitting care unrequited, and in more senses than one. Vincenzo's health mended slowly, very slowly, but mended enough to dispel all fear that the sword of death, hitherto suspended over his head, should fall upon it. To give an idea of the snail's-pace at which his convalescence went on, we will only note that it took him three whole months before he could walk up and down the garden, and more than five before he could venture to the beach.

It is said, and I think with truth, that mothers cling most tenderly to those of their children whose rearing has cost them the most pain and trouble. We suppose that it was in virtue of a sentiment somewhat akin to this, that Rose's devotion to her husband grew in strength, in proportion to his want of her, to her sacrifices for him, to the use of which she felt herself to be. The late sad events had admirably prepared the ground for this transformation of Rose's feelings. The part of guardian angel Vincenzo had played towards her father, the fact that he was indissolubly mixed up with all her last recollections of that adored departed one, his utter disregard of self, which had so nearly cost him his life, all these were new and powerful holds on her heart; and yet, not until she had seen him struck down, helpless, dependent as a child on her — not until she had realized that she could be all that she was to him — not until then was she seized upon by the impetus of that immense tenderness which changes duty into choice, sacrifices into joys; which transfuses, as it were, one existence into another. That he should live, that he should be happy — henceforth Rose had no other aim, no other interest in life. And he, the object of all this solicitude; he, the spoilt child, so gently lulled on that motherly lap, how could he feel otherwise than compenetrated by so much affection, thankful for it, blessed by it? It was long ago — from that day, indeed, on which his godfather, from his bed of suffering, smiled on him again — it was long ago since all resentment for past wrongs had vanished from Vincenzo's heart, and even the remembrance of them, day by day, grew more indistinct, as of things which had only been dreamed. In his morbidly languid state of mind and body, he felt like one roused from a distressing nightmare to sweet everyday realities. It seemed to him as though between the gentle wife who nursed him so tenderly, and the sweet girl who had tended him so carefully in his convalescence after his bad fever some five years ago, there was no solution of continuity, the one was but the complement of the other. Strange, how obstinately his mind would recur to that period. Strange, how vividly he recollected all, even to the least token of partiality which she had then vouchsafed him. And as naturally as sound comes forth from a chord that is struck, so also from these recollections, so fondly dwelt upon, were evolved the sentiments of the time to which they belonged. Vincenzo was going over again his days of courtship.

As soon as Vincenzo had rallied enough to talk at length on any interesting subject, the almost exclusive theme of conversation between husband and wife was, of course, the Signor Avvocato. This proved a new link, which drew them closer and closer together. Death had divested the venerable figure of all its harsh lines, and thrown a halo round those, which gratitude for early kindness and beneficence had engraved on Vincenzo's memory. A son by birth could not have felt and spoken about his own father with more tender reverence than did Vincenzo of his father by adoption. He never tired of enumerating over and over again, one by one, all the benefits he had received from him. Vincenzo and Rose vied with each other in their worship of the Signor Avvocato's memory — only Rose, in addition, never failed to enlarge on the incalculable blessing that Vincenzo had been to her father, always, but most especially during his last illness. Now that Vincenzo was able to bear the suggestion, Rose told him of her great wish that a monument should be erected to her father in Rumelli churchyard; the idea was enthusiastically taken up by Vincenzo, who never more than then regretted his inability to draw. He gave her his notions on the subject, however, and mentioned such rising sculptors at Turin as might be safely entrusted with the execution. The discussing of this project was to both a soothing and constant occupation for months together. On the monument, beneath that of his late master, Barnaby's name was of course to take its place, as it naturally did in all the talks about that dear departed master of his. Need we say that it was never pronounced but with feelings of affectionate respect and regret, more particularly by Vincenzo, who had contracted a new debt of gratitude to his old and tried friend, since his death. By his will, deposited with a notary at Ibella, Barnaby had made Vincenzo sole heir to all his, not inconsiderable, savings.

Rose knew full well that her husband could no more do without mental than without material food; so when she judged him equal to the exertion of reading, she wrote to the Marchioness, with whom she occasionally corresponded, requesting her to send such newspapers, pamphlets, reviews, and books, as the Marchioness thought likely to suit Vincenzo's taste, and to interest him. And thus it came to pass that early one morning Rose went to her husband, with her apron full of papers and books of all sizes, which she scattered on the bed, and said, in answer to his look of marked interrogation, "Have I not guessed right, that you would be glad to see how things were going on in the world?"

"Yes," replied Vincenzo, "but it is not a pleasure I would buy at the price of the smallest discomfort to you."

"I wish it to be clearly understood between us," said Rose, "that nothing which gives you pleasure can give me discomfort. Only don't read too much at a time, and when you get tired, promise to tell me, and to let me read aloud to you."

Vincenzo promised. Severed as he had been for months from all knowledge of foreign or home news, his morning and evening paper were, indeed, an immense boon — but far more precious in his eyes was the phase of toleration, which Rose's spontaneous kindness in the matter so clearly showed. She often read aloud to him, and sometimes articles in which the clerical party was severely taken to task, without wincing.

Rose's next step, as her husband gained additional strength, was to introduce to him, one at a time, such of the acquaintances she had made, as she fancied would be most congenial and agreeable to him. She had plenty of choice; for nearly all the occupants of the neighbouring casini — and they were numerous — had evinced the greatest interest and sympathy for the young invalid, whom they had seen carried into the little house in a seemingly dying state. There had been no end to the calling and to the inquiring after him. Rose made her selection quietly. Three or four of these kind neighbours — the quietest and best informed, as far as Rose could judge — she invited to come for an hour or so on such and such a day, thus affording Vincenzo a wholesome and agreeable change. They were all welcome, as they deserved to be — still Vincenzo had his favourite among them. This was a young and rather consumptive German, who had been ordered to the sea-side for the benefit of his health. The similarity of their situation would of itself alone have attracted the two young men towards each other, even had not another and still more powerful link existed between them — this was their common love of Italy. Herr Wolfgang had been betrothed to a young Italian girl, whom he tenderly loved. She had died in the flower of her youth, and he had transferred all his devotion and passion for her to her country. This enthusiast felt and spoke to all intents and purposes like an Italian, and accordingly watched with an eagerness and intensity, not second even to that of Vincenzo, the signs of the times, which were, if ever, towards the last half of the year 1858, pregnant with decisive events for the destiny of the peninsula. The nature of the conversations between the two young men may easily be guessed; it was such as would, at other seasons, have made Rose draw back in disgust, and hate this new friend of her husband's. No such thing now. She listened now to what they had to say without ever, by word or gesture, showing the least disapproval or dissatisfaction; and to Herr Wolfgang she was specially courteous — nay, cordial in the extreme. Was Rose, then, a convert? Yes, as to the necessity of letting her husband think, and speak, and act, according to his own feelings, so that he might live and be happy. Wolfgang had just finished writing a book — the fruits of his forced leisure — on the subject, or rather, to be precise, against the temporal sovereignty of the pope, which he held to be, with Dante, Petrarca, and Machiavelli, to quote only the highest among ancient authorities, the great stumbling-block in the way of Italian independence and unity. He was now collecting materials for an appendix, which was to consist of quotations in support of his view of the question, most of them from the above-named writers. These quotations, given in their original text, had also to be translated into German — the book being written in German. In this last part of his task Wolfgang had often to apply to his friend for elucidation of the Italian text, which Vincenzo was not only willing but perfectly qualified to give, for he was familiar with most of the passages in Dante bearing upon that vexed question; and as to Petrarca's famous sonnets against Rome, he knew them entirely by heart. But there arose a difficulty now and then not so easy to be surmounted. Supposing the exact sense of an Italian phrase or word ascertained, there remained to be seen whether the German phrase or word into which it was translated was really the best equivalent. Wolfgang, who was conscientiousness itself, could not help continually starting such doubts, which Vincenzo, being ignorant of German, could not solve, save by analogies deduced from his knowledge of English. Wolfgang said to him one day —

"Why don't you learn German? — you who are so well acquainted with English? The one would help you with the other."

"Why, indeed, should I not?" said Vincenzo — "that is, if you think you can muster patience enough to teach me."

So said, so done; and Vincenzo, who had a peculiar facility for languages, in a few months knew enough of German to understand any book of average difficulty. This new study was not entered upon, you may be sure, until Rose had granted permission — not, indeed, until Vincenzo had been eight months at Nervi, when his recovery was so far advanced that it was evident he might occupy himself seriously for a few hours every day without danger.

The Candias' little home was order and comfort itself. A prince of the blood royal could not have been served with more promptitude and zeal than was Rose's husband. His least whims were watched for, guessed, and attended to as if by magic. Rose could not sleep at night for thinking of some dish which might tickle his languid appetite — obstinate inappetence being the great obstacle to his complete restoration. But Rose's unremitting pre-occupation and anxiety about Vincenzo's comfort did not make her for an instant lose sight of the interests she had left behind. She carried on a regular correspondence with Giuseppe, now her factotum, giving him minute directions as to what he was to do, with that spirit of order and practical instinct of business which were among her distinctive qualities. And not contented even with this, she summoned him every three months to Nervi, to hear from him a verbal account of the state of her affairs.

Eighteen hundred and fifty-nine set in. Every one has fresh in his memory the few ominous words which fell from mighty lips over the cradle of the new year, sending a shiver of expectation throughout Europe. It was the shiver of the forest, which feels the coming tempest in the breeze. The Italian question was evidently sweeping swiftly on to a crisis. Not a day that passed but brought fresh evidence to back this anticipation. Austria was strengthening her Lombard frontiers with additional bayonets and new bulwarks. Piedmont, on its side, was arming to its utmost. The spring, the coming spring, was the time universally assigned to the duel between the two countries. Our German threw physic to the dogs, and towards the end of January went off to Turin. Signora Candia, whose keen eyes Vincenzo's excitement did not escape, would fain have said to her husband — Let us both go with Herr Wolfgang. She dared not. Only a fortnight since, the doctor who came now and then from Genoa to see Vincenzo, had pronounced it advisable for him to stay another season at the sea-side, and this time to try the effect of sea-baths.

Just at this moment Del Palmetto came on a flying visit to the Candias. He brought amazing news. Two hundred thousand French soldiers were posted on the other side of the Alps, ready, the moment the signal was given, to come to our assistance. Volunteers were flocking into Piedmont from all parts of the Italian peninsula. The youth of Lombardy and Venetia were emigrating *en masse*. Men bearing the noblest names of Italy were glorying in the worsted epaulets of private soldiers. Garibaldi was talked of as entrusted with the organization of a legion.

"I wish you could see Turin at this moment," wound up Del Palmetto. "It is worth seeing — full as an egg; and as to pluck — I just wish you were there to judge for yourself."

Discourses of this kind were little calculated to allay Vincenzo's excitement. Rose, with a qualm, remarked his increasing restlessness; the little appetite he had had, altogether failed, and his nights were again become sleepless. She set off for Genoa, went straight to the doctor, and placed the dilemma before him. "What was she to do?"

"Take your husband to Turin immediately," was the physician's sensible reply. "The one essential consideration in Signor Candia's case is a quiet mind. All the rest is merely accessory. Who knows, after all, but that the mental stimulus which he will find at Turin will act as beneficially on his health as sea-bathing!"

On the evening of the same day, Rose said to her husband —

"Suppose we go to Turin ourselves, and see all the fine doings Del Palmetto has been telling us about."

Vincenzo's face brightened at this proposal. He said —

"I should like it of all things, I confess — only.. I know you would prefer going to Rumelli."

"No, indeed," said Rose; "the Palace is no longer what it was to me when ... when poor papa was there. Still I shall not be sorry to be nearer to it than I am here; for then I can go over sometimes and look after *our* affairs. Besides, you know I wish to go to Turin about the monument we talked of — and — I like

Turin, and feel an interest in all that is going on there at this moment."

Vincenzo kissed his wife's hand, and said —

"You are very good to me."

"And if I am, is it not my duty to be so to my husband?"

"Only your duty?" asked Vincenzo.

"I don't mean that," exclaimed Rose. "My duty, and my pleasure, too."

Signora Candia wrote, without further delay, to the Marchioness, begging her, if possible, to secure lodgings for them. The Marchioness wrote back that there were no lodgings to be had for love or money, but that Signor Onofrio, who was starting for Paris on a mission, begged to place his apartment, such as it was, at their service. Rose accepted the offer, and on the 23d February the Candias left Nervi, not without regret, for the capital. They had spent nearly twelve months at the sea-side.

CHAPTER XVIII.

Vincenzo's Bark in Full Sail.

Rose could not congratulate herself enough on the step she had taken, when she saw how instantaneous were the beneficial effects derived from it by her husband. After having spent a few days in Turin, Vincenzo grew quite another man from what he had lately been at Nervi. He eat well, slept better, and, along with his activity of body, quickly recovered his serenity of mind. And yet the weather was coldish and wet, far from propitious to delicate people; indeed, contrasted with that he had left, the climate of Turin was a decided change for the worse. Neither did the aspect of the city present any strikingly new feature to one who, like Candia, had seen it as full and far more excited in 1849. What subtle agency was there then busy with him? None other than the current of patriotic electricity in the air, which he drank in with every breath he drew. Vincenzo felt himself in sympathetic communion with one and all of these thousands of his fellow-citizens crowding the streets, and revived in that feeling.

He passed much of his time out of doors. He liked to loiter, with his wife or alone, as the case might be, under the arcades of Via Po, and listen to the political effusions of the passers by, or of the shopkeepers, as they stood at their respective doors, comparing notes upon the posture of public affairs. Not one of the shop windows on his road, in which was exhibited the last political caricature, or the last published map of Italy, or the portraits of the leading men of the day, but he would halt at, staring at these novelties with quite a childish pleasure. Everybody and everything had an interest for him. The first time that he met Count Cavour under the colonnades of Piazza Castello, and witnessed the marks of tender reverence universally shewn towards that great man, he could have leapt and wept for joy. If a drum beat, or a military band played within his hearing, he would set off running, like any schoolboy, to go and see the soldiers file past. If he chanced on young recruits at drill, in one or other of the squares, he was never tired of watching them, straining his eyes to single out who were the volunteers among them. It was in the course of such physiognomic studies that one day Vincenzo discovered, in the ranks of an awkward squad, his German acquaintance of Nervi, and, the drill over, carried him home in triumph.

Save Wolfgang, (who, from this day, spent all his hours of liberty with them), and the Del Palmettos, who called as often as they could, the Candias saw very few people — occasionally two or three of Vincenzo's old fellow-students, met with in his perambulations. As for the Marchioness's visits, they were generally short and hurried. She had more to do than she had time or strength for; besides the epistolary propaganda which she carried on with every part of Italy, and which the pressure of the momentous circumstances had swollen to fabulous proportions, Signora Del Palmetto was the leading spirit of patriotic committees of all sorts and denominations, and the natural central point to which all belonging to the new and the old emigration converged. Ministers were not more busy than she was. Her only moment — we must not call it of leisure, for of leisure she neither would nor could have any, but we will say of slackened work — was of an evening, when, perhaps, between a telegram received and one sent in answer, she found means of discussing the last news, and of anticipating what the morrow might bring forth, with a circle of distinguished visitors — senators, deputies, general officers, &c., who thronged her *salons*. Among these, probably the most obscure, but not the least welcome, were often Rose and Vincenzo. The Marchioness lost no opportunity of marking her partiality for Signora Candia, and her high appreciation of Vincenzo's talents. Her golden opinion of the young man, aided and set off by his becoming modesty and good sense, shortly gained for him the sympathy and good will of all those he met at her house.

Towards the end of the third week in March, Signor Onofrio returned from Paris. The Candias, who knew, through the Marchioness, the precise time he would arrive, had shifted their quarters the day before to an hotel where they had long before bespoken rooms. This arrangement did not please Vincenzo's old friend, who insisted on their coming back and staying with him; a tempting proposal, which, however, they resisted, aware that at a moment like that, a public man in Onofrio's position ought to have entire command of his time, and entire liberty of action. They managed, however, to see each other daily, and without hurry, by always dining together, one day at the Candias' hotel, and the other at Onofrio's house. Onofrio had brought from Paris such a stock of high spirits as made him young again, and the most entertaining companion possible. He made not the smallest attempt at diplomatic concealment of the grounds of his buoyancy — or perhaps more truly, it formed part of his diplomacy to be frank. In order to bring something to pass, it is often only necessary to give it out as certain and inevitable. It was upon no other principle that Count Cavour, assuredly no novice in diplomacy, had been acting when, during the two past years, he had constantly asserted that a war against Austria had been decided on in Paris.

The perfect harmony existing between Vincenzo and Rose could not but immediately and pleasantly impress so acute an observer as Vincenzo's mentor. He was not slow in offering his congratulations. "You have," said he, "achieved a conversion which does you great honour. I wish you could tell me how, that I might impart your recipe to some friends of mine, who stand in great need of some such help."

"It came of itself," returned Vincenzo; "I can claim no merit in it, unless it be a merit to have been long and dangerously ill."

"Perhaps it was just that — women are such queer fishes — anyhow, now that your wife has become a thorough patriot, she will no longer object to your doing something to serve your country, will she?"

"I should say not," replied Vincenzo; "we shall see when the time comes."

"But the time *is* come, my dear fellow. Within a month from this day we shall be at war, and you don't mean, I suppose, to sit with your hands on your knees, while every Italian worth the name is striking a blow for his fatherland?"

"No, I do not; but except handling a musket, which I can't do, I don't see of what use I could be in a time of war."

"By giving that which rules the muskets — brains, sir, brains," cried Onofrio.

"Well, such as I have, and my heart into the bargain, belong now and ever to my country, *only* I don't wish to be hasty, to seem so, at least — it is a whim, perhaps, but I would fain wait until affairs take a decisive turn."

Onofrio interpreted Vincenzo's unwillingness to accept employment as a want of confidence in the completeness and durability of his wife's conversion; a want of confidence which Onofrio shared, and which had prompted him to strike the iron while it was hot.

However, he did not insist for the present. Onofrio was not entirely mistaken. Vincenzo anticipated no difficulty as to his resumption of office from his wife; she had humoured, nay, prevented, all his wishes — in a word, she had lately spoiled him to a degree which excluded even the thought of a possible opposition on her part. But Vincenzo was not sure that her acquiescence to his again entering the service of the Government might not cost her a pang, and, generous and loving as he was, he wished to spare a possible pain, so long as the inflicting of it did not become a matter of absolute necessity; for, if public affairs came to a crisis, he considered that it would be his imperative duty to strike his blow, to use Onofrio's words, in behalf of his country. It was true that Rose, especially since their arrival in Turin, had evinced, on political matters, opinions and feelings quite in unison with his own. But might she not do this out of complaisance to him? The doubt was natural in one who could not help having deep-rooted impressions of her former ways of thinking, and of the tenacity with which she adhered to them. And yet this doubt was unfounded. Rose acted no part. She had to some extent caught the infection filling the ambient air — the judgments passed by the notable persons she met daily at the Marchioness's had not been lost upon her — the enthusiasm which had incited numbers of youths belonging to the most illustrious families of Italy, and with many of whom she was personally acquainted, to exchange their princely homes for the bare walls of a barrack — well, neither had that enthusiasm failed to elicit some sparks of responsive feeling in her own bosom. Rose was on the eve of becoming a thoroughgoing *bonâ fide* liberal.

As days and weeks passed on, Vincenzo had more reasons than one to rejoice over his wise procrastination. The chances of war seemed rather to diminish than to increase. The European Powers, awakened to the imminence of a general conflagration, strove with might and main to avert it. France, apparently at least, vigorously seconded these efforts. There came a day when even Cavour himself, for a moment, despaired of the issue so long coveted. It was on the 19th of April that a telegram from Paris reached him — a laconic, imperious telegram — desiring him to accept, purely and simply, the preliminaries of the Congress as set forth by the Powers. Now these preliminaries imported no less than the disbanding of the volunteers and the suspension of all armaments. It was an awful moment. Fortunately, the gods had struck with dementia those whom they designed to chastise. Three days after, two officers, in white uniforms, traversed the streets of Turin, bearers of the Austrian ultimatum. Its tenour is too widely known to need repetition here. Cavour, and with him twenty-four millions of Italians, breathed freely again.

Count Buol's haughty summons did not reach its destination until the 23d of April, but Austria's rash determination was known in official spheres as early as the 21st. On the morning of that day, while sitting at breakfast with his wife, Vincenzo received a hurried scrawl, worded thus — "*Alea jacta est* — the time for indecision is passed. I have a capital post in view for you. Prepare your wife. You shall hear all particulars *viva voce*. Onofrio." Vincenzo remained thoughtful.

"No bad news, I hope," said Rose.

"Quite the contrary — the news is excellent," replied Vincenzo. "War is all but declared."

"Ah! so much the better," said Rose. "But what, then, makes you look so grave?"

"The fear of giving you pain, dear. Onofrio warns me to get ready for active service."

"Not as a soldier, not as a soldier," cried Rose, springing to her feet, and clutching both Vincenzo's hands.

"No, no, not as a soldier. Alas! I am not fit for one," said Vincenzo. "But even if I were, for your sake, I neither would nor ought to hazard my life. Onofrio expects me to serve my country in some civil capacity, which he does not mention. You understand, Rose, that in this moment, when the storm is about to break over Italy, none of her sons worthy of the name can shrink from his duty without dishonour."

"I would not, if I could, deter you from doing your duty," said Rose, calmly; "only I beg of you, I entreat you, Vincenzo, not to run any unnecessary risks."

"I shall have no risks to run," said Vincenzo — "probably I shall not even have to quit Turin. At all events, I promise, faithfully, to take as much care of myself as I would of you, dear Rose."

When, later in the day, Onofrio came with the details of the momentous intelligence, and broached, not without misgiving, the question personally to Vincenzo, explaining the nature of the appointment which was in store for him, the good gentleman was most pleasantly surprised at the perfectly sensible view taken by Signora Candia of this opening for her husband, and also by her composed manner. Rose spoke like one who had taken it for granted that Vincenzo would not, indeed could not, hold back in an emergency such as the present; and though not dissembling the pain which the prospect of even a short separation gave her (Vincenzo's intended post involved his temporary removal from Turin), she declared that she submitted to it without a murmur, for their country's sake. Onofrio took his leave, quite edified by her plain good sense and quiet fortitude. Signora Candia went through the ordeal with an equanimity which never failed her. What she had said to Onofrio she repeated to the Marchioness, and to all those who, when her husband's appointment became public, congratulated or condoled with her. She made no display of a heroism which she did not feel. Still less did she make any mystery of how much rather she would have had her husband working from morning to night in some office in Turin, than sent to the frontier, on ever so pacific an errand. As it was, she submitted to the force of circumstances, and put her trust in God.

The post assigned to Vincenzo had, in fact, some danger attached to it; but far more on the face of it than in reality. He was to be one of the secretaries to the Civil Commissioner Extraordinary for the provinces of Vercelli and Novara, appointed by royal decree on the 26th. Both these open frontier towns — bearing the same name as their provinces — lying as they did out of the line of defence, forced upon the Piedmontese army by its comparatively small numbers, were inevitably doomed to be occupied by the Austrians. To explain to, and reconcile the populations of these districts, as far as possible, to this dire necessity; to watch that no pretence for provocation was given to the enemy; to re-assure, to guide, to help in every way compatible with the situation, such was the mission confided to Vincenzo's new chief. They had to start for their destination on the very day of their official appointment. Rose, as arranged beforehand, went to stay with the Marchioness till Vincenzo's return. Del Palmetto was absent with his regiment at Chivasso.

Vincenzo's tenure of office was and could only be short. The Austrians crossed the Ticino on the 29th of April; were at Novara by the 2d, and at Vercelli on the 5th of May. As the enemy advanced, so did the Civil Commissioner and his staff fall back upon the points still unoccupied, doing all the little good they could in the restricted sphere of action left them. Indeed, as late as the 20th of the month, they remained in the near neighbourhood of the invading army, an always difficult, and often precarious situation, and one which not unfrequently called for a certain amount of decision and presence of mind. On the 20th, the Austrians retired into their positions behind the Po and the Sesia — a movement which freed the way to Vercelli, immediately occupied by Cialdini; and, a little later, to Novara, at one or other of which places the Commissioner and his suite tarried till the end of the month. This is all that we choose to record as to this brief period of Vincenzo's official career — this, and the fact that he found leisure and inclination to write daily to his wife. As for the rest, we have known him too long not to feel sure that he did his duty thoroughly, and we have every reason to believe that his *pro tempore* superior was emphatically of the same opinion.

Vincenzo, on his return to Turin, met with the two rewards he most coveted; a very affectionate — indeed a positively enthusiastic welcome — from his wife, and the warmest encomium that words could convey, from Onofrio. The looks and words of both friend and wife, testified to how proud they were of him; both anticipated for him a fresh field of action and of honour. Language of this sort, in Rose's mouth, betokened a new and happy phase of feeling, that was hailed with rapture by her husband. The month that had just elapsed had been rich with startling impressions for Rose of many a kind — impressions which had raised her patriotic fervour to the maximum of heat of which her nature was susceptible. Rose was made of flesh and blood after all; she loved the land of her birth, after her manner; probably loved it more than she herself knew — and to see it actually violated and trampled upon by the Austrians, put her into such a storm and agony of pain and passion, as to make her fairly forget that *they, too, were Christians* (one of her famous arguments against the war in 1848), and to see in them only the invaders and the enemies of her country. The frantic exclamations, and tears, and prayers, with which the whole city had accompanied the king and the army on their departure for the camp, the awful solemnity of the days of suspense that followed, the mad excitement of the emperor's arrival at Alexandria, the intoxication of the victories of Montebello and Palestro — Rose had seen and felt it all, and she was still vibrating with the noble emotions inseparable from such indescribable scenes and feelings. Hence her new-born pride in her husband and in the task he had accomplished;

hence her eagerness that he should be again employed.

In this she was soon gratified. On the third day after his arrival, Vincenzo received a hurried note from the Marchioness del Palmetto, informing him that she had just seen Count Cavour, that he had expressed a wish to make Signor Candia's personal acquaintance, and that he would receive him at such an hour of the same day. Signora Candia clapped her hands with delight.

"I only hope," she said, suddenly checking herself, "that he is not going to send you away from this."

"I hope not," returned Vincenzo; "but I don't see how I could decline to go, if he should."

"Couldn't you tell him frankly," persisted Rose, "that you would prefer some occupation in Turin?"

"Certainly, if I had a good reason to give," observed the husband.

Rose blushed scarlet, and said, "All I can say is, that *I* have a good reason for not wishing you to go away."

And this reason of hers, to all appearance, was of so jealous a nature as not to permit of its being spoken aloud; it was whispered in his ear. Whatever it was, it sent a thrill of joy through Vincenzo's whole frame; he clasped her to his bosom, exclaiming, with warmth, "God bless your gentle heart, my darling! Nothing now is wanting to my happiness. I will do my best not to be sent away — at least not for long."

He was not sent from Turin. Count Cavour, after a few kind words, said: "I hear that you know several languages. I require some one to read every morning for me all the foreign newspapers comprised in this list, to point out to me all the passages which might prove injurious to our cause, and to contradict or refute such of them as I shall direct. Can you do this?"

"I think I can," answered Vincenzo.

"Very well. Now, can you also undertake to write occasional articles, or even a series of articles, on subjects suggested by me, and that on the shortest notice, and in a clear and familiar style?"

"I will do my best," said Vincenzo.

"That's it. Be here to-morrow morning at six, and ask for Signor Pietro. Signor Pietro will show you to a room, where you will find all the newspapers for your inspection. As soon as your work is done, bring it to me. You have only to knock at the little door opposite to that of your study, and you will find me. Come in, without waiting, for an answer. Good day."

Vincenzo on the morrow punctually followed these instructions, and from that moment found himself in daily communication with that man, a mere peep at whom in the street had been ever enough to make his heart leap for joy; the man in whom he had for years put his trust, his ambition, his pride. This it was which gave his present appointment its greatest zest. On the other hand, the task was peculiarly congenial to his tastes and powers; its only drawback the frequent inevitable hurry, and consequent insufficiency of the directions he received. Vincenzo was left to guess much, and was lucky enough to guess well, and to give satisfaction. We need scarcely say that his rectifications and refutations of hostile foreign articles, as well as his leaders on such and such a subject, were inserted either in the official gazette, or in the semi-official papers.

Meanwhile, the course of the war, if not smooth, yet run invariably prosperous for the Allied forces; the victory of Magenta had opened the road to Milan; the victory of Solferino brought them to the walls of Peschiera. All eyes were now turned to the Quadrilateral. Venice, from the other side of it, was already stretching her fettered arms towards her deliverers. One more strenuous effort, and Italy was free from the Alps to the Adriatic, and the grand programme of Milan became an accomplished fact. The peace of Villafranca fell like an extinguisher upon these bright prospects. The nation suddenly plunged into darkness, reeled as if drunk. Cavour felt himself in the way, and resigned. Vincenzo would have fain also retired into private life, but the great minister said to him, "Now that the sword fails us, reason the more for sticking to the pen, the sole weapon left us. The appointment I created for you has answered too well not to make me hold to its continuance. I shall recommend you to my successor, and — well, perhaps we may meet here again some of these days." Vincenzo obeyed, and continued to perform his duty faithfully, earnestly, scrupulously; but his heart was no longer in it. Rose shared in his disappointment, and soothed and comforted him like a true wife.

Little by little, however, the sunken spirits of the nation rallied, all hands joined in the manœuvre, and by dint of concord, industry, and perseverance, the vessel which bore the destinies of Italy, stranded for a moment, was made to float again. True enough, that the crew missed from the helm the tried steersman in whom they had put all their trust, but they knew that he was still in the same boat, and that his strong arm and clear head were at hand, if need was, and answered for its safety. Confidence gradually revived, and the course of events justified the feeling. It is not our province to dwell or even to touch upon that series of facts which intervened between Cavour's resignation and his resumption of office, and which must be present to every memory. We accordingly take up again the thread of our simple narrative.

We hinted, not long ago, that the future held in store a great joy for Vincenzo; we may now add, that the happy consummation of his hopes took place in November. Rose made him a present of the most wonderful little creature that ever graced the eyes of fond parents, and which was christened Rose. Vincenzo insisted on the name, as the only one that, by any possibility, suited the tiny rosy fairy. The Marchioness del Palmetto and Signor Onofrio were godfather and godmother to the child. I leave you to imagine the pleasurable excitement and the heartfelt rejoicings incident to such an occasion. Vincenzo had not long enjoyed his paternal dignity, when another piece of good fortune happened to him and to his whole country. On the 17th January, 1860, Count Cavour once more held the reins of government, and that daily intercourse with the great man, so precious to Vincenzo, was again his daily privilege. Cavour was in high spirits, less straitened for time, and much more communicative, and disposed to take the young man into his confidence, than he had had either leisure or inclination to be, during the period of their former relations. The sphere and importance of the work required of Vincenzo increased in direct ratio with the confidence he inspired, and more than one official document, jealously guarded from all profane eyes, was allowed to pass under his, for purposes it would take us too long to detail. The three months that followed after Cavour's return to office passed like lightning for Vincenzo. They were the fullest and happiest of his life.

All the cravings of his nature, all the claims of his heart and intellect, were at one and the same time satisfied. He had, in the first place, just work enough, and that of the sort he preferred, to enhance the hours of sweet leisure and privacy of home; he had the consciousness of being useful, and the prospect of an honourable career, with a seat in parliament as soon as he should be of the requisite age; he beheld his country, his hourly anxious preoccupation, moving on slowly, but steadily, in spite of wind and tide, towards a better future; and to crown all, he was blessed in the affection of his wife, and in the joys of paternity. Withal, his health, without being strong, was good enough. Indeed, if one of those kindly disposed fairies, whose business it was in olden times to bestow gifts on poor mortals, had presented herself to him, and told him to form a wish and it should be granted, Vincenzo would have been fairly puzzled what wish to form.

CHAPTER XIX.

Vincenzo's Bark strikes on Sunken Rocks.

VINCENZO's happy enjoyment of the present, and serene security in the future, met with a sudden check.

In the beginning of the second week in April Rose had gone to Rumelli, as she said, for three days. Her excursions in that direction had lately grown very frequent. The monument to the memory of her father, which had engrossed much of her thoughts and time during her residence in Turin, being now finished, she naturally enough wished herself to superintend the erection of it in the churchyard of the village. This was not an affair of an hour or a day, and her anxiety to make sure that this mark of her filial love should be completed according to her intentions, led to her occasionally making a short stay at the palace without Vincenzo, though, of course, accompanied by her infant, which she was nursing. Well, then — Rose had gone to Rumelli only for three days, and Vincenzo was not a little astonished, nay alarmed, when, on the day of her proposed return, he received a letter instead of the wife he expected. Before making known the contents of this letter, we must premise a few facts indispensable to its being thoroughly understood.

Any tolerably well-informed reader will recollect that, not long after sending an imposing *corps d'armée* into Piedmont, France threw a less considerable force, under the command of Prince Napoleon, into Tuscany. The immediate effect of this move was the evacuation by the Austrians of the Romagnas, which they had occupied militarily for years past. The inhabitants of the Romagnas, left to themselves, were not slack in throwing off the government of the Pope, and declaring their annexation to Piedmont. This was the origin of the Roman question.

Had the Pontifical subjects of the Romagnas the right to dispose of themselves as they thought fit, a right which had been exerted, and successfully, by the Greeks and the Belgians, not to speak of the French? Or were they a kind of *servi glebæ* of Catholicity? In other words, was the temporal power (nobody questioned the spiritual, mind) — was the temporal power of the Pope liable to the accidents inherent to the finite nature of all earthly things, or was it a power *sui generis*, inviolable, immutable, inasmuch as a *sine qua non* of the free exercise of the Pope's spiritual power?

Opinions were and are still divided upon the point. Rose had heard the subject much discussed during the last months, and however strongly her sympathies were enlisted on the side of the Pope, she had shown nothing of them. Signora Candia had determined not to let any difference of feeling upon this, or any other question of the day, interfere with her domestic happiness. Unfortunately, events turned out so, that she no longer deemed herself justified in persisting in this system of outward neutrality, and there came a moment when, short, as she believed, of endangering her soul, she had no choice but openly to act up to her secret convictions.

We said that the Romagnas had pronounced their annexation to Piedmont. The deputation commissioned to carry the wishes of those provinces to King Victor

Emmanuel met with cordial words of sympathy, of encouragement, of hope for the future, but with none of positive adhesion. Diplomatic difficulties stood in the way of a formal acceptance. This occurred in the month of September, 1859. By March, 1860, these difficulties existed no longer, and the earnestly-desired incorporation of the Romagnas with Piedmont was officially decreed. Thereupon Rome issued a bull of excommunication against all those who, either as principals, abettors, or accessories, had in any way contributed, directly or indirectly, to the spoliation of the Holy See.

Armed with this bull, a copy of which he had been one of the first to receive, Don Pio placed it before Signora Candia, and called upon her to do her duty. She must either instantly reclaim her husband, or cut off all intercourse with one excommunicated. Don Pio was not the man to do things by halves. Rose rebelled against this terrible award. Those times were past when Don Pio had only to command to be obeyed. Other feelings, other influences, now counterbalanced his authority. Rose loved her husband as much as it was in her nature to love — he was the father of her child, he was the man she most respected in the world. Impossible to cast him from her. On the other side, the Infallible Head of the Church, Christ's Vicar upon earth, had spoken, and short of unconditional submission, her eternal salvation was imperilled.

Signora Candia, when she went to reside in Turin, had had to choose a confessor there; and her choice had luckily fallen upon a very worthy old ecclesiastic. She carried her anguish of mind to his feet, and appealed to his judgment against Don Pio's harsh sentence.

The old priest's views of her duty under the circumstances proved far less absolute and much more humane than those of the younger man. To get out of harm's way, so as neither to receive nor countenance any scandal, to do this and pray, continually pray for her husband and the afflicted Church, such and no other were the directions she received. Then it was that, greatly relieved in her mind, yet with still an aching heart, she penned the following letter to her husband:—

"My dear Vincenzo, — Nothing is amiss; my health is excellent, and so, thank God, is that of our darling. I begin with this cheering intelligence, my dear husband, at once to dispel the uneasiness about us, which you will certainly feel on receiving a letter instead of seeing baby and me, as you expected. Since it is my fate to give you pain, let me, at least, give none that is unnecessary. Yes, my dear Vincenzo, I must give you some pain; it cannot be avoided; and yet God who reads my heart, God is my witness that I would willingly give up my life to make you happy. But there are interests far more precious than life, and such as I cannot sacrifice even for you. There are — but what is the use of all this preamble but to make you fancy something still worse than what I have to say. What I have to say is, that I cannot return to Turin for the present; nor, indeed, for some time. I never thought it could be so hard to write these simple words. My hand is all in a shake with the effort!...

"Now for the reason which compels me to take this course. I might have hid it from you — I might have easily accounted for our remaining in the country by the fatigue of nursing, or the cutting of baby's teeth —

two are just coming, poor little darling — or the fine season at hand; but I will not, I cannot be insincere. I will not, I cannot repay your confidence in me with duplicity. No, I want you to read in my heart as in an open book. Well, then, my reason for not coming back to you for the present is — I scarcely know how to go on. You will do me the justice, my dear Vincenzo, to allow that I have tried, with all my heart, lately to conform to your ideas and meet your wishes. I have taught myself to believe what you believe, to like what you like, and I have so far succeeded in the attempt as to make you contented with me. I have approved of the war, I have willingly acquiesced in your taking office, I have been happy and proud of your success, and my heartiest wishes have been, and are still at this moment, for the greatness and the prosperity of our country. I have followed you thus far. Oh, Vincenzo, why should there be any point to which I cannot follow you? You guess to what I allude — to one of the results of the last campaign, for which I was quite unprepared — I mean this deplorable annexation to Piedmont of part of the Pontifical States.

"Still, even such an act I might have borne in silence but for the solemn condemnation passed upon it by His Holiness, which makes silence itself a sin. Yes, to keep silent is, to a certain extent, to countenance; and to countenance what the Holy Father has condemned is mortal sin. You must see, therefore, that if I were now to return to you, my position would be a most trying one; indeed, it would be downright wretchedness. Almost all your friends — the Del Palmettos, Signor Onofrio, &c. — and you yourself being in favour of the annexation, I should have no choice but either to remain silent, and thus load my conscience by an appearance of acquiescence, or to protest at every moment, and thus grow a bore to every one, and, worse than all, become displeasing to you.

"I know what you will say to this — you will say, 'Come, and you shall have no such alternative to apprehend. I shall take good care that the thorny question be not even so much as alluded to in your presence.' Yes, but at what cost? At the cost of all your intimacies, of all freedom of communication in your own home? I should hate and despise myself if I could only for a moment harbour the thought of weaning you from your friends, or of burdening them and you with the incubus of a perpetual reticence. No, my dear Vincenzo, there is but one rational way of meeting the difficulty — a temporary separation.

"And now let me beseech you, my dearest husband, not to attempt to combat my resolution, nor to weaken the grounds on which I have taken it. I know you have plenty of cogent reasons to urge, plenty of respectable authorities to quote, against the view I take of this question. I know you have a distinction ready between the Pope, Head of the Church, and the Pope, secular sovereign — between the spiritual and temporal power. All this I have heard over and over again, and without being in the least shaken in my convictions. I suppose (I say so in real humility) that I am far too ignorant to feel the full force of certain arguments. It is a thousand pities that such a clever, learned man as you are should have cast in his lot with a woman who has such a narrow understanding as I am aware I have. But you will give me credit for this, at all events, that I never tried to conceal from you any of my shortcomings. What I am now at twenty-five I was and showed myself when a girl of fourteen.

"Well, then, to me the Holy Father has always been and always will be the representative of Jesus Christ upon earth, and what the Holy Father orders I deem as binding on me as if the Almighty Himself had ordered it. I was brought up in this creed, it forms part of myself; I cannot alter it, nor would I if I could. You see, then, that no good could come of your remonstrances, and evil might. Even to anticipate all possible cases — even if the charm of your voice should be able to banish for a time what you consider my scruples, I know myself well enough to be sure that deep-rooted habits of thinking and life-long associations would speedily reassert their power, and that the struggle within me would begin afresh, fiercer than ever, and make me thoroughly miserable. Now, you don't wish to make your Rose miserable, do you? I rely, therefore, on your generously acceding to my prayer not to oppose, though only by arguments, the course I have decided on.

"Even in my sorrow I must consider myself fortunate that I have no sadder message to send, no crueller duty to accomplish, than such as my strength is equal to. What if, as for an instant I had cause to fear, what if I had had to break off all intercourse with you, unless . . . It makes me shudder only to think what *might* have been, and I thank God humbly and fervently that I have been spared the trial. Yes, my dear Vincenzo, that liberty of acting up to the dictates of my conscience, which I claim for myself, I am happily empowered to leave entire to you. I have no change in the actual tenor of your life to exact, to entreat, or (I am, perhaps, going too far, but God, who sees my motives, will pardon me if I do) to wish for. I have acquired the conviction that regular work of a certain kind is absolutely necessary for your well-being. Go on, then, with your present task; continue to be a useful servant to your country, and a credit to yourself and those who love you. I should not have said this, but that I know how generously self-forgetting you are, and I am anxious to put you on your guard against yourself.

"And now good bye, my dear, my kind Vincenzo. I need not beg you to write as often, to come and see us as often, as you can. I know you will do both without being urged. As for me, I shall write and give you a daily account of both your Roses. Now, I have only to ask your forgiveness for the pain I give you... I am so sorry for it — so very sorry — but it can't be helped. After all, it is only a temporary separation, you know. Matters cannot go on long thus between the King and His Holiness — some right settlement must be made and at no distant period — at least, I hope so, don't you? Adieu! What a pity that it should have come to this? We were so happy together — but I must not murmur. God bless you, my dearest husband, and believe me always

"Your affectionate wife,

"Rose.

"P.S. — Little Rose has kissed the paper here at this round mark, and so have I. Once again, adieu!"

Vincenzo was as little prepared for this ominous

intelligence, as the mariner, who has moored his vessel over-night in a quiet haven, is prepared for awakening on the high seas in the midst of a terrific storm. Not the remotest idea had even as much as glanced across his mind for the last ten months, that the old half-forgotten spectre, which had for so long haunted his married life, might again rise and place itself between him and his wife. And now, here it was, more threatening than ever! Vincenzo was utterly overcome. He laid his head on the desk before him, clasped his temples with both hands, and strove to collect his thoughts.

Presently he took up the letter to re-read it. Some passages scarcely noticed on the first perusal, on the second touched him deeply; traces on the paper of tears, overlooked before, now anxiously sought for and verified, went straight to his heart. With the gush of sensibility broke forth a qualm of alarm. God alone could know, thought Vincenzo, at the cost of what intense agony she had kept up that show of composure, intended to spare his feelings. But he was not to be duped by her generosity, not he; he felt the moral certainty that she was frantic with grief, fairly heart-broken, probably ill.... We know of old how apt was Vincenzo's imagination, in general far from easily excited, to run riot on any subject connected with Rose and her father.

He drove at once to the railway, and within half an hour was on his road to Rumelli — not to combat his wife's resolution, not to argue or expostulate with her, but to soothe and comfort her. Against Rose, exacting, imperious, defiant, he had found it in his heart to struggle; before Rose, tender, submissive, unhappy, he felt completely disarmed. Indeed, if indispensable to her peace, he would lay, as a sacrifice at her feet, all his plans of usefulness, his prospects of worldly advancement — yes, for her peace, he would not shrink even from that.... But Cavour? How account to Cavour for his defection? And yet account for it he must, or what would his kind employer think of him? The locomotive at the head of the train did not work harder than did Vincenzo's poor brain, once set on this track. He reached the palace in a state of feverish agitation.

Rose was not taken unawares; she had contemplated the possibility — nay, the probability — of his coming, and had prepared herself accordingly. We have seen by her letter that what Rose most apprehended, and most wished to avert, was that, in a fit of generosity, Vincenzo should resign his appointment; now plain good sense told her that the more calm and cheerful she appeared to him, the less chance there would be of his taking that extreme step. It was not, however, without a sharp battle with her feelings that she managed to keep her reception of her husband within the bounds of that affectionate cordiality, to which she had accustomed him of late days. She said that she had expected him, and how very glad she was he had come, that they might talk over this momentary difficulty; for, after all, there was nothing like a quiet talk for settling things in their true light. Letters never answered in such cases, they always said too little or too much. Hers, she feared, had alarmed him; had it not?

Rose's assumed equanimity had the desired effect. To see her look, to hear her talk in that easy natural way, to receive comfort and encouragement from her, instead of having to comfort and encourage — in one word, to find her altogether so different from what he had pictured to himself — gave Vincenzo a revulsion of feeling which instantly sobered him. Suddenly divested of the phantasmagoria in which he had clothed it the naked reality, as it stood before him, lost by contrast even somewhat of its natural proportions.

Rose had therefore no difficulty in getting him to adopt her views — the views enforced in her letter. Safeguarding the present as they did, without prejudging the future, they were, in fact, the only rational ones under the circumstances; and Vincenzo, once reassured about his wife, once satisfied that the *short* trial at hand was not above her power of endurance, could not but acknowledge their soundness. In short, Signora Candia had the consolation of sending her husband back to his occupations next day sad — how could he be otherwise? — but tolerably composed in mind, and heartily thankful for being spared the struggle between his duty to her and that to his venerated patron.

Much as the solitude of his home in Turin weighed at first on Vincenzo, he fought against despondence bravely; and to help him to do so with less effort, presently came the excitement of that rush of wonderful events, which opened with the landing of Garibaldi at Marsala, and closed with the proclamation of the Kingdom of Italy. The work of the sword did not exclude the work of the pen, and that of Vincenzo had no rest either by day or by night. Still, whatever the business in hand, however important or pressing it might be, there would peep from the paper before him the image of his wife and child, sitting lonely and disconsolate far away, and a sigh would come. The sight of his dear ones, whom he never failed to visit on Sundays, generally had the effect of sending him back to town in low spirits. These were, however, necessarily fugitive impressions. Vincenzo was too much in the current of exciting events, far too much occupied, to indulge long in melancholy musings.

But when, in the lull of success, both the excitement and the press of business slackened, and the compressed sensibilities found leisure for asserting their own; when Vincenzo measured the length of time since Rose's departure, and looked for the chances of her possible return, and saw them, along with the chances of a settlement with Rome, daily recede and fade away into an indefinite future; then Vincenzo's heart sickened with hope deferred, and he was beset by many misgivings. What came of them, Vincenzo will himself tell in the next chapter.

CHAPTER XX.

Stranded.

"To Signor Onofrio at Naples.

Rumelli, *June 1861.*

"My dear Friend, — I have sent in my resignation; it has been accepted with some difficulty; and here I am again at my starting point. Like an ill-fated ship, over and over again driven back by contrary winds, I return disabled to my moorings, there to lie and rot. It was my destiny that it should be so, and it is so far accomplished. . . . But I have not taken up the pen to complain. Even had I the inclination, the moment would be ill chosen to do so. The insignificant insect shorn of its wings in a cobweb has no right to be querulous, when the king of the forest lies struck down in all his might. All individual woes lose their claim even to utterance in the face of the immense calamity which weighs down a whole nation — the death of Cavour. Prepared for it, as we were for the last four and-twenty hours, we could not believe it — it could not be realized. But yesterday we had heard his voice in parliament; but yesterday we had felt the impress of his large mind on the course of European events; and that to-day there should be nothing left of him! It seemed incongruous, unnatural, impossible, that, so long as his work was not done, the great workman should be missing. Alas! it is even so. Providence has such thunderbolts among its ways. Was the task of Italian redemption too easy with such a man? And was he taken from us that we might grope in the dark, and stumble, and earn, through further suffering, the entrance into the promised land? This is the secret of the Almighty — it only remains for us to bow our heads.

"Happy you, my dear friend, who were spared at least the anguish of the scenes which it was my sad pivilege to witness. Yet why so? There are sights which, however heartrending, still no man who loves his kind would miss, so strongly do they witness in favour of human nature; and the universal homage of filial respect and tenderness paid to Count Cavour, during the few days of his illness, is too honourable to him who received, and to the population who gave it, not to form one of the saddest and yet one of the proudest recollections associated with his name and with the noble city wherein he was born and died. No one who has not seen the thick rows of anxious faces thronging for days together the halls, the stairs, the courtyard of the Hotel Cavour, and the street of the Arcivescovado — no one whose heart has not throbbed in poignant communion with the hearts of the thousands hanging upon a word — can ever realize what *he* was to us. And when the fatal word fell upon the multitude; when . . . but I must stop here. I was there; I saw it all, I felt it all, and still I am powerless to convey any, the faintest, idea of that overwhelming moment. All I can say is, that if peoples are ungrateful — as the common saying is — the people of Turin, for one, was not so. A family mourning over a beloved father, such, literally, was Turin on this lamentable occasion.

"You are not to believe, my dear friend, that I have thrown up my appointment in a fit of discouragement consequent upon the sad event. No such thing. My nature, had it been left to itself, would have prompted me rather to the contrary course. It is not when the general falls that the soldiers are to leave their ranks. Unfortunately, I was not free to act according to my natural inclination. The fact is, that I had predetermined for some time to seize upon the first opportunity for leaving office; the death of Count Cavour afforded this opportunity, and I seized upon it. The forming of this resolution was not the work of a day; it had been forcing itself upon me inch by inch, as it were, for the last six months; and the moment I acquired the conviction that this unlucky Roman question, far from narrowing to a solution, grew daily more entangled and envenomed, and was likely to linger on for years — from that moment, I say, my resolution became irrevocable. Not without a struggle, as you may well believe. I clung to my employment with the energy of despair . . . but in all struggles between the interests of my wife and mine I am destined to be the loser. It has been the blessing and the . . . stumbling-block of all my life, that I should receive so much from that family as to make all return on my part still inadequate to the benefit. I have a kind of superstition on this score.

"Well, then, it was the old story over again — an everlasting contention of mind. You recollect my flight to Turin in 1857, and the miserable failure in which it ended; and yet I had to support me, at that time, the sense of provocation and of the harshness I had been writhing under — while now the case was quite different, I met with nothing but affection and submission. How could I find it in my heart to resist? We could see but little of each other, scarcely once a week. Much as I felt this deprivation, Rose felt it far more. With a man situated as I was, that is, busy from morning to evening, and when not actually at work, constantly preoccupied about it, time flies quick — it hung heavy upon her, whose range of occupation was but limited. I saw with a qualm the colour fade in her cheeks, and her looks grow wan. . . . In short, one of the two was to be more or less sacrificed, and I chose that it should not be my wife.

"'And your duty to your country?' I hear you say. I have put the objection to myself, I have weighed it carefully with the sincerest wish to find it unanswerable, and — I have not found it so. That a man's duty to his country be absolute and exclusive of all other duties I readily admit, but only in a few extreme, and therefore exceptional, cases. Let the country be in danger, the Austrian at the gate of the city, or Catilina in the streets, and no citizen worth the name — whatever his other ties and responsibilities — has a choice but to fly to the rescue. I would for one, in spite of everything. But that in ordinary times and circumstances — when the land has nothing to fear from external or internal foes, when order and security prevail — that a man, I say, irrespectively of, or in opposition to other duties and inclinations, should owe himself *quand même* to his country, under penalty of leze patriotism, the assumption is, evidently, too excessive to be tenable. It may have held good at Sparta, where the State was all in all; but in our modern society, where family occupies so large a place, it is out of date. I lay it down, then, as a rule, that — setting aside a few extreme cases — whenever duty to one's country clashes with other duties, the decision as to which shall take precedence rests with the individual conscience. Now my conscience tells me that my withdrawal from office does not the least harm to the State, while my persevering in it inflicted a very serious one upon my family. It little matters to my country whether the business I have discharged up to this day is performed by Signor Candia or by an equally or far cleverer substitute; but it mattered much to my wife and child whether I should continue to live apart from them, or whether I should live with them. The State has plenty of willing and able servants at its command, my wife and child have only me. Could I hesitate?

"When I said that my absence from my family was fraught with injurious consequences to them, I did not in the least exaggerate. Rose, as I was telling you, was suffering in health from our separation. Her youthful looks and liveliness were fast forsaking her; and some words dropped maliciously by that mischievous monkey, Marianne, gave me a clue to the cause. My wife was imposing fasts and other penances upon herself, to atone for the sins of her husband, I suppose; from which I could not but infer that time rather sharpened than softened her absolute ways of thinking and feeling in reference to our difficulties with Rome. How could it have been otherwise, left as she was for six out of seven days to the exclusive influence of Don Pio? By the bye, there is a rumour afloat that Don Pio is going to leave us. Would to God! To return: be the inference I drew above founded or unfounded, this I must say, in justice to my wife, that I never marked any alteration in her manner to me, and that such as she showed herself at the beginning of this painful entanglement — discreet, attentive, affectionate, submissive — she proved to the end.

"Then . . . I am going to relate a circumstance which will make you, an old bachelor, smile somewhat contemptuously, and which has made me, a young father, nearly cry scores of times. My weekly visit to the Palace had this drop of gall in it, that when I left on Monday morning I had to steal out of the house like a thief, without taking leave of my little daughter, without so much as kissing her in her sleep, for fear of awakening her. This course was forced upon me from the first by the fits of uncontrollable passion into which she would fly whenever she saw me go. Ah me! How the dear little thing kicked, and wailed, and screamed, until she grew black in the face! how her tiny hands clove desperately to me! To avoid such painful scenes — and especially their recoil on her health — I had, as I was saying, to give up even seeing her before leaving; and you can never imagine all the bitterness entailed upon me by this deprivation, all the sad misgivings for the future, which I had the ingenuity to build upon this apparent unfeelingness of mine. You must be a father, my dear friend, to know by how many little tendrils such baby plants can entwine themselves round a man's heart. I fancied that she was getting estranged from me, that she no longer answered my caresses as warmly as she used to do, that my voice had lost its former power over her. I pictured her a grown-up girl, clinging passionately to her mother, and looking at her father with something akin to indifference. . . . That would be a misfortune indeed, the worst of all — not only for me, but for herself. I want my little Rose to love and trust me best after God; I want my voice to be an oracle with her, that she may be happy, and make others happy. I want my sad experience to be of profit at least to my daughter, and to those whose lot in life she may be destined to influence some day. I have suffered too much through her mother. . . .

"Mind, my dear friend, that I don't say this in bitterness. I protest I have not the least shadow of a grudge against my wife. How could I? It is no fault of hers if we could not understand each other on certain points. She has acted up to what she has been taught, poor dear soul; and the responsibility of her not having been taught better rests more with the times and the circumstances of her education than with any living creature. The fault, if any, lies with me, who married her with eyes not blind to her weak points; and, in my youthful infatuation, deluded myself into believing that I might easily modify her opinions. I presumed too much of myself, and I pay a just penalty for my presumption.

"Well, then, as I was saying, I have suffered too much through the mother not to do my best in order that an honest man should not suffer through the daughter in the same way. I am determined upon this, that my daughter shall not be the sort of clog in the way of the man, who casts in his lot with her, which her mother has been in mine. This is a duty of conscience with me, and accomplish it I will. I am not fixed yet as to the means through which I shall accomplish it; a great deal must depend on circumstances. I am no theologian; I have the best wish to live and die a good Catholic, and I would fain interfere as little as possible with my daughter's religious education. My plan for the present is, to teach her to love her country so well, to inspire her with so deep a sense of duty to her country, as may in future serve her as a corrective against the too absolute notions that she may receive on other heads. Time will show if I am to go further, and in what direction. I shall want no leisure to study the subject *à fond*.

"Perhaps you will say, 'All this is very well, and will come in good time, but your daughter is just eighteen months old, and it is rather early to begin your course of patriotic education with her.' May be so, though I am not quite sure of that. At all events, she is not too young to receive and retain certain impressions, which sink into the infant mind, take root there, and become like instincts. For instance, my little one's teaching goes already thus far. When she toddles along the garden-walks, holding by my finger, if I say, 'Rosette, give papa the Italian tricolor,' she will with earnest attention pick a red and a white flower with a green leaf, and hold up the posy triumphantly to me. The other day she almost jumped out of my arms with excitement at the sight of the tricolor banner borne by the national guard, and pointed out eagerly the red, the white, and the green. She also recognises quite well the picture of Cavour, which hangs amongst others in my study, and holds out her baby fingers to it when I ask her which is the *Great Papa*. And then, my dear friend, can it be ever too early for me to lay the foundations of that entire love and confidence on which I rely, in order to enable me to realize my fond views for my daughter's happiness and that of her surroundings?

"Even in this small way I fancy I shall not be quite useless in my generation, for enlightened female education is yet a great desideratum with us. You, my friend, who gave me timely warning of the danger lurking in my path, will not gainsay me on this point.

"And now that I have laid bare my heart to you, good bye my dear and noble friend, and God bless you. I don't ask you to write; I know that all your time is scarcely enough for the thousand duties and responsibilities of your thorny official situation; I only entreat you to come and see me whenever you return home. It will be an act of charity. I don't hide from myself that, after the habits of activity I have acquired within these two last years, time will hang heavy upon me at the Palace. It does already, and I have not been here quite a week. By the bye, do you know that, not a month ago, I was offered a seat in the House by the College of Ibella — an offer which, of course, I had to decline? It seemed done on purpose to distract me. It was an awful wrench. A man does not crush with his own hand all his prospects of usefulness in this world without a pang. A seat in Parliament was my *beau idéal* in life, and — shall I say it? — I felt qualified for it. Forgive me this burst of self-love. It is my first, and will be my last. The victim may be allowed for once to deck itself with flowers. . . .

"But I promised not to complain. What is the use of repining about what is irreparably lost? Let me rather teach myself to be grateful for that which is left me. I have much to thank Providence for — a pure conscience, the affection of my wife, the caresses of my darling, some excellent friends, and all the comforts imaginable, comprising that most precious of all, the being able to add to the comforts of my poorer neighbour. With so many good gifts in my grasp, it may seem unnatural that I should have something to regret, and yet . . . it is so; I cannot help it. I suppose, but for that one forbidden fruit, my lot would have been too happy; and perfect happiness is not a flower of this world. Upon which Christian sentiment I hasten to close my already too long letter, and remain, my dear Onofrio, with best wishes,

"Yours ever affectionate,

"VINCENZO CANDIA."

CONCLUSION.

More than two years have elapsed since the date of the above, and still the contention of feeling under which it was written continues to this day. With the best endeavour to rest contented with the present, Vincenzo regrets the past; with the best wish to be happy, and to make his wife happy, Vincenzo succeeds in neither, and is conscious that he does not. There is a void in his existence which not all his love for his wife, not all his wife's love for him, not all the endearing ways of his daughter, not even her great progress under his tuition, can fill up. Vincenzo misses the stimulus of a regular homogeneous occupation, misses the satisfaction of one of the necessities of his nature — expansion in a certain direction. He guards his secret as jealously as he would the deadliest poison — guards it from his wife, from his best friends, would fain guard it from himself. Never a word escapes his lips which the most suspicious touchiness could construe into regret or disappointment. See him of an evening, sitting with little Rose in his lap, serene, talkative, cheerful; mark the affectionate gentleness of his tones whenever he addresses his wife, who, on the sofa opposite, lulls to sleep on her bosom tiny Urbano, just four months old. Captain, now Major, del Palmetto and, perhaps, the new curate (Don Pio is gone, thank God, and has been succeeded by a tolerant, elderly priest, who acts up to the adage "Live and let live") — well, Del Palmetto and the new curate, while sipping their tea, contribute their quota of news and pleasant chat. If there is a happy man under heaven, could you not swear to that man being Vincenzo Candia?

But see him without a mask — see him in the privacy of his own study, or taking a solitary walk on the terrace late at night — and your estimate of his happiness will sadly abate. Out of the dejected gait, out of the listless eye, oozes his secret, weariness, *ennui*. The assaults from this old enemy, frequent and intense in winter-time, grow less so with the fine season, especially during the three months that the Del Palmettos spend regularly at the Castle, but they never cease altogether.

Need we say that Rose is not the dupe of her husband's kindly meant imposition? Even had she not that kind of divination which affection gives, even had she not heard his broken words in his sleep, she would have read his secret in the premature look of age which has come over him within the last two years. Vincenzo at two-and-thirty has the appearance of a man of forty-five; his hair is going fast, his beard is all grizzly. Rose knows full well the nature of Vincenzo's ailment — knows that it is her own work — and feels powerless, alas! to undo it; for his determination not to live apart from his family is irrevocable. She is fully aware of this; and follow him to Turin, she cannot — her conscience forbids her; and not even for her husband can she endanger her soul. Nothing remains for her but to swallow her tears in secret and — look happy.

And thus they sit, face to face, each acting a part for the benefit of the other, each pretending not to know that the other is doing the same. Sad, thrice sad, is it not, that the schooling and sobering of ten years should abut upon a semblance instead of a reality? Would to God, at least, that the case of the Candias were an isolated one! But no; there is scarcely any corner in Italy, scarcely any corner in Europe, that does not exhibit plenty of such, and worse. God alone knows the number of families whose domestic peace has been, of late years, seriously damaged, or has gone to wreck altogether, on those very rocks which have proved so fatal to Vincenzo.

THE END.

CPSIA information can be obtained
at www.ICGtesting.com
Printed in the USA
LVHW040341110522
718423LV00001B/272

9 783375 004569